T0094458

THE LABORATORY OF LOVE

OTHER BOOKS BY PATRICK ROSCOE

Beneath the Western Slopes (1987)
Birthmarks (1990)
God's Peculiar Care (1991)
Love Is Starving for Itself (1994)
The Lost Oasis (1995)
The Truth About Love (2001)

The Laboratory of Love

PATRICK ROSCOE

ARSENAL PULP PRESS  VANCOUVER

THE LABORATORY OF LOVE
Copyright © 2013 by Patrick Roscoe

All rights reserved. No part of this book may be reproduced in any part by any means—graphic, electronic, or mechanical—without the prior written permission of the publisher, except by a reviewer, who may use brief excerpts in a review, or in the case of photocopying in Canada, a license from Access Copyright.

ARSENAL PULP PRESS
Suite 202 – 211 East Georgia St.
Vancouver, BC V6A 1Z6
Canada
arsenalpulp.com

The publisher gratefully acknowledges the support of the Canada Council for the Arts and the British Columbia Arts Council for its publishing program, and the Government of Canada (through the Canada Book Fund) and the Government of British Columbia (through the Book Publishing Tax Credit Program) for its publishing activities.

This is a work of fiction. Any resemblance of characters to persons either living or deceased is purely coincidental.

Some of these stories appear in previous books by the author of: *Bookmarks* (Penguin Books Canada, 1990) and *The Truth about Love* (Key Porter, 2001).

Cover photograph by © David Pinzer Photography/Image Source/Corbis
Editing by Susan Safyan
Book design by Gerilee McBride

Printed and bound in Canada

Library and Archives Canada Cataloguing in Publication

Roscoe, Patrick, 1967–
[Short stories. Selections]
    The laboratory of love / Patrick Roscoe.

Includes new stories and stories previously published in The truth about love and Birthmarks.
Issued in print and electronic formats.
ISBN 978-1-55152-521-1 (pbk.).—ISBN 978-1-55152-522-8 (epub)

    I. Title.

PS8585.O7236A6 2013   C813'.54   C2013-903256-8
                                            C2013-903257-6

for all those who have survived the laboratory of love

This book is a work of fiction, and any resemblance between its contents and actual people, places, and events might be called coincidental, except that under the peculiar care of God there are no such accidents: every dream of love is the same, and similarly real.

Contents

Part Five: The Laboratory of Love

Acknowledgments

Portions of this book were originally published, sometimes in different form or alternately titled, as follows:

"Rorschach I: The Rough Beast" (as "Autobiography") in *The Vancouver Sun* (Canada)

"The History of a Hopeful Heart" (as "My Lover's Touch") in *The New Quarterly* (Canada) and in *The James White Review* (US)

"Sweet Jesus" in *Blood & Aphorisms* (Canada) and in *Queen Street Quarterly* (Canada)

"Angie, Short for Angel" in *Descant* (Canada)

"Honey" in *The Fiddlehead* (Canada) and in *The Church-Wellesley Review* (Canada)

"The Real Truth" in *Canadian Forum* (Canada)

"Lucky" in *The Malahat Review* (Canada) and in *North Dakota Quarterly* (US)

"The Sacred Flame" in *Christopher Street* (US)

"The Murdered Child" in *Exile* (Canada)

"Phantasmagoria" in *The New Quarterly* (Canada), in *Horsefly Literary Magazine* (as "Harrop") (Canada), and in *Lodestar Quarterly* (US)

"Mutilation" in *The Capilano Review* (Canada) and in *The Danforth Review* (Canada)

"The Beauty Secrets of a Belly Dancer" in *Canadian Fiction Magazine* (Canada)

"Peggy Lee in Africa" in *Prism international* (Canada), in *The Little Magazine* (*US*), and in *Wisconsin Review* (US)

"Beggars" in *Grain* (Canada) and in *Alaska Quarterly Review* (US)

"Wild Dogs" in *Prism international* (Canada) and in *South Dakota Review* (US)

"Shells" in *The Dalhousie Review* (Canada)

"Chiggers" in *The Dalhousie Review* (Canada)

"The Lemon Tree" in *Books in Canada* (Canada), in *Qwerty* (Canada), and in *South Dakota Review* (US)

"What the World Takes Away" in *Queen's Quarterly* (Canada)

"The Tattoo Artist" in *Descant* (Canada) and in *Blithe House Quarterly* (US)

"Only the Bird Knows the Wing" (as "Hieroglyphics I") in *Prairie Fire* (Canada) and in *Harrington Gay Men's Fiction Quarterly* (US)

"Only the Wing Knows Flight" (as "Hieroglyphics II") in *Event* (Canada) and in *Harrington Gay Men's Fiction Quarterly* (US)

"The Truth About Love" in *Prairie Fire* (Canada) and in *Harrington Gay Men's Fiction Quarterly* (US)

"Touching Darkness" in *Exile* (Canada)

"Compromise" in *paperplates* (Canada) and in *Lodestar Quarterly* (US)

"Rorschach V: The Last Word" (as "The Last Word") in *Descant* (Canada)

Some of these stories were reprinted as follows:

"The History of a Hopeful Heart" (as "My Lover's Touch") in *Winter's Tales: New Series Six* (London: Constable Publishers)

"Sweet Jesus" in *Queer View Mirror 2* (Vancouver: Arsenal Pulp Press)

"Lucky" in *Best Canadian Stories* (Ottawa: Oberon Press)

"The Murdered Child" in *Death Comes Easy: The Gay Times Book of Murder Stories* (London: Gay Men's Press)

"The Tattoo Artist" in *The Year's Best Fantasy & Horror: Fifteenth Edition* (New York: St Martin's Press)

"The Truth about Love" in *Contra/Diction: The New Queer Male Fiction* (Vancouver: Arsenal Pulp Press)

"Touching Darkness" in *Bend Sinister: The Gay Times Book of Disturbing Stories* (London: Gay Men's Press)

"Peggy Lee in Africa" received the CBC Canadian Literary Award for Short Story (First Prize) and a Distinguished Story Citation from *Best American Stories*

"Beggars" received a Lorian Hemingway Short Story Award

"Wild Dogs" received a CBC Canadian Literary Award for Short Story
(Second Prize)

"Hieroglyphics I" received a *Prairie Fire* Short Fiction Competition Prize

"Chiggers" received a *Prism International* Short Fiction Competition
Prize

"The History of a Hopeful Heart" was filmed by Jeremy Podeswa as
Touch for Rebelfilms/da da Kamera

"Angie, Short For Angel" was performed by Patrick Roscoe at The
Edinburgh Festival and for CBC Radio

"Peggy Lee in Africa" and "The Tattoo Artist" were also broadcast by
CBC Radio

Part One

BEFORE I WAS SET FREE

*La vie de chacun d'entre nous n'est pas une tentative
d'aimer. Elle est l'unique essai.*

—Pascal Quignard

Rorschach 1: The Rough Beast

"DON'T ASK," I SAY WHEN THE DARK BEAST WONDERS ABOUT MY PAST, AS if the simplest questions regarding personal history are too complicated to consider. Even name and age and place of birth remain for me elusive points beyond the reach of plain statement; I have invented and reinvented my life story so often and for so long that fact can be separated from fantasy only with difficulty, and never with finality. Was I born in 1962 on an obscure Mediterranean island floating off the coast of Alicante, or did I appear upon this planet three years later in some cramped Canadian town? Was my childhood dreamed amid the jungle of Tanzania's Ngondo Hills or in a Mexican village sprinkled beneath slopes similarly tangled with green? Perhaps seven early years were spent in a cold, dark cage where I was persistently starved, beaten, violated; or, for an equal amount of time, until they said she was unfit, I orbited the Pacific Northwest with a mother who danced out of reach of men with eyes that burned in the dark beyond the stage. Say the pale nuns at St Cecilia's had to care for me when I remained mute about what happened before I was found on their steps. When I wouldn't tell who, when I wouldn't tell why. Did my adult voice emerge when I discovered myself at the northern edge of the Sahara, adrift upon the dunes, in search of the lost oasis? Or, by then, was home a decaying rooming house in Hollywood, a corner on the Boulevard, the coffee shop where beat-up angels ruffled wet feathers and waited out the rain? In what year occurred that cold winter in Paris where, from my hotel window, I studied the tops of trees in the park across the way, as if the design they made above grey roofs might explain why I shivered here until spring? An autumn in Vienna blurs into four difficult seasons in Lisbon, bleeds into six years caught within the spell cast by garlic and orange blossoms, lit by gaudy neon on the Guadalquivir. Do you really wish to travel with me through a labyrinth of names and dates and places, in hope of discovering the Minotaur who with hollow voice demands the straightforward, sequential data of a past before he fills on the human flesh which embodies this experience? Occasionally I examine my map of skin for clues about where I have come from and what happened to me there. Lines, marks, blots. Upon my left elbow curves the thickened raised souvenir, shaped like a worm, of my fall from the top of an apple tree (twenty years ago?), from where I believed I could see to the end of the world, to the end of this existence. Adorning my forehead, at the hairline, discernible only by touch, a slight indentation betrays that a white horse's unshod hoof once broke my skull and allowed the eager blood behind to find release. A souvenir from an L.A. knife crosses the right side of my torso; decorating my left knee is a nagging reminder of one more African accident suffered upon the Ngondo hills. Evidence of too many years in southern sunlight creases the corners of my eyes as, in bed, I explain to lovers how these scars came to mark once blank, perfect skin. Of course, this autobiography I spin like some ersatz Scheherazade may vary from one telling to the next. Of course, I'll resort without qualms to any of my dazzling tricks to sustain your interest, to postpone your departure. Really, my torso was torn in Tanzania when I was ten, and not by a knife. Actually, what the knife slashed was my knee; honestly, this happened in San Francisco, not Los Angeles. In truth, I looked from a Paris window in summer, not winter. When conflicting memories disturb me with the notion that autobiography may be a science less than exact, I turn to documents designed to define a human being in the baldest terms. They offer little help: my driver's licence presents a birth date found nowhere on my passport; in fact, there are three passports—one genuine and two forgeries—each sufficiently authentic to allow borders to be crossed without incident. Yes, I've travelled through the world using various identities—not because I dislike my true history and wish to eliminate it, but because of an inability to stay contained within the parameters of autobiography, of any constricting system: I still insist I can be anyone, everyone; anything, everything. For television cameras and journalists, we continually invent ourselves—all of us who inhabit this skin with its multiple layers that will ultimately be dissected and probed and analyzed in the laboratory of love—we stubbornly embark on yet another act of experimentation, creation, rebirth. In the end, I am only a fiction: shaped by editing, subject to revision, open to interpretation, always in danger of going out of print. Every year or so, a *Who's Who* entry bearing one of my names is updated with what are, hopefully, at least approximations of the truth. One day, I may perform this task with greater certainty. Would that indicate evolution, maturity, self-acceptance? Or serve instead as a white flag of defeat, an admission of limited possibilities? Such questions do not apply; the jargon that poses them rings absurd in the dark tunnels that connect longing to loss; it has no relevance to this fumbling journey. "Never mind," I tell the Minotaur, who still insists on concrete fact, before I rewrite myself once again, this time as hero. Now named Theseus, I slay the rough beast and his desire for something more than myth.

The History of a Hopeful Heart

ONE NIGHT, WHEN I AM SIX, I FALL ASLEEP IN MY BED BUT WAKE UP somewhere else. I'm naked and hungry and cold. The room is bare and dark, with walls and floor of rough cement. There are no windows. The steel door is locked. If there's a light socket in the ceiling, the bulb is missing or burned out. As surely as my heart will beat again and then again, I know my parents will not open the door, will not bring me clothes and food and blankets, will not arrive with comfort. They don't know I'm gone, they aren't able to find me, they have decided not to bring me home: the reason is unimportant. It's irrelevant how I got here, or where this is. It doesn't matter why I remain in this room, and others equally dark and bare, for the next seven years.

As soon as I realize my mother and father will not save me, they become only any woman and any man who have as little to do with me as the boy who now shares their pale green house instead of me. I can nearly taste the sweetness of his breath as he sleeps in the bed that held my body. I'm almost able to hear him playing with toy soldiers that once felt my touch. His name remains elusive until I learn from darkness that there's no difference between what is imagined and what is known.

My sense of time is imprecise and marked only by the ticking of my heart. After spending what seems like several days in darkness, I become as old as the ancient wanderer who has searched one thousand years for love. He has crawled back and forth across the world, as I have done between these four walls, to find the holy place where He might appear. Only the desperate are ever truly hopeful.

If you stood outside the door and listened through the keyhole, you'd hear me chant: sky is blue, grass is green, God is good. These are songs I croon, arms wrapped tightly around myself. I wonder if anyone hears. Listens but does not answer. I never call out for rescue. There's no use. I know that right away, before my throat can swell with a single scream.

I lie on the floor, press against the wall. Both surfaces are equally ungiving. Cement soaks up my body's heat but offers none in return. I try to recall sensations of softness and warmth with such strength that there might materialize beneath my head a feather pillow, against my skin a sheet of silk. The more frequently memory reaches for a vision, the sooner it fades. We must add to and not only draw from the images stored inside ourselves like money in a bank, or we become a vault as empty as this room. Cement is hard and rough, I remind myself while darkness blurs the simplest definitions. What's soft, what's smooth? I grope blindly for an answer until I realize only one such thing is present. I touch my bare skin.

As light drains from the chambers beneath my porous skin, darkness seeps in to replace it. Peering through an opened flap of my flesh, you would be unable to discern between outer and inner obscurity. I must fight the feeling that my body has dematerialized into particles of darkness. I savour sensations of hunger and cold because they prove that my physical existence continues. I'd be grateful for any touch that provided further evidence that I remain alive, whatever the emotion to inspire it.

For a long time, I am surrounded by pure silence. The walls that enclose me must be very thick, and this room must be far removed from the world. Eventually I can no longer hear my voice, my breath, my heartbeat. I hold my hand an inch before my eyes, but the darkness fails to thicken with a hint that anything is there. I suspect I've become deaf and mute and blind as stone.

By touch I discover a bucket in a corner of the room, though I'm convinced nothing stood there before. Its purpose is to contain the urine and feces I've been licking off the floor to stay alive. As the bucket fills and the air stews with decay, my nostrils quiver with excitement that my sense of smell remains intact. This emotion toward the bucket turns to gratitude for providing evidence that my hearing has also survived. An insect rustling to and from my collected wastes breaks the utter silence. Each crunch of a roach by my teeth sounds loud as a gunshot. No matter how many insects I eat, there will always be more. I'm dizzied by this wealth of food, this endless supply of company.

When I can't stop shivering, I smear my naked skin with fresh excrement and luxuriate in its warmth. Even as the blanket cools, it continues to beckon swarms of roaches that offer further heat. Their tickling makes me giggle.

Footsteps approach from beyond my room. They belong to a grown man, I think at once. He passes my door without slowing. As the sound dissolves into silence, I'm already anticipating its return. At this moment, cold and hunger are replaced by hope. Breathing mutates into a synonym for waiting. Now my existence has purpose.

My prayers are answered. Three or four or five days later, he passes my room again and then continues to return at intervals. Does longing trick me into believing that each time he comes back sooner than before? Does desire deceive me that each time his footsteps slow further as they near? Has he begun to pause outside the door, then to linger longer and longer? If my heart weren't beating loudly, would I hear him breathe on the other side of a separating inch of steel? Would he walk away for good if I cried out to him? These questions belong to a test that will decide if I am worthy.

A key turns in the lock. The door opens. I treasure what happens next.

Overwhelming weight, warmth. I welcome these sensations with the joy of every explorer who beholds a newly discovered world. Like phosphorescence and gravity, the act of love has always existed, however much we insist it is our own invention.

At my lover's first touch, I understand that the green house was always inhabited by another boy. A second visit confirms that this room has been my only home. Our third encounter instructs me that darkness is the only element to which I've ever belonged.

Sometimes he doesn't enter my room to fill me with his love, but cracks open the door only to toss food inside. It has no flavour, it doesn't satisfy, it could be paper or dirt. I leave the food for my insect friends. I suspect I'm being tested further. My need for nourishment is what has drawn my lover; the end of my hunger would mean the end of his attention. My belly grumbles in the dark as I wonder about the hand that throws the food, then about the heart that moves the hand.

At other times, he jabs a needle into my arm, and I descend to deeper darkness, wake in another room. Except for a slightly higher or lower temperature, and staler or fresher air, a new room might be an old one. Then I discover countless minute differences between the cement skin of the current cell and that of my previous home. But the darkness is constant. A thousand quirks in its character are known and cherished by me alone; like any loyal ally, I would not reveal them though beaten at tedious length. I'll only say that sometimes I believe I've been taken to a room just beside the last one. I'm higher above the world or farther inside it; nearer or more distant from the centre of a city. Yet a thin gold line never shines beneath the locked door. Without this crack of illumination, I have no final proof that the globe has not transformed into a black egg twirling beyond reach of the sun's warmth and light. The moves from one obscure vacuum to the next have no purpose I can discover, except to teach me that every room is dark and cold and bare.

Each time his footsteps near, my heart pounds more loudly in their rhythm. A thin, mechanical cry, like that of a nestling, emerges from my throat. I don't know whether I'll be fed or beaten; my anticipation is an equal measure of fear of hurt and hope for comfort. Slowly these two emotions become inseparable, and pleasure is inextricable from pain. I take satisfaction from each blow of his fists, every brutal kick. Fulfillment floods me when he crams my body's cavities with himself. His generosity touches me. Sometimes he feeds me afterward, sometimes not. Eventually food becomes as unimportant as light and warmth. When my belly groans, it's calling hungrily for his hands; the only tastes I savour are the salty richness of my blood and of his saliva, sweat, semen. If I did not starve, he wouldn't feed me; if I weren't cold, his body would fail to warm me. Without the darkness, he could not offer illumination.

His visits are unpredictable, and always expected. They occur with a frequency that gradually increases; they're marked by an intensity that steadily builds. I wonder where this will lead. Feel him push farther into me, like a brave explorer daring to enter more deeply the dark labyrinth from which he might not emerge alive. Maybe he'll become lost forever in the twisting tunnels, or maybe the rough beast will get him. What glittering treasure in which haunted cave causes him to take this risk?

He has never spoken; nor have I heard him moan, grunt, cry. I don't know his face except as darkness made solid. If he bumped into me on the street, I'd fail to recognize him. I would wonder if each passerby were him. Strangers would glance quickly away from the small boy with starving eyes.

Waiting for my lover's next visit, I try to guess whether his face is lined or smooth. Is his hair dark or light or grey? By his strength, I believe he must be fairly young. But I picture his eyes as old, with the sadness unique to age. Nagging suspicion builds that he's someone I once knew but have forgotten.

Does he miss me when he goes away? Ache for me as I ache for him? I envision him walking from this room—smoothing hair, straightening tie, dabbing handkerchief at a spot of my blood on his wrist. He drives to the supermarket to buy the loaf of bread his wife asked him to pick up on the way home. His blue car pulls into a driveway before a green house. He tosses three pennies to the small boy with hungry eyes who waits on the front steps, then enters the house to greet his wife with a careful kiss. The family eats supper. Afterward the father sits in the living room behind a shielding newspaper. When she looks toward him, his wife reads headlines that scream murder, war, accident. She turns to her husband in bed and he moves away. I should check on Rickie, he says. He stands above the bed in which the small boy lies awake with closed eyes. He looks down at a face as smooth and white as blank paper. His fists are hidden in his pockets. The man doesn't touch his son; the son's eyes don't open. When he sleeps at last, the boy beholds images that make him wish he dreamed pure darkness.

Long ago a small boy was beaten and starved and violated. Even as he grows into a large man, there isn't space beneath his skin to contain all the enormous, lasting hurt. It must be shared. I feel my lover's blind need to rid himself of what he still can't bear. I feel his anger and sorrow when such release does not occur, and the steadily growing violence in his effort to achieve it. He tries again and again to smash through my skin so he can curl his own battered body in my dark room, float in blood like a fetus that knows only warmth and comfort. I would like to kiss away every tear in his eyes, stroke his back with tenderness, suck out all his sorrow. I believe I can save him. Please let me try. Give me one more chance. Yet I automatically protect my eyes and ears and belly from his blows. However much I want to, I can't give myself up completely. The words of love I wish to utter emerge from my mouth as a high-pitched squeal, which resembles the noise made by a pig being slaughtered and which continues until he forces my head into the pail of waste or fills my mouth with himself. I feel inadequate when my lover leaves my room as troubled as he's been for so long, for too long.

When he's gone, cuts and bruises left on my body glow with heat. They ooze sweet pus, which nourishes like placenta. I scratch at the souvenirs of his touch to make them sting more sharply. My throbbing skin assures me that my lover isn't merely a figment of fantasy. It swears that I don't always lack human company in the dark. The pain fills the emptiness of his absence. Two words twist and coil and wrap around each other in my mind. *Love hurts.*

Three times an angel appears. That's what I call her, since she resembles the winged ornament that hovers at the top of Christmas trees inside green houses. She floats down through the darkness and with her presence illuminates my room. My eyes aren't used to such light. It dazzles, it blinds. Soft feathers enfold me, wrap warmly around me. Long kisses feed me milk and honey, then balm my sores that never heal. The angel bathes me in scented water and salves my battered skin with fragrant oils. Her wordless murmur means: one day the darkness will turn to light; or, the darkness isn't so bad; or, the darkness is for the best. With a wave of her wand, the angel's gone. I hate her. Not because she won't carry me away on her strong wings. I don't wish to leave my room and lose my lover and wouldn't go if begged. My subservience has managed to neutralize pain and cold, darkness and hunger. Each visit from the angel turns those forces back into bitter enemies I must fight until beaten once more. Then, in unison, my conquerors chant: We're loyal companions, not fickle friends; it's less painful to live always in darkness than sometimes in light. We'll win every war, they boast.

Time seems to slow when he's not here. While waiting for his return, I repeat my prayers: *Bless him, save him, bring him back.* Or I fill the dragging hours by recalling his last visit. Review that act of love over and over until it becomes a film in my head that can be started with the flick of a switch. Crouched against the wall, I watch the same scenes recur. There are certain favourite ones. Play them in slow motion, make the pleasure last. Scrape myself against cement to approximate, however roughly, the sensation afforded by his loving touch. Smile when my skin screams. Happy.

In the dark, my touch is sometimes clumsy. I fumble with the switch and by accident start a film I don't wish to watch but can't halt. I see a boy of five on the front steps of a green house. He wears short blue pants and a white shirt with short sleeves. His arms wrap around his legs and his head rests on his naked knees. Sunlight warms his skin. Music drifts like motes of gold dust through the open kitchen window. His mother is listening to the radio as she cooks supper. Tonight there'll be macaroni baked soft and warm, with cheese melted among blood-red tomatoes that explode like bombs of flavour. The scent of cooking and the sound of music twine like velvet ribbons around the boy. He narrows his eyes until sunlight enters them like a crack of gold light beneath the door of a dark room. He's waiting for his father to come home from work. A blue car will turn the corner and approach from down the street. If the boy on the steps looks away, the blue car will turn into another driveway. His father will go into another house, pausing to toss three pennies to another boy, who will bury them like pirate treasure.

After the wrong film plays and the wrong images fill me, my lover stays away for longer than usual because there's no empty space in me for him to enter. His sustained absence is punishment for my thinking of something besides him. I rock back and forth in the dark, knock my head against the wall, replicate the rhythm we create while making love.

Acute need to hear my lover come back sharpens my ears or I currently inhabit a room adjacent to one where another boy exists in darkness. Through my walls penetrate muffled sounds of brutal attention being lavished upon a substitute for myself. This boy keeps crying out loud after my lover leaves, when he should be mute with gratitude. He must be younger than me, he must be too little to know better. He's insufficiently evolved to appreciate real love; the precious gift is wasted on him. I seethe with jealousy until I correct my emotion. This is an opportunity to realize how lucky I've been each time my lover has chosen to come to me rather than any other boy.

I hear a host of other boys once I detect the first. They must inhabit rooms not only on either side of mine, but also ones above and below and farther removed. I begin to believe this structure contains numerous floors of long hallways lined with hundreds of dark cells. Sounds of incessant crying travel toward me from every direction. I must fight to hold onto the belief that I was my lover's first choice and that I remain his favourite. It's impossible that anyone else could need his touch as much as I do or receive it with my degree of gratitude. Soon he has to realize that no boy can replace me, soon he will come back.

Until now, my lover has always returned one or two or three weeks after my visions of green houses and blue cars have driven him away. This time is different. I suspect months have passed since I was last graced with his presence. My skin shrieks to be pounded into pulp. The sound almost drowns out the incessant crying of boys who continue to populate the surrounding darkness. I am frightened, I am lost. How many years have I spent in obscurity, and how much has my body changed during this time? I become further convinced that the boys my lover now visits instead of me are as small as I was when he first came to my room. I've grown too big. I'm no longer of any use to him. I will myself to shrink. I refuse to put a single roach into my mouth. If I starve myself sufficiently, love must return.

I become increasingly confused without my lover's guiding touch. Cries of other boys no longer seem to travel through thick walls or steel doors, but sound as clear and loud as though originating within my room. The sobbing bounces between these walls, echoes through the hollow inside me. At last weeping turns into whimpering, which finally gives way to quiet. I interpret this silence to mean my lover has tired of my younger rivals; like me, they're holding breath and straining to hear him come back.

I detect a key turning in the lock, but my door doesn't open. Footsteps move away, leave silence behind. By this point, my skin doesn't hold even vague memories of my lover's touch. I must feel him on me and in me, if just once more. As I've never dared to do, I call out for my lover. When my fists hammer against the door, it swings open. After a thousand failed attempts to open this door, I believed further attempts were futile. Since the long-ago moment when I ceased trying, I now know, the room has been unlocked. The sound of a turning key has always been my heart twisting open.

I'm afraid to leave my room because it's my only home. For a moment, fear of loss holds me here. But I must find my lover. I'm suddenly convinced he will never come to me again. He has given up hope that I'll ever be able to swallow all his darkness. I've failed him once too often. Emerging from my room, I move down a long, dimly lit hallway lined with closed doors. Like the one I've just opened, they're scratched and marked and unnumbered. Through steel seeps the sound of boys weeping softly. As my footsteps approach, the cries cease. I sense breath being held, pulses racing with hope. When I pass by, the painful sounds resume in a higher key. I could open any of these doors, fall upon the waiting boy inside, soothe him with my loving blows. But I need such comfort myself and proceed in search of it. The hallway bends. I turn a corner and reach a flight of descending stairs. I open a door at the bottom and find myself on a street at dawn. Night is leaving the world, a red planet is rising in the sky, I am falling into darkness.

Warm. Soft. White. I presume I'm in the arms of my angel, then realize this is a bed with white sheets in a white room. Equally white bandages cover most of my body. A tube runs from a glass tank filled with clouded liquid into a vein in my left arm. The odourless air is too thin for my lungs to breathe, and the light is too glaring for my eyes to bear. My skin is suffocating beneath bandages, blankets, sheets. Neither the pillow nor the bed beneath me is hard enough. I'm drowning in softness.

I gasp and struggle until hands hold me down. They're not His hands. These pink hands belong to men and women in white whose faces wear expressions I can't read, whose lips issue language I don't understand. Are these looks of love? Words of hate? A needle sinks into my right arm. It fills me with hope that I'll waken in a dark room and that my lover will come to me there. Before falling into blackness, I notice a pale sky gleaming beyond the open window. The fresh air entering the white room stings my eyes and hurts my throat. The drawn curtain flutters white as an angel's wing.

I wake to the same white room, the same bright light. Disappointment. Darkness drains from me in a way that exposes the emptiness beneath my skin, and that leaves me weak and weary and sad. I remain still and silent as the routine around me becomes familiar. Although I continue to wait faithfully for Him, only men and women in white appear. They touch my forehead and wrists with hands weighing as little as air. The tube is taken from my left arm; my right arm is injected less often. My hair and nails are cut. Then the bandages and stitches are removed to be replaced by a thin white robe that rustles like paper. I watch mouths open and close as they make noise I know is meant for me. I strain to summon precious sensations—cold, darkness, hunger—but the bodies that bend over mine refuse to allow me to enjoy my former state of grace. They wish to kill me with cruel kindness. No matter how tightly I close my eyes, some light seeps inside the lids. At night, the lights scattered around me glow like wounds on the skin of darkness.

A man who wears blue visits each day. He sits by my bed and moves his mouth. I wait for his fists to strike. My skin aches more painfully as each sore heals and each bruise vanishes. When the man in blue doesn't touch me and when I remain silent, we're both disappointed. Why won't he lovingly hurt me? What am I doing wrong? I struggle to speak his language as it grows familiar and slowly acquires meaning. Lay me on the hard floor and love me with all your strength, I plan to say when my clumsy tongue learns to move correctly. The man nods as I fight for my first word. It finally emerges. *Darkness*, I beg.

They ask my name and age and place of birth. They want to know what happened before I was found on the street at dawn. Who did this to you? What was done to you? Where? For how long? I tell them about the dark room but not about my lover. Before that? I describe the small boy who waited on the front steps of the green house. Was that you? I hesitate. Then I mention my angel. I reveal that one day she will come to me again. Lift me onto her strong wings. Carry me back to the dark room. Save me.

They move me to another white room. Sometimes I'm supposed to lie on the bed, sometimes I'm supposed to sit in the chair, sometimes I'm supposed to walk around a large space containing other people dressed in rustling white gowns like me. Eat this. Then go to sleep. Now wake up. I know how to be obedient. I speak and the doctors make dark lines on white paper. They look at each other and exchange single words: *shock, damage, amnesia, trauma*. The more darkness they put on the paper, the happier they are. I learn how to please them; it's easy to know what they want. Keep my eyes open and blink the lids. Look at people when they talk to me. Pull the corners of my mouth upwards. Avoid mentioning my angel again, never speak about my lover once. I please the doctors, but they offer no reward in return. No love.

I ask for a pair of blue shorts and a shirt with short white sleeves. They give me a pair of long blue pants and a thick white sweater instead. It's winter, they explain, seeing my disappointment with the clothes. First they say that my parents can't be found, then that my parents are waiting for me to return home. Now the doctors exchange different words: *hope, cure, miracle*. One day, I'm going to learn to swim, to dance, to ride a bicycle—they promise. I'll stroll beside the sea and the sun will toast my skin. Some day I will drive a blue car to a green house where a wife and child are waiting for me. My name is Richard, and I am thirteen years old and I am as good as new.

It's time to leave the hospital. I'm frightened. I curl with closed eyes in a corner of my white room, though I know it's wrong. Heels click, tap, click down the tiled hall beyond the door. The footsteps grow louder, fade away. None sound like His. A hand floats on my shoulder. A voice wavers into my ear, whispers that it's good to cry. My eyes open. I recognize this woman in white. The other nurses call her Angie. It must be short for angel, I think. Angie's eyes hint that she was once loved in darkness, too. One day you'll forget, she vows.

The car is silver instead of blue. The house is grey, not green. The man and woman aren't my father and mother. Their eyes watch me carefully, nervously. This is your room, they say. I close the curtains, shut the door, lie on the floor against the wall. A knock. I don't answer, but the door opens anyway. I can't feel the woman's weightless hand smoothing my hair. The man doesn't touch me. Doesn't love me.

The woman always wants me to leave my room and play outside. I can go to the river or I can go to the park. I'm free. The white winter sunlight hurts my head. The clean air cuts my throat. I search the neighbourhood for a blue car parked in the driveway of a green house, though now I know those things were just a dream. Only my lover's touch was ever real. I'm starting to forget what I need to remember. Too much food leaves me dull, the overheated house keeps me drowsy. I hunger for sharp appetite. Have another helping, invites the smiling woman.

I must go to school. I sit in a small room with a woman who says I can join the other children in a larger room when I catch up. She teaches me this and that; I learn how to please her. A bell rings, and it's time to walk through the crowded hallways. So many boys approaching, passing; they're here, they're gone. Several come up to me. You're Richard, they say. I answer their questions. I look into their eyes and blink the lids of mine. They shrug, turn away. Their running shoes squeak. I think of rats scurrying in the dark on the hunt for roaches whose bodies they crunch with sharp white teeth. I lick my lips with nostalgia.

A boy named John wears a shirt with short white sleeves and jeans dyed a particular shade of blue. Hunger flickers in his eyes. When other boys join him, John's face changes into a smiling mask like theirs. Together they march down the bright hallway in step to some beat I can't hear.

I like the lockers best. Everyone has their own. You spin a steel wheel in search of secret numbers. There's a click when you get it right. The metal door opens onto a small, dark space. Girls' lockers are tidy as dollhouses, but boys throw books into a jumble of baseball mitts and running shoes and uneaten lunches. After banging their lockers shut, boys not named John must always kick the door, making one more dent.

My locker is number 267. I won't say the combination. I carry my books around with me or leave them in the small classroom. My locker is empty, except for a badly battered toy soldier I found in the park. Someone lost him or threw him away. While the teacher draws white lines on the blackboard, I see the soldier waiting alertly in his small dark room. He listens for my footsteps, but when only those of other boys pass he doesn't cry. It's all right to cry, the woman in the grey house says. I'm sitting on the front steps. My arms are wrapped around my legs, my head rests on my knees. Cars pass up and down the street as I drift in and out of dreams.

My angel will never come for me. She thinks I don't need her any more because I am in light. Sometimes she flits with white clouds through the sky. She sees me below and waves her wand in greeting. Clouds break, scatter, dissolve. My fickle friend has gone to a boy who waits in a dark, bare room to be enfolded in her wings.

My skin is white, smooth, unmarked. A good healer, says the doctor. There was no lover, my blank flesh mocks. I dig a knife into a secret place on my body and watch blood rise to the surface. It feels warm and tastes salty.

I write a scarlet word on my arm. *Love.* Lick it up, swallow it away. The small wound burns like fire, but one that dies too quickly. Pale warmth left behind is equal in strength to the weak spring sunshine. Summer will be coming soon, everyone says. That doesn't matter to me. The sun won't ever be hot enough to brand my flesh.

I say some boys and girls have invited me to roast marshmallows and hot dogs over a bonfire in the park by the river. When the flames have turned into glowing coals, we'll sing songs and drink Cokes around them. The man and the woman are pleased. They smile and tell me to have a good time. I dress in blue jeans, white T-shirt, sneakers. I walk past the empty park by the river, along blocks lined with tidy houses, into the city. On a corner I watch for blue cars containing a single man. Count them until I pass number 267. When the fire inside me has burned into glowing coals and my blood begins to sing, a blue car pulls to the curb. The driver reaches over and opens the door. I get inside. As we move down the street, I stare straight ahead to avoid seeing his sad, old eyes. He wants to know my name and age and place of birth. Out of the corner of my eye, I see him glance at me. He's trying to determine if I resemble a small boy who once waited on the front steps of a green house. A boy who was himself.

Turn off the light, I say. When the room is dark, he pulls me toward the bed. The floor, I say.

He strokes my arm. Soft, he says. His touch is light as air. Without my angel's wings, I'm falling through miles of empty sky. Hit me, I say. Feel him freeze. Feel myself thud onto the floor with a force that jars me, breaks me. Don't speak, I say. Harder, I plead. More, I beg.

It's late when I return to the grey house. The man and the woman are waiting up for me. They look questioningly at my bruised arms and face. I tripped, I explain. The man says he drove past the park but saw no fire encircled by singers. We played in John's rumpus room because it was too cold outside, I tell him. I close my door, turn off the light, find the floor.

Sounds of the man and the woman talking in the next room last nearly until morning. I don't try to understand the muffled words. They don't matter. My skin is tingling, throbbing, burning. Evidence of fresh love stays with me through the night. Alive again.

I search for Him one or two nights a week, when I feel the mark of the last hand fade. The man and woman look at each other when I leave the house in T-shirt and running shoes and jeans. They don't ask where I'm going. In the city, I discover certain corners where cars are more likely to stop for me. I learn that I must ask the men for more than three pennies if I want to be taken to their rooms. I tell them this or that; it's easy to know what they need to hear. My name is John, I lie. That's mine too, they laugh. I might go in a red or a black car, if no blue ones stop and my need for more love is strong. Some of the men look puzzled or frightened when I ask to be loved hard. They quickly hand me dollars and tell me to go. Others like to use their hands heavily. Those ones seek me at the corner again. No thank you, I say. A single experience is enough to tell me they aren't Him. None of them are able to love me strongly enough. I'm searching for the only man who can.

At school, the teacher no longer speaks of the day when I'll catch up. I no longer try to please either her or the man and woman at the grey house. I save myself for those who offer the right rewards. One morning, I notice that John has left his locker open. I take the toy solider from my locker and put it into his. In the afternoon, boys and girls are crowded there. They fall silent as I pass. John lives in a yellow house on Jasmine Street, five blocks from the grey one. I walk by on my way into the city, but John is never sitting on the front steps, never waiting.

I bury the money the men give me. Hide it like pirate treasure deep beneath a black circle by the river where once a ring of children might have sung up to the stars. Leave it there to be found one day by a boy who needs to buy a large army of toy soldiers because no one else will fight for him.

One night, I get inside a car and look straight ahead as usual. Richard, says the driver. I turn and see the man who lives in the grey house. What are you doing? he asks. I say that I was waiting for a ride because it's too far to walk home. The man drives in silence. His face is angry; his hands grip the steering wheel tightly. For the first time, I think he might be able to love me. At the house, the man and the woman say they don't want me to go out alone after dark any more. I wait all night in my dark room for the man to come to me. I haven't been loved in a full week; my skin holds no tender memory of a touch. The door doesn't open. In the morning, I walk past the school and into the city. The man and the woman will not look for me, I know.

I live in a hotel. Because the light bulbs are always stolen by one of the addicts or prostitutes in the building, the hallways remain dim. They're lined on either side by scratched, unnumbered doors. Each room contains a boy. Their crying stops as my footsteps approach, only to resume when my key fails to turn in their lock. My room is the same as theirs. It contains a bed, a chair, a sink. I curl on the floor and am soothed by the sound of roaches scurrying in the corners. I've taped heavy black paper over the window, and I keep the curtain closed. I'm never lonely, I'm visited often. My door is opened as many as five times in one night. As the months pass, my visitors leave less money when they go. Soon they'll toss just three pennies at me after finishing with their fists. I can't complain. My lucky skin is never devoid of traces of love; it glows with warmth even in winter, though the hotel's heating rarely works. Tomorrow or the next day, my lover will come back. One or another of the men who visit will be Him. I won't need to see His face because my skin's perfect memory will recognize His touch at once. He will love me hard and He will love me for good. In pure darkness, I await the sound of His approaching footsteps. They will march to the rhythm of my hopeful heart.

Sweet Jesus

THEY SEARCHED FOR MY MOTHER AND THEY SEARCHED FOR MY FATHER, then Sister Mary explained that I belonged to sweet Jesus for eternity instead. She gave me a picture of a man with a long face and yellow hair floating in blue robes amid white clouds. Now they called me Matthew. Like each pair of my cracked shoes, the name felt too tight or too loose, reminding me always of another boy who had worn it first. Doctors peered down my throat for a secret hiding there, photographed the dreams drifting in my head. "If only you would speak," they said. "If only you would tell." They would ask again about the red coat that was found with me in a doorway on Union Avenue among the roaming cats and cars. A woman wrapped the red coat around my body before she left me there, they suggested. "I was lost," quavered Sister Mary. "But now I'm found." At night, the other children cried in neat rows of beds beneath the crosses, amid the smell of onions peeling in the dark. I hid the picture of sweet Jesus under my pillow. He would whisper whenever I moved my head, he would make a promise I kept safe inside a secret box. Sometimes, while the thin nuns cleaned the corners and the bigger children were playing bad games, I could hear another voice reach toward me from an afternoon before all these rainy ones at St Cecilia's. Sweet smoke curled behind my eyes during mass, a bright red mouth laughed through the cloud. Veils fluttered inside my skin, I started shaking, Sister Mary placed the stick on my tongue again. Then the nuns stopped trying to teach me, and the disappointed doctors went away. My broom swept mute years away. It scratched the floor and raised a cloud of dust to Heaven, and the priest with spicy breath showed me a secret inside his lavender robes. In a circle, the nuns clapped their hands at Christmas and asked me for one more dance until I was too big, until I had to go. They gave me to a sour man near the docks. I filled boxes in the back, waited for him to come to me through the dark. His hot face moaned while big boats moved slowly down the muddy river. Another wafer melted on my tongue. One day I found out that I had lost sweet Jesus. My box of secrets was empty. Maybe another boy belonged to Him for eternity now. My feet followed red coats in the street and wondered where my prayers would take me. I'll never tell, sweet Jesus. I'll never ask who, I'll never ask why.

Angie, Short for Angel

ANGIE, ANGIE, SHORT FOR ANGEL, YOU FOUND HIM LYING ON THE SIDEWALK in the tough Tenderloin where you laboured every midnight amid stalled cars and liquor stores and sad scarecrows with sawdust hearts hanging from rows of crosses. Sulky Sue and Beat-Up Betty hugged by your side and slurred: Angie, short for angel, leave alone that little boy who is broken and busted on such mean cement with black tears bleeding from his eyes. A little boy, a beautiful little boy, spoke Angie in a tone of wonder, bending beneath red and blue bars of neon that blinked bleary offers of rooms, rooms, ten dollars for a room. The purple feathers of your wings brushed the boy's bruised cheek, Angie, opening his eyes to see you there above him, your face painted like some exhausted clown, and to wonder if Heaven were this vagrant one-way street.

You were coughing like it was no joke that last September, Angie; however much you ruffled your feathers and swore that being sick was just for sissies, your so-called friends were frightened for you. Since Sulky Sue and Beat-Up Betty could sense a seriously worsening situation, they shrugged up their shoulder straps and huffed: Some girls still got to make a million dollars before dawn. They slow-danced away through a little crowd of ducky boys who were gathered around and singing: Angie, short for angel, please don't jump-start that baby boy while he is down. Didn't you notice that the neighbourhood was dying all around you, Angie; that only echoes from the graveyard tattooed down these streets where on your highest heels, your brand-new stilts, you stalked like an acrobatic child far above this merry-go-round world wheeling and whirling through quanta of dark space? Couldn't you see a flying wedge of winos leap over the boy's body as though it was the famous crack that breaks every mother's back, leaving all those lame lonely women to wonder exactly where they've gone wrong? How his hair was tousled by the breeze that continued to blow hosts of hopeful ones to a state of mind called California, though this sweet landscape melted long ago like multi-coloured candy on your tongue and left a bitter taste behind? Yet Angie, short for angel, irreversibly you pulled the boy's head onto the lap of your robes, which had been pure white before the blues dyed them scarlet and put those ribbons in your hair.

Remember how you took him in a taxi, and up the stairs you pulled tricks on other nights until tomorrow. You were always planning to brighten the grey space with rainbows on the walls and to banish uninvited roaches that wouldn't leave the kitchen where you never cooked, food being what your mother feeds you until home is left forever. But it was cheap to live among the *cholos*, across from the old mission where Spanish priests collected souls in big black hats once upon a time. Now dreams tied to tickets watched through pawnshop windows as welfare mothers slowly waltzed by within the arms of Valium and sometimes Seconal. Now posses of *pachucos* cracked whips to tame each corner, but Angie, you would prance up to squeeze the butter flesh beneath their smooth silk shirts and to whisper: Let's have some rough romance. Causing the brown-eyed boys to droop their double lashes and mumble *shucks* in broken English. They would watch you walk away beneath a moon no longer yours since you had fallen from the stars to land upon these several streets where you were celebrated after midnight closed its fist around the city, holding all the loose ones tight inside the pocket of a pool game played for half a dollar and a kiss.

See how you sat beside the boy on the sofa bed in the front room, beneath the window staring out at Sixth Street. In a voice concocted from smoke and scotch, you urged: Don't try to talk until you learn the words for it. Didn't you press the warm, wet cloth against his cheeks and clean his cuts with stinging antiseptic, every nurse an angel making it okay? He studied you, Angie, until you passed a hand across your face and said that no one ever saw you by the light of day. It made you tremble to see his solemn eyes the colour of your daddy's old blue shirts hanging on the line to dry.

When six days turned to lucky number seven, you asked who did it to him. The boy muttered something about a guy who was a little nice for a little while. Oh, I'm intimately acquainted with that gentleman, he's a famous character, you exclaimed, ejecting a stream of acrid smoke from a corner of your mouth. He has many names and many faces, but always he leaves you hurting the very same way. You watched the boy's petalled lips come together to touch in longing then draw apart in fear. And you thought: Once there was a place anyone calls Kansas, until a tornado twists inside our hearts and twirls us away from the dirt and the dust and the drab voices that say you can't do this, you can't do that, don't go there. So angels finally have no wish to go back home, however much they speak of assorted heavens and weary of strumming their heavy harps. In odd Oz-es they remain to add to all the foolish victims who move inside the eyes of every city like so much grit to cause these tears to fall upon the streets and run in petroleum puddles down the drains. There was Angie, one angel with no umbrella, window-shopping in the rain, the only angel in this boy's eyes.

The Boy

I mean, I hardly knew who she was except for how she explained she was an angel with broken wings and that's why she didn't fly away but lived two flights above a bankrupt bodega. Don't look at me, I'm a mess, said Angie by the sofa where my body was getting better. Again she started to cough on account of the air on earth being dirty compared to how it is up where she belonged. She turned her face away, so all I could see were yellow curls that held a silver crown in place of where a halo had once floated. I would close my eyes to feel hers brush against my skin, like lips that kiss it better, or a breeze that blows you back.

All September I closed my eyes in Angie's front room. What I saw mostly then was Mary, who Earl had never allowed to be my mother. Leave the kid alone, he'd warn if I cried. My mind spied Mary hiding in one of the cherry trees while Earl's boots crushed the long grass below. Little girl, little girl, come to Daddy now, he called, with the belt wrapped ready around one hand. From high up in the branches with the birds, Mary could see across the orchard sloping down the valley. She could see all the way to the town that Earl wouldn't let her visit. It shone in the distance, like the Emerald City.

Sooner or later, Earl would catch sight of Mary's flowered housedress peeking through the leaves. Come down now, he'd say with dangerous softness. I was picking cherries for a pie, Mary mumbled, though no pail was in her hand. She slipped to the ground and followed Earl into the dark bedroom behind the kitchen. The door would close behind them. The hurting noises would start.

Or Mary might mention: I guess I'll go down to the bottom field and see how the peaches are coming on. She'd move through the high grass, holding the hem of her house dress up with one hand, trying not to look back to see if Earl followed, making herself walk as slowly as someone who has no thought of escape. At the end of the orchard sagged a fence with three rusted strands. Once she bent through the wires, Mary would start running down the road toward town. The truck pulled up alongside her. Get in, Daddy wants to take you for a ride, invited Earl. The bedroom door would close again, and the ugly sounds would start all over. I waited in the kitchen with my hands holding each other in my lap. I watched the hand of the clock turn around and around but never get away.

At last Earl would come out of the bedroom, snapping the suspenders back up around his shoulders. He would go out on the porch and make the rocking-chair creak. Mary would wander into the kitchen to start supper, her dark hair with the threads of silver floating down around her waist. In bare feet she moved drowsily across the cracked linoleum, as if against her will she'd fallen asleep in the poppy fields beyond the haunted forest. She would never look at me then. Her face had been locked like the bedroom door. The key was hidden deep in Earl's pocket.

After Earl went out into the dark to move the long lines of sprinkler pipe that kept the ground soaked good, Mary and I listened in the kitchen to the cherry bombs explode. Each sudden bang made Mary jerk. That was when I wished to wrap myself around her and press my face into the cloth of her dress and feel her fingers in my hair. I had a memory of this happening with a much smaller boy who was maybe someone else, not me, in a time before there was any Earl moving through the black night with the crickets screaming at him. Mary sat stiffly, pondering the floor. When Earl's steps returned, she would look at me once in warning, against I didn't know what.

Until one night I thought I heard Mary calling from way beyond the orchard, and even past town. She was calling from some place where her hand would be allowed to touch my hair and where I would be able to feel that her fingers were the same size and shape as mine. I would smell the flowers sprinkled on her dress. I tiptoed into the dark bedroom and found Earl's pants folded on the chair. I took the money from the wallet in the pocket. As the dollars moved into my hand, I saw that Mary was not far away and calling for me to join her there. She was lying on the other side of Earl, between the low hill of his body and the wall. I saw her eyes unlock. They were watching me in the dark. They shone like two moonlit pools that I could never drink, no matter how bad my thirst.

And now here was Angie, holding out the glass of water. It's short for Angel, she said, twisting her mouth into a poignant snake. She set her wand on fire and sucked in magic smoke. Her cheeks hollowed, and her face sharpened until I wondered. She looked like someone I might have known long ago. Not like Mary or any mother, not like that at all. After a jigsaw puzzle is fitted together, sometimes all you see are the cracks between the pieces instead of the beautiful picture spreading whole before your eyes.

Angie would catch my curious look, touch her body and hair. Didn't I fix myself right? she would ask. All the things I never knew until the end. Her hand would reach toward me, then something like a frightened deer jumped across her eyes, and her fingers caressed only air, or some invisible child she would never have. She didn't touch me once, you know. She never laid a finger on me, damn her.

The Angel

Darling, I sincerely believe that every broken boy has lost his baseball glove and lucky marbles, and that's why he finally rests a smashed cheek upon the sidewalk of some queer city with which he has not the slightest acquaintance. (Listen hard, Bitch, because you've never heard me talk this way before, and kindly watch your Royal Ass because in a twinkle I might speak The Truth.) I Confess! I didn't ask his name or where he was from: alas, I remembered! After he no longer hurt, this boy was still severely exhausted, for your first journey away from Home is always farther than from here to any Star. (Please don't Insinuate—it doesn't suit you, My Dear—and who doesn't know that you're the only Poultry Thief around this funny farm?) I told myself I only hoped that one Boy inside my rooms would make them no longer hollow as the tombs where all our Darling Daddies hide. Why don't you stay for the meantime? I invited him on the morning after my magnetic heart drew an adolescent alloy to its chambers, before recalling who but *Moi* could never bear to be seen in the ghastly daylight of this sordid city, which mocks each exiled angel with memories of the celestial sunshine of Before.

Through that soft, warm light, I had grown in my own way. The way that caused my daddy to regard me with puzzles in his eyes and made my mother tell him to leave me be. In the backyard of Before, beneath the bowering maple, I yearned for a vision of the Boy who lived next door. You couldn't see over the tall fence that divided us, you could only hear his mother call him Home to supper when the summer light was everlasting until ten o'clock. In long conversations he shared with me inside my heart, his name was Billy, and only we knew that I was really Angie.

A boy like that has secret places to go when the world is finally dark. Unable to follow, still lacking the wings some beings need for flight, I would be left behind with children playing hide-and-seek around a street lamp they called Home. I could hear the seeker counting quickly to one hundred, then leaving Home to find friends hidden in the dark. I remained concealed behind a bush of red fruit that tasted strange and bitter, that gleamed black in the night. I had no desire to dart back toward the illuminated sphere because it wasn't Home to me. Bright light would never offer me safety, but only expose an imposter of a boy who had stolen my skin. The numbers counted by the seeking children were not my numbers. With the patience of a sphinx, I waited away from the light until long after the game had ended and all the players had gone to bed. I whispered my own numbers. Counted them off like beads strung on a rosary of prayers; believed that one miraculous multiple of seven would bring a Boy to part the chinaberry bush and see me crouched there upon the dirt. I found you, Billy would say, for the first time speaking my real name out loud, and that would mean the final end of being Lost.

Yet Billy could never see me at all, even as the other children teased me for how I walked and talked. Something was wrong with me. I didn't know what, I couldn't fix it. My long sentence to stay inside began. Through the window, I watched other children growing up beyond. They still played hide-and-seek, but now concealed themselves in pairs and didn't wish to be discovered. Only my mother saw through the opaque panes of my eyes, only she always knew what would become of me. There was no choice for me but one day to assume angel robes and paint my face and on unfolded wings fly out into a world that teemed with hidden souls only I could part the leaves to find.

So I became the true self I had always been inside. Yes, God sent me down into this endless exile and gave me strength to lift the lonely ones to choirs above the clouds. I strum my harp and ease their ears, and this is my consolation for being forever unfound myself. Angie, short for Angel, who confuses the minds of mere mortals by describing in a single breathless sentence a Home that is always to be escaped, always to be yearned for. Angie, who walks to the terminal where boys and girls arrive by bus from wherever they cannot stay. Angie, who narrowly watches them descend upon an undiscovered world to look through each other's only eyes. Angie, who turns to tell the man who guards the Lost and Found: I can't remember what I misplaced, but I'd recognize it at once if it were here.

This lost and found boy here. Sometimes he looked at me as though Angie was a poor impostor, and the spirit abandoned behind the Chinaberries had been my authentic self. Fear that there was no going back fluttered my feathers frantically. I wove my words into the most intricate webs, handled my props with the finest flair, performed all the set pieces that only to his brand-new eyes were not sickeningly stale. Explained about the numbers: the lucky ones, the ones less lucky. Don't start your search until the numbers are right, I advised. I prayed this boy would never venture out into the tearful world, for it takes the strength of an Angel to raise the rain back up to the watching eyes from which it falls.

And then, Angie, you sallied through the damp dusk to rooms where happiness is bought and sold. I would like beautiful clothes for a beautiful boy, you announced, plucking possibilities from racks, narrowing your eyes and frowning as you summoned up old photographs from the album of your heart. You chose red and blue, green and yellow, remembering what makes a rainbow call. I'll pay cash, your harsh voice said, removing a fat roll of twenties from your plastic purse and making the sales clerk's eyes cease sneering. You also bought running shoes and a baseball cap, armies of toy soldiers, and books of coloured comics. Plus model planes that can be assembled by a boy who holds his breath and is very careful with his clumsy hands. All this pirate treasure you carried home within your wings, Angie; then the ice in your drink chattered nervously while you watched the boy try on his alluring outfits. He didn't wonder how you knew what size shirts would slip seductively around him, or that each pair of jeans, whether loose or tight, seemed designed to tease a hungry eye. He had no idea you made him look like some boy who is mean until he's touched in the right place, whereupon he melts. You could still wave your wand and make it Christmas any time, Angie, even as you counted on your fingers and realized you were almost out of wishes.

Wasn't that the month of thirty rainy days when you stayed inside, the boy and you, floating together in your odd ark above a sick and troubled land? The telephone would shrill ten times before it quit; *cholos* would call up from the street at two a.m. for you to come out and play. Fat Alice and Beat-Up Betty insisted with fists against the door that a holed-up whore is guaranteed to be forgotten by tomorrow or Tuesday.

Angie, you taught the boy to worship at the temple of the television, upon whose screen were projected numerous glimpses of the way stars once shone white against a background of ebony sky. You communed with Bette and Joan, those beautiful bitches, until the boy believed them to be your dear old friends who heeded your wise words to leave the guy because he wasn't worth the tips of their little fingers. The boy listened to your voice drip with sympathetic scorn when it did not melt with love, and he watched tears fall from your eyes as though in fact those flickering scenes were images escaping from inside your skin. Damn men, you rasped, throwing back your yellow hair, closing your eyes so no careless thief could climb inside to steal your few remaining secrets.

Then darkness would crash down beyond the glass, the hands of the clock would point to holy numbers, your wings would ache to stretch. You had to swallow a round white pill to blur your face into a rainy window and to muffle the voices of all the empty ones who commenced their nocturnal cries to you. You retreated into your boudoir, where the boy was not allowed to follow, according to your only golden rule. Darling, I'm dead, you explained, leaving him in the front room to learn the language of stylized love spoken by stars. Weren't you always careful to close the door behind your back?

Hold me tight and let me stay inside, you beseeched multiple mirrors hanging amid red velvet on your sanctum's walls. How strange that you would worry about your own salvation at this late hour, and wasn't it also quite amusing that a single small boy could make you regret what you'd leave behind? Angels can't afford to feel sentimental, you reminded your reflection grimly; but the truthful glass showed that your system of immunity was failing you in more than just one way. With thinning fingers, you prepared the evening shot like the purest priest arranging Mass. And then it was all right, Angie, you felt heavenly heroin singing in choirs through your blood. You requested Billie H. to breathe bitter prayers to accompany your slow arcs around that perfumed space. Reading yellowed love letters, touching ancient photographs: it was all just another banal goodbye, my dear.

Still there was a boy who watched you emerge from your room with the jerky motions of a puppet controlled by uncertain hands. Who watched you nodding to the sandman. Watched you gazing at all the long-gone boys who were not named Billy, who were not grimacing up from the bottom of your bottle, who were not wondering where you were. Still there was a boy across the room who lightly touched the skeleton of a model plane that one day might really fly. You gave him the whole show, didn't you, you bitch.

The Boy

What happened was there came a night when Angie shook her empty purse and swore that easy street had detoured us by. She hummed for an hour in the bathroom while performing many miracles with makeup, painting silver and gold on her face, draping red satin on her body. Angie fixed the purple feathers to her shoulders and prepared her wings to soar higher than ever before. Does your angel still look ugly? she sniffed, after lining white powder on her compact mirror. I was reminded of the shimmering television women who tossed their heads and snapped their mouths and swung their shoulders everywhere. Joan and Bette would have looked just as lost as Angie if they stepped off the screen into this front room without a carpet or curtains or much furniture besides the sagging sofa where I slept. Their nostrils would have also inhaled white stardust until a wonderful world shifted back into sharp focus. Now Angie looked ready to fly as high as I used to feel on mornings when clean dew sprinkled the orchard grass. Already she gazed toward the far places she was about to find. Like her famous friends on the TV screen, Angie didn't see me even when her eyes turned in my direction. Those tired old hos will have kidnapped my best customers, she fretted. Her voice had changed in a way I couldn't describe; maybe each word was a substitute for a scream. Angie swayed away because there was always too much inside her to trace a simple, straight line. See you in the movies, she called back, vanishing in a swirl of flowers and bluebirds and crosses.

I woke when footsteps fell up the stairs and Angie's key fumbled to fit into the lock. Something sad had happened while my eyes were closed. The woman who had been laughing on the television screen was crying. Angie dragged the drunken sailor in by his tie and shrieked: Just call me Angel! I rubbed sleepy stuff from my eyes and saw that Angie's were glittering like the smashed window of a burglared store. She plucked a pill from her purse, tossed it in the air, caught it with her mouth. I know plenty of tricks, she bragged, spilling whiskey into a big glass then throwing it down her throat. Follow me and don't get lost along the way, she suggested to the sailor. She didn't notice me on the sofa; she was completely concerned with fluttering her wings. I could still hear them beating after Angie closed her door behind the sailor and herself.

It made me wonder extra hard when Angie's laughter stopped rippling from her room, leaving only the sound of the lady on the TV screen vowing she'd had enough and couldn't take anymore. Then Angie started screaming as though she was attempting to call all the way to God, plus there were noises of the sailor swearing and glass breaking and something thudding.

The TV woman's face turned proud and noble, though tears were falling from her eyes. You could tell her heart had swollen like the music at The End. Minus his tie, the puffy-faced sailor came from Angie's room and angled by me out the door. I could hear Angie crying like people do when they think no one listens, then she started coughing bad. Her friend Billie H. was singing the same song over and over, like it was the only one in the world, or she'd forgotten any others. She kept covering the waterfront and watching the sea. Again and again, she asked: Will the one I love be coming back to me?

As she passed through the front room on her way back outside, Angie must have thought I was asleep since my eyes felt like being shut. When I could stand to see again, the TV love scenes had been replaced by repeating patterns of lines and shapes I didn't understand. Through the window, I watched Angie moving along the wet street with her eyes turned to the sidewalk like there were footprints she could follow. Then the corner kids and bus-stop boys began to call her name all the way up and down the block, and Angie lifted her angel eyes in search of another lost someone to find. Even when she was out of sight, and fog from the bay had turned the air into a cold, heavy hand, I left the window open. In case Angie became too tired to climb the stairs in her high heels. In case she wished to fly back home to me.

The Angel

I didn't have to tell him anything, didn't have to explain one thing. The Street insinuated that I taught him the Tricks of my trade, but for an angel there's never a course of lessons with a divine diploma at the end. It must be a Calling. A voice reaches you and convinces you and won't let you go. My voice? Sweetheart, I've told you once and won't tell you again: I wouldn't wish these wretched Wings on anyone. Maybe there was more of a choice for him than there had been for me, but I couldn't help him make it. My insides were spilling into black pools behind the alley trash cans. I was rotting, Love, I was growing weak. It had become more than Fun and Games to save strangers, never mind one darling Boy who peers into the puzzling Dark. I wasn't in a position to tear off my brilliant disguise, or abandon the deep grooves painfully scratched by dull needles into my Heart's round black disc. Yes, I knew about the line that lies between those who save and those who are rescued. I might have invited him into the embrace of my wings and forever placed him on the other side, separate from all us angels. But I couldn't let him into my secret room. I couldn't. And, pray tell, where were you when he needed to enter a precious place like Home, you wicked witches and false wizards? Tin men, cowardly lions, all of you.

It was always like that, Angie. You seemed determined to impress upon the boy how many slack-jawed sailors and sad soldiers there were in the world. Late on mornings after, you would leave your room to lean against the wall and point your cigarette at figments he couldn't see. Your face would be paler than usual, except you painted it a more decisive pink. Around the room you floated and sighed: So handsome, loving, tender. Every stranger is kind in the way he knows how, you murmured wisely, bending over your number book and adding two or three digits from the preceding night into its crowded pages. Each man you touched meant one less to be saved, you believed. When all the orphans from the storm had known your bed of blessing, your work down here would be done. You would be free to unfold your wings one last time and fly away for good, presenting to the guard at the Gate your list of lucky guys to be admitted. I'm almost there, you muttered, gripping a goblet of numbing nectar tighter, taking another sip to tinge the taste of blood you coughed. Angie, you pretended a corner of your eye didn't notice the boy examining your image then turning to his own in the glass. You told yourself that he would touch only toy soldiers, always, and never imitate your state of grace. Your sublime walks on water, your gliding steps upon the sea of love.

The Boy

Sometimes, I didn't know why, they wouldn't like it inside Angie's room. An unlucky number would bust back out her door. And Angie, she'd have new colours on her skin, purple and red and blue. He didn't leave a dime, not one wooden nickel, she'd say, her face set so still. Others would leave her perplexed. That one seemed familiar, she frowned. Has my touch so completely lost its magic that now they must be blessed a second time? Angie would sit by the window and squint through the rain at the church crumbling across the way. Some have hearts of stone, she might mourn, too heavy to lift to Heaven.

But most of the men were grateful for how Angie could heal their hurt; then we'd call a cab to take us to the Chinese cafe. Windshield wipers slapped against the glass; lucky numbers clicked across the meter. Another one down, smiled Angie, waving out the window to anyone at all. Or, rather, up. The men she sent above felt so sad to be apart from Angie that they cried, and every November night was dark with rain. The cab carried us splashing down the nickel, wheeled us nearer the end of another lullaby. The driver sang along with Mel Tormé, and Angie shivered. I bet you never dreamed California would be quite like this, she said, turning toward me in space spiced by old tobacco. Then she leaned against the back of the seat and closed her eyes. She asked the driver to turn up the heat, she asked if we were almost there.

The Angel

There I was, Girl, meeting Mister Midnight on my terribly Tragic corner, when I saw the little Boy idle by into a Bar. The clothes I'd chosen for him fit like a lucky charm: I could barely blink the beads off my mascara before he came back out with a hungry Wolf huffing at his heels. Sulky Sue's small eyes grew big as she watched this temporary twosome wind away like there was only One Way to go. Your pretty Prize has found himself a lucky Winner, simpered the slut. Keep your filthy cunt between your own legs, I advised, and continued counting the raindrops out from which the next wet Wanderer would come for me to Warm.

It's just the Cold and how the fucking fog from the damp bay climbs up my gown, I tried to explain to Miss Misery, who glared at me as if I coughed expressly to disturb her Profoundest Meditations. My latest diet, I informed the other Sidewalk Sirens; I live on Love Alone and lose five pounds a week. Tough enough to beat one Tenderloin winter without Bad Meat around, my fair-weather colleagues mumbled, shuffling away from where I posed with my final loyal friend The Street Lamp and a wreath of smoke twined around my head. I felt all the Forsaken Ones rolling like lost marbles on this globe, which tilted back and forth beneath my feet until I reeled like one more Dizzy Queen who's lost her Cardboard Crown. Darling, I was devastated, too Destroyed to decorate the sewer a single second longer.

In Defeat, I sat inside the Sad Café with coffee kept hot within Styrofoam; but my human hands refused to warm. Shivers were trying to shake the cold from my bones, and for the first time my wings were really wet. Oh, they Drooped; a sour, stale smell drifted from them. Once one glance would have flattened the proprietor of this plastic Palace, the pig-eyed Prince who knew I couldn't pay to sit for an hour out of the rain, which yesterday or the day before I'd found romantic as the young Sinatra. December was Descending, my Time was tap-dancing away. I was too Tired to chase it. There was my number coming up quick and only so much more One Girl could do. Clear out, They'd say. And don't take Anything with you. And don't leave Anything behind. Ready or not, here we come, the Cruel Children cried. One-two-three, we'll find you now, four-five-six, open sesame, seven-eight-nine, abracadabra, ten-eleven-twelve, here's mud in your eye, thirteen-fourteen-fifteen, what to do with the days that remain?

Use them wisely, go with grace, a future Angel whispered in my ear, stilling my Silly Heart.

I turned to see the boy beside me, looking like he'd learned something new and pulling three twenties from his pocket.

And then I really knew. Every angel can leave one gift behind when She is found to be a He behind a curtain of chinaberries, or on the far side of any forbidden fruit, and brought Home at last to where the Light shines bright. This is her unexpected Salvation, her undreamed-of reward, unseen until now.

They could at least give you crisp, fresh dollars instead of these dirty ones, I said. They could at least do that. Look: your halo's crooked, I croaked, reaching out to bless the seven points that shone above his head.

Can I buy you coffee? asked the boy.

And so it was, Angie, that you took to your bed to lie awake all the hours of every poisoned night, no time to waste in sleep. Sweat seeped out between the countless cracks of your rusted armour, and you melted into one of any number of puddles that children splash through on their way to school. Billie H. sang you forward into the darkness where she waited, crooned you through the black sickness of the lost ones against which your vulnerable self had refused to be protected. You listened for the boy to come running lightly up the four a.m. stairs. His knock on your boudoir door would signal a wish to relate new adventures you had originally experienced several centuries ago and since repeated beyond all numbers. Alas, I'm dead asleep, you called through a quarter-inch of separating wood, then listened to his restless movements on the other side: switching TV channels, dissatisfied with all movie queens; picking up the telephone to abandon it without even dialling Information. It was never easy to return to earth after experiencing the marvels of first flight, was it?

The feathers of your wings fell from you one by one, drifting to the floor around your queen bed and lining it like the bottom of a nest. You were becoming lighter, Angie, you would need no wings to ascend finally to the green and yellow stars. How much did it cost to keep your back straight on the infrequent occasions that you inched into the front room? Can you lend me a little? you asked the boy when rent day came around again too soon. From a box beneath his bed, he plucked several bills from among many crumpled others. His whistling was jaunty as he dressed himself; his loving eyes embraced his image in the speckled mirror. Did he glance toward you when your hand picked up the arm of black plastic and your thinning finger dialled what you hoped would prove at last to be the lucky combination of an infinite number of possibilities? Mama, it's me, you said across Long Distance, nervously clearing your throat. Angel, you repeated, biting your blistered lip. You have the wrong number, you echoed the operator, returning the arm gently to its cradle. The number was not right.

Go softly, Angie. You were silent when the boy brought his game to play in the front room. Go easy, Angie, you told him on mornings after, when all you saw was one more blind believer in the religion whose only tenet promises that touch can redeem every pawned heart. The power of love, the power of illusion. Surprise, surprise, Angie. Without your wings, you were never really here.

The Boy

Then Angie couldn't get out of bed until evening, or not at all. I'm such a lazy girl, she would drawl if she did manage to shuffle from her room. The six steps made her pant like someone who's run six miles. Angie seemed surprised to find me each time she emerged, as though I was only ever what her heart had dreamed.

She still squeezed chunks of shining glass onto her ears and wore rings around every finger, yet Angie didn't look much like an angel any more. I wondered if a crazy child had scribbled crayon on her face. The yellow hair was always tipsy on her head. I could tell her wings were really broken now, though sometimes she would flutter them weakly within the walls, wishing they might work again. From a hiding place inside Angie, someone smaller was coming out a little more each day. Someone with lighter bones, a sharper face, and shy eyes that hadn't yet learned to dance. Angie was shrinking inside her angel robes; her eyes were sinking into her face. I thought she might be getting ready to go away because she kept asking if I'd seen her cardboard suitcase anywhere. She couldn't stop repeating that three yellow stars were stencilled on one side of the suitcase and three green stars on the other, as if describing the colour of stars could force them to appear.

I could feel my own wings grow a little bigger each time the lonely men touched me. First the feathers felt like a heavy weight on my shoulders that made walking almost as hard for me as it was for Angie now. Then I learned how to use my new wings. I became crazy about flying, I liked to fly just for the fun of it. I was always swooping in and out of the Sixth Street windows, back and forth above the city, here and there and everywhere. I soared up to rooftops bumping like wharves in the fog. As Angie must have done a zillion times before, I let currents of air carry me far over the bay to islands made out of mist.

The rain grew icy and silver angels shimmered in all the stores. Christmas is coming, I told Angie. She didn't often ask about the world outside the window. Just once she wondered if Fat Alice and Sulky Sue were still bragging on their corners, and if Beat-Up Betty was in the junkyard yet. It's nice to stay inside at last, she said, keeping quiet in her chair to save up energy for her trip.

Angie's eyes were turning into glass as they sank deeper into her face. They didn't blink no matter how long I looked into them. I thought each of Angie's eyes had become a crystal ball where what you wish to see or need to know appears. There was Mary, looking back at me. I didn't let him touch you once, not one time, she said. Then Mary faded away. Only I was left hovering upon Angie's glassy eyes. Like there was two of me now.

Angie stirred. Remember living way up on the top floor of the Holiday Hotel? We could order anything we wanted from room service; we never had to come down from the sky. The rug was so thick beneath our feet, it felt just like walking on clouds, and our big bed drifted like a boat through green and yellow stars. We were rich enough to throw ten-dollar bills out the window just to watch them float down to people who believed that God was shaking the treasure tree in Heaven. Do you remember going to the National Circus of Argentina? Do you remember seeing the white horse in his field of yellow flowers? Can you remember the butterfly man?

Angie talked more and more often about the time when we had always been together, but I couldn't remember any white horses or butterfly men or Holiday Hotels. Sometimes I thought Angie was becoming mistaken about how things really were, like believing she heard Barbara Stanwyck when it was plainly Susan Hayward speaking from the TV screen. The way she felt positive that all the *cholo* boys below our window were named Billy, when every one of them was a Juan or José. Like how she called me Angie now.

After falling asleep each night in the grey house amid the cherry trees, maybe I flew away with Angie. Maybe she had been with me from the beginning—always, forever. I picked up one of the wands Angie no longer liked to wave. Fire burned inside my heart and smoke curled through the air, shaping only lucky numbers. Suddenly I saw Mary perched atop a cherry tree, squinting into the sun to see the writing of my wand before it vanished into sky. I swooped down toward my mother and passed so close that the tips of my wings brushed her face, causing her to smile.

Angie, Angie, short for Angel, the first day of your true life dawned. You opened the door you had never entered and found the place for an angel to rest between her soaring, with many mirrors to remind her of the impossible image she has achieved. With drapes of crimson velvet to filter the harsh world's light and to render this room the rosy chamber of a beating heart.

Look. On the soft wide bed lay the body of a boy grown old and tired with waiting to be found. His face had finally been washed clean of the juice of bitter berries. On a nearby chair rested locks of yellow hair.

Angie, you walked across a feathered floor to where angel robes were hanging, and you found two small pillows upon which weary men, climbing into the warm bed of your body, could rest their heavy heads. You fixed yourself, Angie, for the first time adding curves and curls to your lost boy's body, for the first time painting your face. Making it no longer frightened. Making it right.

Wasn't it just like you had always known it would feel, Angie? Look at you lighting your magic wands and tilting your mouth toward the liquid gold of gods inside the glass. Hear the stars lilting about love from the front room's TV screen, listen to every angel's sainted sister singing for the needy to take all of her. Take your lips and arms and eyes into the night, Angie, and give them generously. Soon there will be heavenly heroin and round white moons of pills to give you strength to put on ruby slippers and set out on the road of yellow brick. Into your big black book you will enter the names of those you save, the long list of all the ones to be allowed through the Gate and back into the Garden, where fruit hangs heavy and sweet from every tree.

It was Christmas, Angie, and a child of God was born again to man. You unwrapped presents you had bought for another angel; you gave them to yourself. A carolling choir drew near. A host of angels lifted a boy's bones off a bed in order to plant them behind a bush of bitter berries. A lucky number of boys would grow from that sacred ground. One day you would find them and comfort them and shelter them, until on some silent, holy night they would assume your wings of love and embark upon the ecstatic flight for which they longed, Angie, short for Angel.

Part Two

AFTER THE GLITTER AND THE ROUGE

After the glitter and the rouge
There's nothing left to lose
And everything to win
The world, you feel it spin
The music starts again
It's time to let it in
Another dance begins
After the glitter and the rouge

—Patrick Roscoe
"After the Glitter and the Rouge"

Honey

THEY TOOK ME AWAY FROM HONEY, THEY SAID SHE WAS UNFIT. THAT WAS the end of us being on the Jupiter Circuit together, orbiting between Tacoma and Portland, Seattle and Spokane. All the rooms above the bars where Honey danced her golden self before men hungry for something sweet beyond their reach. "We're troupers," she'd say each time we unpacked our old things and spread them around to make every place like home. *Live Girls!* stuttered various neon letters I learned to read at six. For eight years I listened to some dangerous heartbeat below, *boom boom*, while waiting in the musty bed for Honey to finish her last show. Then she would float upstairs with Diamond Lil, an aging star, huffing at her heels. There was always ice down the hall for sticky drinks, there was Lil becoming blurred and calling me her Little Ladykiller as I fought to stay awake. No life for a boy, they said; it was all the life I knew. Or sometimes late at night a man would trail Honey's sweetness into the room. She was always a little breathless then, fixing me a bathtub bed until the man quit making noise and the door clicked goodbye, so long. "He's gone," Honey breathed above me in fresh perfume, in her silver robe. That was when we would curl before the window and watch drunks fall to prayerful knees in the street below, see coloured lights shake scared when it rained. "This isn't so bad," Honey might say between a sigh and a yawn, a blue pill and a red. Tomorrow we could sleep all day, tomorrow we could sip thick milkshakes in cafés. Lil stitching a million sequins onto costumes, Honey swaying before the speckled mirror, being sad on Sunday: all these things I would first try to remember, then try to forget. How at the Greyhound station Honey wrapped her smooth scent around me one last time. "I could never change enough to please them," she said, flicking yellow hair from the ruined makeup around her eyes, taking one step back to look at me once more. She held my arms so tight, she left red marks that would fade too soon. "You'll run away from Ruth like I did," she promised quickly; then her heels tapped away, my bus started north. *Miss you like crazy*, read the first postcard I received at the trailer on the outskirts of Brale where I came to stay with Ruth. "Out of sight, out of mind," muttered the old woman when I asked why there was no second or third card from her daughter, my mother. Ruth scrubbed the trailer some more. It was always too small and she could never get it clean. Boys were dirty. So she gave up again, fixed herself another drink during the commercials, told me to go play outside. Behind the trailer spread a field dotted with stumps, weeds, rusted machinery. On blonde afternoons bees buzzed there, nothing better to do; later, Jupiter would rise from darkness, float beyond my reach. One stump was hollow, bees flew in and out of its secret space. Honey was inside. I reached in to take some for myself, the stinging started, welts rose like a red constellation upon my skin. It hurt until the world turned once. In September, school would start; then other things would happen.

The Real Truth

FOR A LONG TIME, THERE WAS NOTHING SOLID TO REACH OUT AND TOUCH to remind myself of the real truth when Ruth swore that she'd never heard of anyone called Honey. My grandmother spit out the two syllables like something tasting bad, wondered what kind of whore's name was that; it belonged to no daughter of hers. There was only how I remembered Honey sounded telling me about Eureka, California, while we curled together on the fire escape overlooking Spokane or above the bar in Bellingham. The way my mother's voice turned scratchy in the Greyhound station when she wouldn't say goodbye; this was only adieu until we reunited in Eureka one day. Diamond Lil, always the wise sidekick, shook her experienced head, swayed some more upon her heels. "He's only eight, it isn't right," she kept repeating like a prayer, kissing another cigarette pink then squashing it like a burning beetle beneath her toe. A cardboard suitcase decorated with six shiny stars rode with me on the bus north, across the border to Canada, when they took me away from Honey and Diamond Lil and the Jupiter Circuit. Orbiting across Washington and Oregon was the only life I'd known. Inside the suitcase was a photo Honey made me promise not to lose. You could touch our paper features, feel my mother and I squeezed together inside the arcade booth. Making funny faces and wearing our favourite hats as quarters fed the hungry slot, during the pop hiss flash. Plus Diamond Lil gave me one of her eight-by-tens from way back when, the good old days when stripping meant show business and dancers were entertainers, smiling coy with her boas and feathers, the stilettos and the big bouffant. Also a plastic whistle from a Jupiter dancer named Jewel. "Just blow when you want me," she liked to pucker and wink beneath her Bacall bangs. A Cracker Jack ring from the sad-eyed girl named Star who

Harry was always advising to Sell it, sweetheart, with a smile. Just several things you could touch to help you believe in the truth of what wasn't there. "Cheap goods," muttered Ruth, pursing her mouth and unpacking the suitcase when I arrival at the trailer on the outskirts of Brale. "Cheap as cheap." The next morning everything except my clothes was gone. I later found the empty suitcase out in the field, blistered and warped by sun and rain, hidden among those tall weeds that scratch. The six green stars were no longer shiny, but now each one as faded and sad as Star. I never learned what happened to the photographs, the whistle, the ring. "What're you talking about?" demanded Ruth when I wondered. "Wake up, kid. You're dreaming." My grandmother deemed that everything I remembered from before Brale, BC, was make-believe. Those identical gyrations of the Jupiter Circuit across Washington and Oregon had never been; that once-upon-a-time with Honey was a figment of my imagination. I couldn't rub the real truth between my fingers to feel its texture, gritty and smooth at once, like sand in the sheets at Salem. When Ruth took her bottle to bed, I would wander from the trailer, lose its lone light to distance, allow the dark to touch me everywhere. Wind shoved down the mountain, pushed a smell of rust across the river. Slowly the glitter and the rouge of before receded; Diamond Lil's sequined shape shimmied out of sight. Now was separated by a border from then; bygone Eugene and Olympia belonged to the map of another country and not to me. All those towns where Honey still danced moved as far away as stars in the big black sky above the stumps, the brush, the thorns. A boat drifted up there, too. My daddy floated between Jupiter and Venus, traced circles among the constellations, orbited a sickle moon. His sailor cry sounded clearer than the crickets, closer than the owl up in the twisted oak. He was still a child, Honey said, just turned eighteen, another tall boy on a three-day pass. Too far from home, he stumbled in to see her dance. He never said he'd stay. So how could he know that I was breathing, folded inside such dreams, while Ruth's TV snowed static through another winter and time scuffed by? Drop a curl of bark into the Columbia River, cold current pulls it south toward Spokane where Honey always liked entertaining cowboys, over from Idaho on a dare, their faces frank or sort of shy. The Circuit was unwavering, its rotation so fixed that I could still know where Honey was headlining this week, when it would be on to Walla-Walla again. The itinerary was written on my heart, along with messages on picture postcards that Honey never sent me. *Miss you, love you, wish you were here.* A lipstick kiss for a signature, sure. One night I realized that something had happened to Honey: her lilt no longer lifted to meet Daddy's high *ahoy* inside my head. Abruptly the air around me lacked the singular, sweet arrangement of ions—insinuating as any aroma, subtle as some pheromone—which had wafted through my blood ever since Honey gave birth to me in Eureka, California. Now my lungs inhaled a thinner, flatter element; my tongue tasted the zinc from the smelter stacks that puffed like Lil's cigarettes in the down-river distance. Maybe Honey and I would never meet up in Eureka some day after all. Maybe she did her bump and grind in Heaven now, burlesqued with stage-struck ghosts above. Down here, the world was holding its breath; more than ever, the landscape was formed out of longing. In Portland or Tacoma, Diamond Lil had laughed thinly with just Jack Daniel's, or else her sad pal Jimmy Beam, about the weirdos and the creeps who filled the blackness before the stage, shifted tensely beyond the spotlight's glare, unseen. For years Honey had sensed a bad number out there, the unluckiest one of all, anxious to stop her dance for good. She could almost glimpse his face if a blue pill didn't work at five a.m.; that was when she would lullaby to me about Eureka or discuss the sailor until dawn. After I was ten, it got darker on the outskirts of Brale. Ruth stuffed cardboard over the trailer windows for insulation; the next spring she wouldn't take it down, said perverts liked to gawk at her, the curtains weren't enough. At the end of the dirt road, across the frozen mud beyond the ditch, the school bus jounced by without me. River kids flattened features against the windows; their glassy eyes slid out of sight. They liked to caw *Yank go home* across the playground when Ruth didn't keep me home because Sodom and Gomorrah ruled the classroom. I didn't need to learn more lies. "Filth begets filth," Ruth fretted in her gumboots before I learned not to mention Honey. Her stick poked into the burning barrel, turned the trash, stirred sparks. "Flesh and fornication." She brooded aloud about dirty boys more often as I got older; the ragged wind flapped her complaints like flags. It was always the stink, the stench of sin, enough to make you sick. No wonder Ruth's throat retched vomit; the poison needed to get out. A rank pool of everything gone wrong beside the bed at dawn. A sharp, angry language, almost English, in the dark. In the end we couldn't have the trailer lights on much; they would attract attention. The social worker and her fellow spies snooped plenty already and there was an abundance of Satan's interfering agents around. Beelzebub buzzed secret code through telephone wires strung above the road to town, belched smoke signals from the smelter stacks. Something dirty over there in the sky. Ruth gurgled another prayer to her own sweet Saviour until, *Damn it to hell*, the bottle got knocked over again. Scotch stained more thin Bible pages, soiled the skimpy trailer air. The way things were made me picture an abandoned car rusting in some February field. I wasn't old enough to leave the outskirts of Brale in search of the real truth. I was still too young to discover the magic door leading to how it ought to be: the secret way to all Eurekas. It wouldn't be until I was thirteen that my daddy's call would reach out and pull me to the cities by the sea. Late at night, I'd prowl harbour shadows in a tavern full of tars hoping to find a hungry touch that was finally his. I would lick away the anchor Honey said was tattooed on his shoulder— the left, or was it the right? Who can recall, that long ago? It was back so far, when Diamond Lil was still a reigning star. I would kiss and not forget his salty lips, I would slide inside his gap-toothed grin. Waking to receive his squint, sometimes blue and sometimes green, just like the sea we'd sail across, far from Ruth slurring to the sandman, from cramped space trying to squeeze my dreams. "Hold on," counselled Honey in my heart. "Sustain." To pass the time until my turn came to abandon Brale, like my mother had done before me, I strung shiny sounds into a necklace in the night; names of strippers we'd trouped with sparkled the dark like sequins. Brandy, Crystal, Ruby. Champagne, Jewel, Star. Maybe people like Ruth would say those weren't their real names. Maybe Diamond Lil was just Louise and Honey only Hannah. But I came to believe that what is really true and more than true is always what you wish, how you hope, the way it all must be. Beyond the facts, besides what's black and white, more lasting than anything carved in stone: the real truth shines the colour of your stars. Six green planets glittered above the trailer and the wind and the dark. Emerald islands, Honey. Pacific ports of prayer to sail toward during sleep. One day we will waken where we need to be.

Eureka, California

UNTIL THE END, I'LL BELIEVE THAT EUREKA, CALIFORNIA, FORMS THE heart of every prayer sent to Heaven to describe what means the most to you on earth. Maybe that's because of how Honey spoke about the place where she delivered me into the surprising world. Eureka was more than the backdrop to the famous year-long sabbatical she and Diamond Lil took from the Jupiter Circuit on my account and reacquainted themselves with civilian life with mixed results. Afterward, Eureka served as the setting for each one of Honey's poems and psalms. On her lips, its name always sounded less like a ringing exclamation at some original discovery than a murmur that what's been forgotten is now recalled.

Eureka, I remember.

"Sure, I'm coming with," said Diamond Lil when she learned about Honey's intent to have her child in California. She could use a break from show business herself, get that shine back in her star. She'd always wanted to play fairy godmother. For a moment Lil felt miffed at not being given any hint as to who my father was. But she couldn't let Honey head off alone in her condition, not a chance. It had been eight years since she'd found the girl strung out on speed and spreading in the rough Red Room in Seattle. She had taught Honey costumes and music and lights, paved the way for her to join the Jupiter, shared star billing with her ever since. Although Harry didn't appreciate the prospect of losing his headliners for so long, and sulked with his cigar over who could fill their spot, they left Seattle that October on the southbound bus. There were different stories later. Diamond Lil claimed they ended up in Eureka by chance. Their ticket money took them that far; twenty more dollars would have meant another town. According to Honey, she'd always dreamed about Eureka.

It had floated inside her head forever.

They found a small wooden house, once painted green but now faded almost grey, with a deep front porch that slanted toward the sunshine and movie stars in the south. There was a living room and a kitchen and a bathroom, and two bedrooms with gable windows like curious eyes upstairs beneath the eaves. "A real house," Honey would repeat in wonder on the fire escapes of the hotels that afterward became our only kind of home. A backyard with a crooked plum tree. A front yard surrounded by a low wooden fence, faded the same green as the house, that tilted this way or that, like it couldn't make up its mind. On one side lived a blind old woman who wore her white hair in a long braid down her back. Her fingers read cracked photographs taken at a time when she could still see. On the other side was a family with two small children, one boy and one girl, who would have been my friends if we'd stayed on in Eureka, California. They would have lent me their tricycles and invited me to spend Saturdays in a tree house, up among the apple blossoms and the birds.

Honey would tell me about Eureka, California, whenever I felt sad or frightened on the Jupiter Circuit. She and Diamond Lil had resumed orbiting on stage six months after my birth. Other girls on the bill helped look after me. Star and Jewel and Crystal changed diapers in their G strings and pasties, shook rattles in stilettos and silver robes. Harry groused he wasn't running a day-care, but bought me a miniature banjo for my third birthday. Sometimes things would happen in the hotels that made my heart *boom, boom* like the music in the bar below. That's when Honey's voice felt like a soft hand on my head while reminding me again that on the street where we lived in Eureka, California, no one locks their door at night. Children play hopscotch all afternoon on the chipped sidewalks, old people slowly walk arm-in-arm around the block at evening, and through the cool dark, couples dance on front lawns to the radio even when it rains. They waltz over the wet grass, *one* two three, they twirl beneath the dripping trees.

Honey didn't dance a step the whole year she spent in Eureka, California. Instead she caught up on a decade of missed sleep. It was so quiet she could be out like a light all night and for most of the day. Maybe that's why it would sound like a lullaby when Honey later told me about the place where you don't need pills even on mean Mondays. More things my mother didn't do in Eureka, California: paint her face into a meal for the eyes of hungry men in the dark; strap her feet into tall shoes like stilts that made her sway with each step; pile her blond hair high on her head with quantities of rhinestone pins. She wore ballet slippers and a ponytail in a rubber band in Eureka. She learned to click knitting needles while, two blocks away on Main Street, in the Rise and Shine Café, Diamond Lil waited tables to keep the wolf from the door. Breakfast shifts started at the crack of dawn, though Lil was used to stumbling to bed at that hour. She complained that her arches were falling faster than the rain that sloped past the mountains all winter; she moaned that in this two-bit town, her love life was as extinct as any dinosaur. Lil left the Diamond part of herself behind on the Jupiter Circuit, along with her sequined costumes and her love life; for a year she was plain Lil who poured coffee and served eggs over-easy and asked if you wanted pie with that. She had a polyester uniform of cheerful yellow and low white shoes like a nurse and a name tag with a crooked star dotting the *i*. In the evenings, she would soak her feet in a basin of warm water and sigh that the sleaziest stage was starting to look pretty good, never mind the weirdos and the creeps, while instead of scotch Honey sipped a big glass of milk so I'd grow strong and tall. If you listened, from the plum tree in the yard an owl would hoot once, twice, three times.

"It wasn't so big in those days," Honey would recall, as if Eureka, California, had happened long ago, as if she'd been back to see how it had since grown like me. Often I had the feeling that my own eyes witnessed the whole year there. I didn't so much hide inside Honey for the first half of our time in Eureka as hover near her on that slanting porch where she rocked away the hours while radio jingles floated from windows as yellow as Lil's uniform, from cars slowed by teen-aged boys wanting a look at Honey even when she was big with me. Their horns honked like passing geese. Light from street lamps had to reach and find its way through leaves of maple trees that lined the sidewalk, and from the mountain sank the smell of bears bumbling through berries while Honey muttered *knit, purl, knit* beneath her breath, worked the wool that would keep me warm. Eureka can be cool, though it belongs to California. You shiver when fog strays inland from the sea. It reminded Honey of a tall boy's breath made visible by condensation, shapes of unheard words fluttering like salty flags along the shore. We must have paced the sand with the wind in our faces, Honey and I; we surely held a shielding hand above our eyes and squinted at the grey Pacific for sight of a sailor's boat. Sometimes late, when the town was sleeping, Honey slipped from bed and through the quiet streets wandered beneath the same stars he steered by, out at sea. He was just eighteen, still almost a child, another frank boy on a three-day pass. In Tacoma, too far from home, he stumbled in to see her dance. He never said he'd stay. When he left, he didn't know that I was floating in Honey's saline sea, turning with her tides while the sunshine and movie stars remained stubbornly in the south, as distant as any sailor. I could see Eureka, California, so clearly as Honey described it. Every photograph in the album of your heart shows where you've been happy, even if you were blind.

But once in a while I suspected I was mistaken in my memories of Eureka, California. "Honey was sick as a dog the whole time," Lil might mention. "For months after your birth she worried every minute, sat up night after night to watch you sleep. Tips at that greasy spoon were so lousy Yours Truly had to steal from the supermarket more than once. There wasn't a decent bar in town where a girl could go for a little drink or two. The neighbours wouldn't talk to us. The roof leaked. It never stopped raining. Don't ask what I had to do to get the landlord to let us have that shack in the first place. Talk about your weirdos and your creeps."

Then I would wonder, while Honey spoke about Eureka, California, if she were remembering another town instead. The red pills could make her mix things up. Maybe she was really talking about where she had lived as a girl in a wooden house painted green but now faded almost gray. While she described children playing hopscotch and dancers in the rain, Honey stared straight before her, as if she were blind as the old woman next door and couldn't see me beside her on the fire escape above Tacoma or Portland, Seattle or Spokane. As if she were speaking about a time long before a shy sailor, long before I found my secret way inside her. "It was just any place," she answered when I asked where she had been born. "Any place," she echoed in the flat voice that answered the hungry men who sometimes trailed her sweetness into our room late at night. "It wasn't Eureka, California." She would hardly talk about a time before the Jupiter Circuit; neither did Diamond Lil, even when the sixth sticky drink made her slur secrets. After she swallowed a blue pill instead of a red, or when I asked at the wrong time about the sailor, Honey would tell me to shut the fuck up, leave her alone for once, could I please just do that? She would disappear from the hotel until the next night's shift. I rapped on the wall five times to invite Diamond Lil over from her room next door where she was practicing bumps and grinds before the speckled mirror, doing what she could to fight off the competition. There were always more young girls coming up. "She had to go like that," the aging star would say to explain about Honey slamming her way out of the hotel now. Or about her escape at sixteen from whatever town had been too small, too slow, too far from the sea. Honey never had a mother or a father. I knew that from the way she held me tight, whispered into my neck, licked my eyes to make me shiver. No one told her, when she was a frightened child, that there was a place like Eureka, California.

Lil would shake her head. Under a mask of slathered cold cream, a pensive expression might have played. "Honey wasn't like this before Eureka," she said. Restless, nervous. Missing cues every night on stage, her mind a million miles away. Sometimes that happens. A girl takes a step away from the gig, she can't come back to it with the same feeling. Maybe she recalls what should stay forgotten. When Honey returned to the hotel from feeling bad, she would explain that she had gone to Eureka to have me because she thought it would be something to be born there. She couldn't give me a tricycle or a tree house, but she could give me Eureka, California. "Always remember," she'd say, putting on her face for the early show once more, preparing for the next shimmy and strut. "Always remember that no one can ever take Eureka, California, from you. Can you please just do that?"

I tried. After they took me from Honey, during years of waiting until I was able to run away at sixteen, just like she had, from a town that was too small and too far from the sea, I tried as hard as I could to remember the place where she promised we would meet again one day beneath a crooked plum tree or on some slanting porch. Once more we would be three in Eureka, California. A new kind of three. Not Diamond Lil to make Honey and I one more than two, but a sailor whose eyes like mine were sometimes blue and sometimes green, and sometimes faded like every forgotten dream. In the waterfront hotels of the Pacific ports I orbit between now, on the salty wharves and docks where sailors lurk with aquamarine eyes that are never his, I still try to remember Eureka, California. It was the only promise I could make you, Honey, the only promise you asked me to keep.

Lucky

YOU COULD CALL HER LUCKY OR YOU COULD CALL HER LUKE, BUT NEVER Lucille. That name belonged to a sap who cried and tattled and was frightened of the dark, not to someone who could spend night and day outside in winter without feeling cold, plus run swiftly, climb high, jump far. When I was ten, two years after I had been taken from Honey to live with Ruth, Lucky appeared in the brush at the far side of the clearing behind the trailer. The world can be such a sudden place; a door closed for so long opens in a pulse. My eyes understood at once that without knowing it, they'd been waiting to be filled by just this figure made of sharp angles and brusque lines. Sometimes you realize you're hungry only after taking the first bite. Lucky was building something from old boards—a fort, it looked like—but stilled when my shoes crunched the frozen grass and weeds. Eyes as grey as the November sky narrowed to judge whether I was an enemy— or, as Lucky would say, one of Them.

At first I thought Them referred to a gang of older country kids; later I realized it meant almost everyone. Maybe I wasn't one of Them because, like Lucky, I didn't own mittens or a winter coat or such. Maybe because on Saturdays, when Ruth went into town for a minute that lasted until closing time, she would lock the trailer door so my dirty hands didn't touch her things. Lucky knew I had to crouch against the double-wide to protect myself from the wind, had to shove my hands deep into the heated pits of my arms or range the fields and think of warm subjects such as California and Honey's eyes and how Diamond Lil would laugh like hot chocolate in those rooms above the bars where she and Honey danced. Maybe the reason was just because. Camouflaging her fort with brush so They wouldn't detect and destroy it, Lucky asked: "Are you going to help or not?

"Incidentally," she mentioned. "My name was never Lucille."

From the start I called her Lucky instead of Luke. She liked that name best, how it fit. Just as Billy described the boy I was. "You're not a William," agreed Lucky. "And you're definitely no Bill." All the Jupiter Circuit dancers had names that told you what they really were; for instance, Ruby and Crystal and Star.

I wondered if Lucky could be someone I'd known in a place far away. South across the border, in Washington or Oregon, in any of the Jupiter Circuit towns over there. It felt as familiar to see her smoking Marlboros, or aiming a stream of spit at a difficult target, as it had been to watch Honey paint her face for the next show. That happened sometimes now. A face in the schoolyard turned, and the turning traced a face once glimpsed quick as a camera flash in a café window in Tacoma or Eugene. Another instant photo would stick forever in the album of my heart.

"Over there," Lucky answered, with the wave of one long thin hand, when I asked where she lived. No houses or trailers lay in that direction, only partly cleared fields dotted with weeds and stumps and rusted machinery, more clumps of brush and a tumbledown barn, then the bald, black mountain. I puzzled why I'd never seen Lucky in school or, if she did live nearby, in these fields I roamed whenever Ruth started slurring about Satan who had turned her precious baby into a whore named Honey and had burdened a clean Christian woman with a dirty boy like me in return. Filth begets filth, sin always stinks; Ruth could smell it on me. *Get out.* Soon I had a notion that Lucky had been nearby since my arrival here at the outskirts of Brale, BC at the age of eight. I'd been unable to see her not only because she had a way of blending in with the landscape but because my eyes needed to learn to find her. They hadn't discovered how to detect what was waiting to be found right there before them. My daydreaming was the reason, suggested Lucky. She'd seen me plenty of times herself: following the train tracks by Waneta Junction, climbing the creek up the mountain, hiding in the tall summer grass while planets shimmied in the sky. It made me feel funny to think someone had been watching me when I believed I was alone. I remembered how, during the first year apart from

Honey, I thought she could still see me, however far away she danced. That feeling slowly faded, taking Honey with it.

"I have to go," Lucky announced abruptly on the first afternoon I saw her, though the fort wasn't finished and light still tried to wash the muddy sky clean. She didn't say goodbye, so long, meet you tomorrow by the bridge. That wasn't her way, I'd learn. Each time she left, you didn't know if she'd appear again in the same grey-green skirt whose hem drooped around her bony knees and bounced against thin white legs that were always scratched. This skirt had once been part of a Girl Guide uniform, admitted Lucky, though she wouldn't belong to such a pack of dopes if you paid her. Instead of shoes, she wore big gumboots without socks. She would have to pull off the left boot and empty melted snow that leaked through a hole in the toe. Lucky always wore a brown sweater with yellow buttons that looked like it was meant for someone's grandmother, shiny at the elbows where her sharp elbows poked the wool. She didn't have any other clothes, I suspected, but she had other things instead. Her ears worked much better than mine. She could easily hear a snake coiling through the grass, a deer at the far side of the field. I grew used to watching Lucky move quickly toward a voice I couldn't hear, then slip beyond the elderberry curtain at the edge of the next clearing. I realized eventually that she could see in the dark, as though her feet had eyes that allowed her to step surely when there was no path to follow, only unlit stones and lurking roots. Sometimes Lucky would freeze—in one motion, without slowing—and push her face into the wind. Her grey eyes closed. She was concentrating on what the chill air carried. Clues that could solve distant mysteries. Evidence of apples in Oregon, of sweetness in the south.

It might be getting dark by the time the bus dropped me at the end of the road after school. In the trailer, Ruth would be changing channels and working on another bottle while she waited for Dear Jesus to save her from all the filth and trash. It wasn't hard to pass that lone light, head back to where Lucky might be. Like wading into cold black water. Even after learning about some of her secret places, I could never find Lucky. She always found me. I wouldn't know anyone was near until she stood right there, breathing light and quick from running. Or she'd be a bit farther away, at the edge of my sight in the dusk, bent near the ground to study tracks left by some bumbling brown bear. Before I reached her, without any hello, Lucky would already be continuing a conversation in a way that made me think we had never been apart except in my imagination. "Incidentally," she would add.

I never did discover exactly where Lucky lived, or whether she had a mother and father, sisters and brothers. There were certain subjects she didn't care to discuss; if I brought one up, she would say I sounded like one of Them. "Twelve," she replied, after a minute, when I asked her age. Many things that mattered to Them, like school, didn't have even incidental significance for Lucky. Maybe that was why I couldn't picture her in town, or in the classroom with its neat rows of desks alphabetically arranged. She didn't fit with Ruth in my mind at all. They refused to share the same snapshot, shoved each other out of the frame. I knew never to mention Lucky in the trailer because of Ruth's way of speaking about what counted most, how her tongue turned Honey into that filthy whore. And although she knew where I lived, Lucky didn't knock on the screen door for me. Ruth was only one of Them, not worth our while to talk about even when the back of her hand made coloured lights dance inside my head. What mattered was a fire that we guessed a hobo had left to smoulder beside the tumbledown barn. Or steam rising from the creek as an invisible housekeeper ironed the water. A raccoon hat that Lucky pulled from beneath the broken seat of one of the cars, abandoned and rusted, that littered our landscape. We took turns wearing it like Davy Crockett, despite a smell of something gone bad. Lucky had such things hidden far and wide. She liked to spread herself around, claimed for her own this whole area that wasn't wanted much by Them. Suddenly she'd bend down, push some rocks aside, and from a shallow hole lift two wrinkled apples wrapped in dry grass. "Damn squirrels," she swore when nuts saved for supper were missing from another hiding place. We didn't really mind. Thick milk could always be coaxed from Old Man Johnson's bad-tempered cow if you were careful. I began to understand that these fields, all this wide, open space, was where Lucky lived. Picture a big room without walls and slate sky for a ceiling. Stereo birds, light bulb stars. Lucky would curl beneath the cottonwoods when it rained hardest. She spent the night in a boxcar or in a wrecked Ford or in the tumbledown barn. She slept here or there. It reminded me of following the Jupiter Circuit with Diamond Lil and Honey—those different towns, a new one every week.

Lucky liked shiny things especially, such as tin whistles and steelies and brand-new coins. Whatever caught and gave back light had value. "Possession is nine-tenths of the law," one of Lucky's favourite sayings went. So I didn't ask where she'd gotten the army knife with seven blades that could pry open the door of a boxcar forgotten on the Waneta Junction siding. A blanket and a half-burned candle took up one corner of the splintery floor, plus three comic books starring superheroes who could rescue anybody no matter what the danger, who would save the most desperate situation. "Sort of," she replied, when I asked if she'd settled here for the winter. Lucky answered my questions more often now, though each one still made her stiffen, as at an alarm.

I found out that Lucky didn't need to go to school because, as she pointed out, knowing the fuddy-duddy Fathers of Confederation wouldn't do her an ounce of good when she became a rodeo girl. She would ride in a western saddle when she had one, but in the meantime went bareback, with a bridle fashioned from binding twine, on Old Man Johnson's mangy horses. Lucky had given each one a name; they sounded like dancers. There was Jewel and Satin and, her favourite, Champagne. In secret, they cantered down to the dam at midnight, galloped along the flat, hardpacked gravel bank. Her specialty was racing barrels. Lucky had a length of rope that was worn as a belt around her waist when she wasn't twirling it above her head, snaking shapes in the air, capturing stumps with the noose. "Watch this," she bragged, showing me another trick she'd mastered while I was learning fractions and capital cities and *je suis, tu es, il est.* The rope floated a circle through the dusk like one of Lucky's smoke rings; it snared a fence post gleaming white as her legs with first winter snow.

Beneath the bridge, while Lucky discussed Spokane, three hundred miles to the south, where big rodeos with cash prizes were held every summer, I tried not to shiver like a sap. If the air that licked my skin inside the trailer was at once too sour and too sweet from Ruth's bottles, at least I would be warmer there. I wondered whether it was becoming too cold even for Lucky to live in a room without walls, beneath such frigid sky. I wondered why she didn't find some long pants and a heavy jacket to possess nine-tenths of. Then I understood. That was what a Lucille would have done, not a Lucky or even a Luke.

One Sunday in December, Lucky's legs were marked with red stripes that looked like they'd been drawn carefully there; a few days later, they might have been outlined, just as neatly, with black crayon. My eyes had missed seeing the real truth before them. All along, the scratches on Lucky's legs had been something else.

"That Lucille is such a sap," said Lucky, when she caught me looking. "She's too weak to fight back and too stupid to run away. It serves her right, what They do to her."

Lucky began to speak often about Lucille, as if that girl mattered more than incidentally now. She sneered about the sap the same way she did about any of Them; but her voice held more than scorn; there was a further sound behind the sound, like a river in back of a wind. I learned Lucille loved sweet things, every kind of candy. If she became a rodeo girl, Lucille would curl her hair, put on makeup, and wear fancy costumes with rhinestones and fringes to barrel race. And, of course, Lucille was excited that Christmas was almost here; it was just the kind of holiday a sap like her would enjoy most. She adored the coloured lights and the carols and the presents wrapped in shiny paper beneath the tree. Lucille was crazy about all that jazz.

"Naked dancing?" demanded Lucky in disbelief when I told her about the Jupiter Circuit, and how it had brought Honey and me to Spokane lots of times but never to a rodeo. "People pay to see that?" As I described Diamond Lil's feathers and boas and fans, then Honey's long blonde hair and high silver heels, Lucky's grey eyes narrowed as if refusing to allow such complicating visions to interfere with their clear sight.

"Well, maybe in the States," she admitted finally, as the only possible explanation for naked dancing. In a grudging way, apparently against her will, she asked over and over about the music the strippers swayed to on the stage, about staying upstairs from the bars, about the funny men who sometimes followed Honey's fragrance into our rooms late at night. How I'd have to sleep in a bathtub bed until they stopped creaking the big one and the door clicked goodbye, so long, at last he's gone. Lucky asked me about such subjects over and over, just to express her astonished disdain; yet each time I could hear the river more loudly behind the wind, a yearning flow.

Lucky's sharp eyes peered south toward the Washington border, just beyond Waneta Junction. She could see a host of dancers spinning in a spotlight on the other side. A shiver passed over her face; fast as a minnow's dart and flash; it resembled the ripple that would follow her glance at the smelter stacks rising above distant Brale. Maybe Lucille flickered half-formed in her features. I wasn't sure. Before I could decide, Lucky's face had become extra alert, more intent than ever.

Something dropped from her skirt pocket as we skidded through the snow to scare bats in the tumbledown barn. I picked up the rag. There was just enough time to unwrap an old lipstick and a little compact before Lucky grabbed. "See? This is exactly what I mean," she spat. "It's Lucille to a T." Her strong arm pitched the things across the fence, that far. They flew like birds, then suddenly plummeted to make you think a hunter had taken good aim.

"Unless you wanted them," taunted Lucky, running on toward the barn.

I stole a pack of cigarettes from Ruth and a bag of Hershey's from Kresge's in town. Christmas presents for Lucille as well as for Lucky. I had to leave them where they would just be found and could just be claimed, since Lucky wasn't a sap who hoped for presents. She was easily able to steal whatever she needed, incidentally. On my way to the boxcar at Waneta Junction, I wished for once that Lucky wouldn't find me. I hid the cigarettes and candy beneath her blanket, then sat to reread the best comic book, about the hero who always saves the day. The inside cover had been blank when I'd opened it before; now it looked like someone had been practicing printing there. Unsteady as Ruth after a bottle, the letters might have been made by a six year old, or by an older person using the wrong hand. Lucky was spelled a hundred shaky times.

When we discussed a comic book, Lucky sometimes got the story wrong. That can happen, if you read just the pictures.

"The only thing worse than a sap is a sneak."

For the first time, I heard the voice Lucky used to speak to Them. The bruises on her face, dark against the pale, had been there before. Accidents were bound to happen when you were practicing a new rodeo trick, Lucky would explain. Standing up tall on Champagne's back as he loped around the ring and you twirled a lasso, you were going to fall a hundred times or more until you learned to keep your balance. It didn't matter, it didn't hurt.

The banged-up face was gone from the open boxcar door. I didn't see Lucky during the following days. Maybe there was a grey-green flash past the camouflaging pines. The crunch of gumboots on snow. Two alert eyes piercing the air's invisible wall.

On Christmas morning, Ruth gurgled with an empty bottle cradled like a precious baby in her sleeping arms. I searched the trailer in case some presents were hidden somewhere, then stepped outside. Cigarettes and candies were sprinkled over the snow, as if they'd fallen out of the sky, or been dropped from a sleigh speeding through the air. I dumped them into the barrel whose smoking contents Ruth liked to stir with a stick while she muttered about filth and trash, trash and filth.

Lucky still found me after Christmas, but less often. For weeks, I could wait long hours beneath the bridge, by the boxcar, or inside the tumble-down barn without her showing up. Then one day she would appear again. Now Lucky spoke as if I were incidental. She looked intently toward the trees, like her words were really meant for them. Her shiver at the sight of the distant smelter had turned into a shudder. Lucille never came up at all anymore, as if she had died before she really lived. But without asking further about the dancing there, Lucky mentioned Spokane more often. You could ride to the rodeos in the back of a truck, she mused. Anyone could easily cross the border beyond Waneta Junction in the summer, when only college kids worked at the little building with the gate across the road. You just walked around when the big dopes weren't looking. Once she showed me an American quarter she'd saved, though it didn't shine brand new. "It's worth more," Lucky said, suggesting that it could buy anything you wanted: quantities of cowgirl costumes decorated with rhinestones, and fancy fringes everywhere. I didn't like to hear about Spokane so much. It picked the scab on my heart to remember the Paradise Hotel where Honey and I had always ended up for one week every second month. The desk clerk with one glass eye and his wooden leg. Lonesome miners over from Idaho for a good time on the weekend. Honey's face appeared to me through a thick, foggy window these days. I could wave and call, but she didn't see me, didn't hear.

Lucky's blanket, candle, and comic books were gone from the boxcar. I couldn't find them in the tumbledown barn or in one of the wrecked Fords. It was hard to say where she slept while January turned colder. Her eyes wouldn't let me ask. "This damn smoker's cough," she complained as it got worse. The snow was brown where she spit. Her hardest rodeo trick, standing on Champagne's back without holding on, didn't get better; from the look of her face, Lucky fell more often than before. Now when she said she had to go, I tried to follow her tracks in the snow once she was out of sight. At a certain point, they would suddenly trace tight circles that crossed each other in confusion, with no one clear path leading from the maze. I bent over the puzzle, words I should have known how to read, then lifted my head at a snort of laughter. There was no visible source for the sound.

"Hurry up," said Ruth when I came home from school one day in February.

We were moving into town right now. I'd heard many times how a house on Columbia Avenue had been robbed from Ruth by the City, like everything was stolen from her. Somehow, the place was hers again. Ruth wore a tight, satisfied smile, like she'd pulled a good trick.

Old Man Johnson's truck had already been loaded up with the treasures that belonged to Ruth, the ones that my dirty hands were never allowed to touch. There wasn't time to run to Lucky's secret places to say goodbye if she were there. I couldn't dart beneath the bridge where I had buried three things Ruth had missed when she burned the contents of the cardboard suitcase that travelled with me from the south. They were three things I promised Honey I would never lose.

Town was just five miles away, but everything was different beneath the smelter hill. Smoke from the tall stacks made my throat burn, my eyes itch. I couldn't see as good as before; it grew harder to make out the real truth of things. Honey had been a girl in this old house with a slanting porch and peeling paint and one front step missing. Her room above the porch was kept locked. The door wouldn't pry open with the army knife I'd taken nine-tenths possession of from Kresge's. I slept on a cot in Ruth's room; she liked to keep an eye on me these days. That was different, too. Before, Ruth never minded if I stayed out all hours in the fields with Lucky trying to trap rabbits with a snare of string. "Why'd you bother coming back?" she had asked when I came through the trailer door at last. "Since you're going to leave like that slut in the end." Now I had ten minutes to make it home from school or else.

For the first few weeks at Columbia Avenue, Ruth didn't buy bottles. We cleaned the filth and trash, scoured the stink of a slut from the floors and walls. Then Jack Daniel's started hanging around again. He made Ruth sick and sad; he made her lock me in the closet with the coats. Ruth prayed to Dear Jesus on the other side of the closet door; coloured lights danced in my head when it finally opened and her hand lifted. I tried to remember that all this was incidental. I reminded myself that the world was one big place without walls. "Sky for ceiling," I repeated in the cramped darkness. "Light bulb stars."

I had to go to a different school because it was closer. From the far side of the playground, other kids still yelled *Yank go home*. One recess, I thought I saw Lucky over by the swings. I rubbed my itchy eyes, tried to see better. This girl had the same sharp face, thin legs, slate-grey eyes. Although the March air felt cold, she wasn't wearing a coat or mittens or scarf.

"Lily," called a boy about my age and size. As she turned to him, the girl noticed me. Her grey eyes narrowed; she frowned. Then Lily ran away.

Three times, after the snow began to melt, I caught the school bus out to Waneta Junction as if I still lived in the trailer at the end of the dirt road. An old man and woman had moved into the place. I saw her wandering across the field with one end of a rope tied to her wrist, the other end dragging on the ground. "Marie," the old man called toward the thistles. "Marie," he called again, when the woman didn't turn toward his voice. She wasn't wearing shoes, not even ones with a hole in the left toe.

I waited for Lucky at the same places as before: a wrecked Ford, a boxcar, a tumbledown barn. There were no signs that anyone visited there anymore. Lucky refused to emerge out of the empty air. Now she really believed I was one of Them, I guessed.

"Lucky," I called loud as I could, but my voice sounded doubtful of its power to summon what my heart hoped for most.

"Luke," I tried.

"Lucille."

No matter what name I shouted, Lucky wouldn't come. I realized that. "Are you insane?" she asked the one time I tried to call to her across Old Man Johnson's field, before I knew her very well. "Do you want Them to hear?"

It was dark and late by the time I walked back to Brale. There was hell to pay. William was too weak, he couldn't fight back or run away, he deserved what he got. This time was worse than the others, like falling from a horse in the sky. I had to stay home from school for a week so it wouldn't show. That was when I began to think about the sailor Honey had sometimes said was my father. I was reminded of him by the tall man who lived down the street. I thought his eyes were blue-green from squinting at the sea. His back must have become strong and broad from pulling up the heavy anchor. Another man, also young and tall, lived in the same house. They were worse than filth and trash, said Ruth. In the closet, I pictured them and thought I heard my daddy's voice calling from a city by the sea. There was the sound of waves behind wind.

I knew I could go out to the fields to look for Lucky just once more before Ruth made certain I never went there again. Before I left Brale the way Honey had left for good; the way she promised I would. The last try had to count. I planned carefully while Ruth's marks faded from my skin, like memories of a mother.

All the snow had melted. The creek splashed loud and fast with run-off from the mountain. The air felt nearly warm at four o'clock. Soon it would be summer, time for rodeos in Spokane. I waited in Lucky's secret places, though now I didn't really believe she would appear. It might be Lucille, I thought, or maybe the girl named Lily.

The three things I had buried beneath the bridge were gone. Someone had found them and taken them, though they weren't shiny, though they were just three small things.

When the sky started to get dark, I walked to Lucky's favourite spot for practicing rope tricks. It was a clear patch of ground behind the tumble-down barn. Once, we guessed, a corral held dancing horses there. The world twirled like a lasso in the air as I bent to scratch big letters with a stick into the ground.

"Incidentally, I'll never be one of Them," I printed as neatly as I could, though I knew Lucky couldn't read my promise.

After the Glitter and the Rouge

"At least it's only the one side," says Diamond Lil, the last of the old-time strippers, appearing out of the pale Portland sunlight to take Honey from the hospital. The doctors have been only able to do so much, the grafts failed to take as well as they hoped; there were certain complications. Lil doesn't flinch at her friend's face; she's witnessed worse. A stiff blue body on the bathroom floor. There's nothing for Lil to do but unsnap a roll of twenties and settle the bill and hand Honey dark glasses. Then the marquee outside The Golden Arms makes a promise, *Live Girls!*, that grows bigger as the taxi nears. Honey watches the driver try to keep his eyes from the rearview mirror; he would have stared for a different reason before. "Everything heals," Lil tries to gloss over in their room, packing feathers and boas and fans, preparing to follow the Jupiter Circuit on to Eugene one more time. They drink a champagne toast and, to the tune of shattered glass, vow to work together again some day.

"Maybe a mask, maybe a bit of classy kink," muses Lil, snapping her makeup case shut on that remote possibility, hardening herself to the fact that she's pushing forty like it's a boulder you have to heave uphill or be crushed by. The Circuit is unaffected by accidents; it will orbit Lil back this way again. She'll bump into Honey here or there or in Eureka, California. Lil laughs at all the lies life makes you tell, grimaces at sentiment too expensive even on installment. Honey stays on at The Golden Arms with her costumes and Camels, with the lotions and the pills. Lou lets her keep the room till the end of the month for old time's sake. Food ordered in, curtains always closed, a strange face floating in the speckled mirror. One night she tries to see what glitter and rouge will do; they only make the left side flame more brightly. Crimson neon clicks *Dancing Nightly!* across the curtain, buzzes through Honey's dreams. Each week fresh dancers troop in stilettos and robes down to the Showroom; their grumbled dissatisfactions are known to Honey as well as her own name. May rain slices in straight lines onto Centre Avenue. Traffic lights switch like a lost boy's eyes change colour according to which arcade photo of him hovers inside your heart. Then quarters drop into a pay phone during the northbound Greyhound's ten-minute Tacoma pause. "I'm coming home," she says, after Ruth's voice needles through a bad connection. "Frances," she says, knowing it's time to forget being Honey. Or Blaze or Star or Crystal.

"It's not pretty," comments Ruth, opening the screen door Frances slammed shut sixteen years before. "Ran off same as you," she offers to explain the absence of the boy they took from Honey and sent to Ruth when he turned eight. The old woman sighs. Like mother, like son. Now look what charity's brought to the door; this beat-up whore back beneath her Christian roof. Ruth glances at the cardboard suitcase, pushes at her wig, goes into the kitchen. Reheated coffee spreads bitter fumes while Frances unpacks in her old room above the porch. She balances on the mattress edge, tries to detect a hollow that held her sleeping son. Possessions left behind here at sixteen were burned in a backyard fire; Ruth hissed *slut* into the sparks and smoke. Now that thin voice calls *supper* up the stairs. It becomes obvious that Ruth goes out only to the Safeway, to the liquor store, to cash her monthly cheque. "The house is paid for," she volunteers, a rare revelation. Apparently, the bank tried to take the place at some point, and Ruth was in a trailer out by Waneta Junction when the boy arrived to stay with her.

Frances can't ask how tall Billy had grown by the time he left, can't wonder where a boy of twelve would go except eventually out to sea like some sailor whose arms are known for a single salty night before he must be back on board. She can ask only who lives next door these days. "Same ones as always," Ruth sniffs. Plenty of neighbours have moved away, the smelter keeps laying off, good riddance to bad rubbish. Still too many dirty dagos around East Brale; they'd be better off up in The Gulch with their pervert Pope.

Frances walks past the old high school, over the bridge. There are few people to gawk at her, none she recognizes. The town itself appears unchanged. The same metallic taste to the air, same banks of black slag. Smoke still coughs from the stacks up on the hill. The doctor told her to stay out of the sun; whatever the weather, she won't take more walks. Instead, the days are spent inside with Ruth and the TV on an endless loop. "Greasy Italians," the old woman mutters in the midst of boiling potatoes, frying meat. "Filthy Wops." They eat early, while the afternoon is still hot. Heavy meals steam the kitchen damp, curl the corners of Frances's sight. Afterward, Ruth climbs the stairs and closes her bedroom door. She clinks the bottle against the glass; whines prayers to Jack Daniel's and to Jesus. Frances sits out on the front porch; the boards are warped, grey paint peels. *I'm your private dancer*, moan cars cruising Columbia Avenue on those summer evenings. Drivers are boys with last names like Lorenzo or Catalano, with grandmothers who've never learned English. Maybe they're heading down to Gyro Park with gallon jars of papa's homemade wine. They'll get brave enough for the cold fast river, try to swim to the flat rocks midstream. That last summer, when she was sixteen, the boys didn't call her Little Orphan Frannie any more, but Brale girls still didn't trust her. Rough red wine, cast-off clothes upon the bank, moon touching a current white. The first time she made it to the rocks, Frances knew she'd be gone by fall.

"It was an accident," she finally says in September, when Ruth still hasn't asked. Frances reaches for her mother's hand, guides it to her face. Where the skin is puckered, pink.

First doctors then police explained that he must have planned it well in advance. The acid was quite rare, difficult to obtain, used only in specific laboratory experiments. He'd lurked beyond the purple and the pink for years. One of the unseen angry men who cloud the stage lights with Camels, who wait for the next blonde move. Honey had felt him out there ever since Lil found her strung out on Seattle speed, spreading in the rough Red Room when she could get herself together. "There's more to the business than young pussy; little girls burn up in a week," Lil chided Honey, teaching her costumes and music and lights. Soon they were trading off the Jupiter's headline spot, doubling up in hotels, living steady and sober and straight. A Eureka winter away from the glitter and the rouge for Billy's birth; back on the Circuit while he grows into a gaptoothed boy. Social Services send him north at eight to become the kind of memory a dancer can't afford; one more phantom haunting the no-man's land between a blue pill and a red. Then the audience seems to glower with greater rage each night, makes Honey nervous as sixteen. "I come every time I'm on that stage," cracks Lil, parking herself inside their room with paperbacks after the last show, going through pages like some love-story junkie. On all those nights, in Salem or Olympia or Eugene, Honey tries to stay in with Lil and sew sequins by the window. She tries not to wonder which of her moves will make something click in his head, tell him she's the one who needs to wake up in a motel room with fire feeding from her face. He'll stop her dancing, he'll make it so the hot lights never dim. They'll bore into her skull always. White current wiping away what made her restless, burning pieces of before into ash and cinder. "I don't remember," she said when they asked who he was, how he looked, what took place on that night she grew tired of waiting for it finally to happen. Afterward, she felt relieved.

Frances goes up to her room above the porch as soon as evening cools. Once her midnight ladder, then perhaps a trap for Billy's paper planes, the pear tree outside the window rises twisted, gnarled. She wakes with heat like stage lights on her face, with a shadow shifting on the wall. At the end, she could pick up cues blind, close her eyes and feel the difference between a red spot and a gold. "When a Man Loves a Woman" and "Misty Blue" and the one about the rain against the window: she swayed to them all. Downstairs in the dark, her fingers discover the piano hasn't been tuned since the last time she practiced for her Friday lesson with the teacher with the cats. She's forgotten how the pieces went, or eighteen years have flattened them into something else. Behind her, a black shape looms in the doorway. "I always knew you'd be back," says Ruth, satisfied at last. From now on, everything will be quiet and slow.

Part Three

WHAT THE WORLD TAKES AWAY

We need, in love, to practice only this: letting each other go.
For holding on comes easily; we do not need to learn it.

—Rainer Maria Rilke
"Requiem for a Friend"

Rorschach II: The Black Hole

It's time to achieve the top of a giant tree rooted deep into America. Lofty in your sixth summer sky, a halo of white cloud circling your head. Sweet cherry already rich in your mouth; further fruit tempts nearby, a branch breaks as it's grasped. The roar past your ears, the drop faster and faster. Falling feels long and dark, though your eyes are open and your heart beats just six times before you thud onto East Africa. A white cast on your left arm rusts the same red as the dirt beneath blazing bougainvillea. When Dorothy descended from particular sky, she learned how the world can change completely in the blink of an eye. In every Oz, colours are too brilliant and smells too pungent, and light falls in angles unknown to either Canada or Kansas. Stare at the scar on your elbow that promises to fade but never to disappear; will misshapen bones float until they reassume a perfect shape. Stars drip from the heavens, stones sink through sea. Only some elusive, obscene wizard can lift you back through time to the top of the sky, where you viewed the New World before the fruit was plucked.

The black hole lacks the dimensions of time and space; it is without darkness or light, warmth or cold. Existence inside this void resembles deep sleep induced by a field of poppies, except there are no dreams or even nightmares to remind you that an undistorted world waits nearby. It is the blankness that stretches between losing consciousness in a bland suburban house and waking in some cage without a key. Between injecting the needle in Sacramento and withdrawing it in Winnipeg. Once you enter the black hole, cackles the wicked witch, you will never escape it entirely. (Back in her drab farmhouse kitchen, prairie dust sifts upon Dorothy as she gazes out the window, across flat fields of corn, hoping and dreading to be torn away by another tornado.) You will always walk carefully upon the earth, peering at ground that can suddenly open like a hungry mouth to swallow you up and then spit you out, nearly whole, beside the Sphinx, on the Equator, inside Hollywood, upon the lonely moon. Or say the globe is mined with spots as fragile as the kind that decorate a newborn baby's skull. Turn a corner of any unassuming street to find yourself inhabiting a different city, another year, a distinct skin: you are Rick or Rickie, Richard or Reeves; he is ten or twenty or thirty; this may be Salobreña, Sidi Ifni, Santa Cruz. You learn not to seem surprised by the most abrupt change: it has always been like this; it will always be this way.

Once I tried to touch the top of the sky, you mumble to your smirking shadow on Santa Monica Boulevard, on ghastly Geary Street, on any number of forlorn sidewalk strolls. It slides away in fickle search of a more substantial form to follow. Sailors who've lost their dog tags huddle in doorways, drift unanchored through slick night, whistle as you trickle past barred-up bodegas and burned out streetlamps and madwomen dancing in rings in the rain. In the distance, another siren shrieks its lullaby; one more alarm punctuates the Tenderloin's bitter bedtime tale. Each splattering drop further rusts your metallic skin and corrodes your tin-man joints: by dawn you will creak and groan your way through vacant lots littered with fetuses butchered then abandoned among the gaudy debris, all the blooming weeds.

Wake cautiously at morning's aborted birth; with suspicion open eyes. What room emerges from darkness into daylight? Who is this sad scarecrow leaking straw beside you? Do the lines and angles of his cloth face draw the map of a continent you know, a landscape you love? On your skin are fresh marks of damage, betraying how hard you crashed to the ground this time. Beside the bed, next to the bloodied syringe, are clothes that fit. Feel in a pocket for the slip of paper printed with a name and address. You've learned to hang onto this scrap as fiercely as you clutched the broken branch during the first dizzying descent, the original journey to alien earth. In another pocket hide dollars, keys. You prowl the unfamiliar rooms in search of enlightening evidence; but you are no longer a confident detective; there will never be sufficient clues to solve this puzzle perfectly. To seam the crack yawning between the jungle of the western slopes and junkyards of queer cities. To explain how and why you ended up within these generic walls, these anonymous cement embraces.

Baptize yourself with the name on the slip of paper. Take a taxi to the address printed there. Open a door with keys that fit the lock. Enter bare rooms as strange as those just left. Home? The word echoes without end inside this vacuum; repeats until it garbles beyond meaning into only ironic noise. Empty space sucks at memory, hollows your hurting head. Outside the window, leaves spin in autumn wind, whirl through the pale Portland sky. A splotch of black ink stains a wall that might have been blank white yesterday. A souvenir of the same intruder who during your absence leaves hieroglyphics in the notebook—signs and symbols you attempt to decipher into language that might explain how to escape the haunted forest? Your mind skips over a question without an answer, ponders the mark upon the wall instead. Inspect it closely then lean nearer, until air whistles past your ears again. Once more you plummet through darkness. One day, hope's bad habit stubbornly believes—foolishly insists—you will emerge from the black hole as another brave explorer who has patiently been waiting to be born.

Peggy Lee in Africa

AT NIGHT THREE CHILDREN FLOAT IN BED AND LISTEN TO THEIR FATHER play Peggy Lee records at the other end of the latest house. This one is built of cinder blocks and a tin roof; instead of glass windows, there are wire-mesh screens to let in breeze and to keep out snakes. The cool voice slips through another hot Tanzanian night, *I know a little bit about a lot of things*, silencing crickets, hushing cicadas. For a moment, the music mutes. Maybe the father no longer revolves around his room like the record, no longer sits on the edge of his bed, large hands curved around knees, head bowed, listening. Maybe he has finally switched off the light to drown in darkness like his children. Then Peggy Lee begins to croon again, over and over incanting the same spell upon a man who is fearful of snakes and who won't ride roller coasters and who feels faint at the sight of his own blood. Tangled jungle pours scent down the Ngondo hills, poisoned perfume wraps around the house.

Sometimes during the day, when only the houseboy is home with him, Donald tiptoes into the father's room. On the record covers, Peggy Lee's face is pale and smooth beneath short waved hair that is more white than blonde. Her lips are painted deep red. Donald last saw his mother two years before, during a June picnic in the yard behind a relative's house in Canada. Cousins and aunts and uncles balance paper plates of cold fried chicken and potato salad, ride coloured blankets that hover like magic carpets just above the grass. "Look!" cries Madeleine, his father's oldest sister, pointing upward. Behind the fenced yard rises the hill with the hospital on top. A woman in white stands on a balcony high up there and waves to everyone below. Donald believes he can see her short blonde hair, her deeply red mouth; it will be years before he learns how distance can distort or damage vision, transforming any coiled length of rope into an asp. Someone also wearing white appears behind the ascendant woman and leads her back inside. A game of croquet begins at the picnic, bright balls are sent spinning across the lawn, there's a hollow sound of wood knocking wood.

Soon Lily and MJ are asleep. Donald can hear his sister and brother breathing in their nearby beds, oblivious to the messages still transmitted by Peggy Lee through the Morogoro night. *I know a little bit about biology,* she confides. "She's not here," the father once replied to Donald, running one hand through short black hair, squinting at the sisal fields in the valley below the cinder-block house. Lily squirms in her sleep; something's always trying to get her. Now the father has stepped with a flashlight from the kitchen door. A weak beam plays through darkness, searches for danger undulating nearby. Tentatively, the man takes several more steps forward, retreats back inside. Peggy Lee sings on until dawn.

"That old snake in the grass," Lily will write to Donald twenty years later, from inside visions of vipers. "'Honey, what does Peggy Lee have to do with anything?' Mitch asked, the last time I saw him. Apparently, Mitch still thinks MJ will be found; he says he's doing everything in his power to make sure his boy is brought back home. Of course, he never mentions you," writes Lily from the clinic in Canada that Donald pictures poised high on a hill, with innumerable balconies from which hosts of mothers and sisters wave to people playing summer games below. "You're smart to refuse to step foot back on our native soil," adds Lily. "Don't return, it's not safe, venom abounds."

The father is clear-eyed and energetic during daylight. He changes out of his teaching trousers, white shirt, and thin tie; in an old pair of shorts, he throws a basketball at a hoop fixed to the side of the house. The children sit in the shaded doorway and watch the father's skin darken to the colour of an African's. He dribbles and dodges past an invisible opposition, scores two more points. "How many does that make?" he asks excitedly. Inside, the houseboy prepares food; when it's ready, he goes home to the village for the night. Supper cools and hardens on the table, unpacked crates from Canada loom in dimming rooms. A moment after bright sunlight rules, it is nearly dark. The father attempts one more lay-up. The children can no longer make out his leap toward the hoop, his drop back to earth. It doesn't matter that they're no longer able to see something round spinning between his palms. They know already that he holds the world in his hands.

While the evening is still early, and MJ and Lily are playing the Canada game, the father might listen to Frank Sinatra or Ella Fitzgerald. He hums around the house, practices new Swahili words aloud, interrupts the children's activities to tell stories of when he was a boy. "I was the only one in town to swim the Columbia River," he brags. "Everyone else felt afraid of the currents, the rocks, the undertow." Especially perilous swims are described in detail as the children's eyes grow heavy in their nodding heads. Later, if wakened by Peggy Lee, they'll know that in the morning the father will be silent over his coffee, with skin swollen beneath eyes which do not turn toward children who squabble or bicker or cry.

While the father is "bringing home the bacon," as he calls teaching history, Lily and MJ attend a makeshift school in the nunnery at the top of the mission, where the jungle begins and colobus monkeys sway the palms. Weary of following the silent houseboy from room to room, Donald walks up the road and among the scattered mission buildings. The father's voice is suddenly close, clear. Through an open window, Donald sees rows of young men and women with dark skin and white teeth gazing at the father. He sits with swinging legs on the edge of a desk, then springs up to write on the blackboard. "If we know what took place before, we may understand what happens now," the father explains. His eyes travel around the classroom, come to rest on the window. He continues to speak smoothly about an impersonal past, as though Donald did not interrupt his line of vision, as though his son were not there. The boy crouches between freshly watered shrubs and digs hands into damp dirt. He paints his face with the markings of a lost or extinct tribe, reels at the rich odour of excavated earth.

One night Lily finds a snake curled in a corner of the children's room. The father pales. Gripping the machete, he stares at the intruder from a distance of several feet. "You can sleep in my bed," he tells the children, closing the door of their room tightly and leaving the snake undisturbed, alone, coiled around itself for warmth. The children crowd into the father's big bed; he has moved with the record player to the living room for the night. *I know a little more about psychology*, suggests the singer, charming the snake into lifting its head, extending its muscled length, swaying in sinuous circles. Peggy Lee performs magic until morning, when the house-boy opens the door of the children's room to find the snake is no longer there. The father carefully inspects the window screens, fails to find flaws.

"If I could get back to Africa, I'd be okay," Lily writes Donald from the clinic they won't let her leave. "There, at least, the snakes are real; you can close the door against them. Peggy Lee makes them vanish in a puff of smoke. Do you remember the time Mitch suddenly decided we had to learn to swim, packed us into the white Peugeot, drove all morning until we reached the coast? 'Anyone can learn to swim in the Indian Ocean,' he said. 'The water's so salty it holds you up when you don't know how to float. You couldn't drown if you tried.' He shouted instructions from shore, he refused to get even his toes wet. 'I already know how to swim,' he said. 'Float!' he called. And we did, didn't we? We floated all afternoon in water as warm as blood, while on land Mitch turned over rocks in search of cow-ries. 'I won't always be around to save you from drowning,' he said when we were allowed out of the water at last to wobble on legs that had forgot-ten how to navigate solid ground. 'I can't always save you from this or from that,' he frowned, holding a shell to his ear. What faint music did he hear? I no longer hear Peggy Lee in the night. Do you? Does MJ, wherever he is? MJ would get me out of this place if he were here. I keep thinking he drowned, though I know that's not what really happened. MJ is still with Peggy Lee in Africa. Like Sister Bridget, they disappeared into the jungle, in search of the river's source, somewhere at the top of the Ngondo hills, which we could never find. *Missing*, is the official word. Not *dead*. Did you know Mitch has started collecting stamps since he retired? 'Honey, I have to have a hobby to keep me busy now that my babies have abandoned me,' he explained in a postcard from Thailand. I take it the wise Buddhists wouldn't have him; anyway, he's in Budapest now. Stay away, little brother. Remain in Spain. The snakes have briefly vanished, which only means they'll be back in greater number soon. Everything would be all right if I could smell the frangipani by the river just one more time," writes Lily in another of the letters Donald will fail to answer, not wanting a message to his sister to be read first by doctors and nurses with clean pink skin, with cold Canadian eyes.

MJ claims that she's in a hospital; Lily insists she's dead. "Who?" asks Donald. Lily and MJ agree that the mother didn't really have short waved hair that was more white than blonde. She didn't use deep-red lipstick, and she didn't sing the same song over and over until you fall asleep. "You can't remember," they tell Donald. He remembers riding with her on a roller coaster, while Lily and MJ occupy the car behind, and the father watches anxiously from below. Climbing slowly, falling fast, snaking swiftly all the way to the end. The children lurch off the ride, join the father on the ground, watch the mother ride again. Her head is thrown back, short blonde hair whips; her laughter shrills above screams of other passengers. She rides a dozen more times, laughing like she will when they come to take her away. (Then Donald stays with Aunt Madeleine during the day, and the house on Aster Drive is quiet at night; the father plays Peggy Lee and prepares to take the children across the world, far from everything.) Finally descending from thrilling heights, the mother is silent in her summer dress. Her red lips press tightly together. Children and father melt cotton candy in their mouths, throw rings at gaudy prizes. Lily wins a big stuffed snake she calls Honey.

Nothing grows around the cinder-block house yet. The bare dirt is red and cracked from lack of water and too much heat, or it's a field of mud during the rains. "It would be a waste of time to start a garden," says the father after three years, twiddling his famously green thumbs, "since we're here temporarily." The Peggy Lee records have become worn and scratched; a constant hiss threatens to drown her voice out. Sometimes the needle skips over damaged grooves. Peggy Lee jumps from one unfinished phrase to another, fails to make sense. Donald has grown old enough for school, up where the butterflies are brilliant, but the convent that contains the classroom has been abandoned: after Sister Bridget disappeared in the jungle, the other nuns returned to Holland to walk in wooden shoes through poppy fields and to skate like Hans Brinker across frozen canals. Occasionally, the father gathers the children around the atlas or dictionary for an hour in the evening; more often, he retreats into his bedroom after supper. "When are we going home?" MJ asks once. "This is home," the father replies, kneading his left bicep slowly, then saying he has lessons to prepare. His door shuts behind him; Peggy Lee starts to sing again. The children's hair blanches beneath African sun, until it's more white than blonde. They climb the river that rushes down through jungle, search for the source somewhere at the top of the Ngondo hills. Sometimes they believe Sister Bridget flits beyond thick vines, no longer lost. They eat green mangos until their stomachs turn tight as drums. Oldest to youngest, they file along a narrow path with grass higher than their heads on either side. This order is unfortunate for Lily. When they meet a snake, it will be too startled by MJ, in front, to bite him; it will already have had its fill by the time Donald comes along at the rear. Unlucky Lily, forever in the middle, sees serpents in the clinic. They are always long and thick and tattooed with intricate designs whose brilliant colours appear only in the jungle or in dreams. "Don't bother," Lily replies to the father's last long-distance wish to visit her bare white room. "You can't save me from the poisoned fangs. That never was your strong point."

The father cries for help. The children find him at the kitchen sink. A knife has fallen by his feet and deep-red blood flows from his thumb. He leans against MJ. Lily runs for bandages and tape. Donald watches the father's legs tremble. *I'm a little gem in geology*, boasts Peggy Lee, knowing nearly everything. "I'm bleeding and it won't stop," Lily tells MJ one day. "I don't know what to do." "Neither do I," replies my brother.

"Dear Lily," Donald could have written. "Peggy Lee is still alive and kicking, though I hear she no longer resides in Morogoro, Tanzania. 'The climate,' she murmurs, stroking her velvet throat, 'was not good for my voice.' Now the notes are no longer perfectly pitched; now she's old and ill. They prop her on stage in a blonde wig and dark glasses and she snaps her fingers through "Fever" for the millionth time. Mitch wrote to me that you refused his offer to fly across the world to see you. He said it breaks his heart that he can no longer save his children from this thing or the other thing. I always thought everything would be all right as long as Peggy Lee kept singing. She could save us from anything, I believed," Donald doesn't write to Lily, who finally coils around herself for warmth. The clinic and Canada are always cold. Sometimes my sister unwinds her length and flicks her tongue. A slow hiss is her only language now.

Fireflies float through the window screens, drift around the children's bedroom. They blink like the coloured lights of an airplane in search of a safe place to return to earth. "One day we will fly away from all this," MJ tells Donald. Lately, the children have picked through the father's things; careful detectives, they leave the Peggy Lee records exactly in their place. A hunt for photographs of the mother produces only a letter from Aunt Madeleine in Canada. "You must do something with those children," read MJ and Lily. Donald, who hasn't learned letters, stares at the smooth pale face on the record albums and remembers Peggy Lee laughing all afternoon behind her locked door in the house on Aster Drive. She wouldn't release the bolt. They had to smash through the wood and force their way inside. "Before it's too late," adds Aunt Madeleine. Yes, it's late. Fireflies bumble sleepily around the dark bedroom. Donald hears MJ ask Lily if she's still awake. "I think so," she answers. "I don't know," she says a moment later. The father sets the needle back down on the black disc; it will trace a million revolutions before dawn. *But I don't know enough about you*, Peggy Lee finally admits. Her voice is playful, light, certain that tomorrow she will understand everything about the ones who pray to her at night.

Beggars

ARDIS SLIPS FROM THE WHITE PEUGEOT AND PAST THE BEGGARS SQUATTING in front of the greengrocer's. Five or six of them are always there, wrapped within rough brown cloth, eternal victims of flies. From cardboard islands floating in the dust, they reach out insistent hands, they whimper and moan to me. Although we speak a separate language, and they have moved beyond words anyway, I understand what the beggars want: we need the same thing. Their limbs melt in Tanzanian sun, shrink before my sight: shortened fingers, toeless feet, bare rounded bones like handles of old walking sticks smoothed by constant touch. They could be male or female, young or old. Leprosy, Ardis has told me, on one of her good days. Inside the store, my mother's firm, clear voice requests oranges and mangos, rejects imperfect produce. The main street of Morogoro bakes in the middle of afternoon; it is empty except for the beggars and me. Once a month, police with clubs herd them out of town; through the night they shuffle or limp or crawl back to their place before the store to wait for me again: they will always return, I know. Lily and MJ say that if a beggar touches you lightly, even once, you will catch what it has, and no medicine will ever cure you. The features of your face will crumble into dust, blow away across sisal fields, scatter upon the four corners of the globe—until even your own mother and father would not recognize you. Then you too will squat in the dirt and moan eagerly when anyone comes along to spit on you; you will accept anything as alms. *Don't touch*, says Ardis, if I reach toward the red ring on the stove, the crimson circle of her mouth. I kneel beside the beggars. They fumble at my empty pockets, then stroke my ordinary limbs. My eyes close. I feel the imprint of a unique touch; I shiver beneath hands shaped like no others in the world. A lipless mouth kisses the centre of my forehead. I am blessed. All outcasts are holy, says the Koran. Ardis emerges from the store, her string bag filled with brilliant tomatoes, perfect papayas. We stretch our eroded hands to her, we whimper and moan. All we want is a single coin, small and round and flawless, to hide within our rags. We have learned not to ask for much; give us only a token of pity, please. Now I am missing one ear, a nose. This is only the beginning: one day my soul's strait-jacket may disintegrate with divine disease, my heart lose its cage of bone. Ardis glances indifferently down, her cool summer dress flutters just beyond my reach, the white Peugeot pulls away. Then the street is silent, empty.

They let her out of the clinic too soon or she returns to us too late. In 1969, three years after she unwillingly enters the cold white rooms in Canada, Ardis flies with one light suitcase to where we have ceased waiting for her on the Ngondo Hills of Morogoro. Mitch explains to Lily, MJ, and me that our mother will seem different after having been apart from us for so long. He doesn't prepare us for muscles twisting like taut ropes beneath dead white skin, for eyes looking beyond whatever lies before them, for a head constantly turning to see whether someone watches from behind. "Did you get the presents?" she asks at the arrivals gate, in a voice roughened and deepened by medication. In Occupational Therapy, Ardis fashioned gifts for us. On her eighth birthday, Lily received a clay ashtray painted with anguished faces of flowers; for my sixth Christmas, I was sent a papier mâché paperweight supported by more wiry legs than any spider has. In the airport, Ardis looks at us evenly, taking in who we are and what we might ask of her. Then she looks away, and she will not see us again, except as another feature of the landscape, like the bent baobab at the end of Mitch's recently planted garden. During the drive home from Dar es Salaam, Lily and MJ and I hang over the front seat and watch our mother silently bite her lip. Perhaps she is struggling to find appropriate words, suitable sentences. "Judy Garland died," she finally remarks, flatly. "She died to save us all." Mitch's hands tighten on the steering wheel; Ardis looks beyond what lies ahead of us. Apparently this continent that she's never seen is familiar to her nonetheless. Schizophrenia has shown my mother everything already; nothing can surprise her now.

I believe the beggars in front of the greengrocer's suffer so I will not. Their sickness is my health; their need, my wealth: we're that closely connected. Later, I come to think that the beggars are blessed with wisdom that increases in direct proportion to the gravity of their disease and want. Their compensating powers transform each of them into another kind of wizard or witch who, with a wave of wand, can alter flowers into fetuses, change sticks into snakes. Now, as before she was taken away, Ardis can't touch her children: despite the doctors, her hands are still poisoned. They would leave a pale patch on my skin; the first sign of sickness that spreads and erodes and eats at bone, tissue, cartilage. When I fall and scrape a knee, my mother's mouth twists, and her hands clench in her lap. I stare at the entwined fingers, squint at stains of nicotine. I would like to tell Ardis that I'm already contaminated from need, and that it's too late to worry about my being infected by her power to transfigure terrain into symbols that speak its truth. The baobab beyond the wall, the armies of ants that file relentlessly through the garden, the mica glinting on the road: what do these things mean beyond themselves? Ardis has learned to hoard knowledge that would be cited as further evidence of madness if it were revealed. This is all that is left to her; she will not speak. Doctors propose that her visions are the product of a biochemical disturbance of the brain, a tendency toward which may or may not be hereditary. I do not know then that I will spend my life fearing Ardis's secrets, which I am convinced are the same enigmas guarded by all the indigent and infirm, and in denying that they are only distortion. I am persistent as any unwanted thing: if you drive me out of town with your blunt, heavy clubs, I will always crawl or limp or shuffle back.

Upon her arrival in Africa, Ardis steps as carefully as every parolled prisoner who dreads being returned behind bars. After her most casual comment, she glances toward Mitch to read his reaction: he has become the doctor with the drugs, the warden with the keys. This is only a conditional release, my mother knows. In the afternoon, her limbs flail the Morogoro Country Club pool, churn enough laps of murky water to equal the width of any ocean, pull her finally out to pant in a puddle on burning cement, short blonde hair darkened with wet, dreaming. Lily and MJ and I are supposed to play healthy childish games in the distance. Instead, concealed by fences and camouflaging shrubs, we stalk Ardis like spies, watch her stride back and forth across the roughly stubbled golf course; swinging her club at the ball, sailing it out of sight, she plays one round after another until, with burned skin, she drives us home at sunset. There she sits on the verandah and stares down into the valley. Her cigarette's smoke winds through the air like the steam from the train snaking through sisal fields below. Mitch stands amid his gardens, shades eyes with one hand, watches Ardis sink into her private shadows. This is more than he bargained for; perhaps my father is already planning his famous disappearance into the desert, twenty years in the future, far from the acrid taste of medicated kisses. Inside, the houseboy fixes food, makes sure our clothes are changed, our faces washed. I separate myself from Lily and MJ, who dance rings around the lemon tree and in weak voices sing the song about the circle game. Stealing up on Ardis from behind, I lean toward her neck. *Mother,* I whisper into a shelled ear. Her back stiffens; the cigarette falls from her fingers. She rises to walk swiftly to her room, where behind the closed door she whimpers and moans, pleading for Mitch to pity her with a pill.

For several months, the heavens remain clear and calm. Ardis makes careful lists in handwriting that does not waver, composes intricate menus with many courses for the houseboy, at the market requests perfect produce in firm tones. Then clouds return, and she dozes on pills in the afternoon, wanders from her room to ask what time it is. Her face is puffy, the short blonde hair uncombed, a trail of fallen ash betrays her route of aimless roaming around the cinder-block house. Halfway through the rainy season, she no longer makes an effort to keep up appearances, doesn't hastily comb her hair and apply lipstick on hearing Mitch whistle home from work. She stops offering casual comments that might meet with anyone's approval. With one finger she pokes at the wire-mesh screens that keep out snakes, makes minute openings that Mitch will not notice. Escape is always on her mind.

Before sleep, I chant my prayers to Judy Garland and Jesus, then wait for lipless mouths to impart essential information into my dreaming ear. The world beneath the Ngondo Hills requires interpretation; five senses aren't enough. From sleep's abraded ovals, however, emerges only moaning. I waken to realize this is the painful sound Ardis and Mitch make together in the dark.

Later, she begins to vanish. When Lily and MJ are at school, and Mitch away at work, Ardis puts on crimson lipstick, ties a scarf around her head, drives off in the white Peugeot. The grey house beats with silence. The houseboy will only answer yes or no; he pushes me away firmly when I try to touch his smooth black skin. The dirt road to the village beyond the mission is wide, and shaded by ancient trees. Smoke scents heavy air around a confusion of huts; tin roofs glare at the blinding sun; drying clothes drape like bright flowers in the shrubs. Children as small as me flee when I approach. Garbled and incomprehensible as the language of beggars, Ardis's voice emerges from a hut before which the white Peugeot waits. When I knock on the door, my mother falls silent; birds still whistle about over the rainbow and way up high. The door won't open, there are no windows, thick darkness must reign inside. Ardis must be feeling the ruling blackness with her hands; it will dissolve her form, render her invisible for another three years. I crouch in the dirt before the hut, while shadows stretch into exaggerated shapes and the hills above turn deeper jungle green. Now Lily and MJ will be home from school, colouring pictures and playing crazy eights in our room. Then Mitch will also return, change out of good teaching clothes, work in his gardens that bloom with the speed and brilliance of hallucination. Supper will be silent except for screams of crickets outside in the dark. Later we will lie in bed and listen for the white Peugeot to crunch the gravel drive. The car door slams, the kitchen door opens. Mitch begins to beg in their room at the other end of the house. Lily and MJ hold breath in beds near mine. Years later, I will study the photographed features of my brother and sister, inspect faces thinned and hardened by the effort of not asking for anything.

Once Ardis takes me with her. When the white Peugeot has passed the edge of town, she stops to kick off her sandals and to open all the windows. Then we are flying faster and faster along the narrow road that winds all the way to Dar es Salaam. My mother's bare foot presses hard against the pedal; wind whips her scarf and my eyes tear. I blink to see soldiers chewing sugar cane beside the road, spitting pulp at our swift passing. Ardis gazes fixedly ahead; she doesn't glance or talk to me. When her foot pushes right to the floor, the engine begins to whine and the car's metal body shudders. Sometimes, hitting a rough spot, the Peugeot seems to lift into the air for a moment as mad and timeless as a skipped heartbeat. We rise and fall across the hills until the sky blooms red and clouds seep blood and the Indian Ocean stretches beyond a foamed shore before us. I ask Ardis what lies on the other side of the water. She bites her lip; a fleck of crimson sticks to a tooth. Now the palms are disappearing and dhows drown in darkness. We sit in the car and watch waves turn silver as the moon, the stars. There is a great gulf between us, as much salty space as separates this shore from Zanzibar. I can't see what waits across the water, and I can't see her face when, at last, my mother speaks. "Don't ask me for anything again," implores Ardis in the dark, before she vanishes back into the clinic at the other side of the world. "Please," she begs, as she turns the key and takes us slowly home.

The Lemon Tree

MITCH SURVEYS THE ROUGH, SCRAPED REALM AROUND THE NEW HOUSE and proclaims that gardens will grow easily here. "Sun, rain, rich soil," he chants, indicating with a powerful hand his kingdom of infinite breadth and wealth. This lofty gesture says that everything is already in the earth; you only need to seduce it up. Mitch squints into tropical sun; his dark eyes glint like the mica on the gravel roads. In a row beside him, three children wait for what their father will conjure next; they can never guess what that might be. If Mitch envisions fantastic flowers and plump bushes and trees offering unlimited shelter and shade, he doesn't wish to share these pictures. He kneels to rub red dirt between two fingers, to contemplate potential. In the valley below, the afternoon train whistles through the sisal fields; Mitch's face jerks upward, crazy with confidence. "All you have to do is plant," he states, then strides away in boots that make the gravel crunch. MJ, Lily, and Donald stand stiffly on unrealized landscape as if tough roots bind their feet into its alien earth, preventing them from moving freely, allowing only dreams of escape. He can plant them in Spain or Panama or Greece, Mitch believes; they'll grow easily anywhere. All it takes is sun, rain, rich soil.

Mitch waves his wand three times, and grass sprouts around the cement-block house. Three times more makes buds blister, leaves widen, flowers unfold. A father can change the world that quickly. There is no way of knowing that finally his powers will fail, or be exposed as just cheap tricks. In torn shorts held up by a belt of string, he bends tenderly over the earth, turns it with expert hands, sure fingers. The children watch his broad back brown, see his wedding ring flash amid the dirt until the sun descends.

After dark, Peggy Lee serenades unpacked crates, croons to their suffocating contents. In the back bedroom, MJ and Lily recall other gardens in other places. Are they still alive, those gardens in Spain and Greece and Panama? Or does what Mitch plants die once his restless eyes wander toward a new horizon, once his hands travel to touch unknown terrain? Do they wither like the mother in the clinic, in Canada, in the cold?

Mitch sets three saplings into the ground. "They're yours," he explains, stamping lucky circles around the buried roots. MJ has an orange tree, and Lily's is lime. For Donald, always the youngest, there is the promise of lemons. Each child is responsible for his tree: to water it, to pluck insects from first fragile leaves, to prune so branches grow shapely and strong. Owners will dispose of produce as they please. They can sell the fruit for shillings beside the road that leads to town, like the sugar man does his cane. The children pose tensely beside this source of future wealth while Mitch hunts for the camera in the house. Here is another moment that will not last; it must be captured by any means at hand. ("Don't say I never gave you anything," Mitch will later say, scratching his head, bewildered by his children's unvoiced accusation that certain necessities were withheld from them. "What about those trees?" he will wonder, peeking cautiously into the past.) They wait for their father until they can't see each other for quickly fallen darkness, MJ and Lily and Donald; perhaps this is preparation for the day when they will lose each other for good. Three thin voices carol; the song about the circle game twines into Tanzanian night. Mitch can't find the camera. Was it lost in Italy, forgotten in France? There will finally be no evidence of what this man provided for his children, of what was not enough.

In the nunnery at the top of the mission, Lily and MJ recite multiplication tables after Sister Anna and capital cities after Sister Ruth. At home, alone except for the stubbornly silent houseboy, Donald tends his lemon tree. Each morning, he runs to see if overnight it has shot up as quickly as the beanstalk that can be climbed all the way to where God watches. He totes buckets of water across the yard, spills it around his tree, practices patience on a flat stone nearby. Surely the lemon tree will grow with extra speed because of the special care bestowed upon it? The heavy sun presses like an iron against his head. He imagines an abundance of broad leaves above, protecting him and casting coolness over him. "If you water too much, it won't grow," warns the father, appearing suddenly in his teaching clothes as Donald carries another brimming pail across the yard. Half its contents spill along the way, create a trail anyone could follow to find a boy praying to some green-thumbed God beside a spindly tree. (How much should you give and how much should you withhold? Donald will spend the rest of his life seeking to balance this impossible equation.) Upon the slender trunk, within a crooked heart, he traces certain initials below his own. Later, his head buzzes from the sun; he can't eat supper. "Don't you want to grow big as me?" asks Mitch. Apparently, this is not a rhetorical question; there exist myriad possibilities of who and what a boy may choose to be. Donald can sense a wealth of treasure concealed beneath the earth's skin: sunken cities, subterranean spirits, buried selves. All of this may be compelled by Mitch to ascend into the light.

When MJ and Lily return from school, Donald entertains visions of a trio skipping rings around three trees with joined hands, incanting spells of safe and swift and steady growth. But his brother and sister are reluctant to leave the back bedroom; facing away from the windows, they play intricate games involving distant landscapes where snakes do not slither constantly past the corners of your eyes. "What I really wanted was a dog," mentions Lily, when Donald reminds her and MJ of their neglected gifts out in the yard. Her thin face and crooked teeth will one day inhabit the same clinic in which the mother currently shivers. "I never asked for any kind of tree at all," Lily flatly adds.

Sun whitens Donald's hair; it tinges his skin gold: in shade, he might be yellow. Folding arms around knees, he makes a shelf to rest his heavy head on. Africa consists of one long dream. He tastes intangible lemons; chews phantom, slippery pulp. (Why is he always thirsty now and why won't water slake this thirst?) Above the dozing boy, just out of reach, dangle golden globes, a whole galaxy of flavour; if he were taller, he could pluck them, peel them, devour them. As it is, he can only view the tart contents of his unconscious with proprietary interest, find slim consolation in owner's pride. If there were justice, his lemon tree would be twice as tall and broad as the untended trees of Lily and MJ; it would be as majestic as Donald sees it in his sleep. Something is not right that the three trees remain equal-sized—each still hardly taller than Donald himself, with only hints of branches, the illusion of buds. It is difficult to believe that though they continue to appear identical, and belong to the same genus, they will one day bear fruit of varying colour and size and shape.

Mitch's gardens insist on growing with the speed of hallucination, on swallowing up space around the house. They consume sunlight and gulp water and block out sky. Do they steal all nourishment from the vicinity, deprive the children's trees of elements they need? Donald must poison what his father cultivates in order for the object of his own hope to flourish? Only the death of one may permit the other life?

Soon Donald fears losing himself in Mitch's tangled gardens. They become like the jungle that presses around the mission: aswarm with wild animals always on the prowl, too rich in scent and colour, enough to make anyone feel faint. It seems possible that the way will never be found from this maze of twisting paths already choked and leading to no clear destination. Donald will wander such wilderness forever, searching for a sign to point him back to a time when there was order on earth, and when a canopy of dazzling green did not lie between himself and watchful eyes above. Then his lemon tree appears, something safe to run toward. Its trunk is still slender enough to wrap arms around, but insufficiently thick to fill them.

"*Citrus limonia*," states Mitch. "Once it flowers, your lemon tree will bloom all year and never stop bearing." He peers down at his youngest child. "It will be worth the wait," he vows with such assurance that Donald will always remember this promise even as it is broken over and over in a whole multitude of ways. In spite of a scrupulously nurtured talent for revising the past, Donald will never be able to erase the image of his father's face imposed upon the sky like some extra planet, another sun. Mitch adds that soon there will be more lemons than Donald will know what to do with. Fulfillment has its flip side too, may be the implication. It would be safer if dreams did not come true? Were not allowed to materialize as ordinary, as unsatisfactory, as more sour than sweet? Donald's mouth puckers; his face twists.

When it's too late to know anything for certain, Donald will wonder if their trees were given to the children as some kind of perverse joke. He learns that citrus does not flourish in the tropics; one season of intense rain, on the Ngondo hills, would have illustrated this fact. (In the Morogoro market, there is an absence of lemons and limes; confusingly, oranges are always green.) Mitch must be aware of the climate's unfitness for a citrus crop—even as once again he describes in luxurious detail how Donald's tree will look when it matures: here are pale, pointed leaves and short, stout spines; there reddish buds growing singly or in clusters, there blossoms of pure white exuding strong fragrance after dusk. Does something sly, even malicious, cross Mitch's face as upon a canvas of air he paints these pictures? Is there some simple lesson here to do with life being one long series of small disappointments, and might Mitch intend the early transmission of such knowledge, which he himself has learned too late, to be his real gift to his children?

Before Mitch decides that Catholicism corrupts, Donald is sent with MJ and Lily to the mission church where the Dutch priest collects souls in his big black hat on Sunday. While monkeys screech in protest beyond the stained-glass windows, Father Franklin explains that in one God are housed three divine Persons: Father, Son, Holy Ghost. The Son is of the same substance as the Father. The Holy Ghost comes from the Son through the Father, or, theologians alternately propose, from Son and Father jointly. This is much too fine a distinction for a child who can glimpse no ghosts, sacred or otherwise, nearby. The son closes eyes against wavering incense, views the father stalking through a world of his own creation. Dwarfed by papayas and mangos that thrust themselves toward the sky, three small trees stand in a row. On the pew beside their brother, MJ and Lily inhabit an apparent trance. Donald will not be able to save their bodies; he will be unable to save their souls. The Holy Ghost, invisible in shadows, whispers another acidic promise of divinity.

When the rains arrive, and there is no need to water the lemon tree, Donald hovers with MJ and Lily in the back bedroom. Mist creeps down the hills in the middle of the morning and wraps itself around the house until dusk. It isn't possible to see the lemon tree through the window, at the far reach of the dripping garden. Donald tries to remember how it rose before him. Faith is required to believe it stands there still.

Already artful at reminiscence, Lily and MJ discuss the past while the heavens leak. Lily says that in Greece the garden was on a cliff, and MJ says that in Panama a muddy river ran where the garden ended. "There were paths among the stones and roses," muses Lily. "And apple trees," MJ recalls. Where was that? What garden contained roses and stones and apple trees? For every garden outside every window there exists a previous garden; always another room lies beyond whatever walls hold the present. Each in their own way, Lily and MJ will finally wander from sight of everyone. They will press through the neglected gardens of the past—wild and overgrown, conquered by armies of thistles and weeds and thorns—in search of the original garden that flourishes far from the mirage of an oasis beside which Mitch's skull bleaches white. "Don't forget the bench next to the willow," reminds Lily. "Or the swing beneath the oak." Perhaps it is the mist outside that makes her voice muffled, turns it into sound travelling through thickened time and space. In the future, Donald will wander lemon groves of California and Crete, trample fallen fruit alive with wasps and ants. Then his sister's voice will sift through leaves in the way it speaks to him now, recollecting citrus secrets that reach fruition only in the orchard of Mitch's mind.

It is the hour when MJ and Lily sigh in unison across the dark room, when Mitch meditates to music down the hall. Outside the air is clear and cool. The rain has ceased until morning; mist has retreated up into the hills. Too large and heavy, the axe trails like a plow behind Donald; a furrow follows him from the house, deep into Mitch's gardens now muddy and slippery, and occupied by hoarse frogs. The lemon tree shines in the dark. Its green trunk resists the axe. Anyway, Donald is too young and small for such a task; like MJ and Lily, he should be in bed dreaming of somewhere far away where every promise bears fruit and the wait is always worth it. For a moment, Donald doesn't see the shape that looms beside him, the darkness made solid as spirit was once made flesh. "It's not sharp enough," explains Mitch, taking the tool from his son. Despite this fact, he is able to sever the trunk with one blow. The lemon tree topples, causing not the slightest tremor of the earth. Two trees remain; a trinity is broken. There is the father and there is the son, but where is the Holy Ghost?

Wild Dogs

DURING HOT, STILL AFTERNOONS, WHEN ONLY WASPS DISTURB THE GLASSY silence, Lily hunts for ticks. On the hard, shaded dirt to the east side of the house, beneath the bougainvillea, she holds our dog tight between her legs and combs fingers through secret places of his coat: below the neck, beneath flaps of ears, within the pits of legs. The swollen pests are pinched between a finger and a thumb until the tight skin of their sac bursts and Ginger's blood spurts over my sister's hands. She sprinkles white powder where the parasite has nestled; this is supposed to discourage further infestation. But a hundred more ticks will fasten to Ginger on his journeys through the brush tomorrow; especially during dry season, there are always too many to be killed. Our dog squirms beneath Lily's ministrations. Dissatisfied with our company, he is forever slinking from sight, losing us easily when we try to follow. Lily says that Ginger hunts for the tail that was chopped off shortly after his birth as a boxer pup. ("It's the custom," our father informs us. "Something people do," Mitch adds weakly, when our puzzled faces request a better explanation.) Only the stump remains, scarcely enough to wag. One day Ginger will return home with his missing tail between his teeth—instead of the usual rats and snakes. Perhaps then he might become our loyal companion, our faithful friend, no longer prone to prolonged disappearances or battles with other dogs that leave his torn ears as permanent attractions for flies. "These ticks will drink all his blood," Lily tells me, not looking up from Ginger's coat. Lips pressed tightly together, she ignores my suggestion that we venture down the hill to visit the sugar man beside the road. If we sing a number from *Mary Poppins*, he will give us as many lengths of cane as we can carry. All afternoon, we'll be able to chew the sweet, stringy meat his big machete has peeled and spit out a trail of exhausted pulp that shows where we wander through a Tanzanian translation of Hansel and Gretel's haunted forest. Still disregarding me, Lily moves her thin, freckled face nearer our dog's coat. She doesn't look up when a ripe pawpaw falls with a splitting thud from a nearby tree; within ten minutes, its sweet flesh will swarm with ants that feed so ravenously you can almost hear the click of small, sharp teeth. Suddenly Lily loosens her legs and claps three times near Ginger's ears. Our dog bounds away. My sister holds blood-stained hands to the sky, squints at them with satisfaction. With broad, sweeping strokes, she paints her face with crosses; the marks are nearly the same colour as the ochre earth. After the blood dries, Lily must be careful not to smile, or her face will crack.

Our dreamy father has few rules, all laxly enforced. Mitch forgets to check the correspondence lessons we're supposed to do each morning, and he doesn't remember about bedtime and brushing teeth and writing letters to our mother. Also overlooked is his law that we three children must stay close to each other. "There's strength in numbers," Mitch likes to points out. That we do sometimes play together, MJ and Lily and I, is from necessity. There are no other children on the Catholic mission—except for black ones who sing taunting rhymes to our backs, or throw bowls of white mush in our faces if we come too near. Mitch encourages us to explore as far and wide as we can, and doesn't express fear for our safety as long as we're home before dark. "Where did you go today?" he asks eagerly each evening, when secrets concealed from light come out to prowl in the darkness beyond the door. "What did you see?" We look at each other and select the stories Mitch can be told. Our ability to move as a trio across the disturbing landscape is often impaired because MJ has to lie with tightly closed eyes in bed. His head hurts. You can see veins beneath his brow beat with blood angrily trying to get out. When he comes home from teaching, Mitch will massage MJ's temples, rub his scalp with strong fingers. "It's just the heat," he says again. With MJ waiting to heal and rise, Lily loses what little loyalty she has to our broken group. I turn to see her nearly out of sight, one of the old, pleated skirts donated by the nuns swishing around her scissoring legs. When I try to follow, my sister walks more quickly, or she pushes me efficiently aside, as you do a branch or vine that blocks your path. I never know where Lily goes alone; upon returning, she will not tell me and deflects Mitch's inquiries neatly. I suspect she follows the trail that climbs above the mission and twists through jungle to where the Ngondo River roars between the rocks. Up high, the air turns into a thin, cool element that feels alien to me, unsuitable for human lungs. There birds cry too loudly, flowers bloom too boldly, the jungle looms too thick and dark. Lily meets Ginger by the river, I think. I never fear that Lily might become lost up in the jungle, like Sister Bridget did; two years older than me, eleven, she can surely find her way back down with Ginger. They will arrive home when they're hungry; they will be home before dark. I believe that, like our dog, my sister searches for something severed from her shortly after birth. What is it that Lily hunts during those afternoons above, when at the dazed house below the only sounds are the ancient gardener's machete striking stones in the yard, the houseboy's croon as he wrings dripping clothes behind the kitchen, the whimper of MJ from his dim, painful room? What will Lily bear between her teeth when she returns?

I'm sure Mitch had the best of intentions when he gave us a dog. "I had one when I was a boy," he says; then we hear once more about his tough Regina youth. Probably Mitch holds in his head some clear, focused photograph of three children frolicking with a happy pet. Caring for their dog, the children will learn responsibility; in return, he acts as comrade and strengthens their number. Mitch doesn't seem to notice that from the start our attention to Ginger goes unreciprocated; we're neither interesting nor necessary to him. We are unable to teach him to fetch or sit up or to roll over and play dead. "He's getting big," Mitch observes happily, as in the kitchen, Ginger lifts his head at the bark of wild dogs in the distance. They bay at a rough beast who slouches through the night, says the houseboy. Our dog scratches on the door until we give in and let him out. Returning the next morning, he will smell of something rotten, bad. Lily disregards the stink, picks more ticks from his coat, tries to brush it smooth. Perhaps things would have been different in a more bland setting, without the scent of wild blood to lure our dog from us. Mitch's hopeful vision may have unfolded more perfectly against a background of neat lawns and fences, tidy sidewalks and maple trees. It is our father's fatal tendency to disregard the landscape upon which he sets his fantasies. And to believe that as long as we reach home before dark, everything will be all right.

During our latter years in Morogoro, Lily stands taller than MJ and me, with hair hacked by Mitch into the shape of a bowl. He enjoys playing barber, shaves mine and MJ's and his own head to the scalp, pronounces pleasure in the cool results. My sister's face is sharp, her new teeth grew in crooked, scabs always decorate her knees. I am not aware that other girls play dolls and house or dress up in a mother's clothes; Lily doesn't mention such things. She likes to swim and run, and climbs to the tops of trees. She enjoys silent activities, such as our visits to Father Joe, the mission natural-ist, who keeps guinea pigs and snakes. The biggest boa doesn't like to eat when watched by curious children. You must be very still and patient to catch him strike at the guinea pig shivering at the far side of the cage. Lily stares hard as with a gulp the live meal is swallowed whole. Later, I will always envision my sister intently studying what lies before her eyes, while MJ and I have to turn away. It seems to me that I was usually watch-ing Lily rather than the world; she saw for all of us, I think. When we're shown how a cow is slaughtered then skinned at the prison farm, Lily's eyes widen slightly; then they quickly narrow, seal the sight inside herself. Later, Mitch attempts to butcher the beef in our kitchen. He scratches his head at a puzzle of sides and quarters, waves the saw through aromatic air, clutches his famously weak stomach. Lily splashes in pools of blood alongside our father with suggestions and advice. From where I hover with MJ in the doorway, I believe I see my sister's nostrils quiver as they inhale the stench of intestine, the stink of death.

While MJ sometimes tells stories about where we lived before Africa and what happened to us there, Lily refuses to discuss the past, and shows scant interest in what isn't plainly visible now. My brother recalls the dancing goat on the white island in Greece and the little one-armed girl in Spain. He describes our mother, Ardis, far away in Canada. "She has blonde hair and red lips," MJ muses again, while, without a word, Lily wanders from our secret place beneath the lemon tree. We find her occupied with an army of soldier ants. In an endless file of perfect pairs, they move toward a distant destination we're unable to fathom. You can stir the marchers with a stick or douse them with pails of water, but this interrupts their progress only for the moment it takes to scramble back into rank. MJ says the ants are returning home. I suggest maybe they are lost. Lily insists they're going to war. We agree that these insects can strip the flesh from a large beast in seconds. Leave bones clean as a whistle in the blink of an eye.

Before Sister Bridget vanishes in the jungle and the other nuns are sent home to Holland, they often seem to appear out of nowhere, in the most unlikely locations. We glimpse a dozen of them filing across the golf course at the Morogoro Country Club early in the morning, or clustered in the back of a pickup truck whirling down the road. Moving with surprising swiftness, a pack encircles us to flap black habits like wings in our faces. When MJ and Lily become a class of two taught up in the convent by Sister Cecilia, the nun who speaks English best; we're still unable to distinguish the others easily. Their costumes lend them anonymity. Gradually we learn that Sister Bridget is tall and thin, Sister Ingrid short and plump, Sister Elsa always flushed. The nuns sigh and cluck and pat our heads. In guttural Dutch, they discuss us between themselves, seeming to search for the solution to a difficult problem. They attempt sentences of severely accented English that we barely understand. "By the sea of Galilee," I think Sister Elsa says. MJ believes they're telling us to prepare for the Second Coming. Lily doesn't like the nuns; she won't look at them but glares at the ground instead. When they pull skirts and blouses from beneath their robes like magicians and offer my sister these clothes donated by the Dutch to dress a little native girl, she accepts them rudely. They pat our heads once more, then turn toward their convent perched at the mission's highest point, where a confusing tangle of jungle begins. During the months before the nuns leave Morogoro, MJ's head hurts almost every day, and Lily refuses to attend Sister Cecilia's makeshift classroom without him. She and I slip past the convent to explore a universe of thick green vines. The sound of sweet voices raised in hymn follows us. Rather than soothe, the song seems to add a jarring note to the setting, as if the air were incapable of receiving words of praise and thanks.

When Lily turns twelve, she begins to pick at her blouse, lift the cloth that chafes her budding breasts. The unconsciously repeated gesture reminds me of the way Ginger shakes his head in a violent, vain attempt to banish flies clustered on his bloody ears. The flaps aren't able to heal; his hind paw scratches them constantly raw. The houseboy is left to feed Ginger during our frequent safaris through East Africa, and whenever we make a longer trip because Mitch decides it's time for us to see the Sphinx or the Suez Canal or the Wailing Wall before it's too late. During the fifth year in Tanzania, Ginger doesn't show up for three days after one of our returns to the cinder-block house. He stays away for two weeks the next time. Soon he's at home only intermittently. Between his visits, I forget the shape of Ginger's nose, the colour of his eyes. We spy him infrequently in the distance, among the pack of wild dogs that makes wide-ranging expeditions through the area. They run in a loose cluster, with noses near the ground, direction determined by invisible forces, snarling at each other. I try to call Ginger, but he no longer knows his name. "Leave him alone," says Lily, turning away. "It was a stupid name. His coat was never the colour of ginger." Although Mitch might be unaware just how elusive our dog has become, he appears to sense things are somehow not the same for us, and tries to put a finger on it. "Do you have everything you need?" he asks once. Our father seems less confident of holding the winning play for each of life's hands like a wild card up his sleeve. He inquires less often at evening about where we've been that day. Perhaps Lily causes him particular unease; his eyes ponder her, glide away. He suggests she spend time with Prima, the stylish young East Indian woman who lives in the house below ours. Lily stares at him. "Why?" she asks. Mitch rubs his head, glances at his watch, hums. Suddenly, his fingers snap. "Chess!" he exclaims. "Which of you kids thinks he's smart enough to beat the old man?"

As the pack grows larger, people begin to say the wild dogs are getting out of hand. No longer skulking warily at a distance, they become bolder, more threatening. They will circle a house with howls all night, trapping sleepless inhabitants inside. They kill chickens in the village beyond the mission. More than actual damage, they cause disturbance, fear. "Rabies," it is muttered. Africans want to get rid of the wild dogs with axes and machetes. Our houseboy says these animals are evil spirits arisen from centuries of tortured sleep. They are demons escaped from nightmare. One night, we listen to the wild dogs tear Prima's pet colobus apart. "Go back to sleep," says Mitch, a black shape in the bedroom doorway. The monkey's screams die. In his bed between Lily's and mine, MJ moans. His headaches have grown worse, though the Morogoro doctor, a graduate of the Bombay Institute of Dental Hygiene, promised he would grow out of them. Lily slips from bed and stands with her face pressed against the wire-mesh screen that's supposed to keep out snakes. "What are you doing?" I ask. Lily's nightdress, an old gift from the Dutch nuns, falls too short around her thin, scratched legs. It gleams in the darkness. "Where are you going?" I whisper, as my sister's bare feet pad from the room. I hear the kitchen door click open then shut. In my safe, hot bed, I fall asleep while Lily searches outside for secrets contained within the mutilated carcass of a monkey. I dream her eyes burn yellow in the dark. Her mouth froths white. Thick blood smears her nose.

What did I see, what did I dream? Later, I will never know for certain if I glimpse Lily poised at the edge of the sisal field below the mission, encircled by wild dogs that leap up to snap at her face. With her back straight and arms folded across her chest, she stands unmoving amid the whirling beasts. Do her lips move? Is she speaking to the dogs? All at once, she turns on her heels and runs from the writhing ring. The dogs take after her, barking madly; they are hunting Lily or they are following Lily. The pack enters the sisal that grows taller than my sister. All I can see is a dense green field, with no hint of what it contains, unfolding still and calm before me. Troubling my eyes.

Finally we return to Canada and to our mother, who manages to stay out of the clinic as long as she takes her Lithium. None of us speaks about Morogoro much. Mitch seems disappointed that we aren't grateful for his gift of an exotic experience. My father's efforts to settle down in the small British Columbia town seem half-hearted; his temper grows uncharacteristically short. In five years, he will go away again. This time alone, this time for good. Lily refuses to remember anything about Africa; she barely admits we lived there. In Brale, BC, my sister says she can't recall our chameleon with the leash of string around its neck or our hunts for frogs in the gutters above the mission church. Or seeing the Milky Way creamed above the Serengeti during a night drive home, when Mitch stops the car and insists we climb out to view the sky. "The stars are closer when you're in Africa," he tells us. I believe that still, as I continue to believe many of my father's patent untruths. But Lily denies knowledge of the shape formed by a baobab against Arusha sky and the shriek of a colobus when you pass beneath its jungle perch. In Brale, she disguises herself with makeup and drinks home-made wine with Italian boys down by the Columbia River. Now she has long hair hanging over her eyes. From beneath the bangs, Lily watches Ardis warily, sniffs at our mother from safe distance, tries to determine whether this stranger poses danger. "Go back to the loony bin where you belong," she snarls, when told by Ardis to be home before dark. Our mother retreats behind the closed door of her room again; in the basement, MJ watches another hour of TV. Despite a battery of tests and medications, my brother's headaches are never diagnosed or treated with success; in cold Canada, they're clearly due to more than just the heat. MJ is unable to attend high school frequently enough to graduate. At eighteen, he disappears on his way to Montreal, where he's headed to look for work. I think he can't stand for us to see the veins still throbbing with angry blood beneath his brow. He needs to lose Africa, to lose us. I continue to believe a dark continent lies concealed beneath our skin. A sharp knife could peel away a layer of flesh to uncover the rich taste of mango, smells of charcoal and dust and rotting fruit, the mocking laughter of hyenas in the night.

Perhaps Lily was seeking such things when she used the razor on herself. By then—like MJ, like Mitch—I had left the haunted house beneath the reeling crows, below a white sift of icy powder. We went our separate ways, abandoned the possibility that safety lies in numbers. Only Ardis remained in Brale when Lily entered the regional hospital's psychiatric wing. ("Jesus," Mitch wrote to me in London. "We should have the family name engraved on the place.") During the next three years, while Lily stayed stubbornly silent at the far side of the world, I would sometimes think of Ginger. By the time we left Morogoro, he had become one of the wild dogs entirely, no longer ours at all. He never came to the cinder-block house even to snarl over a plate of bones; his teeth would have sunk into our hands if we reached out to pet him. We heard that disease had swept through the pack of dogs. For a while, their number did seem smaller; then they appeared as many as before. Several times, in the car, we might have seen Ginger loping along the ditch beside the road. We weren't sure. I said yes; Lily disagreed. "He's dead," she flatly stated. "He died a long time ago." When I finally heard from Lily, she said she had found Jesus. Intermittently, He allowed her to leave the clinic and live with Ardis in the Columbia Avenue house below; then the burden of sin would drive my sister back to her cold white room upon the hill. I couldn't help but imagine Jesus wandering lost amid the bamboo shoots beside the Ngondo River, impractical white robes tangled in vines and roots, waiting for Lily to find Him and to bring Him home before dark. My sister wouldn't see me when I visited Brale in 1986 and 1995. On both occasions, she retreated into the hospital before my arrival and remained incommunicado there until I left. On my return to Europe and then North Africa, she sent me poorly printed religious tracts and urged me to save myself before it was too late. Through post-cards mailed to me from Thailand and Indonesia and Tibet, I understood that Mitch also received warnings of a Second Coming. Apparently, his strategy to avoid final judgment involves fleeing ever farther from its reach. And mine? Today, in Morocco, skeletal dogs haunt my step, whine in my ear; the market teems with icons whose obscure shapes tug my mind. The mosque bell clangs hollowly just before dusk; below my balcony, the street suddenly fills with believers scurrying home before dark. Night creeps into the *derbs* of El Jadida, descends on barren desert beyond. Stars rise in the sky. "They're closer when you're in Africa," I used to write to Lily. With Ardis and Jesus and medication, beside the Columbia River's frigid sweep, she attempts to stitch calm years out of cleaning and dusting and other careful rituals. The last time I heard from Lily, she enclosed a photograph. I couldn't recognize the woman with puffy face devoid of freckles, with hair pinned into a neat bun, with untroubled eyes. Lily looks into the camera without smiling, as if afraid her face will crack. As if parted lips would allow a wild dog's howl to swell the air.

Shells

"Bury or boil," replies Rogacion when Mitch asks our houseboy what to do with the shells. We've brought them home from the coast for our mother. They need to be rid of what's starting to rot inside them before she arrives from the clinic in Canada in three weeks. It isn't clear to MJ, Lily, and me how long our mother's going to stay; whether this time she might remain. Mitch wouldn't answer when my sister asked. "She'll be the old Ardis again," he vowed in his jaunty way instead. Maybe then our father recalled how badly the same promise had been broken two years before. It wasn't either an old or a new version of our mother who haunted these Ngondo hills for several months. The muscles of that woman's face would twist at the sight of us three children; a jolt, some powerful electric shock, made her twitch and stiffen if we approached too near. What happened once the rainy season began , how that got bad then worse, until she had to be sent back to Canada—suddenly, ahead of time, with a nurse. Mitch peers toward the fields spread below our cinder-block house, as though sisal might conceal an elusive key to a difficult puzzle. Everything worth finding hides. My father's eyes clear. Fingers snap to announce another of his famous inspirations. "Shells," he exclaims.

Things went badly last time because we failed to welcome Ardis with presents, Mitch seems to suggest in the days leading up to the shell-gathering expedition. Three years apart from us were sufficient to turn our mother into a member of some savage tribe that must be appeased by the right token. Or it isn't the amount of time away from her family, grown to five years now, but where that exile has occurred, that makes Ardis a threat. As if Canada, not Tanzania, were the more dangerous, uncivilized influence. Like any primitive, our mother would be simple as well as savage. Vulnerable to being tricked into swapping her most valuable possession for the cheapest trinket. It might as well be plastic combs that gain us what we want.

It's not enough to drive an hour to the coast and gather shells from some convenient Dar es Salaam shore. Commonplace conches might do for the damn Brits, but not for Ardis, not for our Cedar Bay girl. We can manage better than that. Mitch claims to have extracted, from his most reliable source among the ancient men he likes to squat with in the village dust, the name of the best shelling spot in the Indian Ocean. An unspoiled island offshore from Kunduchi, known only to natives; a speck of land not on the map. Good old Christophe, the best shell man in the business, would take us out in his *ungalawa*. Such outriggers were navigating these waters long before the white man arrived. Thatch sails, palm-trunk pontoons: the crudest kind of handmade craft. An authentic African adventure all the way, another Robinson Crusoe experience for the whole gang to enjoy. "Don't you remember Lanzarote and Ios and Formentera?" our father wonders to his less-than-enthusiastic gang, showing us implements resembling fireplace pokers with bent ends that will assist the imminent hunt for treasure. As if we ought to understand that every island encountered since we wandered away from Brale, BC has served as one more stepping stone in a plan whose secret purpose is to offer Ardis what she needs, what we don't have.

"You never find what you're looking for in plain sight," warns Mitch, when Lily and I bring him shells quickly gathered from the island's stony beach. We definitely won't run into any damn Brits here. An hour out from a shore now beyond view, this scrap of rock barely interrupts ocean; it has no fresh water to drink, no bushes or trees for shelter. The sun is fierce by midmorning; already it has inflicted another of his headaches on MJ. A bad one, I can tell. My brother sits stiff as a wooden voodoo doll near to where the best shell man in the business has crawled into a slice of shade cast by his boat, after a vague wave to indicate where treasure waits. For once, Mitch doesn't accuse MJ of being a stick in the mud; doesn't sulk because his oldest son won't participate in making a fantasy real. "Everything valuable always hides," Mitch reminds Lily and me again, brandishing his tire iron as though it were less a tool than a weapon drawn against some invisible enemy. Three birds—resembling oversize, prehistoric pelicans—circle patiently above. I don't know what these birds are called; nor the names of shells we're searching for, what they look like. "We'll recognize them when we see them," declares Mitch in the extra-hearty tone that, even at age ten, always makes me doubt him. Rather than reliable fellows and the best men in every business, don't we need one or two plain facts to help us to interpret this landscape, and to elicit its secrets?

Shells valuable enough to be offered to Ardis apparently lurk in tidal pools where soupy water slaps, gurgles, sucks at ankles. Under rocks, in fissured pockets, intricately swirled or spiked shapes conceal their pinks, their golds from sunlight that bleached my sister's and my heads white soon after arriving to this continent. (MJ's still-dark hair evidences how much his headaches keep him inside; as for Mitch, it isn't so easy to change an old dog's coat, he smirks.) You have to turn over rocks with your tire-iron lever; you have to wrest shells from the wet, salty darkness to which their mantles cling for life. Mitch dismisses each specimen Lily and I offer. "Good try," he says, "but I guess you don't have the old man's eye." He wants us to witness his discoveries instead of making our own; he needs us to share his excitement on capturing one more exotic prize. "Found another beauty," he crows again. Lily and I flutter starfish limbs in a separate tide pool, pretend we can't hear. "He doesn't have a clue what he's doing," my sister scorns. We watch our father's tanned back glisten as it shifts the landscape for our mother's sake. Muscles jumping beneath skin like kittens drowning in a sack. Then glare drains away definition, blackens Mitch into only shadow. The *ngalawa* no longer provides any shade; exposed to the sun, Christophe still snores. MJ's pale face has turned paler and an angry blister blooms on one corner of a moving lip. I know my brother will silently count until he reaches the number that marks that this too has passed.

Five buckets of shells slosh in the back of the white Peugeot, spit and hiss all the way home. A strong smell, briny and gamy at once, becomes increasingly heavy as we drive inland, thickens as though we're nearing the same pungent element we're trying to leave. "Phew," exhales Mitch, cracking his window an inch wider, while MJ gags again.

"Bury or boil," Mitch mutters like a mantra all evening. After our houseboy offers us this choice, something distorts his fixed mask, exposes itself in his eyes, makes him move quickly away from the house. (*Disgust*, I think, twenty years later.) Rogacion spits, once, at the end of the yard. Without sending a child over with an excuse, he fails to show up for work the next morning or on following ones. Village sources won't shed light on our houseboy's whereabouts. Sometimes the toothless old fellows don't seem to understand Mitch's Swahili, pretend it's a whole other lingo they speak. My father's face shadows, as it does whenever an obstacle comes between him and the elevated source of an earthbound dream. "Boy," he says, shaking a disappointed head and dishing out a version of one of his boyhood Regina suppers on Rogacion's first AWOL evening. "Some fellows sure are quick to jump ship even when the old gal isn't sinking." A row of five buckets just inside the door emit an aromatic question, pungently pose it throughout the house all night.
Bury or boil?

Mitch lowers a test bucket of shells into bubbling water. "Quicker this way," he hazards, leaning back from an overpowering stench as steam rises from the pot. On the surface black scum gathers, thickens, obscures what's happening to the shells below. "Maybe we should have done this outside," my father grimaces, wrinkling his nose. Suddenly he grabs his stomach, lurches out the kitchen door. Lily turns off the stove. We find our father kneeling on the grass, near his portulaca patch. Heaving, gasping, panting. Unable to breathe an alien element.

We allow the house to air out all morning before venturing back inside. Then Lily reaches through a crust of scum. Are the shells she removes the ones Mitch dropped into boiling water? Can inner death alter outer appearance so completely, so quickly? Reduce lustrous beauty into its plain, dull opposite? Effect a change more permanent than, for example, all the fleeting transformations of Gary Cooper, MJ's chameleon, before his disappearance? The kitchen whispers about forbidden treasure whose tempting glitter tarnishes at the lightest touch. Lily shakes an emptied shell to determine whether it's lighter without its secret. She holds it to one ear, reveals her crooked teeth. The smile fades. A pearl leaks from some deep chamber of shell, slides down my sister's neck, hangs there. She touches a finger to the viscous drop, lifts it to her mouth, licks lips.

"Look," says MJ.

A small crowd has formed at the end of the yard, where it meets the mission road. Village children and church beggars and the cassava women whose baskets appear to brim with large white maggots. They look expectantly at our house, murmur unease across the yard. The crowd gets bigger, louder. As if steam has shaped a lingering signal visible only to African eyes. *Approach*, it invites. *Come and see*. At the same time, the perfumed air might be warning: *Not too close*. "Everything's a movie in Morogoro," Mitch says lightly, when our restless audience still hovers outside in the dark.

My father plays the Peggy Lee records in his room that night. Her voice slinks out the window, seduces the crowd beyond to disperse, teasingly instructs Mitch what to do. By morning, he has learned that burying is slower than boiling, but less malodorous. What's in the earth will devour what's in the shells without diminishing the latter's beauty, he hopefully adds.

How deep is deep enough?

Not having all the answers will always throw Mitch off. "What do you think, gang?" he asks, hesitating with the shovel. If the hole is too shallow, it might not allow access to the deep life-forms that can devour the essence of a shell. Worms thick as pythons, I imagine, which with one flick of fangs extricate every meaty morsel from the most withholding mollusc. Maybe wild dogs would detect a subterranean stench, be attracted to something rotting below, want to dig it up at night. Not for eating but to carry off and scatter like fragments of gleaming skull through the brush. Or it would be hyenas that skulked out from the dark and danced atop an aromatic grave that would be laughingly exhumed by dawn. Yet shells buried too deep might be destroyed, crushed by the weight of too much dirt, dissolved by too much darkness. At lunch Mitch slips home from teaching to inspect the patch of earth that holds our secret at the far end of the garden. He stamps already hard-packed ground as though to keep what's down from forcing itself up; to discourage any unwanted element from breaking surface, bursting through. Maybe my father recalls old country spells shared by his dusky Regina aunts, incantations originally uttered by women in black around smoky village fires. He sprinkles a ring of lime around the spot, sets a stone in the centre, adds ash on top.

At midnight Lily shakes my shoulder, whispers so MJ won't wake.

"He's out there again."

My sister and I kneel before the bedroom window, squint through the screen at a flashlight prowling the darkness beyond the lemon tree. "What is he looking for?" I dreamily wonder, as though the purpose of my father's investigation of the night were to invoke a question whose answer would illuminate not only this dark moment but also the meaning of the whole obscure search that MJ, Lily, and I have been taken on against our will. I must fall asleep with my head on the window sill. In the morning, the texture of the bedroom floor patterns my stiff knees. A temporary tattoo. Intricate as one decorating the Carnelian cowrie, say.

MJ notices that the sugar man doesn't come by anymore, though we're always good for a shilling of his cane. All the Africans who habitually took a shortcut across our yard appear to give it wide berth now. My father's classes become sparsely attended when they were notably popular before; even the Dutch nuns, whose pink faces poke concern through the doorway while he's teaching at the mission, prove conspicuously aloof. "I'd almost welcome a couple of damn Brits at the door," Mitch mentions one quiet evening. Perhaps the atmosphere around us remains subtly fragranced by warning of dangers contained within this sphere. Say we've grown too accustomed to the scent to detect it. Maybe it clings to our clothes, skin, hair. Strong soap won't be able to decontaminate us of longing; no amount of fresh air will eliminate need's last rank trace. Still one more invisible, permanent brand.

"A week," my father guesses when we ask how long it will take the earth to clean out the shells. For the first time I am attuned to how desperately the famished globe beneath me starves; it would gobble up the most unappetizing nourishment. Any carcass, carrion, corpse. In sleep, sounds of chewing, slurping, munching rise around me. They're muffled, almost inaudible; they're insistent. My dreaming stomach groans with phantom hunger. I salivate with sympathy in sleep.

Lily salvages the shells robbed of beauty by boiling. She strings the smallest of them into a dozen bracelets to adorn her thin wrists all at once. Every swivel makes them click like teeth. A larger, sharp-spiked specimen dangles around my sister's neck. Her jewellery resembles the ceremonial kind that is assumed after completing a tribal initiation or test of courage or rite of passage. Some shells are carried around like good luck charms in Lily's pockets, others placed in significant locations. The bowl Ginger ate from before he ran away to join the pack of wild dogs. The nook of the mango tree where we left never-collected letters to Sister Bridget until it became her turn to disappear. At the spot where we found Gary Cooper, at the spot our chameleon was last seen. Five years have been enough to ensure that this geography will always be defined by the associations to loss with which it swarms.

As the date for Ardis to arrive draws near, our father's eagerness for the event wanes. A flashlight no longer plays through the darkness where shells are buried; he doesn't dash to the site at noon. "She can take them back as souvenirs," he offhandedly mentions once, acknowledging that our gift may be insufficient to induce Ardis to stay. More and more, my father looks resigned to failure; inspiration has let him down again. At this point, climbing up into the jungle in search of the rarest butterfly would be too little, too late. To enchant Ardis into sharing the spell in which we are uneasily sunk will require some far more potent totem. A rhinoceros tusk, the claw of an Arusha lion, a shrunken human head.

We unearth the shells a day before Ardis arrives. They need to be cleaned of dirt, then polished. Mitch inches shovel into ground, tosses the tool aside, burrows with bare hands to prevent the metal blade from inflicting damage. The hole reaches the depth at which the shells were buried without revealing them. Mitch digs deeper. MJ, Lily and I look down into yawning darkness. Not one sliver, not a shard of shell. Rising breaths of cold make me shiver in the burning afternoon. My eyes lift from what isn't below, detect movement beyond the frangipani's gaudy screen. Dark stirring transforms into a trio of village children. Our witnesses scamper away.

As if it were an open, obscene grave, we turn hastily from the hole. Inside, the house appears all at once derelict for reasons related less to Rogacion's recent neglect than to long abandonment by the life it once contained. Floors waxed dark red have dulled the colour of dried blood; a company of army ants feeds from dirty dishes; cocoons and webs have sprouted in the corners. Mitch makes a half-hearted stab at marshalling his troops to swing into Operation Clean-Up. It's hardly worth the effort. Accustomed to an antiseptically clean, painfully neat clinic, Ardis would be unimpressed at being brought even to a spic-and-span house from the Dar airport tomorrow. Mitch swipes his rag at dust like he's swatting away a persistent ghost. MJ retreats to bed with what he says is another headache. Through the bedroom window, I glimpse Lily slipping toward our father's overgrown garden. The contents of her arms are indistinct in failing light; then my sister herself is blurred by distance, finally buried beneath black.

"I knew it," says Lily, when our mother is not among the passengers of what was supposed to be her flight. Without a magic magnet, minus shiny, seductive gifts, we lack the power to pull her to us. Mitch is subdued during most of the drive back home. "We'll get a letter that explains everything," he says, without conviction. By the time we near Morogoro, my father has bucked up enough to start laying out a new plan. A sojourn at the Mombasa shore will be just the ticket to make us all A-okay again. When the Peugeot pulls into the driveway, Rogacion is hanging laundry on the line. My father walks past the houseboy and through our cleaned house. His bedroom door doesn't open when, several minutes later, I knock to announce news. In our absence, the hole at the end of the garden has been filled in, smoothed over, made to vanish.

A letter must have arrived to explain Ardis's failure to do so; that memory must have seeped from me to linger in the Morogoro air like a signal visible only to some cassava woman's keen eye. Everything valuable hides. Although the sugar man begins to show up at our door each day again, and the path across the yard becomes redefined by all the feet to cut across it, and Mitch's classes teem as before with students attracted to his eccentric take on history—even then the air around us remains somehow offended by what we have done: how we tried to fulfill our need at this landscape's expense. It was wrong to take the shells. Within a decade, some varieties will become rare enough to require protection by law. As valuable as my father wished them to be.

I move in dream through each Morogoro night. A secret path is marked by chips of white whose gleam draws me away from the cinder-block house, invites me deeper into darkness. Past the farthest reaches of Mitch's gardens, through the frangipani, into brush beyond. Leopard cone, hump-backed cowrie, prickly drupe, spider conch, orange-mouthed olive: now

I know their names, what these shells were called when filled with life, when beautiful. The white that guides me across the earth exactly matches the white of stars strewn above. My footsteps could be tracing patterns of Pisces through the sky, following the Milky Way forward. I hear muffled rushing, the echo of a roar. The river appears, a black glint for Lily to kneel beside. My sister looks up at me, looks back to the white object in her lap. She is trying to rub three wishes from what's hollow, what's hard. Her prayers are answered or her hope for them dies. Lily holds the shell up as high as her arms can stretch. A scepter, an offering, a symbol.

Ardis's aborted visit seems to end our Tanzanian experience abruptly, though we linger for three more months. "She'll join us in Sri Lanka," Mitch ventures, getting out his maps. "Or in Seville." As if location were the sole factor in deciding whether Ardis does or does not come back.

I never again see the shells Lily rescued from a dull, plain fate. Where loss occurred is now unmarked; what's absent may become forgotten. My sister appears vulnerable without her ceremonial baubles, unarmed against an inimical world. A sound of clicking teeth no longer betrays her furtive explorations. I don't hear Lily slip from the cinder-brick house in the middle of the night or come in later from the dark. Mitch frowns at his maps, mumbles about Seville or Sri Lanka, prays to Peggy Lee for new inspiration. MJ whimpers through another Morogoro afternoon. "I'm burning up," he says. For a moment I think I smell incineration. I can feel MJ transform into smoke and ash inside. There are ways besides burying and boiling, I might tell Rogacion. "It's almost over," I lie to my brother instead. As if we haven't, MJ and Lily and I, already told each other goodbye.

Chiggers

SOUNDS OF PAIN REACH THROUGH THE DARK. A SMALL ANIMAL MUST BE caught in a trap on the other side of the bedroom. To escape, it will have to gnaw through bone that metal teeth already crunch. It will have to leave a limb behind. Survival has its price, every mangled body says. Now I realize the whimpering travels from where my brother's bed floats on the far side of our sister's. It's MJ who moans. "What's wrong?" I ask the darkness, as if it were responsible for all emotion voiced within its obscure walls, and were aware of the reasons for my brother's distress. The room falls silent. MJ wants me to suspect he's asleep. He needs me to wonder if this is just a dream. At eight, I've learned some sounds are made only when you're certain no one listens. Beyond the window screen, another Morogoro midnight swarms with insects that wait until light leaves before they emerge from hiding. Their rustle and stir infiltrates wire-mesh pores to fill the void made by MJ's quiet; but the world outside the cinder-block house is always too restless to be any kind of balm. I wonder whether in her bed Lily also listens to MJ struggle to remain mute. If my sister hears him try to hide how much it hurts. The effort is deafening. A stifled scream swells.

"You don't take aspirin in Africa," chuckles my father when Lily proposes this as a remedy for MJ's first bad headache. It occurs within a month of our arrival to Morogoro from Brale, BC—via several years of apparently aimless wandering across seemingly random swathes of the globe. According to Mitch, Western medicine has no effect on the Ngondo hills; illness occurs beyond the reach of pharmaceuticals here. Let the damn Brits swallow what the quacks claim prevents malaria, dysentery, typhoid. Mitch's gang is as tough as any out of his hardy 1930s childhood on the east side of Regina. Able to adapt to anything, to survive anywhere. MJ will buck up before we know it.

The headaches continue. They're something bad; they need to be kept secret. Once or twice a month, MJ slips away from Lily and me unnoticed. It could be during a butterfly hunt in the misty jungle above the mission. Instead of capturing some winged specimen, our gang of three loses one of its earthbound own. Later, my sister and I trail in with nets from another glinting afternoon, blink in the bedroom doorway until a shrouded shape emerges out of dimness. Lily lifts the sheet to inspect our brother's peaked face with the same fascination she shows for the boa constrictor for sale in the market in town. You can always tell how much she wants to poke a stick through the mesh, jab at the coiled length, make the snake strike. She feels MJ's forehead, though its heat could brand. She holds his wrist to count his pulse, then commands me to run to the kitchen for a cool, damp cloth. My brother's eyes won't open or tear. He refuses to say where or how much his head hurts; what the pain is like, if it's better or worse. Our offer to read aloud from *Robinson Crusoe* is rejected and a glass of water is declined. Lily grows impatient with such an unresponsive patient. "He wants to be alone," she decides, searching the cupboard for firefly jars. It's almost dusk. Soon a flickering will decorate the darkness above our reach. In Africa, we're always trying to catch something.

The Old Country collection of stick huts and smoky fires remembered by Mitch's quartet of immigrant aunts is never far; here, it's closer. A path connects the mission to the village. There Mitch squats in the dust with toothless men after his teaching day is over. He practices Swahili slang and soaks up tribal wisdom and consults about MJ's condition. The old fellows are sure to know a plant that can be ground into powder or distilled into a tincture or concocted into a potion capable of curing his boy. Some jungle root, blossom, leaf. Or it will be a spell that saves MJ from slicing the darkness with screams. The chant of a crone living alone in a hut at the end of a path that twists and winds through elephant fronds, choking vines, clouds of purple moths. A flinty throat releases sparks of sound; ancient hands conjure amid smoke, encourage what hurts MJ's skull to leave. Invite my brother's pain to release itself into the charcoal air, where it may be diffused into an ache subtle enough to be borne, and shared, by all who breathe it.

My father shakes his head when the old fellows won't help his boy from fear that their secret remedy might end up as one more colonial acquisition. The damn Brits have ruined Africa for everyone. MJ isn't always able to wait until we're sleeping before he moans anymore. The sound begins earlier in the evening and lasts longer into the night. Mitch has to retreat to his room at the other end of the cinder-block house. He can't stand to see his children suffer; he can't bear hearing any of them cry. Once more his record player unwinds Peggy Lee into the dark while Lily presses a fresh cloth against my brother's forehead. Covers the vein bulging on his left temple. Purple blood beats, purple blood can't get out. MJ's lashes flutter with each pulse. They're dark as his hair remains while Lily's and mine become bleached white by Tanzania. My brother's eyes won't open all the way until what burns inside him has seeped out to soak his sheets. Then the bedroom blooms with a sickly sweetness. Some fruit might have split on the cement floor, what's beneath the skin become exposed. Ripe meat immediately starts to rot and just as quickly teems with insects drawn by a tantalizing aroma. It will be a full day before they finish feeding. When the too-sweet scent has begun to fade and MJ is almost able to heal and rise, my father might appear in the sickroom doorway to ask how his gang is coming along. "MJ will buck up for good before we know it," he guarantees again. "Just wait." Mitch hovers, tentative. Then he knows exactly what to do. He'll shimmy up a pawpaw right now. He'll risk his neck to bring an anodyne far more powerful than aspirin down to earth for his oldest boy. Lush orange-red flesh will be just the ticket for whatever ails MJ. An elixir for us all. Africa is not the disease, Africa is the cure.

The headaches occur more often, except during the rainy season. Say for those moist months the tin roof is pounded and beaten instead of my brother's skull. Say drumming water can substitute for drumming blood. Subdued by a liquid din, MJ, Lily, and I play inside; beyond the window, red dirt hemorrhages downhill. Untouched correspondence lessons accumulate in the corner. Mitch has become too preoccupied to ask what we've done all day when he returns home from teaching. Africa is not working out quite as he planned. MJ, Lily, and I embark on another round of the Somewhere game while in the kitchen the houseboy rattles pots in counterpoint to rain's percussion. Rogacion won't come into our room even when MJ's okay. He is spreading stories through the village, according to Mitch's sources there. "Those damn Brits sure did their job on the fellow," my father comments, when the stiff houseboy won't unbend enough to squat with him in the dust or mud. What Rogacion says occurs inside the cinder-block house could only take place at night, when he goes home after making supper. When he's not there.

Each headache leaves my brother paler and quieter than the one before. Each requires more time to be recovered from. "The last thing he needs is an audience," explains Lily, as we ascend without MJ into the jungle where Sister Bridget is lost, where the missing nun waits to be found. My sister believes that MJ doesn't want us to witness how, more and more, he counts beneath his breath when it gets bad. If the right number is reached, the hurting might end. Nor does our brother wish to hear where we've been and what we've done without him. His face turns to the wall when Lily tells about climbing to the top of the mission to ask Sister Elsa to remove our chiggers. To dig out with her heated needle the parasite that burrows through skin to lay eggs in the rich, warm flesh below. "You must roll them out," stresses the last nun left since Sister Bridget vanished and the rest returned to safe Dutch soil. She grips a foot in one hand, while the other aims her needle at the red swelling that betrays an intruder's point of entry. Sister Elsa swivels her wrist subtly, turns the silver sliver like she's opening a dangerous door, withdraws the necklace of miniscule, transparent beads. She holds this shining string up to light, swipes at her dark blue habit to clean it off the needle. Intently, not flinching, Lily observes as the operation is performed on her. When it's my turn, I close my eyes and hear Sister Elsa intone: "You must not allow the chain to break." Her guttural accent makes these words of the sole remaining nun sound like ancient, sacred law; they linger as a warning in the almost-emptied structure's air. If a chigger string breaks while being removed, my sister and I know, eggs left inside the skin will hatch there. They'll grow larger and swell fatter. They'll find their way into your blood. You could lose a limb, as some of Mitch's village fellows leglessly attest. That's why we aren't supposed to go barefoot in the dirt, Lily and I. That's why, when we do, we have to climb to the nunnery at least once each dry season. Like Mitch, MJ never gets chiggers. My brother isn't outside enough, I think. Not sufficiently to be infiltrated by this landscape. Mitch claims it's because his oldest boy has skin as tough as his. At other times, it's because they're the dark-haired duo. The lucky pair.

Between each headache, my brother looks on-guard against the next. Strained by the suspense of when it might begin, alert for the first twinge of returning pain. MJ becomes listless even when he says he's okay. He's unable to lead our trio during increasingly brief respites from what's wrong. Was he this quiet on Ios? Wasn't he livelier in Lisbon? Or was MJ crushed from the start by the weight of being Mitch's oldest boy? Paled by that swarthy shadow? I can't remember and Lily won't say. My sister doesn't like to discuss anything before Africa. "It's the moon and the stars," she mentions, when we're walking back from the river with lucky frogs after dark, once again shoeless in spite of chiggers. Lily means that the headaches imitate the rhythm of lunar cycles; come and go according to the whims of Pisces, the dictates of Virgo. My sister cranes her neck to study intricate, illuminated patterns spread above. "It's going to get worse," she predicts.

Lily shakes the thermometer, frowns in our father's doorway. "He needs to go to the doctor," she says again—as if it wasn't, in part, to move beyond the reach of the quacks that we left Brale, BC, in the first place. To escape the damage they inflicted on Ardis. Treatment that turned her into a long-term inmate of a cold Canadian clinic. Transformed her into a mother lost at the other side of the world. My father looks at Lily, looks back at his maps. "It's all in MJ's mind," he explains, tracing a finger slowly across the Aegean Sea. "He just needs to buck up." The thermometer is missing the next time Lily sends me running for it. Now we have no instrument to measure the heat of the fire burning our brother's brain.

Sound hardly ever emerges from our room while Rogacion is around; dry season or wet, it still isn't as bad during the day as after dark. MJ's first cry makes the houseboy freeze each time. He leaves the kitchen, sets out on the village path. Tells more things that make African tongues click against teeth as Lily and I pass. When Rogacion returns several days later, it's freshly apparent that he never approaches within six feet of my brother. Eventually, Rogacion won't wash MJ's sheets, clothes. Lily and I scrub them in the sink, hang them on the line. Mitch doesn't have to know everything, my sister says about this secret.

Then the headaches seem gone for good. Glaring sunlight doesn't bother my brother after he finds Gary Cooper. He ties a string around the chameleon's neck and leads him all afternoon through Mitch's gardens. Our father is satisfied that once again he's been right. His oldest boy has bucked up, just like the old man said he would. "It was in your head the whole time," he repeats. A moment later, my father adds: "I knew you'd be better once we reached Africa." As though we came to this continent expressly to search for a cure for MJ. As though his condition preceded our arrival, rather than the other way around. My father watches MJ promenade his pet with an intentness that suggests a boy can camouflage himself from sight as easily as a lizard. In the end, it's Gary Cooper who vanishes. The string around his neck frays then breaks. He slips away to freedom, where survival will depend on luck, and on his skin's ability to be both change-able and tough.

After he loses Gary Cooper, MJ's headaches are worse than when Ardis flew across the world to us during our second African year, when she fails to arrive for a scheduled visit three years after that. I waken to the sound of my brother's head knocking the wall above his bed. Let me in, let me out, let me reach the right number. One night it's noise from beyond the cinder-block house that disturbs my sleep. MJ's and Lily's beds are empty. I'm drawn across the rough grass by sound I can't identify, by a voice I can't place. Need to know pulls me deeper into Mitch's tangled shrubs. My brother is curled into a ball in the dirt, beneath the frangipani. He's naked, growling. A stick is clenched between his teeth, in his foaming mouth. Lily squats nearby. Satisfaction shines on her face as I retreat unseen to the house. In the morning, I might believe it was just another dream if flecks of red dirt didn't nestle in the corner of my brother's left eye, in the lobe of his right ear, between two front teeth. "I slept just like a log," Lily yawns luxuriously.

Mitch begins to mention his Aunt Lil. He remembers her fits. The frozen blood, the spells, the special sight. He peeks across the supper table to where MJ droops above his untouched cassava, while Lily complains about her fate as our most eccentric ancestor's namesake. "It could have been worse," Mitch says. Instead of explaining the comment, he glances at MJ again, winces as though his own head hurt.

Mitch hopes a sojourn at the Mombasa shore will make everyone A-okay, but his gang hasn't bucked up by its return to the Ngondo hills in time for the summer rains. Rogacion fails to materialize at the kitchen door after we get back. He's left the area, say some of Mitch's sources; according to others, he died suddenly in our absence. No one else will come from the village to save the cinder-block house from assuming an aspect of neglect that deepens each rainy day. MJ remains inside throughout this season, whether his head hurts or not. Or because it always hurts. Five years have thickened the bougainvillea that Mitch planted around the cinder-block house. Leaves press wet against window screens, block sight of the world beyond, make our already dim bedroom murkier. An over-sweet smell hangs ever-present in damp air; it won't wash off my brother's sheets, clothes, skin. MJ never whimpers across the dark room anymore. He doesn't growl through the dark night again. His head no longer knocks numbers against the wall. Or maybe I don't hear it. Maybe the rain's too loud. Maybe I don't waken. Maybe I have already fallen into an enchanted slumber from which I will always struggle to escape.

To be heard above the rain, Father Franklin has to pound our door. Mitch has failed to show up to teach again. "He took MJ to the doctor in Dar es Salaam," says my sister, as though the white Peugeot was not drowning in the drive. As though MJ wasn't in bed in our room down the hall. As though lately our father hadn't been wandering out in the wet almost every day. The same too-sweet smell that haunts MJ will steam from Mitch upon his soaked return. Again he'll shake off raindrops and look toward the door shut between his oldest son and himself. Again nervousness will seem to shade into fear as my father towels his dark hair dry. "It's Africa," he says, coming in from the deluge one afternoon, as though Lily and I should understand that these recent days have been spent searching for the cause of his oldest boy's suffering. Here is the diagnosis that would elude the quacks; a source of pain whose removal could thwart Sister Elsa's needle. For once Mitch shares a revelation without a ringing tone of triumph. The tin roof falls silent, as if rain has halted at my father's announcement rather than commenced an ordinary four o'clock caesura. Sudden quiet always feels unsettling; first words spoken after its arrival sound too loud. "Where are the suitcases?" asks my father in a voice seemingly amplified into a shout. "And where are the trunks?"

In Copenhagen, Jakarta, and Rio de Janeiro, my brother doesn't demur when Mitch declares that our departure from Morogoro cured his oldest boy. He smiles wanly when Mitch states that ever since the whole team has been tip-top, A-okay, dandy. My brother won't share the glance Lily and I exchange when the leader of our gang brags about its toughness. As we drift farther and farther from the Ngondo hills—without, it seems, ever reaching anywhere—Mitch starts to imply that the damn Brits drove us away. Or else it was the Catholics who made us leave Paradise. "Or the chiggers," Lily sarcastically suggests. She and I wear anklets of pin-sized scars that fail to fade even as our bleached heads darken. Africa got inside our brother and burrowed so deep that even Sister Elsa's needle could not roll it out cleanly. "It's the chiggers," MJ grimaces when no longer able to conceal that, whether or not they ever went away, the headaches have definitely returned. This happens after we finally make it back to Canada. In Brale, BC, it's not so easy for Mitch to prevent the quacks from getting at his oldest boy. He tries to suppress satisfaction when their tests fail to reveal what's wrong and their drugs don't succeed in easing what hurts. Lily and I try to express surprise when MJ disappears at seventeen. Two years later, Mitch vows to bring my brother back home, vanishes with unmistakable finality himself. After the lucky pair has left, and my turn arrives to abandon Lily and Ardis to their uniquely private, similarly painful Brale devices, I'll wonder if any of us managed to escape Africa unscathed after all. Without abandoning one of our own, without breaking the chain, without leaving a limb behind. In my Santa Cruz or Seville or Sidi Ifni dreams, during an exile's anodyne sleep, the cinder-block house has become entirely swallowed by bougainvillea, transformed into an oversweet secret. The bedroom at one end is as obscure in day as in night. Sounds of pain burrow through the dark, penetrate pores, sliver through flesh to multiply over and over in my poisoned depths.

What the World Takes Away

AFTER EVERYONE ELSE STOPS, WE STILL SEARCH FOR SISTER BRIDGET. "They didn't look hard enough," explains Lily. "They gave up too soon." My sister insists that she and I will find the missing nun up where jungle distills Africa into a cool green element you can taste, mist you feel on your face; there beyond vines twisting and coiling into letters of some secret alphabet, beneath the mossy clouds. Her blue habit is soiled and torn after one week outside. She has lost her rope sandals. A wimple no longer looks white. Idly, purely from custom, Sister Bridget fingers her rosary, counts beads beneath her breath in Dutch. Her expression appears enigmatic and serene at the same time. You can't tell whether she wants to be found and brought back, or whether she'd prefer to stay missing. Only Lily and I realize she became lost trying to escape. Only Lily knows why we would hunt someone whose flight from here I thought we always wished for. "Of course, she won't be the same," is my sister's sole comment concerning the discovery we hope to make, who it is we'll find. Lily gnaws her lower lip; a fleck of red sticks to a tooth. "No one could expect that. The jungle changes you."

From our hiding place behind bamboo, Lily and I would watch her emerge from the nunnery at the top of the Morogoro mission then pause to ensure this exit had not been detected by the sisters still communing mutely inside with God. The screech of a parrot in a coco palm lifts her eyes, impels her up the path that climbs into the jungle. Or the church bell will make Sister Bridget move away when its pealing floats up this high. A dark green tangle swallows a deep blue habit after twenty steps, allows Lily and I to follow unnoticed. The third twist in the trail is marked by a bent mango tree. A hollow in its trunk holds another note for Sister Bridget to find. She passes the spot without a glance; she'll come back after dark. It would be unsafe for her to pluck our message from hiding for a quick glance in daylight, as it's always too risky to carry any of them away. *Help is near*, this one invisibly vows. You have to hold lemon-juice ink near to direct heat—say, to the candle flame that will illuminate Sister Bridget's journey back here through the dark—to see what it says. To an unknowing eye, the scrap of paper appears blank. Waiting to receive a communiqué, rather than to impart one. "They're all she has to hold onto," says Lily, whenever we substitute a fresh message for one that has already given strength. At first it puzzled me how lemon words revealed by the heat of Sister Bridget's candle could fade from sight by the time my sister and I remove them for careful disposal. Why those paper scraps appear innocently blank, not dangerous at all, when Lily burns them at the far end of our father's garden. Then I understand. It would be equally risky for Sister Bridget to leave an exposed message in the hollow where she found it as to slip one into a pocket of her habit for a souvenir. Evidence mustn't fall into the wrong hands. No one can know. At midnight, beside the mango tree that bends where a trail twists for the third time, Sister Bridget holds a message her grey eyes have just absorbed in one hand and the candle that revealed it in the other. Her flame relieves the surrounding darkness only enough to throw a confusion of too many suggestive shadows. Only enough to draw nocturnal jungle life to watch and wait just beyond the feeble glow. Sister Bridget closes her eyes, moves her lips. She is reciting a silent prayer or mutely repeating our several words of faith and hope. Before returning the scrap of paper in her hand to its hiding place, Sister Bridget licks our secret citrus secret from it. Her mouth twists as she erases one more tangy clue.

The messages are always short and simple.

You're not alone.

Sister Bridget knows little English. She must memorize our words on the spot.

We know.

No need to sign our names. Sister Bridget will realize it's us.

We understand.

Who else could it be?

"Which nun is she?" Lily asks the African inspector who appears at our door while the church bell appeals for darkness to deliver what it withholds. Although Sister Bridget is discovered missing before dawn, Father Franklin waits until dusk to alert the police in Morogoro. The next day they return with dogs. Lily and I hear distant barking as we discover the hollow of the mango tree to be empty for the first time. Sister Bridget has taken our last note with her, along with a candle stub and a box of matches.

Don't lose hope.

As if that were something you could misplace, something you might not find again.

It falls from your pocket as you rise higher above the world; it hides in a snarl of fronds and leaves.

Shines like an alert eye through shadow. Winks through pools of green.

"She's watching us," says Lily when we reach the old teak forest, on the other side of the river crossed on bridges of fallen trees. My sister's nostrils quiver, dilate, flare. She can smell how near it is, what we're looking for.

Sister Bridget was just another Dutch girl who skips along dikes and skates like Hans Brinker across frozen canals before the Catholics kidnapped her to the Ngondo hills of Tanzania. Father Franklin forces her to wear a blue habit with a white collar and white wimple; Sister Elsa straps rope sandals to her feet. Immediately, the captive realizes how difficult escape will be. She knows little English and less Swahili. She doesn't possess a passport, a ticket, one East African shilling. The other nuns rarely let her out of sight. Sister Bridget counts rosary beads and inhales incense and moves her lips in obedient prayer. She paces a long, narrow porch while the jungle pants promises, shrieks invitation beyond. She sustains a serene expression. Twelve dutiful years will lull the mission into forgetting it holds a hostage.

Then it's simple for Sister Bridget to slip from the nunnery during afternoon hours meant for solitary devotion. A bent mango tree always appears at the third twist of the path. The path always leads to the Ngondo River. On a wide, flat shelf of stone carved by the cascade, within its liquid roar, Sister Bridget rocks herself away again.

For a week, search parties move in rows across the fields, jungle, brush. Their sticks beat the earth, punish it for concealing Sister Bridget. You can hear whistles shrieking like alarmed birds in the distance, you see beams playing through the dark. The dogs fail to pick up any scent; a body is reluctant to be found. When not even a scrap of deep blue cloth will show itself, everyone except Lily and me gives up looking. Only we know that Sister Bridget remains alive and well and near. She curls to nap beneath elephant ferns. She sucks stems like straws to slake her thirst. She nibbles berries and insects and leaves. Each day she becomes slightly less lost. Faint tolling from the world below can still make Sister Bridget shrink; yet slowly she is growing more frightened of retreating irreversibly beyond the sound of the bell than of being returned to the place from where it calls.

Sometimes Mitch claims it was his plan for us to end up in Africa all along. From the day he removes MJ, Lily, and me from Brale, BC, while we wander the world for several seemingly aimless years, my father knows that our journey leads inevitably to this cinder-block house with a tin roof and mesh-screen windows. In spite of too many damn Brits in the vicinity, the spot will be A-okay for his lucky gang. As long as we stay out of the clutches of the Catholics, Mitch always adds. At first, my brother and sister and I do seem to glimpse the mission's score of Sisters only from a safe distance. Filing to or from their residence that hovers high above the church. Dangling rakes and hoes over shoulders like crosses, singing guttural hymns to stay inspired and in-step. We learn their names when they appear at the door to give Lily the skirts and blouses donated in Holland to clothe a little black girl. Even when my sister and I start climbing up to have Sister Elsa dig chiggers from our feet with a heated needle, we fail to notice that one of the other nuns is trying to communicate with us. After our mother arrives from Canada then returns too soon; after Ginger grows dissatisfied with a pet's tame existence and runs off to join the pack of wild dogs that prowls the brush beyond the mission; after MJ's chameleon, Gary Cooper, transforms into one more loss inflicted by this landscape: only then does Lily realize that Sister Bridget has been sending us signals from the start. We're not the only ones here against our will, she silently says. Not the only ones who dream of escape. The signs are so subtle they still elude me after my sister points them out. All I see is an inscrutable face framed by a white wimple. Paper skin that must be held near the flame of Lily's fierce gaze before a message appears on its blank surface.

Hold on.
Stay strong.
Don't give up.

Lily clutches onto hope of finding the lost nun as tightly as she once did a belief that, no matter how much time might pass, we'd cross paths with MJ's chameleon one day. We would recognize Gary Cooper by the string embedded in his neck, where skin has grown over one end of what was originally a leash. On the Ngondo hills, Lily remains alert to everything that tries to camouflage itself from our sight; everything the world would take away. Her grey eyes narrow into a permanent squint as, despite their scrutiny, elements of the landscape one by one become lost and never found. Sometimes, as if faith were a habit she isn't able to break, Lily still speculates that Ginger bares his fangs among the pack of wild dogs snarling across the sisal fields. As we walk to buy a shilling of cane from the sugar man down by the road, she might mention: "We'll find Gary Cooper when we least expect to." A moment later, my sister idly adds: "It's funny how that works."

Lily no longer suggests, even casually, that our mother is going to fly to us from Canada again. Not after what happened the first time, not after Ardis wasn't well enough to leave the clinic for a second scheduled visit. "Why not?" my sister used to shrug, about the chances of a repeat trip, as though all the missing might materialize with ease. Didn't Ardis just need to buck up in order to get better? Didn't our father still say it was all in her mind? I misunderstand Mitch. I believe he means that every facet of our African existence, all of it, is my mother's fantasy. This experience upon the slopes of the Ngondo hills occurs solely inside her skull. When Ardis is cured, a diseased dream will end.

"We're going to look for Gary Cooper," Lily fibs in the dim bedroom, while the sun beyond beats another afternoon into submission, forces our brother to remain out of the glare again. MJ's head started to hurt when we arrived to Tanzania. Or maybe it was after we left Spain; maybe before waving goodbye, so long, to France. As his headaches worsen, fewer of Lily's and my adventures include our brother. We return to the cinder-block house to find him silent beneath the sheets. We share less of where we've been, what we've done. We don't tell MJ the truth about Sister Bridget, before she vanishes or after. Too many afternoons spent inside have made our brother just like all the others, according to Lily. "Gary Cooper's probably out there in plain sight this very minute," she speculates with an airy wave. Her other hand flutters a paper scrap to dry the lemon ink on it.

"I bet we just can't see him." MJ shifts to face the wall, leaves Lily and me to ascend through air that cools as we pass the classroom where Mitch barely pretends to believe the truth of what he teaches to rows of enraptured Africans. Our father never worries where we explore or how far we roam. He doesn't fret over undone correspondence lessons that gather dust every dry season, mildew during the rains. He isn't able to ask Lily why she needs yet another lemon from the Morogoro market. Our father has his own secrets. They swallow him like hungry flowers in the dark.

Mist would suspend itself above the river, drift down to make Lily and I shiver where we spy. Sister Bridget rocks like she's riding a camel. Her habit twists around her knees. One hand reaches up to urge the slow beast on.

She shudders, it stops. When her eyes open, maybe they're surprised not to discover some dune-filled desert far away from here. Every Morogoro morning can be as startling as that. Just ask Gary Cooper.

Now Lily drops any number of notes at seemingly random intervals during each day's search for Sister Bridget, as if delivering the mail of an unmarked postal route. She no longer worries that messages might fall into the wrong hands. I'm no longer sure whose hands they are meant for. Lily has never liked to explain every little thing. Paper scraps proliferate in the under-growth like a white flower unique to this tropical forest. Unshared secrets accumulate. Stumbling across them, we're surprised at evidence that we've been here before.

Only Sister Elsa stays on at the top of the mission, only for a while. The other nuns are sent back to Holland immediately after Sister Bridget dis-appears. It isn't safe for them here anymore, frowned Father Franklin. No quantity of incense inhaled behind stained-glass windows can provide complete protection; not even sweet Jesus is able to keep all danger from everyone. I picture a score of blue-robed nuns clomping in wooden shoes beneath windmills or with ruddy cheeks pacing amid the tulips, happy to be back where they belong. With a covert glance at Lily, I wonder if you must lose a sister before you can go home. Together we approach an aban-doned structure where geckoes wait to be brushed from walls, scorpions shooed from the shadows. We peer through frayed screen into the porch nuns paced with hands folded like delicate secrets inside their habits, with tasselled cords swaying from their waists. They would click wooden beads and murmur prayers and beseech sweet Jesus to save the little black chil-dren. They never bother with Lily and MJ and me; we make all the nuns shake their covered heads. In the end, even Sister Bridget knows we can't be rescued from this dream. It would be pointless to include us in her plan to escape. Futile to invite us along. "It's every man for himself," Lily says, clutching her scabbed knees and casting a slanted glance toward the other side of our bedroom, where MJ whimpers.

Lily will no longer tell me what she writes in lemon ink. "The usual," she evasively answers. I suspect heat would reveal a terse plea for salvation. Conveyed not through language or even code, but through hieroglyphics, Rorschach symbols.

The sugar man says his nephew glimpsed Sister Bridget in Dar es Salaam. She was buying pigs' feet in the market, claimed the boy. Mitch calls that an African story. Like the one our houseboy tells about slaughtered children who transform into spirits that haunt the Ngondo hills with slit throats streaming endless blood. About sparks ancient women send into the charcoal night that return as butterflies in morning, or as firefly atoms to decorate some future evening; in both cases, as vivid as Gary Cooper at his most brilliant—posed against the colours rioting Mitch's gardens, say. Just before each sudden nightfall, the end of the sky shades into the exact blue of Sister Bridget's habit. Once more I count the million stars that spangle my mother's mind.

I am forgetting her serene expression and the timbre of her voice. She never spoke to us directly; she was silent in our presence; conversation with another nun would break off when we neared. Only a handful of Sister Bridget's words lingered long enough or carried far enough for Lily and I to be surprised by how deeply they were pitched, how roughly delivered. The last time we followed her up the river path, as if she knew we were there, Sister Bridget looked over her shoulder with the serene expression that is fading from my memory like stars before each dawn.

"We never asked her to take us with her," Lily suddenly says. Every day we climb higher into the jungle; every day we push deeper into its secret places. Every day I wonder if my sister and I

will become lost ourselves before we can find anyone. Now fireflies are always out by the time we return to the cinder-block house where our father lingers with the last light in his gardens, where our older brother stays as quiet as he can in bed. "She would have taken us if we had," Lily states in a voice that sounds raised to defend Sister Bridget against some unspoken charge. Of abandonment, of carelessness, of neglect.

Lily glares out the bedroom window when another rainy season arrives. Like our mother would do, she bites her lower lip. A fleck of blood sticks to a tooth. Sister Bridget must be impatient to be found now that she's no longer lost. Waiting alone in the dripping jungle day after day must be tedious. Soon she won't be able to resist slipping down to the mission after dark. Her bare feet will step around mirrors of puddles, crush mica shards gleaming on the road. She peers through a mesh screen beyond which nuns slept in neat rows beneath mosquito nets. She descends farther to circle the church, to skulk outside our similarly unlighted house. "Who is it?" Lily wonders when knocking wakens her then me. "Who's there?" I hear my sister ask the darkness. It's only MJ hitting his head against the wall above his bed, trying to stop what hurts at night that way. It only sounds like knuckles rapping on a door that won't open. It's locked; no one's home; someone has lost the key. "Who is it?" Lily asks, night after rainy night, though there's never an answer.

"She would have been able to reach anywhere," Lily says, "if she'd brought us with her." My sister's voice takes on a bitter tone whenever she mentions the missing nun now. Lying awake to listen for knocking in the night has made her as pale as MJ, as all the others. "We know there's safety in numbers," my sister adds ironically. As if we could still believe that old dictum of our father's, after first Ginger and then MJ deserted our already thin ranks. Reduced a supposedly lucky gang's number to a vulnerable two.

More and more I wonder if Sister Bridget ever wanted Lily and me to part a curtain of green and find her. Maybe she has concealed herself a hundred times behind bamboo, just as often held breath until we're gone from a guava grove. Maybe we should leave her alone. Stop pretending someone's lost when she's hiding. I am several decades from understanding that the desire to be found and longing to remain concealed can co-exist in permanent tension. "You're just like all the others," Lily would say if I shared my doubt. She bickers with MJ while the sky leaks too heavily for exploring outside. Once again she blames our brother for losing Gary Cooper. Her mouth twists in anticipation of the next tart words she will lick up, swallow, turn into a secret inside herself. No one will ever know. Three tolls of the church bell command the roof to stop drumming. Then my sister and I climb past the nunnery, ascend above the mango tree in a recurring waking dream. We move through steaming ferns that immediately leave us drenched. My eyes are no longer alert for a flash of blue. They fix on Lily's push through thick green in front of me, her quick step over gleaming vine and root. By the end of the rainy season, we're not looking for Sister Bridget anymore, it seems. Lily is trying to escape from me, instead.

"We'll find her tomorrow," my sister promises when MJ starts to moan in perfect time to the knocking of his head against the wall. As if that dubious assurance could be the certain answer to each question contained within this dark room and the simple solution to every mystery prowling an obscure world beyond. At once, our brother falls silent. "Her?" he asks, perhaps thinking Lily means our mother; unaware that after three months Sister Bridget still waits to be discovered. She has long ripped her wimple into bandages for cuts and scrapes inflicted by an outdoor existence. A matted tangle, the very corn silk we always imagined, falls half way down her back. Soon her blue habit will become tattered beyond wearing. Soon there will be sightings of a spirit dressed in leaves and vines, with enigmatic symbols painted in berry juice on its parchment skin. "I meant him," Lily corrects herself. "I meant Gary Cooper." For a moment, Lily's words confuse me as much as they must do MJ. At eight, murky zones of my mind already swarm with a vast cast of the vanished. Take your pick, Gary Cooper might say. I wonder who or what my sister will decide we need to look for next. I don't realize that for our lucky gang this is only the start of searching. I can't foresee a time when it will be each other we try to find, MJ and Lily and I. Only a quarter-century later, here in this *derb* at the end of the world, while I lie awake and listen for a three a.m. knocking on the door—still, even now, after all these silent years—do Sister Bridget and Gary Cooper become linked in my memory. The blue nun leads the green lizard by a string leash toward the river. Say the path curves where a leaning tree holds a secret, where the scent of mangos and lemons mingle. Say the unlikely pair disappears around that third bend. Or they're right before me, camouflaged or in plain view or written in invisible ink upon paper air. I just can't see them. I am unable to see through acidic darkness to where MJ and Lily breathe. The knocking starts again. Whoever stands outside the closed door still won't go away. It's funny how that works.

Part Four

HOW MUCH THE HEART CAN HOLD

Nothing human is alien to me.

—Terence
"Heauton Timoroumenos"

Rorschach III: Ventriloquism

AT THE BACK OF THE FURNACE ROOM, THE TIN CAN LURKS IN MUTE darkness. It is large and heavy and painted pale green, with silver showing at the dents. The tight lid eases off with a genie's sigh. An acrid aftermath rises from inside; the scent of smoke mixes with those of oil and dust. I dig deep into my inheritance: pale cat's-eyes, opaque agates, gaudy globes. The glass warms to my touch, burns and moans and whispers. Bubbles burst inside my head. The furnace beside me switches on and the earth trembles beneath my feet.

My uncle swallowed too much smoke before my birth, leaving behind his hockey sticks and baseball gloves and a universe of stunted spheres. In photographs his face looks pinched, unlike those of boys who in springtime lay stomachs against muddy grass, push hair from winter-white foreheads, with a squint send one more marble twirling toward its target. *I got you!* they crow at the click of glass on glass. They spin me across the field until the world revolves dizzily, until I can't see straight. Crystal can't help clouding. My agate eyes fog beneath some Billy's breath.

We never visit the cemetery on the hill where my uncle and grandparents practice patience. Driving us past, my father stares straight ahead; rows of white crosses blur by. The wiring of the Christmas tree lights was faulty; one night, my grandfather forgot to unplug the cord. Since his wife dug herself into the graveyard seven years ago, he and his youngest son have been sleeping in the basement. Five older children, my father and his sisters, are already out of the house. Now empty rooms crackle overhead. Gaily wrapped presents turn brown then black beneath the Douglas fir. Smoke steals down stairs. They find the old man halfway between his bed and the window. The boy appears asleep. A lucky marble hides in one of his clenched hands.

They give me his name. *Donald*, they say, and his voice emerges from my mouth. *Dummy*, they taunt when he refuses to move my lips. My bed is in the basement, beneath the surface of the earth. The world twirls slowly; now I'm older than the other Donald ever was. I grip a favourite marble and sniff smoke. Without moving lips, I chant childish prayers; seven miles away, they ascend through the graveyard's skin, muffled by snow as white and clean as the bones it blankets. I have passed through flame, I am as fearless as the phoenix.

There are a dozen years of frozen winters and fiery summers in the small town split by a river that runs swiftly, icily, dangerously in every season. From the bank I toss marbles; liquid mouths gulp greedily. An empty can floats from sight. I'm free to twirl and spin across the world, though the scent of smoke clings to me always. I chip and crack. I'm easily lost and sometimes found. Indifferent hands heat me, roll me away. My cooling skin awaits the next warm touch. *I never dreamed it would be like this*, the other Donald murmurs from my unkissed mouth. Smoke from strangers' cigarettes curls into the corners of my cold, hard eyes. I drown again and again with desire for incinerating flame. On the river bottom, marbles turn to stone.

The Sacred Flame

A FIRST FLICKER APPEARS IN THE UPPER EAST WINDOW OF THE HOUSE. This is the room where the two girls sleep. Francie and Grace must be around eleven or twelve—I'm not certain—they aren't the object of my focus. The fire spreads quickly, like alcohol through blood. Long months of cold darkness are blotted out here and now; for the first time since last summer's blaze, I cease shivering. Smoke puffs languidly into the calm night. From my hiding place, I'm currently the only witness to this vision, though a dozen glass eyes in my pockets are eager to share what I see. They become hot to my touch, they begin to whisper: *Yes, yes*. My Father, who hovers nearby whether I'm aware of Him or not, murmurs His approval too. *Yes, yes*. It's not panic that prevents me from calling out an alarm; my senses are at their most lucid right now. I study how flames soar thrillingly up curtains. I observe how their colours change according to the substance they encounter. My new skin—it will always be new, it has never fit, after twenty years it still itches—prickles with suspense. Will the blaze move this way or that? Shift to the right or to the left?

I am familiar with fire, though it often proves an unpredictable force, a fickle friend. I could tell you that every blaze is unique and that each one's character depends partly on the qualities of the night on which it comes to life—temperature and humidity of air, whims of wind—partly on the intentions of its creator. I take pride in my fires. They're good ones. Vibrant, spirited, swift. Red and orange and yellow dominate my palette, though swathes of purple or blue or green can make my paint-er's blood sing. Especially at the start, while taking shape, my fires bear the unmistakable imprint of my touch and respond obediently to my needs. Inevitably, like any headstrong adolescent, the raging flames will insist on going their own way.

I wait for a first cry, a muffled moan, a scream. The two girls must lie open-mouthed in their twin beds. By now they have sucked considerable smoke into pink, tender lungs. It wanders freely through their throats. Caressing, violating. In the next room, the sisters' parents undergo transformation into a single charred heap. I see their joined mouths, the last kiss. Possibly there was time for her to waken and turn to him. If she'd touched his shoulder one moment sooner, he might have made it out of bed and half way to the window before my hot hand laid him down.

So far this fire has proceeded in surrounding silence. That can't last. Soon a scent of smoke will select the dream of some nearby sleeper to infiltrate. ("I don't know why it was me that woke," the chosen one will later puzzle to the local paper and then repeat a hundred wondering times over kitchen tables up and down the block.) The fire department will be summoned, nearby households alerted. Porch lights switch on. In nightgowns and pajamas and slippers, neighbours mill over the sidewalk. Half awake, confused, they wait for the shrieking trucks, the flashing lights, the uniformed men. The futile effort.

By then, I'll be gone. I have no wish to see my work ruined by water and chemicals, turned into a soggy, disgusting mess. They told me I never saw the burning house after I flew from it with wings of fire unfolding from my shoulders. They insisted I ran into the blanket that was held out for me. They repeated that I didn't hide behind the chinaberry bushes at the end of the yard, didn't watch alone amid the bitter fruit. The blanket folded around me, they swore, it swaddled me inside a skin of pain I wasn't able to see through. The first of their lies.

This moment belongs to me. (My Father has fallen silent; He understands how much I need to savour such scenes undisturbed.) A long wait pays off at last. Myriad details that have been impressed upon my memory finally serve. I can see the pattern of the carpet that's being singed, the grain of scorching wood. The particular combination of ordinary materials that distinguishes this house from the one next door. Love has made the burning structure mine.

My searing vision eats its way toward what waits to be devoured below. The boy's room is on the ground floor, below those of his parents and older sisters. Why does he sleep alone down there, where at midnight he can waken to hear a doorknob turned by a gloved hand, the sliding open of an unlocked window? (His apprehension is unusual; in general, they believe themselves so safe, the innocents in these small towns.) I've seen how exhausted he looks in the daytime from too many nights spent straining to hear the intruder, to detect my stealthy step down the hall. Once when I was in his room, gently touching model planes and wondering if they could fly, I felt myself under observation. Light from beyond the window blanched the watching boy's face, his throat. His eyes gleamed. He was waiting to see what I'd do next. I branded the air with the shape of my twisted cross.

Hello, Timothy.

Now he listens to crackling above. I wave my conductor's wand and modulate the voice of the fire from dull to sharp. Smoke creeps down the stairs. *They better wake up before the smoke hurts their eyes,* I thought on the night it was my turn to be purified by flame. Cigarette smoke had always travelled directly toward me. If I tried to move out of their path, the acrid plumes would alter direction to follow, as though my grey eyes held a special attraction. As though they wished to water and sting. As though their clarity asked to be clouded. How boys blow warm, wet breath on marbles, send them twirling across the grass.

Timothy. The right name, the right age. Once again, for the tenth time, I've chosen carefully and chosen well. The summer hay, the timothy. Hot scratches on my bare legs. In the middle of Harrop's field I threw a marble as far as I could. I wanted to lose it so I could find it. I searched all afternoon in the timothy, though it made me itch all over. My hands, my arms, my shoulders. My new skin. Don't scratch, you'll only make it worse. I always find what I've lost, the ancient itch is always soothed, for a moment at least.

Timmy, Timmy, his mother has summoned a million times. He thinks he hears her calling from above now. A voice draws him up; the stairs feel warm to his bare feet. At the top, he can go no farther. Fire fills the hall. When he tries to push through the flames, they lunge back at him. *Don't touch.* Crimson feathers fasten to his arms; sparks shoot from his shoulders. Fuel his flight back down the stairs and out the door. The night is shockingly fresh. He doesn't see the well-intentioned, who wait with the blanket. (Later, they'll say: *We saved you.*) He is thrown past any possibility of help, flung onto cool dew beyond. He rolls across the lawn like he's done with Francie and Grace all summer; their clothes have been stained emerald shades since June. I was gasping amid the chinaberries, by the leaning fence at the end of the yard. You couldn't eat the bitter fruit; you could only throw it or squish it between your fingers. Explode the smooth, tight skin; smear your face with what's soft and wet and warm inside.

No one followed me down the front steps with wings fluttering from their shoulders. Only when the fire trucks screamed around the corner did I turn inflamed eyes from the gaping doorway to the Thoms and Booths and Carpenters gathered on the sidewalk. The uniformed men pointed spouting hoses. They were able to save the houses to the left, to the right.

It will be an hour before the liquids and powders do their work tonight; before this fire can be controlled, quenched, killed. It will be another hour before four bodies are carried out. The boy behind the bushes is shivering; suddenly it's so cold. Not until dawn begins to bleed the sky will this year's Timothy emerge from hiding. (It didn't happen that way, they'll always say. We rescued you, we held you, you weren't alone.) He's done wrong, he must be punished. First with questions. *What happened? What did you see? What do you remember?*

I remember. I remember all of it now. Yes, yes, whispers my Father. Memory swells inside me like marbles fill my pockets. It warms, strengthens, purifies. My pajama shirt is stained grass-green. My fingers drip with the juice of chinaberries. I paint my face; in red, write hieroglyphics that will never wash away.

I believe in the sacred flame. When my Father asks me to spread fire, I obey quickly and without question. Ours is not to wonder why; we're here to carry out His commands. On one level, my duty is to cleanse through fear. At every funeral, the survivors look like they've been shaken hard by their near escape from flame; despite television and Xanax, they'll never feel safe again. Extreme heat destroys germs, eradicates disease. Sin purifies into cinder. Ash absolves. Sprinkle it on wounds and sores. Strike the match and set them free. Let them feel the holy heat, raise them with smoke above this sick and troubled land, dissolve them into divinity. Then my work is done and my Father allows me to leave. The traumatized town will not notice I'm gone. There's never a goodbye.

You would think my existence an empty, drifting one. I say this apparent aimlessness conceals His plan from unfriendly scrutiny. During the cold months between one summer blaze and the next, I admit, it can be difficult to maintain clarity of vision and resolve of purpose. I must steel myself against the crash of spirits and the plummet of mercury that follow every fire. The current winter seems particularly long and hard; warmth drains too quickly from memory of the most recent Timothy. My tenth Timothy. I wait out frozen months in an obscure room in a sprawling city. *Lie low*, instructs my Father. Behind closed curtains I turn scrapbook pages, study yellowed clippings. Several thousand pixilated dots of black display my ten-year-old face beneath a headline. FIRE KILLS FOUR, ONE SURVIVOR! From more recent reports with similar headlines, faces of other boys stare back at me. Or are they each the same thousands of dots, subtly rearranged? Has only a single boy ever peered through curtains of flame? FOUL PLAY SUSPECTED! bold font exclaims. CAUSE OF BLAZE UNKNOWN. I smile at such stupidity. It amuses me when it doesn't make me sick.

This is not a confession. I have done only right. You will not find the secrets of my method here, nor the keys to a coded art. Ask my Father, He knows. Despite its criminal incompetence, our Mounted Police will stumble on me eventually. I'll offer no resistance when they lock me up. Pride will keep me silent; my deeds speak for themselves. Yes, I realize that the fifth estate will pounce on my story and, in typical media fashion, misconstrue, misinterpret, malign. It will try to diminish the importance of my achievement, to tarnish the beauty of my handiwork. So I must leave behind these pages, these clippings, this testament. My Father wishes it.

And my souvenirs sustain. During the months between autumn and spring, I become enraged by careless accidents. Faulty furnaces and live wires and open hearths are strewn across this cold land; from coast to coast, cigarettes smolder beneath sofa cushions. FIRE CLAIMS FIVE! I weep with anger. Mishaps like these can diminish the power of my art, obscure its effects. *Easy*, admonishes my Father.

Huddled beside the radiator, I envision the tenth Timothy. He walks beneath trees stripped of leaves without realizing where he's heading. He finds himself before a black, gaping hole. His new family says: *Don't go there anymore*. They don't matter; they don't belong to him. *Don't touch*, they warn when his puzzled fingers explore his new skin. It itches; it doesn't fit; it doesn't belong to him either. He can't stop shivering; before, he never felt the winter. I could tell this Timothy that it will get colder each year and that numbing decade will succeed numbing decade. Or is it only me? I understand that the atmosphere is becoming increasingly smoky, warm. Brown and yellow filth rises from several million factories. Grey exhaust trails from countless cars, buses, planes. We're racing heedlessly toward the final fire. Our star will soon explode in a shower of sparks that will dazzle Heaven then die.

My own ice age seems unending; this frigid season threatens never to thaw. I must stir to keep my blood from congealing. I am the figure you don't see walking alone down the street, head bent to pavement. Your eyes glide blindly by my ugly clothes, my thin frame, my peaked features. You fail to notice me hunched over cheap food in plastic places. I have shrunk deep inside myself, away from the fear that surrounds me. This city poses danger. I wouldn't be effective here. The impact of my fiery touch would be lost amid random stabbings, overdoses, rapes. My hand would falter, my aim would miss. *Steady*, He commands. I see young boys, already sick, polluting the corners. So many Timothys I can't save. *Soon*, promises my

Father. I must take care not to be infected. *A little longer*, He instructs. I try to stay inside, I try to stay clean. I turn scrapbook pages and pray upon a galaxy of glass.

My marbles are a secret inside a tin can that's old and dented and pale green. The full, heavy weight of the container anchors me. I take off the lid and remove the varicoloured globes. Each one warms quickly to my touch. I count slowly, careful not to lose track when the tally grows awkwardly large. I count again and again. There is only one holy number. By the time I count the last marbles, the first ones have grown cold. There are too many; they can't all be warmed at once. Then I feel His firm hand on my shoulder, pressing away my panic. Patiently, touch by touch, I warm my secret world once more.

I can dream all day over a single flicker of colour caught in a single crystal cage. The trapped bubbles of breath. In the street, I keep my hands in my pockets (the scars make people flinch) and caress several special marbles hidden there. Like smooth boys, they whisper when you touch them. They moan to be released. *Hey*, breaking voices plead from the corners I quickly pass by.

When they let me out of the hospital, they said I was as good as ever. Brand new skin on my shoulders, arms, hands. *It's yours*, they assured me. Another lie. It was shiny and hard and artificial. Not my skin, not anyone's. It still chafes like hot August hay. Don't scratch.

And they gave me the green can. They said it was all that survived the fire with me, but I couldn't recognize this container, I didn't remember any boy who'd hoarded treasure inside green tin. I wondered if this was another of their lies. *Everything else burned*, they insisted. I still stank of smoke. The scent clung to me, it wouldn't wash off, the new family kept catching their breath. Some people tried not to stare at my scars; others nudged each other in the stores. *He's the one*. I didn't listen. Now there was a murmuring in my ears. He had found me.

In the spring, His sun uncovered the schoolyard from beneath soiled snow. There was a month of playing marbles. Before and after classes, during recess and lunch. The other boys were startled when I joined in.

Each day I'd choose lucky specimens from the green can, send them spinning across the field. The click when two marbles touched made me inhale sharply. *I got you!* crowed Billys and Alans and Todds. Their pants were smeared from kneeling on the muddy grass. Their faces looked pinched and winter-white. They opened their mouths, pushed back hair. They squinted and took aim. *Mine!* they cried when I let them win. I felt them roll my glass self between their palms; they made me moan. Then I narrowed my smoky eyes and won back my treasure. The boys became bored with marbles, abandoned them for baseball.

My Father's voice becomes louder and more insistent as the days lengthen with spring at last. He believes me too dreamy. He worries I will forget the radiant plan. Temperature rises. I feel heat reach toward me. A force that has waned across vast distance. I stretch like a cat, blink. My head jerks up from a glass universe at His curt command. *All right*, He snaps. *Get to it.*

There's nothing to pack except for the scrapbooks and the green tin can. I go where I'm told, arrive where He needs me to be. Licence plates tell me this is Beautiful British Columbia. Another small town. They're all essentially the same. One main street, two traffic lights. In summer, this place is complacent as a cat curled on a warm ledge. I am the ball of fur that will stick in the town's throat and make it gag and choke and gasp for air. Until then, there are backyard barbeques and picnics at the lake. Children are out of school and men take three-week holidays. These people are so unsuspecting, I pity them.

My operation is swift, smooth, skilled. A waitress feeds me information while across the café her boss glares with eyes that nip like little girls. Twelve thousand, smelter work mostly, quiet. Good. Next, the local paper with its badly focused photos of Kinsmen congratulating themselves at their annual banquet. The sports-page promise that the high-school basketball team will try harder next year. Ads for used cars with low mileage, announcements for auctions rain or shine. There it is: basement apartment, furnished, immediately.

The stucco house is on one of the older streets on the east side of town. It's been too large for Gladys since George passed away five years ago this fall. No number of over-stuffed chesterfields can fill so much empty space, too many vacated rooms. At night Gladys lies awake in the big double bed, presses a hand between her legs, listens to the house shift. It groans like the bellies of vanished children she spent twenty years filling. I've rented rooms from a dozen varieties of Gladys, from here in the west all the way to Prince Edward Island. They never charge enough and are always eager to believe any story offered them. Gladys stares openly at my hands; revulsion and fascination wrestle. I know she wants to touch the shiny skin just once, quickly. "The car went off the road and rolled three times, my world turned upside down," I explain. Gladys's lips tremble. She apologizes at length for the basement furniture, which graced the rooms above until they bought new ten years ago. When I go out, this woman will creep down the stairs to pick through my few things. (The suitcase containing my history is locked; the green can hides behind the furnace.) She wants to see if I've burned holes in her carpet or left water rings on the table. She is quickly impressed by my neatness; it's enough to make her like me. I don't smoke or drink—they're filthy habits. And I'm so quiet.

To further the necessary illusion of striking roots, I must secure some sort of work. Any job will do, as long as it keeps me inside, safe from the ball of fire in the sky that makes my blood roar, my fingertips itch. (Summer has its own dangers.) *Caution*, warns my Father. High unemployment figures reported by the government constitute one more lie. I easily find something within a week of arriving anywhere in the true north strong and free.

This time it's a small outlet of a large chain of CD stores. "Just call me Junior," winks the manager. He's another fool who'd keep smiling on learning that his mother and father were asphyxiated last night. I stare at Just Call Me Junior until the two marbles in his face start rolling around like they're loose. Immediately I see that the store is mismanaged. I make a report but let Junior know that it won't be sent to the head office for now. He's relieved and worried at once. I smile because the big boys will soon smell this rat even if I don't toss it in their face. Junior glances at my hands, gulps.

June jumps into July. I'm set in motion now, I can do no wrong, temptation is easily resisted. Stay out of the sun, though its warmth attracts and I'm always cold. Even intense solar heat can't thaw my core; it only makes me yearn for the force of stronger fire. *Cool it,* He advises. *Chill.* Hours in the murky basement after work are like being underwater. Submerged from the sight of boys dressed only in shorts, they're everywhere, bare flesh toasted by sun, but not dark enough, I could make them burn. *Relax,* my Father chuckles, shaking His head in bemusement. "Roll up your sleeves and loosen that collar," suggests Gladys. "It's hot enough to make anyone wish for a holiday in hell." The formality of my attire baffles the woman until she decides I keep completely covered from respect for her. She purses her mouth, pats her wig.

At the store, I straighten files and invoices, free Junior for long liquid lunches at the Kootenay Arms Hotel. I breathe easier when he's not around leering at the little girls dressed like candy. They all come in, the dollies and the dopers and the dumb dancing bears. Their heads bob to the music as though their necks lack bones. They don't buy; they drift up and down the aisles exchanging secret messages with deadened eyes. *Can I help you?* They see my hands, leave. I return the pawed CDs to their proper place. The alphabet is holy. Work quick, work right. My true purpose runs in seconds and minutes through each day, advancing to the shining hour. Air-conditioning hums and blows cool air in my face. Outside, Cedar Avenue wilts at one p.m.

The long evenings draw me back. Old sounds enfold. Lawnmowers whir, and roller skates rumble across sidewalks. I hug myself, rock back and forth. Gladys treads heavily above, someone walking on my grave. My mother liked to go barefoot around the house. I had to strain to hear her light step overhead. Soon Gladys will call downstairs, ask me to join her on the front porch. The evening has cooled, and she's made a pitcher of lemonade. In a drone, she repeats stories of her dispersed children and dead husband as an occasional car drives past. I fail to discern any significance in these banalities; the way people speak about family mystifies me. A dog barking at the end of the block interrupts Gladys's litany of loss. She sniffs, her face looms like a splotchy moon. "You don't want to sit around with an old dame like me all night," she announces, then resumes her lament before I can disagree. The tenth car to go by will be my signal to embark on tonight's reconnaissance, I decide. If I weren't here, Gladys would slouch before the television, stare at cancerous images until shaking herself awake and wondering what she's been watching. Like all the others, she can't see.

"Go on, stretch your legs." Gladys waves me away. Now is the night time, the right time, my time. With black cats I slink over fences, through dense shrubbery. Our glassy eyes glitter. I turn a corner and find myself in the landscape of my childhood. It always happens that easily. The neighbour-hood would hold no significance for you. Modest stucco houses, cracked sidewalks, a maple in the front yard. At ten o'clock, children are still play-ing hide-and-seek. They scatter to conceal themselves up among branches and inside tool sheds and behind the chinaberries. At a lamp post that serves as Home, a boy counts to one hundred with closed eyes. He runs numbers together to shorten the length of time before he can leave Home to search for the hidden children. They'll try to steal back while he's away, they'll close the door to Home against him, they'll shut him out for good. His face is familiar. It's the face of a boy who lies awake at night waiting, listening, fearing. Like the others whom darkness hides, I hold my breath. I think my next Timothy has been found.

I'm careful not to build premature hopes. This boy is the right age and the right size, but that's not enough. So many boys spoil too soon these days; most show signs of early rot before I can reach them. Over the course of several weeks, I study the two-storey house of my prospective Timothy. I learn the rooms' arrangement, acquaint myself with their occupants. Two parents, two sisters. And a chinaberry bush at the end of the yard, beside the fence. The major requirements for my next blaze are met. Details that don't fill in the background perfectly can be overlooked. *This is earth, not Heaven*, my Father points out dryly.

Certain scenes bring me closer. Timothy and his father are playing catch in the backyard. They toss the baseball back and forth. When the mother calls from the house, the father drops his glove and turns inside. Timothy remains in the yard, waits for his father to return, finally picks up the abandoned glove. He tries it on, but it doesn't fit. Later that night, he'll watch his mother apply lipstick. She leans into the mirror, tilts toward her son's reflection. "Are you ready?" the father calls from the hall, jingling keys in his pocket. The mother turns, brushes the boy's cheek with her mouth, leaves a scar he rubs deeper red as the car pulls from the driveway.

Closer, closer.

August 7th. I have ten days left. This time has the heightened quality of hallucination. Everything seems drawn with unusual clarity; everything appears sharply focused. What was blurred and muffled by distance has drawn near. Unexpected meaning emerges from the surrounding world. Junior takes blondes to Christmas Lake each weekday at noon and leaves the store in my charge. There's a sad dripping from the bag of ice Gladys places in front of an ineffective floor fan. She leaks sweat and swears this is the worst summer in fifteen years. The town rations water. Sprinklers twirl like graceful dancers over lawns on alternating days, repeat perfect spirals. The forest service bans campfires in the woods. Men are recruited from beer parlours to fight a fire raging a hundred miles to the east. At work, my head bobs to the constant music. Really, I'm nodding agreement to my Father's instructions. *Yes, yes*, I repeat. *Yes*.

At midnight I drop ten marbles in the yard behind Timothy's house, where I know he'll find them. One for each soul saved so far. I feel their spirits with me. Timothy will wonder where these marbles have come from and if they're missed. He won't mention his discovery; it will be added to other secrets he hoards in some incarnation of my tin can. With feline sight I prowl the dark that presses around the house then scout inside. There's no alarm against either fire or intruders. Stupid faith. I take exquisite pleasure in my caution, my daring, my dancer's perfect poise. *This one's for you*, I breathe as I slip an eleventh cat's eye beneath the downy pillow of a boy feigning sleep. Upstairs, a man and woman make noisy love. I dream a new child's conception.

As the anniversary marking my death and my birth draws nearer, momentum fades. This moment's balance is delicate; the slightest error can upset the scale. I don't know what's wrong, I say to my frowning Father. Usually, during these final days, I experience what I imagine lovers feel while reaching toward climax. Pleasure in drawing out for as long as possible the urgently sought moment. Explaining to Junior that my mother has died and I need a day off for her funeral, I travel to the nearest city to buy materials with which to construct my fire. My Father's voice becomes louder. He demands and insists and urges. His voice contains an edge of anger I haven't heard before. For the first time, it occurs to me that I might be only one of His many chosen sons. If I prove unwilling, there are others who would feel honoured to carry out His important work. Perhaps I'll be dispensed with when no longer of any use. I saved you from fire, and I can sacrifice you to it, too.

In hope of re-igniting an extinguished spark, I study my scrapbooks and measure my accomplishment. It suddenly seems insignificant. Only one fire a year. (I'm not allowed more; He prefers quality over quantity.) For one mad moment I long to take a torch and start a thousand fires at once—quickly, carelessly, desperately—to illuminate the earth with one brilliant blaze.

Stop! he shouts.

I study the photograph of my favourite Timothy, the one from five years ago. He must be fourteen now. I'm filled with questions: How tall has he grown? How often does he study the four glass gifts I gave him? How close does he sit to the campfire that's sung around on summer nights? I long to return to that town and to find that Timothy. To pass him one more time in the street. To allow him to see my loving eyes again.

No, it would be foolish. *Look forward!* shrieks my Father. *They would remember you, they would recognize you. Strangers are uncommon there and tragedies rare. Stay away.*

I'm exhausted by this unwinnable war. I'm weary from having fought the world for ten tough years. Before me stretch longer, colder decades. With time, it will become increasingly difficult to warm myself with a single fire just once every four seasons. I'll freeze as scrapbooks fill too slowly. My glass universe will chip, crack, shatter.

I picture a cabin on a lake. The scent of pines is fresh and sweet. Breeze off the water feels cool. There's a mist wafting over the lake like smoke. It lifts to reveal ten boys on the farther shore. Their limbs are thin brown sticks. Smooth, unscarred. They're daring each other to be first to plunge into water that's cold even in summer. They arc marbles through air; induce the lake to open its throat and swallow with a greedy gulp. Then ten divers attempt to retrieve what's sunken. A surface becomes smooth and blank except for bubbles escaped from the aquatic searchers' lungs. I hold my breath, wait for submerged heads to burst into the air above. *Be careful*, I call too late.

Careful. Something's wrong. I've never needed sleep during the week before a fire. There wouldn't be enough waking hours to hover at the edge of the ten-year-old life about to feel my scorching touch. To sate myself with a sense of how a Timothy tastes, of his flesh's tender texture. But this time I'm unable to fight off sleep filled with the kind of dreams that unfold so vividly you can't believe they've vanished at morning. I don't know what's happened to my Father. He has taken Himself away without even a token farewell. He's disappointed by my sentimentality, disgusted by my self-indulgence. Now another servant is being seduced by the same intimacies He breathed into my ear. After a decade of undivided devotion, His forsaking seems unbearable.

Then I detect new voices. Through the dark I can hear Joan of Arc at the stake and the widows by the Ganges on their raging pyres. They're calling me. *Come in from the cold, leave darkness behind for good. Enter the light, feel its warmth, let us take you back to Him.*

I wake shivering. I've slept too long, it's nearly too late, there's hardly enough time. I try to hurry, but my fingers are clumsy with cold, my almost-frozen blood is sluggish. I keep forgetting what needs to be done next. I can't stop thinking, irrelevantly, that at this moment Junior is leafing through *Billboard* and nursing his morning hangover. Without my Father to guide me, I can barely ascend the basement stairs and stumble past Gladys. She's drinking cold beer and fanning herself with a piece of junk mail on the porch. Her face reveals surprise that I'm not at work. Each moment of the following hours, while I prepare my fire, resembles a sharp sliver of glass. Some pane has shattered. I can crawl through the blasted window, but its jagged edges cut. In the end, I'm not sure this blaze has been set correctly.

Then I'm behind the chinaberries once more. I twirl ten marbles in my pockets, the dizzy world revolves. Dew has gathered on the grass, children have been called home, screen doors have slammed for the last time tonight. Around street lamps, yellow yawns. I wait for the block to settle into its bed, turn on the pillow, and fall asleep with one sigh.

For a moment, I don't understand. Why are red and yellow tongues licking the ground floor of the house already? They should be starting with the rooms above, where the man and woman and two girls sleep. Have my hands failed me? I glance down and see fingers smeared with the juice of chinaberries. They gleam black in the dark. I feel Timothy's chest rise and fall with even breath. I envision what his closed eyes behold: the blue surface of a lake waiting to be broken by tomorrow's dive.

I am running toward the house. Toward Home. I trip over a sprinkler, am sent rolling. I know my trousers are stained green at the knee, as though I've been praying on damp grass. Marbles have fallen from my pockets. They revolve across the lawn, they scatter from sight. Unburdened, I'm all lightness. I am lifted to my feet and carried to the house. Inside the front door, I hear one of the girls call from above. *Mother!*

I have forgotten how hot it feels inside fire. Such intense heat shocks after the cold I've inhabited for so long. Yet it's easy to push through veils of flame fluttering between me and an eleventh boy's bed. Everything is simple since wings are restored to my angel arms.

Timothy is fire. My Father's voice snaps and crackles. I ignore Him; He has come back too late. I am gathering Timothy in my arms, I'm folding him within my feathers. Already his agate eyes are fixed on the Kingdom that reigns above the smoke. I must go with him there. I can't remain here alone. I melt upon him, spill over him. We're joined. Together we soar upward, away. This moment is so warm. This embrace so pure, so sweet.

The Murdered Child

ONCE MORE SOMETHING IN THE NIGHT, PERHAPS THE COLD DARKNESS leaking from the lake beyond the window, urges me to telephone my sister. Lily continues to live in the same square of stucco in Brale, a hundred miles from this cabin, where we were children. In otherwise abandoned rooms, the only one left, she guards secrets that refuse decent burial; meticulously tends souvenirs of skeleton, flicks dust from bone. She won't or she can't shed light on what more than two decades of widening distance have failed to illuminate for me: nagging questions not hushed by a silencing Sahara; the image not choked from view by Guatemalan jungle.

That unseemly sprawl upon the surface of memory.

That obscenity in the snow.

Yet my reasons for being drawn to this cabin on this nearby lake hardly seemed fuelled by the need to make specific discoveries with Lily's help. My end-of-summer arrival here from Lisbon—it could have been from anywhere—represented merely the latest in a long series of geograph-ical dislocations executed partly with reluctance, almost against my will. Sometimes you go back in order to move forward, I explained vaguely to myself, as if nothing more than that were at stake, as if the business of surviving history were as simple as a mumbled mantra. Placing myself within sight of my past—close enough to squint at the source of its tug and pull, sufficiently removed from reach of its danger—did not mean that one single mystery clamoured more loudly than others for immedi-ate solution. Several questions wavered and twisted through the air like smoke from bonfires of October leaves at Sunshine Bay: Why did my father and brother both vanish off the face of the earth—each in his own time, in his own way—before I embarked on my own less final flight from

Brale? What was life like for my mother, Ardis, during the years preceding her death in that small town? How has Lily managed to hang on there, in spite of everything? And what has happened to me that I don't know these answers? While summer people closed up cabins and retreated to town— leaving the lake to just a scattering of souls, allowing it to reassert the indifferent essence of a place not created primarily for human pleasure—I delayed letting Lily know I was—am—this near. She could continue to believe I'm anywhere, nowhere, one more of the disappeared. For the moment, proximity seemed sufficient to dissolve any urgency in my need to see my sister. I might thumb a ride or catch the bus to Brale one after- noon or another. Instead, I scuff maple drifts in Lovers' Lane and row to the cliffs at Christmas Cove and prowl a landscape almost familiar, nearly known, faintly remembered. I imagine it's enough to understand that the evening train whistles along the opposite shore just after eight o'clock. I tell myself that the source of needed wisdom lies in comprehending why wind sweeps down the valley always from the west. I was able to convince myself, during darkening days, that the purpose of my journey here is to re-learn the Vee shaped by Canada geese against mountains, upon sky.

With the arrival of cold, which felt harsh after my years in southern climates, at my first sight of snow in all this time, I began to shiver, in the way I once had as a child. I felt the same sense I did then of a boy wan- dering out in bitter weather. Again—still—he is nine or ten or a stunted twelve. A second mouth has been slashed, beyond healing, into his throat. In bare feet and wearing little more than rags, indifferent or at least accus- tomed to the elements, separated from home and school and other chil- dren, he steps lightly through two feet of snow to pause at the end of the beach, near the ferry landing, where he skips three stones. Before disap- pearing into the cluster of pines on Greene's Point, he turns to look back through my uncurtained windows. A face indistinct in dusk, clear only to my memory's eye, gazes into rooms where I am illuminated, as on a stage. As in another country, a warmer sphere, a separate zone.

Each half-glimpse of the wounded, wandering boy made it more necessary, and urgent, for me to see Lily. To sound out the feasibility of a visit—whether my sister's condition would permit—I telephoned our Brale aunts. (If you call one of the four sisters, I still knew, you have to call all three; these are women who take offence easily, who like to nurse slights like a teetotal does drinks.) Each aunt sounded unsurprised to hear I'm in the area after being far away for so long; to their minds, only outlandish behaviour could be expected of anyone eccentric enough to leave Brale. "There's no work around here," Dorothy informed me, puncturing what could be the sole sensible reason for turning up anywhere. "A cabin on the lake," echoed Madeleine flatly. "At this time of year." Just hippies and crackpots and people who don't bowl would make such peculiar living arrangements, then pretend they're the superior choice. "She'd love to see you," Kay decided doubtfully, giving me Lily's telephone number.

That was in November. This is January. I've been to Brale and I've seen Lily. No deeply buried secrets were excavated by our encounter. Or was one? There is this: now the snow outside the cabin windows often holds footprints at morning; conceivably those of a child, they are sometimes confused by tracks of deer and bear. A handful of pumpkin seeds, twisted within a scrap of silver paper, waits in my mailbox beside the road at noon. And nearly every week, something in the winter night, perhaps the smooth glide of ferry lights across black water, insists that, despite what was or was not unearthed during our recent visit, I must call my sister.

This is never simple. If nothing else, during the past months I've learned that Lily tends to allow her telephone to ring unanswered. She disconnects the cord, forgets it's not plugged in. Or a recorded voice says her number is not in service. For reasons I can't guess, my sister frequently changes or cancels or unlists her number. I consider then decide not to call the aunts to ask if they know the new listing. To their injured puzzlement, they have little contact with Lily. I'm left to check directory assistance until a new number appears under—and this always startles me—our shared last name.

It has never been easy to reach my sister.

If she does happen to lift the receiver tonight, Lily won't speak first. Like a secret agent trained not to reveal herself to a possible enemy, she waits silently for callers to identify themselves. Learning it's me on the other end of the line will fail to ease suspicion; nothing resembling a conversation will follow. She's well, the house is fine, weather isn't unusual for this time of year. No, she hasn't been away. Yes, her number has changed again. Lily won't ask how I am, what I am doing. She won't refer to my November visit. She won't explain why she hasn't called me since that meeting.

My sister has grown even more guarded than the child who concealed herself behind stony features and covert movement and silence. If I spent my first sixteen years living with Lily without fathoming her interior life, such ignorance wasn't only mine. MJ, my older brother, and our parents, Ardis and Mitch, also remained uncertain why Lily's bed yawned on summer dawns, whom she met on the mountain in spring, where she went on nights as cold and dark as this night that conceals the answer to a question, the identity of a corpse.

Lily finds him on the mountain when the November world is frozen and stiff, yet still unsoftened by snow; five months before we will search for pussy willows in April thaw. "Come," she says, materializing in the furnace room doorway in an unfamiliar grey felt coat that looks several sizes too large. Lily has stolen it from the school cloakroom or from the change room at the skating rink. In a dim cave carved out of discarded furniture and abused boxes, and of hockey sticks that belonged to an uncle from whom I inherited a first name and sharp features and fear of smoke, I look up from my latest letter to Jesus. The furnace switches on; the blue pilot light hisses. The house suspends itself uneasily in Saturday quiet: Ardis escapes into sleep in the big bedroom upstairs; Mitch has shut himself in his study across the basement; and MJ spends most of every weekend with television and treats at Aunt Madeleine's, by the river. "Come," my sister repeats. It's neither a command nor an invitation. Lily's speech is usually uninflected; scant emphasis lies behind her words to lend them nuance. Her communication is blunt and flat as that of cardboard Indians in the westerns Mitch drags us to at the Royal Theatre, where from the front row he watches John Wayne, another simple man, with wide, admiring eyes.

"Hurry," says Lily, beckoning with one reddened hand. She invariably loses the mittens our concerned aunts give her. She doesn't seem to feel the cold, roams without a hat or scarf in winter. Lily has been outside all morning, I can tell: waves of chill pulse from her poised form. She knows a way of leaving the house unnoticed; only half way through a weekend afternoon, or not until after the streetlamps blink on, might her absence assert itself. Where does she go? Mitch and Ardis don't ask; it's better not to. They accept that Lily fibs as lightly as breathes. "She's different," sigh the aunts, applying Brale's catchall adjective for harmless eccentrics and non-practicing homosexuals and tentative pedophiles to a thin girl of twelve who goes where she wishes, takes what she needs.

Surprised by Lily's rare summons, I emerge from the back of the furnace room. I believed that my hiding place, amid the asphyxia of oil and dust, was a secret shared only with my buried uncle; but Lily always knows how to find me. Even after she stops looking, even while I conceal myself beneath thick blankets of time and distance, Lily knows where I am.

On a late November afternoon I walk down Aster Drive to meet Lily for the first time in two decades. During two brief visits to Brale, in 1986 and 1995, when she was in the hospital on the hill, Lily wouldn't see me. The lingering power of that double refusal, and the weight of all the years since then, made me nervous upon dialing her number from the cabin. When I spoke my name, silence followed. "Donald," I repeated. Fumbling to speak words that received little response, I tried to believe the awkwardness of the call came from our not having spoken for so long. "If you want," said Lily to my suggestion that I visit for a few days.

My small suitcase brims with questions concerning what happened to my parents and brother while I was embracing distance. Knowledge of their fates has been gleaned from what lay behind and between the lines of several brief notes from my aunts that somehow happened to find me during those years. *We thought you should know*, each one began. There is too much I don't know, much perhaps only Lily can tell me. Did she ever hear from Mitch and MJ, anything at all, after they evaporated from

Brale's air? Was Ardis's death easier than her life? And how has Lily been able to sustain herself?

Approaching the house, I wonder if anything will be learned inside it after all. The place looks small and shabby. A single-storey structure, similar to others on the block, with bare front yard and a vacant driveway. Although dusk hasn't fallen, the curtains are closed. I ring the doorbell, touch it again when no one answers. Has Lily forgotten about my visit? As I am about to test the door, it opens.

Although thirty-eight—just two years older than me—Lily has turned mostly grey. A neat bun rises above a face whose sharpness has been replaced by puffiness, perhaps from medication. Grey eyes loom behind thick glasses, fail to blink at my hello. Grey skirt, white blouse, and dark sweater are as plainly cut as a uniform, and look homemade. The contours of Lily's body have blurred like her features, but without concession to softness. She would feel stiff and cold in my arms, I suspect.

Lily glances at my suitcase, retreats down the dim hall. It strikes me that each of her steps is precisely measured to cover the same distance.

Taken aback by her failure to offer a token greeting, then recalling her distaste for words, I follow my sister inside. She pauses, partly turns. "You can sleep in your old room," she says. Toneless as ever, her voice is pitched lower now. "The bed's made. Supper's at six."

Perhaps because she didn't initiate this visit, Lily continues with the housework it has interrupted. The living room she is dusting appears painfully tidy and clean already. I notice that old furniture retains its old arrangement. The bedroom that belonged to our parents stands shut, like Lily's across the hall. Curtains from my childhood have faded in swaths; paths betray where the carpet has been most heavily trafficked. If the walls have ever been repainted, it was with the same colour. Turning on the stove's back left burner, I hold my hand above it. The element still doesn't work.

"Yes," says Lily, not looking up when I mention that the house appears unchanged. "No," she says when I ask if she'd like help with supper. I linger in the kitchen, uncertain how to give Lily the present in my suitcase.

It's a book about what I imagined happened to all of us.

Descending to the basement, I place my luggage on one of the beds in the room I shared with MJ, then glance into the furnace room. It remains crowded with broken tools and rusted skates, and with empty jars that hold breath beneath a film of dust. The scent of oil entwines my head, shuts my eyes. As if a finger of bone traced my spine, I shudder. In Mitch's study, out-dated history texts weigh the shelves and the manual Olivetti still squats on his desk. Avoiding a sharp, exposed spring at one end, I curl up on the rumpus room couch that was once upstairs. At card-table islands, MJ, Lily, and I bent over homework in this sunken space, while Ardis lurched through medicated hours above and Mitch toiled at his memoirs. Without irony, my father titled them *A Simple Man*.

"Time to eat," Lily calls down the stairs.

The kitchen table is set with two plates, two forks, two glasses of water. Lily serves a casserole made with macaroni and tuna; a child would enjoy such soft, bland food. Eyes focused on the wall behind me, Lily pauses eating only to sip water or to reply briefly to my tentative remarks. The neighbours to the east moved; she isn't sure who lives there now. Yes, down-town Brale has changed some. No, she prefers to clear the kitchen herself. She knows where everything goes. Lily's movements at the counter look carefully considered and cautiously executed; each one hints of obscure ritual, of secret significance. I realize how difficult it will be to ask the questions that have brought me here. Back turned to me, hands plunged into scalding water, Lily allows her shoulders to loosen then sag. Steam seems to rise from her body, drift from her skin; it hovers around her head. Lily stands before the sink as if she's forgotten what she's doing or where she is. The tap drips a persistent reminder. Abruptly, my sister's back stiffens. She pulls the plug, dries her hands. "You must be tired from your trip," she says, still faced away. "Good night."

She turns the corner of the hall toward her bedroom. Or does she sleep in our parents' old room now? Water runs in the adjacent bathroom. A door opens, closes. It's seven o'clock.

What have I expected? What do I deserve? To be eagerly welcomed as a long-lost brother? To be greeted with open arms? Yes, Lily, I'm tired from my trip. My trip has been longer than a hundred miles from a cabin on a lake; I hadn't realized how long my trip has been until circling back now to where it began. My trip's been too fucking long, and it isn't over yet. Not by a long shot, not by half. I grimace at my reflection floating on the kitchen window. Although I can't see through the image, I know a maple tree, nude this season, rises half-way across the back yard. Beyond the fence runs another row of single-storey houses; past that, the highway. Then the mountain looms jagged and tall; bare rock even during summer, always splintering a chemical sky. Sometimes we tried to reach the top to discover what lay on the other side. But we never could conquer the peak; the slope was too treacherous, too steep. "I'll reach it without you," Lily said, after allowing me to attempt the ascent with her one last time, before she began, at twelve, to scramble alone upon the mountain, beside the cold, swift river.

No. Not the last time. There was at least one more time. Yes.

A November Saturday in 1972.

Something like a scrap of paper stirs in a dark room in my mind.

The house stands silent. Has Lily already gone to sleep or does her light still burn? She lies on a narrow mattress and looks up through the dark? Or tosses in the wide bed where Ardis sweated pills, where Mitch planned his escape? I'm tempted to steal down the hall and look for a stripe of light beneath a door, then remember that several floorboards creak.

All I know is that, for ten years after she turned nineteen, Lily passed in and out of the psychiatric unit of the Brale Regional Hospital previously haunted by our mother. I know only that, five years ago, just after Ardis's death, she was permanently released. As far as I understand, Lily has never held a job and doesn't own a car and rarely visits our nearby aunts. Although everyone in Brale knows everyone, she is without friends. There has been no lover. A solitary existence in this quiet house may be essential to maintaining a fragile stability. Lily may be unable, rather than unwilling, to answer questions. It may be reckless if not wrong to remind her of the past. It may be necessary for her to forget.

And me?

Downstairs, I sift Mitch's study for his memoirs, without hope. Failing to discover a manuscript during my two earlier Brale visits, I was convinced my father had destroyed the work-in-progress or taken it with him when he vanished in 1978. I inspect the basement bedroom for any evidence of my brother: unblinking cat's-eyes, model airplanes, baseball gloves. Although his transformation into thin air was apparently planned less carefully than our father's, nothing remains of MJ either. Not anymore. The last time I was here, several such tokens still survived.

The house is the same, yes, but with a difference. Every artifact to evoke those who abandoned it has been scrupulously removed. Hidden away, destroyed. I envision Lily clearing out closets and drawers, wiping fingerprints from surfaces, stripping space of clues to crimes and keys to secrets until only intangible evidence remains. She stands before a backyard bonfire without flinching while flames leap at her face, inhales smoke as wisps of ash snow on her head. With a stick, she stirs coals; prods until they hiss, forces fiery eyes to blink sparks.

I lift my eyes to the narrow window set high in the wall above MJ's bed, at ground level.

It lies out there, in the cold, dark night, the question I need answered.

It's not a question concerning Ardis or Mitch or MJ, after all.

Hours later, sliding into sleep, I'm disturbed by a sound from above. The click of the front door. My watch glows three o'clock. I shove away sleep and wait for Lily to return. Didn't she always come home eventually: when we were children, when we saw the truth?

A child stands above my bed of frozen earth and jabs her stick. "He can't feel anything," she informs a presence hovering behind her. The wooden point presses at my bare belly, seeks to pierce the skin, wants entry to entrails. The child pokes harder with her tool, she needs to see inside. Her grey felt coat flaps from the effort; her sharp face frowns. She's angry that I don't cry, moan, plead for her to stop. My eyes refuse to close against the intent face above. My gashed throat grimaces. A bubble bursts from my blue lips, escapes into sky. "His name is Billy," she says, dropping the stick and turning away. The pulsing shadow separates from her, nears me, bends low. A warm hand, the same size and shape as mine, strokes my stone cheek. Scented breath urges me to speak.

At the kitchen table, Lily bows her head before a cup of coffee.

"Good morning," I say, foggily filling a mug. My hands wrap around heat. I'm cold, despite the groaning furnace. Although it's early, I feel like I've slept too long, too deeply. I can't remember hearing Lily return last night. She wears the same neat skirt, blouse, and sweater as yesterday. Has she been to bed at all?

"Did you sleep well?" I stare at the scars. The one on her right wrist is thicker than the other. She did it in the back of the furnace room, Aunt Dorothy wrote me at the time. Ardis was the one who found her; the rest of us had left Brale by then. *Come here,* my asphyxiated uncle summoned Lily in the blue basement light. *Dig deeper,* he urged. *See what's inside.*

"Yes, I did," replies Lily, rising from the table and leaving the kitchen. The front door opens then closes. I move to the living room and part the curtains. Lily passes without a coat beneath the slate sky, between the frosted yards.

This house has to tell me something that Lily can't or won't. I open the door to our parents' room. Obviously, Lily hasn't made this room hers; the wide mattress below the bedspread lacks linen. Nothing litters the dressing table; closets and bureau prove bare. The adjacent bathroom contains toothbrush and paste, soap and towel. The medicine chest holds several vials of pills, with a prescription made out to Lily several years ago. Chlorpromazine. Across the hall, Lily's old room is uncluttered as a nun's; even during her childhood, it lacked girlish touches. The narrow bed is neatly made. A Bible rests on the night table. One bureau drawer contains underwear; like the closets, the rest are empty. Not even a small white valise, locked tight, lurks anywhere.

Wandering back to the living room, I realize with fresh force that it has no television or music system, no framed photographs or magazines or books.

A small radio perches on the mantel. Turning the switch, I find it tuned to static. The buzzing seems to rise in volume inside me. It says these curtains upon the street are never opened. The telephone and doorbell rarely ring. My sister wears the same clothes and eats the same bland food each day, and late at night walks to the same dark place.

She lives simply, that's all. Not everyone hoards old photographs and love letters, torn ticket stubs and tattered maps. Lily exists on a monthly government cheque that probably isn't enough. She can't afford sleek machines and the latest gadgets and an extra pair of shoes. Apparently, she no longer takes what she needs. Or no longer needs.

I move toward the old-fashioned rotary telephone. Aunt Madeleine expects me to visit today. In her house by the river, we'll sip tea and nibble cake and skim lightly over the past and present. Lily will be mentioned cautiously, if at all. Then we'll visit Ardis's grave in the cemetery where my grandparents and uncle also shivers. We'll drop in on Dorothy and Kay, end up playing dice and cards for quarters. I'll catch my aunts peering at me sideways for clues to how their youngest brother might have looked if he hadn't swallowed too much smoke at twelve. I won't ask if they remember the murder of a child more than twenty years ago. I know their resentful answer already. Children have never been murdered in Brale, BC.

"This way," she says over her shoulder, walking quickly. Where are we going, Lily? She won't wait for me, I know. I hurry to follow my sister across the highway and through brush on the mountain's base. Lily threads her way surely up the lower slope. Her breath puffs signals that vanish before I can read them.

She stops in a narrow gully and bows her head toward the ground.

What is it?

I don't want to see, don't want to know.

"Look," says Lily.

A boy. There's something wrong with him. He's wearing only running shoes and socks. The left shoe is torn at the toe; green peeks out. It's cold, he should be dressed, why didn't we bring him a shirt and pants? My drawers are filled with clothes that would fit; he's the same size and shape as me, nine or ten or a stunted twelve.

Something else is wrong. His throat shouldn't look like that.

A second, messy mouth. Torn lips caked with rust.

"Who is he?" I ask Lily. I don't recognize him. I haven't seen him among the boys who yelp like wild dogs across the schoolyard. Maybe he goes to the Catholic school with the Italians, lives up in the Gulch or down in one of the shacks on the river flats.

"His name is Billy," says my sister, poking his stomach with a stick.

His hands curl around something that isn't there. His legs twist at odd angles and dirt sticks to his white chest. He stares at Lily as she jabs the stick. He won't close his eyes, he won't cry. His lips are blue. He must have been eating berries. That's not right. Berries don't grow on the mountain in November, we slather their juice in July.

"He doesn't feel anything." Lily drops the stick. She turns, faces me.

"He's mine," she says.

I bend over the boy and touch his face. Cold skin tingles my hand.

"It's going to snow," Lily says behind me. "It's going to get dark."

"Billy," I breathe. "It's time to go home."

After my walk from Aunt Madeleine's, the house seems very warm. It feels empty, though something cooks in the oven.

A muffled thud sounds from below. Steps ascend the stairs. Lily walks past me to the stove. "Greetings from the aunts," I say, attempting lightness. Silent, Lily peers into the oven.

Downstairs, I throw my coat onto MJ's bed, where the contents of my suitcase are strewn. I start to leave the room, turn back. Is something different about the things on the bed? In their appearance? Arrangement? The book I brought for Lily is gone. I search the space carefully, even kneel to look beneath the bed, without success.

"Time to eat," Lily calls down the stairs.

We have the same supper as the night before. I suggest we take in the movie at the Royal Theatre. "We'll sit in the front row," I propose. "It wouldn't surprise me if John Wayne still exterminates Indians on that screen. My treat."

Lily declines. "It's going to snow," she says. As she clears the kitchen, refusing my help again, I feel I've sat in this room every evening of my life and never gone away. There's been only a single supper, a single evening. Long ago, time stopped, stiffened, froze.

Before Lily can finish at the sink, I move to the living room and turn the radio on. I fiddle with the dial until I find the CBC. Voices cant about Quebec. Perhaps Lily will settle on the opposite couch; even if we don't talk, that would be something. A start. Water runs in the bathroom down the hall. Lily enters the living room, walks to the radio, turns it off. Before I can speak, she's gone. Her bedroom door closes.

I can't remain in this silent house. I slip on my coat and step outside. Cold jabs me wider awake. Lily's window is dark, the empty street is quiet. I move past curtained squares glowing with yellow light, with television screens leaking cancer. Lily, is it going to snow?

"He's still there," says Lily in 1972, parting the curtains and looking into the dark street. Although Brale stores preen with Christmas decorations, the ground remains bare because the snow is late this year.

I haven't been back to the gully since Lily showed me what it holds. "Stay away," she's sidled up to warn me. In the schoolyard, I've studied yelping boys and wondered whether one is missing. Maybe Billy was among them; maybe I didn't notice him before. His parents must know he's lost. They are looking for him, or they have given up looking. His toys no longer wait for his hands to curl around them. He shivers where he lies. I want to bring him clothes, but I'm afraid. There was something the matter with him, something more than blue berries and a second throat, I can't remember.

"Don't tell," says Lily, dropping the curtain.

When she slips from the house now, I know where she's going. Perched on a flat rock near Billy, she tells him things she won't tell me, describes what's locked in the small white valise at the back of her closet. He will never betray her secrets; my uncle won't reveal mine.

Down in the furnace room, at the warmest part of the house, I curl in my hiding place. My uncle inhaled too much smoke when he was twelve. The Christmas tree caught fire, something was wrong with the wires of its lights. The boy tried to crawl to the window; the smoke was too thick and he couldn't get out. Now his can of marbles sighs in the corner; his hockey sticks stir the shadows. My pencil presses against the pad of paper I've taken from Mitch's study. *Dear Jesus*, I print. *Dig deeper*, my uncle whispers. There's something different about his voice. My uncle sounds like Billy now. *Dig harder*, they plead. I press the pencil until there is only a hole where Jesus was.

I can't find the gully in the dark. Dear Jesus, it's cold. Stumbling across loose rock, I wonder if the features of this slope could have changed since my childhood, if a million years of weather since then have done their work. Or has sly memory played another of its tricks? "It was just a game," Lily told me in January that year. "He was just pretending. Billy lives up on Shaver's Bench. He goes to the park there all the time. He's probably on the swings right now. We just wanted to see how your face would look." His face looked pale and thin; a smudge of dirt clung to his risen ribs. I saw the shoe with the hole in the toe and a clue of green sock so I wouldn't see something else. As that winter passed, memory of Billy froze into a picture of my uncle in my mind. The same face. Speaking shadows in the furnace room turned muffled, then mute. Only the deep-freeze hummed. He was silenced so he would never tell.

Lily walks quickly toward the mountain as snow finally falls. I believe she doesn't know I'm behind her, at a quiet distance, until she stops and turns. "Don't follow," she calls, standing still, becoming white. Snow will bury Billy until spring. It's too heavy and too thick; he can't dig himself out from the hole where Jesus was. I retrace a dozen steps; my trail has already been covered. I stop to look where Lily stood a moment ago. A dark shape moves through falling flakes. The white curtain closes, the white valise snaps shut. Billy's heart beats against my chest, hammers its cage of bone. *Let me in, let me out.*

No longer a nimble child, I fall with a grunt. A small, sharp stone presses into my spine. I can feel it, Lily. My hands curl as sky begins to shred white scraps of a letter from Jesus. Something glassy glints toward me; a shape of darkness breathes nearby. I'm trying and failing to close my eyes against the intent face above me. The puffy features. A white blanket covers me with warm weight. I'll never tell, Lily. These blue lips will never ask why.

Snow won't stop falling through the past or through the present. It fills the timeless hole as quickly as I dig, forbids me to find the face. I can't reach Billy. *Dig harder*, he calls up to me. *Dig faster. Dig more.*

The house on Aster Drive hovers in darkness amid descending snow, though I left the living room lit. My iced feet feel their way quietly down the hall and stairs. *This way, Billy.* In the black hole, I fumble for the edge of a bed. Objects fall to the floor as I pull back covers. We've climbed into MJ's abandoned bed by mistake. It feels the same as mine. Billy's skin feels as cold as mine. Until dawn, we shiver in synchronization. Our teeth chatter in time.

At morning, silver light gleans the kitchen. The snow has stopped. Six white inches conceal the features of the landscape. The blanched bones of the backyard maple rise as foreground to the black-and-white mountain. A cup of cold coffee rests on the table.

"Lily?" I call. My unanswered voice sounds thin and frightened as a child's.

Let's go, he says. *Hurry*, he urges.

My suitcase is packed. Should I leave a note? *Dear Jesus* ... Fresh footprints lead from the front door, bend in the direction of the mountain. Shivering, I stall. My feet start to follow my sister's trail, then turn the other way, toward downtown Brale and the bus that will carry me back to the cabin on the lake.

The fire in my stove has gone out and the cabin is cold. Beyond my wall of windows, the small ferry still floats across a black hole yawning between white shores. Still pursues the endless back and forth. On the farther side, lights from scattered cabins peer down into liquid darkness, seek the contents of the depths. Steam rises through falling snow, from the lake, as someone down there sighs.

The receiver in my hand is warm. How many days have passed since my telephone has rung? Since my voice has spoken? My lips kissed? I glance around the cabin. After four months, it still looks unknown. There's no television or music system. No framed photographs or sleek machines or glossy magazines. Only a few pieces of shabby furniture left behind by previous tenants. I don't hold a job or own a car. My clothes are washed in the sink, hung to dry on a string above the stove. Taking what I need for warmth, I steal wood from distant neighbours. There's no money to buy a cord of larch for the stove or curtains for the windows. I am exposed in this cabin hugged from behind by brush and cottonwoods and ponderosa pine but, in front, perched boldly upon the shore. Anyone driving on or off the ferry can see inside. "He's different," locals have begun to mutter.

How and why have I ended up in this flimsy structure, this unlikely location? I sense I'm undergoing someone else's experience. My own existence has ended; this is afterlife, though the empty shell of self still sings. In some indeterminate season, the source of my ghost wanders the clearing above Lovers' Lane. Hand-in-hand with my uncle, he roams among berries and thistles and weeds, up where the cold wind blows.

I dial Lily's number. A measured sound fills my ear. He was raped and killed and left on a mountain. Searching the slope for pussy willows the following spring, I once found myself by accident in that narrow gully. Not even a pair of running shoes remained there after the April thaw. "You lied. He doesn't play on Shaver's Bench. Where did he go?" I asked Lily, who had turned more silent that season. Inside a locked white valise, she was already storing razor blades and pills with other secret things. My sister didn't answer me or turn her face toward my question, as if it had failed to reach her.

Is it possible? In a small town, children are apt to hear disturbing news that adults might try to keep secret. The sexual murder of a boy would have filled the *Brale Daily Times*. The town would have bristled with panic, shuddered from fear. Doors would have been locked at night. The park and other places where children play would have turned deserted after dark. Uniformed men would have combed the mountain and dragged the river until they found a body or gave up looking. They would have gone from house to house with questions. They would have had no reason to look in the closet of a girl on Aster Drive. No cause to notice the white valise at the back, no motive to discover a green sock inside.

A sound like fingernails scrapes the window at the back of the cabin. Or it's just a branch. I've been here too long. It's time to leave. I can no longer share the cold with you. Donald. Billy. Whatever you call yourself. My shell of self must seek a warmer climate in order to keep singing.

Snow shakes steadily through the dark; the cabin roof groans beneath its weight. A buzzing in my ear swells in volume as it persists. I glance at my watch. Is it too late, Lily? Ringing violates the house on Aster Drive. It won't stop until I put the receiver to rest or my sister disconnects the cord. I never told, Lily. I never asked who, I never asked why.

Phantasmagoria

THEY SAY THAT YOU WERE JUST A DREAM, BUT NOW THE NIGHT IS OVER. At chill dawn I waken once more in the cabin on the lake, with pines pressed behind and the meadow farther back. There is the shape of your head indented upon the pillow, the scent of your last cigarette stale in the air. Night turned traitor, inhaled, and held its breath while you stole away, while I slept unaware.

If I believed them, we never scattered yellow leaves on the road to Redfish Creek or rowed the boat to Sunshine Bay to drink wine upon the midnight cliff. I search drawers and corners and beneath the bed for proof of your presence. Where are your shirts that furled within the closet, the razor rusting beside the sink? All evidence has been immaculately removed (by you?), and now with insistent voices empty space demands to be filled. You were here, I know—even as they repeat that imagination plays pranks and desire conjures phantoms that hover like mist above cold water before they fade. I remember that you never said you'd stay.

The long grass stiffens with frost and the kettle steams upon the stove and a boomerang of birds slides above the slate lake. Sometimes the damp morning earth betrays the spoor of prowling through the dark. Claws, hooves, paws.

So at night I turn the pages of my books and hear the ferry cross back and forth nearby, connecting this side to the other. Tomorrow I will see you standing on the farther shore, shrunken by distance into anyone at all, dissolved into blue and green and grey, reflected upon the still water. And I will glimpse you walking through the woods above the old man's farm.

You turn once to glance behind, then continue toward the clearing where we lay in tall weeds through summer afternoons languid with bees. Even now I know the shape and size and texture of the muscles that strode your legs from me. From a distance, well-intentioned neighbours arrive at noon to say that I will soon forget, or will dream a new lover in the night.

Each week darkness arrives earlier, and the snow-line lowers. A descending lake exposes small stones that were concealed by water before. Already it is winter and summer people have retreated into town. Cabins are locked tight; they twitch with ghosts. We listen for the last train to whistle above the water; we split enough wood to warm us from November until March. There is coffee in the morning, a candle for the night. The refrigerator buzzes. Mice rattle between the walls.

Perhaps your voice draws me out this afternoon, and I find myself on the point beyond the wooden bridge. I realize I've been here before. I know this landscape that you are coming back to breathe with me. In the meantime, another Kokanee wind sweeps down the valley, and my warm breath puffs above Lovers' Lane. Bears curl in safe, dark caves, and deer descend the mountains in search of food beneath the snow.

Marie

DURING THE DAY, HE HAD HIS BUDDY, OLD JACK D, WHILE MARIE GOT by on the hard food he put down for the cats. He didn't know if she fell or what. Comes in from the other room, finds her licking the floor on hands and knees. She seemed to like it down there, Marie. At dark, they attempt to chew off foil plates while first frost creeps past the county line. Not many souls out this way: another trailer across the field, smoke in the sky above the stumps. He made her feed herself supper; she could do it if she tried. Her noise starts, her left arm floating stiff in the air. You had to knock it down. The spoon hits the floor, scares the cats out into the cold. They stayed inside, Marie and him. TV voices ricochet between the pasteboard walls, echoes carry him way back. Marie by the grill, behind the smoke; him at the blurred counter. That's how it began. Ammonia ascending from bent spoons, eggs twitching in café grease. Praise the Lord, and praise the holy hunchback. His heart jumped, she flipped it over, squinted at the edges curling crisp and black. Seeing what was there, if it was any good. You never know what will happen. Just ask Old Jack D; maybe he holds all the answers, deciphers static scratched from radios as years slouch by. Taking the truck to town alone, having to tie her to the trailer door to keep her safe. Having to avert eyes from the rearview mirror. How she looks in clothes she fights him not to change, grey eyes still fierce sometimes. It's for her own good, sure. A knot left over from fishing trips up in the Suquamish, loons crying to the lake. Once he rattled back to a tilted porch, hollow bottles, no Marie. She'd left him before, when she could. Tried more than once to stay away across the hills. Another awkward woman off-balance awhile in another small town. Now, at the same time, she's here and she's gone. Marie, he called. Where are you? The name steamed the air, smoked inside his heart. For forty years he'd liked to call her, even when there was no need. Marie, my own Marie. Something stirs the brush past the next clearing. He sees her barefoot in the stems and weeds, the rope trailing from one wrist. Time to cut her hair, to put plastic on the windows, to find a winter coat for the stoic scarecrow. He could do it if he tried. Marie, he keeps calling while she snaps November twigs brittle as old bones. This time her face would turn and know him. Next time, another time. Some magic time. Come on, Marie. She starts that noise, loons at lakes. The ammonia circle swells. Back home, it's time Old Jack D grinned him to sleep. Marie curls on the kitchen floor, a purring corner.

Part Five

THE LABORATORY OF LOVE

Hay quien muere de amor y no lo sabe.

—Antonio Gala

Rorschach IV: Mutilation

FLIES GROW DROWSY AND DRUNK IN TANZANIAN SUN, BUMBLE AGAINST the mesh-screened window, burst with the promise of blood. Beside the sill, a small boy kneels on the floor of red tiles polished once a week by the silent houseboy; a scent of wax lingers like an eternal reprimand in the air. With a pin pinched between thumb and finger, the child contemplates the flies, discerns which is the fattest or biggest or most lazy. His left hand holds the chosen one in place and his right hand guides the pin into its body. Time holds breath while the insect's thin hard encasing is penetrated, exhales in relief as a silver sliver eases into softness. The wings of the fly beat and buzz as red drools onto the window ledge, glues the body there. With one finger, the boy paints lines and shapes upon his blankly anonymous arm. He can draw numbers, letters of the alphabet, more elusive symbols. Recently, he has learned to spell his name.

The ants are always very quick. Before the blood can dry, they march toward the tantalizing aroma of an easy prey. Tiny, efficient jaws nibble the helpless fly; tear away choice morsels, tender meat. Some ants are over-excited by the bounty, can't decide whether to eat on the spot or take food to a safer place to savour. Insane with greed, deluded by hunger, they pile more plunder on their backs than they can carry. The boy intently watches the scene he has created, scatters objectionably voracious ants away. Only once do his eyes look out the window. He is immediately overwhelmed by the sight of a world too much larger than the immediate kingdom under his control. At the edge of the yard, beside the frangipani, the houseboy and gardener each hold one end of a thick, long snake. Swahili twists and tangles across the air; like a branding iron, sun strikes flat and hard. The snake drops; the gardener's machete slices; the boy blinks. He can't remember the place they say is his real home, on the other side of the world, where a mother hisses and coils in a cold, white room.

He decides to save this fly, for no reason except that the choice lies within his power. He withdraws the pin, nudges the insect away. Surprisingly, it appears little worse for the impaling, barely more dazed than before. The other flies seem unalarmed by what has occurred nearby; disaster is always far away, deceptively drone sun and heat and dust. Perhaps the boy will sever the head of the next fly with one quick slice of pin. Will tear off only the wings, only the legs.

His bare knees have grown stiff and sore against the hard tiles. Shifting, he intuits a presence behind him. He turns to encounter the houseboy's stare. Black eyes floating in pools of white; dark skin stretched tight across high cheekbones of a face as void of expression now as when the boy's father whimpers in the back bedroom after dark. Without a word, on soundless soles, the houseboy turns out into the yard. There he will burn garbage in the barrel, surround the house with smoke, encircle it with scattered ash to keep death and demons away.

The boy reverts his eyes to the window ledge. He is suddenly sick of greedy ants, bored with flies that are fat and foolish and easy to kill. He looks out the window again, down the hill that slopes toward the west. At the end of the dry season, red dirt has been baked hard and cracked by heat. A secret earthquake might have broken the surface of the earth. From the mission above, where encroaching jungle looms and spreads, the bell tells pink priests it's time to chant feeble prayers, to fumble through wishful sacraments.

There is no telephone in the apartment the boy occupies ten years later, when he learns the truth at seventeen. Mail declines to arrive; a knock refuses to sound; other residents of the building remain unseen and unheard. The days are silent; nights equally still. Several times a week, it is necessary to go out into the cold to buy food, to attend a nearby university. In classrooms his face is without expression. He stares at the instructor as if trying to read lips. The pages of his notebook remain blank, white, pure. They say he's supposed to understand the words marching into his ears; they say this country is where he belongs. Such concepts are sliced in two as soon as they are spoken. Alone in the apartment, he forces sound through his throat to ensure his voice still works. Noise swells the space. Perhaps it is Swahili, perhaps some secret language. At night, cars glide along the street below, crawl their headlights like a phosphorescent snake across the wall. The boy prefers the rooms dark, when just a circle of red glows upon the stove. Rest the blade against the element, bend to feel burning heat. When the metal is ready, press it against skin. A subtle scent rises from one arm. The knife must be reheated several times to remain effective during repeated applications. Later, when a light has been switched on and the room jumps out from blackness, the boy will study a pattern of marks on his arms, as if trying to interpret hieroglyphics or to read a muddy map. The design seems to possess almost-remembered meaning; from beneath the skin of surrounding silence slivers a whisper that is faintly familiar, nearly understood. Years later, the marks will have faded into small pale scars. When the skin that bears them tans, they are almost invisible.

At evening, in one of a cluster of white houses on an Andalucían hill, a young man lights the kind of candles old women dressed in black burn beneath miniatures of the Holy Virgin or the Saviour. A skin of red plastic encases wax; translucent tubes offer a roseate glow. A trio of flames barely waver in air drifting inland from the Mediterranean, carrying the scent of spice all the way from Africa.

On his narrow bed, the young man lies suspended by the voices of the family living below. After three months, they have given up inviting him downstairs to sit with them around the heater on chilly evenings; the kindly señora has stopped asking why he never goes out, whether he is sick, if anything is wrong. Two fingers of his left hand pinch a burning cigarette; continually, unconsciously, the other hand explores the flesh of his face. From this prone position, it is possible to look through the window, across the terrace, toward the *faro* of the next town along the coast. Its light sweeps a circle, performs a ceaseless search through darkness. Gaze at the orbiting beam, as if it will extinguish without attention; glance away only to strike another match. It hisses like a snake at the cold, white room. After twelve, when his last cigarette of the night has been stubbed out, Spanish still carries from the street below. Although this is a language the listener can understood as well as any other, a lifetime spent in scattered landscapes have taught him how to flick a mental switch and transform immediate idiom into mere sound. Now three candles burn vigil through the night; now three pink planets float in a dark room as its inhabitant drifts into dreams of fireflies leading the way through jungle on the Ngondo hills, flickering a path through another thick Morogoro night. At morning, it is time to look into the truthful mirror at a forehead marked by a dozen small wounds inflicted by fingers in search of something hidden, something concealed. The scent of wax hangs heavily; the injured forehead creases with puzzlement. Three candles still burn. Three candles are carefully blown out.

On the terrace, the light is very clear. Mountains to one side and sea to the other are sharply focused. January sun feels almost hot. The young man leans back in a chair, tilts his face toward the sky, closes his eyes. When he opens them an hour later, his vision is darkened until light pricks painfully back into the retinas. It is time to look again into the mirror. The marks on his forehead resemble tattoos of some primitive tribe. Already they are vanishing into an expanse of darkened skin. In a few days or a week, their last traces will be gone, and the mirror will reflect no information regarding name or age or place of birth.

The Beauty Secrets of a Belly Dancer

"DON'T ASK ME ABOUT LOVE," WARNS THE BELLY DANCER, THOUGH SHE'S a survivor of as many affairs as there are grains of sand upon the Gobi, when I mourn the latest lover who's left. "I still don't know the first thing about the subject." At three a.m., she returns from a corner tapas bar in my Sevilla neighbourhood, where a wealthy American has bought her drinks. "Older," Reyna describes the man without enthusiasm, sautéing garlic in olive oil. (Garlic is good for the scalp and relieves menstrual discomfort.) "The guy's taking me to the bullfights. He has season tickets for the shade. We'll watch Curro Romero try to do his thing." Reyna kicks off her heels, wriggles out of her tight red skirt, sighs into a sheer Egyptian robe that floats and flutters around her thinness. (In dressing rooms for cattle-call auditions, she can change beneath the garment to guard her secrets from other dancers' knowing eyes.) Reyna lights candles and incense, puts on a salsa CD, settles down to eat garlic over bread in my living room, where she sleeps during the annual visits she makes from New York. From my bed in the curtained alcove, I hear Luis Enrique sing the same song over and over. *San Juan sin ti*, he laments endlessly above a throbbing beat. I know my houseguest is rocking rapidly back and forth in her chair, like a camel's passenger who bobs for hours on a humped back, dazed by hallucinogenic heat, surrounded always by the same parched expanse of sand, apparently not moving at all. *Cuerpo a cuerpo, de sexo a sexo*, sings the lonely boy too far from Puerto Rico, needing a body he can hold onto like it's home. Reyna expertly rolls high-grade grass that she smuggled through Spanish customs, deeply inhales something more essential than oxygen. (She has long ceased trying to weigh the narcotic relief gained against the physical damage done: ice cubes beneath her eyes will be the only answer on yet another morning after.) Sweet smoke insinuates out into the Sevilla night; travels toward the south, the east.

Just before I fall sleep, the belly dancer changes the CD. Now Middle Eastern music jangles my neighbours' dreams. Reyna has switched into one of her working costumes, perhaps the silver halter with gold lamé harem pants beneath a bared midriff. While I dream her into a tent beside the mirage of an oasis, she kneels on hard tiles in the next room, hands resting on the floor before her for support. Her neck begins to pivot in frenzied circles, long black hair whips the air, candle flames shudder and shake. The head dance, this one's called. ("Let's give them a little head," she jokes to her partner before they slink onto a Manhattan stage for their final set.) Somewhere in the distant desert, jarred by tambourines and drums, camels lift their necks from a pool of precious water; it drips like gems through heat that sucks the moisture from air, from skin. The dancer's hair lashes more wildly at all the men who have failed to take her from this place: she would like to stripe their backs with blood. The slowing beat jerks the dancer from side to side. Although unable to escape the percussive blows, she smiles slyly beneath her veil, full of secret power. Jasmine and myrrh smudge the shadows; coils of controlled muscle twist beneath skin still smooth and soft. The men with money in her mind gaze intently, not missing a move. As flutes shrill toward a finale, the dancer's face falls against the floor. She freezes into a posture of submission at the feet of her invisible audience, waits for bejewelled hands to clap her out of sight. (Always save your best moves for the end; leave them wanting more than you'd ever consider giving.)

Long after I'm far away in sleep, half-way to the home that waking never lets me reach, Reyna cleans makeup from her face, washes away the black kohl around her eyes. (In the end, blinding kohl saves dancers from witnessing the disappearance of their beauty and the growing indifference of lovers, the melting of water into only mirage.) Sallow skin emerges in the unkind bathroom light. Reyna's head pounds after the unwitnessed exhibition she's just completed. When the show is over, dancers don't dare attempt escape across the sand: sun would singe their skin until it was without worth, or the moon would drive them mad. There's no easy end to the desert; another dune rises beyond every one that's climbed. (There is no simple way back there, either; that will be a further lesson learned too late.) Sighing, Reyna heats olive oil in a teaspoon over the stove's gas flame, applies thick warm liquid to lines of fixed smiles around her eyes, her mouth. Gorgeous young girls are always elbowing their way onto Gotham stages; but can they work a rough room, transfix an inattentive audience, sidle smilingly through club owners' tricks and traps? The belly dancer pins up the hair she will never blow dry, and washes only with a special shampoo found in a single East Village store. ("Imagine if I lost my hair," she laughs on April afternoons when dark glasses conceal her eyes, though my living room is always dim. She fondly strokes the thick braid that's slung over her shoulder like a favourite pet snake. "A bald belly dancer. Wigs never work. How would I pay the rent?") In my dreams, members of a harem wait restlessly for fresh summons of clapped hands, for warm wet lips pressed upon a veiled mouth. They glance mistrustfully at each other and wonder who'll be chosen this time to be bobbed into oblivion on the sea of love: the dance always leaves you needing arms that can hold you here if they can't take you there. Reyna abandons the mirror, leaves her image to peer myopically from that window in the wall. Only opium permits us peace until the next performance—I am, in my fashion, a dancer too—some slumber in spiced shade. Beyond these canvas walls, no skyscrapers rise to break flat terrain or to interrupt empty vistas. Reyna, once we could see far through burning air, deep into our common destiny. Did heat refract the reality wavering before us into illusion? Twist the truth that one day we must add to the dust of all the dancers who believed beauty could lure a lover strong enough to carry them back to where they belong? Finally Reyna breathes drugged, disturbed sleep; I call out my departed lover's name; garbage trucks groan through the dawn.

Why doesn't Reyna save the ten-dollar tips tucked into her shiny costumes for vacations in Cairo or Beirut, rather than always here in Spain? I wonder but don't ask, out of respect for secrets as fragile as my own and from knowledge that explanations for apparent incongruity are hidden for a reason. ("How did you end up here?" they incessantly want to know. "Why don't you go there?") After five Aprils spent in Sevilla, Reyna's Spanish vocabulary remains restricted to words for dishes, drinks, and sexual positions. As long as she stays mute, she passes as a striking señorita, thanks to Mexican blood on one side of her family. Her grandfather was a professional gambler who robbed his bride from a Guadalajara convent and carried her north to California. The old woman mutters broken-English prayers in San Francisco, and sends rosaries and crucifixes to a granddaughter gone astray. "Reina?" they ask on these streets, confused by spelling and phonetics, not believing the name hasn't been assumed for the stage, one more showgirl aspiring to royalty. "Queen of what?" they wonder.

"When I was little, I wanted to be a nun," confesses the belly dancer over a salsa pulse, "but I realized that wasn't my true calling." In the weak, late-afternoon light, before candles can be lit, she appears tired and pale and almost old until her hips begin to sway. Then her fingers entwine in an intricate arrangement to produce a snapping as loud as a pistol. (This secret took her seven years to master; others remain to be discovered.) Arabs love the noise, but my upstairs neighbours bang their floor in irritation. "Some people wouldn't know a free show if they heard one." The belly dancer rolls eyes heavenward, cracking the air on the beat. Copper bracelets clink, scarves swim through space. "Customers have to pay a lot for this," she says, then abruptly separates her hands to reach for the bottle of rough red wine. (Never drink before five, always swallow a glass of water for each one of less pure liquid.) We make them pay and pay and pay: they can never give us enough; they always leave us wanting more. ("Just once more," I beg into the telephone, before he clicks a disconnection.) For consolation, Reyna and I will hire a carriage with bright yellow wheels to roll us through the park at dawn. While the *gitano* driver slaps reins against the horse's back, we lap champagne and laugh along the leafy avenues, hear harness bells and hooves announce our approach as we draw nearer to the end of what we've chosen to be: entertainers who ignore that the tent has been emptied and taken down, leaving no trace of spectacle behind, abandoning us here in Western twilight to insist that once we were not only ghosts in the Kalaharis of your mind.

"There's plenty where he came from," the belly dancer reminds me again. She studies my skin. Radiant afternoons on the roof have turned me dark as an Arab boy. "Sun is the worst thing for you," she chides, spreading the whipped white of an egg across my face. The mask hardens; if I smile, it will crack. (Don't show them how you feel, let them read their own emotion in your eyes.) The Queen of What rushes to get ready for a date that was scheduled to start two hours ago. (Never show up on time unless cold cash is involved; anticipation will increase both their eagerness and your beauty.) Married men and impotent cab drivers and unemployed waiters come and go, while surely somewhere sheiks in billowing white robes race Arabians across the sand, dark eyes unsmiling above dunes of cheekbones, every one of them an elusive Valentino in the moonlight. In ten days, Reyna must squeeze back into two rooms in the least lucky letter of Alphabet City, negotiate a crack-heads' neighbourhood anew, wait once more for the agency's orders to appear exotic for fifty dollars at another bachelor party or bar mitzvah. (A good man also expects her return; she carefully conceals fleeting infidelities from him: he has his uses, she may need to resign herself to his sober steadiness in the end.) "Go out and find another," my friend advises over her shoulder, clattering to the door. "Get it while you can." Tonight I stay at home with my sentences instead: seduced by their punctuated rhythms, how they can sweep me breathlessly toward The End. Once upon a time, Scheherazade told tales to divert the master of her fate and to forestall her certain doom: this was her way of dancing; this is also mine. Outside, a sudden sirocco stirs the palms along the boulevard, then dies to make them droop once more. I touch my leathering skin. It will be sufficiently tough by the time mocking laughter swells around me like a dense sandstorm of sound through which I'll stumble until enough grit has been swallowed to end my hunger for good. Thinly sliced cucumber placed on the face eases aridity. Beyond this secret lies another secret, just as above Saharan stars exist more stars, though we can't see them. We must hang onto the belief that they are there, as we must keep searching for the lost oasis: this is our story, Scheherazade. Once upon a time, it always starts. You know the ending, but please don't reveal it yet. There's time for several more dances still.

"Semen's the only moisturizer that really works," the belly dancer remarks idly to her bullfight date, lifting his hand from her thigh, inspecting her face in a compact mirror. "It's the protein or something." In the ring, Curro Romero illustrates just how far he is past his prime. Each year his costumes become flashier, his moves with the cape less elegant. Reyna remains in her shaded seat while the rest of the *corrida* audience rises to turn its back against Romero's bungling of another bull. The belly dancer blows the matador a kiss. He bows low before her, then tosses her an unearned ear that causes the crowd to roar louder disapproval. Afterward, Reyna's wealthy American date mistakenly believes he's purchased something beside seafood and wine for five thousand *pesetas*. "I'm going to make myself beautiful," she evades, heading toward the restaurant's Señoras to slip out a rear exit. "My kisses aren't for sale," she proclaims back home, undulating anxiously before my eyes. "Feel this," she says, placing my hand on her belly. Something inside hits my palm; a secret child bangs the wall of imprisoning flesh. Long ago, Reyna brutally rid herself of who she used to be. She left a fetus with her face in miniature floating by the foggy shores of San Francisco and a decade later was reborn as an exotic dancer who crowned herself Queen of Anything At All. (In illegal clinics in this country, embryos aren't wasted; they become the chief ingredient of expensive oils, lotions, creams.) I too have shed former selves as easily as snakes squirm from skin, freeing myself to coil around cacti, beneath flat stones. Reyna, we could spin from this city on the early morning bus, cross the Strait of Gibraltar beneath birds and breeze, be back on the desert before shadow has stretched into darkness on the sand. When were we last there?

In what lifetime long ago? It becomes more difficult to remember with every night we dance for sad fugitives of some Foreign Legion of the heart. In a week you will leave here for your tenement across the sea, and we will not reunite to share a sixth Sevilla spring. It's clear that one of us doesn't make the other stronger. Our journeys back to where we started must be undertaken separately or not at all. Perhaps it's already too late to return. Perhaps we have forgotten how to exist on dried entrails of armadillo.

"If I get another, we can make a Mickey Mouse hat," suggests the belly dancer, jaunty once more, holding up her trophy. Blood from the ear has dried brown on her skirt. Reyna dabs at the stain while the unanswered telephone is forced to ring by one of the weak men who wish her or me to sway the hot, still night. Already the severed ear has begun to fill the room with pungent scent; we'll need no further incense this evening. On the other side of the city, Curro Romero practices imperfect pirouettes before an accusing mirror. He stumbles, shrugs, reaches for the bottle. He accepts that the game is over. (His hotel room is otherwise empty; there is no one to remind him that alcohol as well as salt will bloat.) I paint the belly dancer's fingernails—one red, the next black. She is twenty-five or forty-five or somewhere in between; anyway, the end of her career is also near. The night will be shockingly cold, though the day was much too hot: you're never prepared for the desert's swift, extreme changes of temperature, no matter how many of them you survive. Like bullfighters, belly dancers don't usually have bank accounts, social security numbers, or pension plans to soothe the future; it's difficult to save for a rainy day when you have been raised to believe that no precipitation would ever fall upon a sere landscape around you. I blow on Reyna's long, thin hands until I'm breathlessly unable to call out the name of the lover who left no footprints in the shifting sand. *San Juan sin ti*, grieves Luis Enrique one more time, exiled always from his island. In the Andalucian air beyond the window, flutters and wails of Moorish music evoke camel caravans and somber Saharan sunsets and bands of thirsty Bedouins. "Please don't ask me anything about love," repeats the belly dancer, before we retire to our separate pillows. We lie awake in the narcotic night and hope for a breath of breeze to stir the air, caress our crumbling skin, touch our kohl-blinded eyes with one more kiss we cannot see.

The Tattoo Artist

It was not easy to find the tattoo artist, though his skill was renowned throughout our town and far beyond. Away from the boulevards and cafés, away from lights and crowds, he lived among the narrow, twisting alleys behind the *quartier portugais*. These were lit only by weak lamps attached sparingly to the cold stone walls, and rats roamed freely after dark within the gutters and the waste. Few people passed over the rough cobblestones then; occupants were silent, if not sleeping behind closed doors to either side; the doors were unnumbered as the alleys were not named. Except for a cat's sudden scream, or the squeak of a bat, no sounds but the footsteps and heartbeat of a solitary searcher would echo against stone. It was possible to find the tattoo artist only on a starless night, when he did not prick coloured constellations into the black skin of the sky.

A sign did not hang helpfully upon the artist's door; nor did the door stand open in invitation. Within the labyrinth, the tattoo artist's whereabouts were as elusively unfixed as those of a fugitive, though it was purported that his room was always a bare, cement space illuminated by one candle, half-burned, whose light transformed his ancient dyes and needles into substances sheened with gold. If you were able to discover the secret way to the tattoo artist, the path of your life would be changed forever, it was averred in the tone of absolute certainty only ignorance can evoke: nothing and everything was known about this man whom the mute would describe in clear, precise detail if they could speak. Perhaps he strolled through the *souk*, unidentified though not disguised, to hear the stories told about him—all contradictory, all unproven—when we wearied of discussing the sixty lessons of the Koran or the reason for changing tides.

Each of us grew up with a mother's warning that, if we were not careful, the tattoo artist would etch hideous, permanent pictures into our sleeping skin. Later we learned that perhaps his designs could attract the ideal lover who does not waver, who never strays. Some said the artist substituted poison for ink when sought out by an evil man, and some suggested that in certain worthy cases his handiwork could cure sickness and even extend life. There were those, too, who claimed that his instruments were the tools of Allah, and his images the Prophet's revelation. It was agreed that one needed to seek the tattoo artist at the correct time of life: overly tender skin would fester, blister, and scar beneath his needles, while tough and weathered flesh would break them. The tattoo artist was a Jew from Essaouira, a *marabout* from Tarfaya, a Berber murderer or thief. Perhaps he was a distant cousin on your mother's side, the leper disintegrating in front of the Cinéma Le Paris, that pilgrim glimpsed yesterday on the road to Azemmour. Stories shifted like Sahara sand blowing through the *derbs*, and they changed shape and form from one day to the next, according to the wind's whims. I did not puzzle at never seeing an example of the tattoo artist's work during my yearning youth: by the time I grew into a man, I had come to believe his design would remain invisible upon a subject until that being stretched his soul into a canvas tight and strong and broad enough to display the beauty that it held.

On the starless night I finally felt compelled to find the tattoo artist, I had to ask infrequent strangers hurrying through the alleys for directions. Often they wouldn't pause to answer or muttered brusquely that they didn't know; many spoke a dialect I hadn't heard and could not understand, as if they came from the other side of the Atlas Mountains, or far beyond the Rif. If I knocked on a door to ask my way, those inside remained silent or warned me off with a shout. I remembered how it was said that numerous people had vanished in the course of the search I was undertaking. Whenever a restless, dissatisfied soul disappeared from our town, the assumption would be that he had passed through the gates of the *quartier portugais* and had failed to emerge. Some said these narrow alleys, dark even during day, teemed with lost spirits who on each starless night reached out with hungry bones of fingers for anyone foolish enough to seek the tattoo artist they had not found. This was home, it was rumoured, to countless beings fallen into disappointment and despair, and that they sought consolation in narcotic and carnal pleasures was evidenced in the sweet smoke and moans rising into the blue sky above our sensible town. "See what happens," mothers told their discontented children, hoping one day these offspring would grow satisfied with the prospect of a harmless tattoo of the kind offered every day at a reasonable price in the market; for example, a green cross of Islam, or a yellow star of hope.

I wandered until north and south became indistinct and time and distance lost proportion, before finding someone who would help. She looked at me with suspicious eyes under the lamp where we met and appeared undecided whether to speak or not. Slowly a knowing smile twisted her face, which was scarred and disfigured beneath heavy powder. "The next crossing," she said finally, placing ironic emphasis on each word. "The third door to the left." She turned and walked swiftly away, drawing a scarf more closely around her head, leaving behind light, mocking laughter.

The tattoo artist did not answer my knock; but when I pushed the door, it opened. In a room off the entrance, he sat on a wooden bench between the small table holding his instruments and colours and the chair in which his clients sat when they were not required to lay on the floor or stand erect to receive his mark. He looked in my direction as I entered but did not rise to greet me. The old man wore a dark robe, with a hood concealing his hair—whether black or white or vanished—and partly curtaining his eyes. The garment made it difficult to determine his body's size or shape. His fingers were long and thin and naked of rings. No tattoos could be seen on the skin uncovered by the robe. Appearing absorbed in thought, scarcely conscious of my presence, the tattoo artist did not speak.

I sat in the chair and explained I wanted a tattoo unlike any other in the world. Commonplace tattoos—a lover's name or initials; an eagle, lion or snake—did not interest me, less the heart, the arrow, the bolt of lightning; nor did I wish for some rare symbol of obscure significance. I wanted a singular tattoo that would reveal my unique essence. If I couldn't describe it, or refer to it by name, this was because my desired design existed only in the tattoo artist's imagination as yet. With absolute certainty, I knew that the mark should be imprinted upon my heart.

The tattoo artist listened, then left the room by a door to the rear. He returned and set a tray holding a silver teapot and three glasses on the floor. After a moment, he poured pale tea into two of the glasses. Steam began to rise. Suddenly I wanted to tell the tattoo artist many things about myself: where I had come from, what I had seen and done, whom I had loved. I needed him to know how long I had anticipated this moment, and how difficult it had been to find him, and that any doubt I had felt about receiving his mark was gone. He should hear me and see me, I believed, in order to know exactly what to place on my skin; but the artist only watched the rising steam with seeming disinterest in the material before him, and I could not interrupt his silence. He shifted the candle slightly, then studied the shadow it cast on the wall. He sighed. Removing a small square of folded paper from his robe, he opened it above one glass and spilled white powder into the tea. He handed me the glass. I drank the hot liquid quickly, then loosened my shirt and lay on my back. The cement below me warmed as I fell asleep.

It was cold when I awoke. The candle still burned halfway down. The tray that held the teapot still rested on the floor. One glass was empty, one glass was full, the third was gone. There was a burning sensation at my heart. I bent my neck and saw my tattoo. At once I knew I had never seen such a shape before. It was unique. I didn't know the significance of the symbol; it called nothing definite to my mind, yet seemed at once to suit me and to describe me. Was there a suggestion of a cresting wave, the hint of a half-closed eye, an allusion to an outstretched wing? Refastening my shirt, I watched the tattoo artist wipe his needles of dye with a wet cloth. He replaced them exactly in their former position on the table. He stared at his instruments with an expression that contained amazement or horror or pleasure, or a mixture of those three emotions. He appeared unable to hear my thanks or my offer of payment. I left his room.

For several years, I was pleased with my tattoo, though the pricked skin continued to burn long after it healed, in a way that wouldn't allow me to forget its presence. When exposed, it caused astonishment and envy, and those with apparently ordinary tattoos sought my companionship and approval. My mark became famous in the town and occupied a central place in conversation. On the corners, old men argued endlessly over its meaning, and small children tried to trace its outline with sticks in the shore's sand. Seers used the shape to predict the future. Holy men proclaimed it evidence of Allah's touch. In the dark, lovers pressed lips against the brilliant colour; tried to lick off the resistant ink, travelled its complex contours with their tongues. It became fashionable, for one season, for other young men to have my design copied onto their skin by the tattoo artists in the market. Such imitations, however skilled, proved inexact and appeared grotesque. During this time, I felt that even with my shirt buttoned to my neck, passersby could see through the fabric and spy the colours stained upon my heart.

Later, though unchanged, my tattoo seemed to evoke a different response—distrust or pity or fear. People fell silent as I approached down the street, and hands were placed over children's eyes. No longer did lovers line up to lie with me on the sand; perhaps they realized their kisses would not erase my mark, that it must always fail to slake their thirst, that it could never be swallowed to ease an aching hunger. Now I was lonely and separated from others by what I once hoped would permit them to see me clearly and to know me intimately. As if it were obscene, I tried to keep my tattoo hidden by wearing a heavy burnoose during the hottest season. "I hope you got what you wanted," said my mother, as another wedding procession wound past our door. Now ashamed of my mark, I wished it would fade or wash away, or alter into an unremarkable design. At night, dreams of an unbranded existence afforded me brief release; waking at morning brought bitter disappointment. When I offered the tattoo artists in the market large sums to remove my mark, their refusals were nervous but adamant, and I was driven to prowl the dark alleys behind the *quartier portugais* once more. Hoping its creator could alter or eliminate my unwanted design, I searched for him on many starless nights, yet in those narrow passages encountered only youths with blank, unmarked skin. "Go home," I told them. "Before it's too late."

My tattoo seared more sharply one day, as if freshly pricked onto my skin. The pain would not permit me to sleep or dream or pray. At this time, I began to wonder about the tattoo artist, seeking to reconstruct every detail of my experience with him, and to find in memory a clue to the meaning of my mark, or a way of living with it. I mused upon the possible landscape of the artist's past and the likely geography of his present. What were his intentions when the canvas of my skin had faced him? Why had he used his dyes and needles on me in one way and not another? This was the period when I hoped to understand the implications of my mark by comprehending the artist who placed it there, as we turn our eyes toward the heavens to contemplate the creator who fashions us here below.

In this way, my long journey began. I roamed first our town and then nearby ones in search of somebody with the same tattoo as mine. I had faith that at least one other man wore the brilliant shape that hovered over my heart; even accidentally, it must have been drawn more than once. It had to have a twin. As years went by, and my search met no success, I journeyed farther and farther, crossing mountains and valleys, deserts and plains, rivers and oceans and streams. In distant lands, I saw many things and met many people, but the man whose tattoo exactly mirrored mine did not materialize before my eyes. When it finally occurred, I still believed, our meeting would possess the symmetry and grace of a balanced equation: my mark vanishes beneath his gaze as his dissolves under mine, and we no longer each feel the same constant pain. "One glass was empty, one glass was full, the third was gone," I repeated as the road stretched far before me.

Although my end is growing near, I continue to roam from place to place in hope of discovering someone marked like me. The skin above my heart still burns; I haven't grown used to the ache. While some colours of the world have surely faded, and stars have dimmed like faith, my tattoo flames as brightly as ever. Now it is many years since I have been to the town of my birth, and I don't know if my family and friends still live. I don't know if the tattoo artist still practices his esoteric art within the dark alleys behind the *quartier portugais*. I don't know if he still pricks needles into flesh, staining it differently each time, leaving upon our hearts the unique designs from which we seek release.

Hieroglyphics 1: Only the Bird Knows the Wing

HIS TOUCH UPON MY SHOULDER WAKENS ME.

Finding the room empty except for myself, I innocently believe the slam of a neighbour's door has disturbed my dreams. On this virgin visit I am unequipped to understand how, in the instant it takes my eyes to open, he is able to steal away unwitnessed, his escape betrayed not even by a discreet closing of the door that leads to the courtyard common to each *piso* of the building or of the farther one that issues upon the street beyond. My senses have not learned to detect a blur of his warmth, just the slightest smudge of scent, lingering in chill air whose darkness is relieved only by the candle that always sits on the desk beside my pallet and that invariably illuminates my labour in the notebook there. Let it burn, urges my drowsy mind, not attempting to explain the resurrection of a flame surely extinguished before sleep, trying instead to determine the time by means of aural evidence. Heels do not tap over cobblestones in the street outside; the bar directly across its narrow width is silent; voices fail to float from San Eloy twenty farther steps away. I have been roused at night's deepest hour when, on the other side of this room's wall, in their ascetic beds, nuns clutch rosaries in unconscious, callous hands. When only whores and *maricones* of the barrio witness my vanished visitor slip through its twisting streets, perhaps to interrupt the dreams of any number of other souls before dawn.

The nearby pearl of light overcomes my unwillingness to rise, tugs me toward its wand of dripping wax.

Shivering, I lift my body from bed, shrug on clothes, move toward the desk.

Face the open notebook aglow with candlelight, confront his violation of it.

At first, I suppose that at some point in the night my somnolent self ascended to scrawl the substance of a dream. Yet the marks do not resemble an identifiable script, appearing to be neither Arabic nor Sanskrit nor characters of Oriental cast, less those of any Western language; rather than words, they approximate a combination of crudely sketched concrete nouns and, possibly, symbols of intangible concepts. Runes. More exactly, hieroglyphics. While failing to adhere to a straight line, either horizontal or vertical, they do not look to have been placed haphazardly. There is no indication that this is the feverish work of some dream-dazed being; no sense of an intruder's furtive, hasty effort. In both colour and shade, the carefully employed ink precisely matches that which is contained within my pen. I pick up the implement from its unassuming position beside the notebook. Try to detect the warmth of a hand's recent grip, fail to reach a definite conclusion.

What author other than me could be responsible for this coded composition? Is it the work of an invasive ghostwriter? The classified communication of some secret agent in whose covert operation I am unwittingly involved? I check the door, discover its bolt undrawn. Sliding the bar in place, I wonder if my apparent carelessness in regard to both unextinguished candle and unlocked door might have resulted from retiring preoccupied to bed. Did the evening's writing somehow disturb me? An aspect of the material was unusually upsetting? Instead of seeking to answer this question through referral to my most recently composed words, I study the puzzling page further. Certain stylistic flourishes of its script—a slant of line, the curve of a curl—almost look familiar; my mind is nudged by suspicion that it contains a deciphering key. I gaze at the scattered symbols until my focus unlocks. The hieroglyphics blur, shift, double upon themselves; then they seem to lift toward me, to assume a third dimension. For a moment, it seems possible to hold the substance of this unrequested communication in my hands; understand it by its texture, shape, weight. Then my vision corrects itself and the hieroglyphics possess a purely alien aspect again. I shiver not only from several centuries of the cold preserved within these stone walls and turn to the notebook's previous page, gain comfort from sight of line after straight line of clear words, sensible sentences, plain paragraphs. As quickly as it arrived, my sense of reassurance fades. Prose that seemed elusive and rich before sleep now strikes me as unsatisfying, blunt, bare.

Blow out the candle, return to bed. As if impatiently awaiting me, sleep quickly wraps its warmth around my cold self. Just before consciousness is quelled, the inscrutable page appears illuminated upon the darkness overhead, floats at a remove that permits me to believe its meaning is contained not within each elusive element but rather in the larger design they shape.

A variety of Rorschach.

A wing, I think, as feathered arms enfold me, sail me into darkness.

"Only the bird knows the wing," read your penultimate postcard, delivered from Delphi after that final flight from my arms.

During the days that follow, it is possible to dismiss the initial incident as no more than an isolated accident, some freakish phenomenon. That unrelieved, unrelenting solitude will occasionally play tricks upon the mind can only be expected. Tearing the perplexing page from my notebook, on the morning after it appears, I stuff it deep into the garbage pail. My pen resumes composing paragraph after precise paragraph. Is my handwriting now particularly neat? Do my words cling with especially strict obedience to each ruled line? Am I turning to the dictionary constantly to ensure that the most commonplace words exist beyond my mind? This work is a craft, like carpentry or masonry; nothing more or less. The result of my labour pays for these rooms, this electricity, that food. Hours away from the desk are never spent dwelling upon what is written there; my words have long seemed to lack any link to me; I would falter if asked to explain their substance, purpose, meaning. Such distance between my self and my work has not previously appeared to subtract from the latter's power.

I straighten the rooms and prepare simple meals and press my ear against the wall to hear the faint, muffled chant of prayers on its other side. The building's cleaning woman makes her weekly visit, bangs a bucket and slaps a mop over foyer, courtyard, stairs. Half of the dozen apartments facing onto the patio, both on this bottom floor and on the two above, are unoccupied; usually all hover in silence. Only infrequently does a couple visit the *piso* directly above mine, for several afternoon hours, with the obvious, express purpose of making loud love. The sound causes me to cringe. Has it been five or seven or ten years since I left all that behind? Since I began my endless, ineffective attempt to recreate from words the lover abducted by erasing air? To hazard even a rough calculation of that painful number is to flirt with danger; unremitting solitude can be survived only by avoiding certain sensitive subjects. This city has been chosen as my residence precisely because it is not mined with associations to a wounding past, not littered with trip wires that would detonate history's explosive bombs. That I have failed to become known by any figment of this new landscape is something to skip over as hastily as contemplation of my notebook's contents. If my voice often offers an extended monologue into empty air, I remind myself, this merely indicates a primal, natural need to exercise muscles of lips, tongue, throat.

Now each night I close my notebook immediately after putting down the pen. I check and recheck the door to ensure it has been bolted before bed. Sleep is entered with a degree of wariness, some suspense. Waking in the middle of several nights, I am relieved to find the room entirely dark, with not even a sliver of light intruding through tightly sealed shutters from the patio beyond. Sight of the undisturbed notebook, dawn after dawn, solidifies a sense of re-established safety. Perhaps one morning the candle on the desk looks shorter than when blown out the night before. It seems possible, on a subsequent day, that my empty pen had been half full of ink upon being set down before sleep. Yet as long as the notebook remains unviolated, I am able to disregard these signs as easily as I do my endlessly recurring dreams of love.

"Only the wing knows flight," your last postcard told me from Tangier, completing the riddle to which our experience would now forever be reduced.

Just when the first incident has almost been forgotten, a second occurs.

This time I waken with the clear sense of his touch upon my shoulder; it is an impression so definite that the mirror might conceivably reflect a handprint's singular shape and unique lines upon my skin. Insufficiently experienced to realize the futility of my action, I leap from bed, stumble naked through dimness, feel for the door. It has been left ajar tonight. The courtyard looms vacantly; other apartments are dark; silence seeps. As if from the bottom of a well, I look toward the square of exposed sky that spreads two storeys above. A quarter-moon is visible; its sickle scythes my mind, carves a forbidden shape upon my memory.

The crescent of your body against mine; your arched throat beneath my lips.

The notebook lies defiantly open on the desk. I squint at a fresh confusion of characters sketched upon a page. Are these hieroglyphics identical to those of the first incident? Do they replicate what I discarded? I slowly draw my face away from them, search for the shape of a wing to emerge from their mass, fail to discern any larger design. Flipping to my most recently written page, I discover it has been torn from the notebook. Now my previous day's effort ends prematurely, abortively, in mid-sentence. Although composed only hours earlier, the missing words are typically vague to me; a final unfinished phrase does not encourage what followed to swim into memory's murky pool. It is unlikely I can recreate those lost words again. When pursued tomorrow, the text may take a tack entirely different from my original intention. Assume some shattering shape; evoke unbearable emotion; lead to an unacceptable end.

I switch on lights and hunt for the missing page. Bare as a nun's cell, uncluttered by sentimental souvenirs or mementos of romance, my rooms afford scant potential for concealment. I search the same few possible places any number of times without success. Before turning off the lights,

I deliberate over the notebook for another moment. In what might hopefully be received as a gesture of appeasement, to discourage future theft of my words, I leave the page of hieroglyphics intact. His page, I think automatically, again. There is no reason to suspect that the intrusive writer must be male, except for the weight of historical record: every rape of my heart has been performed by a man.

Taken the first time by surprise, still a child, I naively believed he was struggling to penetrate my nave and apse.

Over the course of the following days, it becomes surprisingly difficult to proceed with my text. Surely the fact that each day's labour has always been undertaken with little awareness of, or reference to previously composed sentences should mitigate the damage incurred by a single missing page. Yet I find myself haunted by those several hundred stolen words—what did they say? what power did they possess?—to the point that my progress finds itself seriously impaired. It seems more and more likely that the page in question was taken not because it happened to be the last one written but because it contained my most valuable sentences, least replaceable thought. Long hours are wasted studying the fresh set of hieroglyphics from wistful hope that decoding them might not simply reincarnate my abducted material in its original form but, more than that, convey love's truth in a fashion less flinching and more evolved than my own abilities could achieve. Yet his signs and symbols insist upon growing increasingly confusing with extended study, despite almost seeming to plead for rather than resist my comprehension now. While previously able to concentrate upon the work at hand with such intensity that only one moment would seem to pass between sitting at the desk at morning and rising from it at evening, my attention currently becomes drawn, time and again, to the world beyond my rooms. Eventually, I am always listening for the street door to open, for his footsteps to cross the courtyard, for his voice to prick the skin of silence. Always waiting, in bed, for his hand to pluck my blanket's shroud, to cup my hidden heart.

You mumbled in sleep the foreign language of your dreams, offered your most subterranean secrets to my wakened ears, released fantasies of escape from our imprisoning passion out of their deep, dark cave.

My gesture of appeasement fails.

On the next occasion I am disturbed, candlelight reveals that he has absconded into the night with twenty pages of my text. Just as many sheets of hieroglyphics have been left in their place. At first, I am more concerned with what has been given to me than with what has been taken away. Having access to multiple examples of his symbols may aid in their deconstruction; perhaps analysis of significantly repeated combinations holds the key to deciphering a code. It swiftly becomes apparent, however, that each page contains hieroglyphics so unique from those of others that they might be the language of a distinct civilization, of some unrelated form of life. As my head grows heavy and dull from fruitless study, I become aware that the landscape of skin touched by his rousing hand throbs with steadily intensifying pain. Examination in the mirror reveals not a bruise but rather a handprint on my shoulder. When the mark refuses to wash off, however scrupulously scrubbed, I inspect it further. A wing, I dully think, covering the shape with an awkward bandage, as if it were an obscenity that required censoring beyond any afforded by a shirt.

The wounds you left refused to heal for years, insisted upon commemorating the damage inflicted by a thousand and one betrayals.

The twenty pages that have been ripped from the notebook are not contiguous, I discover; it is rather a case of three missing here, of four taken there. Resulting textual gaps are of a breadth that each remaining portion of prose might belong to a separate manuscript. My mind lacks the power to cross these dozen yawning chasms, to seam together the material on their distant sides. My work seems hopelessly mutilated, butchered far beyond the point of repair. Love, I can only grimace, as usual just able to recall my subject's most general gist; after all, my theme is always the same.

Instead of embarking upon an effort to recreate my text from scratch, I sketch without purpose upon a blank page. The idle activity is surprisingly satisfying, like soothing a troublesome itch. Meaningless lines gradually float a question into my mind. Can I be drawing his unseen image? Has my hand unwittingly traced his unglimpsed face?

All photographs of you have long been abandoned, lost, destroyed; the shape of your mouth and the slant of those grey eyes exist only in a black cavern located deep beneath the surface of memory, far beyond possibility of mental excavation.

I gaze at the doodled designs until realizing, with a shudder, that they bear a certain resemblance to his hieroglyphics.

The next time, I am prepared.

Immediately alert at his waking touch, in shoes and clothes left on for sleep, I spring from bed. Rush past the burning candle, scarcely glance at the notebook spread open beneath a flame shaken wildly by my swift passage. Tonight the door has been left further ajar behind his departing back, as if to encourage me to slip through its gap and attempt pursuit. Yet my rapid response goes unrewarded: the courtyard taunts with its vacancy; unfilled by his form, the street door gapes mockingly wide. Stepping from my building, I look in both directions. Too narrow to allow automobile access and only one block long, Calle Fernán Caballero is obviously deserted. He has already slipped up San Eloy to my right or stolen from view around the church at the street's other end. I turn uncertain eyes toward the cobblestones. They shine from the nightly effort of street cleaners who, after the general population has forsaken the streets for sleep, loose hoses and brooms upon the pavement and refresh the city for another soiling day. A single set of footprints, defined by being drier than the surrounding surface, urge me to follow their lead toward the left. I place one shoe upon a print, try to determine similarity in size. Bend down to learn from close inspection whether his sole is smooth or has a textured tread. Rise before arriving at an answer. There is no time to linger;

with every moment, he moves farther away. Lifting my eyes only once, to find the moon has achieved half its full potential, I quickly follow the trail left for me, submit my gaze to the silver street.

By the time I return home, the sky has lightened to grey and the city is slowly waking. Wearied by a long, fruitless search, I fumble to unlock my building's door. The key refuses to turn. A forceful push on heavy wood, painted dark brown and studded with brass, produces no result. Suddenly the door is opened from the other side. Eyes confront me coldly from a face surrounded by a scarf made from the same grey cloth as the habit of the nun. Apologetically, I step backward. My mistake is explainable. As though some secret link existed between the structures, the door of the building in which I live and that of the adjacent convent are identical in both colour and design.

Despite brightening dawn, my shuttered rooms retain near total darkness. The candle that was left burning has been reduced to a lifeless pool of wax. Without bothering to glance at the notebook on the desk, lacking the strength to face his latest mischief, I fall fully clothed upon my pallet. Exhaustion fails to encourage unconsciousness to come; sleep during day is alien to me. I lie stiffly beneath the blanket, press my eyes tightly closed, review the path of my search through the city of night. See that success was doomed almost from the start: when his footprints began to fade before reaching Fernán Caballero's end; when they disappeared entirely in front of the closed church at the limit of the block. How despite this evidence that he evaporated inside the sacred structure, and without a trail to follow, I press onward: into the maze of La Macarena, across the bridge to Los Remedios and then Triana, up Avenida de la Constitución's wide sweep, through the pooled shadows of Parque de Maria Luisa, all the way to Nervión. I peer into each infrequent stranger's face from foolish belief that his features will announce themselves to my eyes; I hope that from one of those unfamiliar forms might float pheromones whose unique chemical composition would be known to my senses from his fleeting visits to my rooms. At the inkiest hour before dawn, I finally find myself lost, bereft of bearings, befuddled in some distant *barrio* crawling with edgy addicts and forlorn gypsies and scores of souls for sale. It is there, until my eyes erase the image with one blinding blink, that a possibility of him poses within the doorway of a barred *bodega*, awaits a buyer for his body. Something in the wide span of those winged shoulders, in the slope of that strong back. Both fit the figure my unconscious eyes have spied sitting intently at the desk, bent above my open notebook. He casts a glance toward my sleeping form upon the pallet, slightly shakes the candle's flame with his turn of head. Puts down the pen, tears pages from their binding. Rises from the chair, reaches down to touch my shoulder. Is his expression concerned, amused, indifferent? It is there and then, at that uncertain point in my mental journey, as if now his phantom hand urges unconsciousness rather than the reverse, that I fall asleep.

How much did you cost, and was your price finally too high?

This time, without a sense that he has touched the spring on my shoulder that releases me from sleep, I open eyes in darkness. No flame casts its golden nimbus above the desk; street sounds indicate the flurried activity of early evening. My body rises from the pallet, aches as though pummelled for hours by heavy fists. Reluctant to switch on lights, I fumble to find a new wand of wax. Strike a match, induce a sulphur hiss, inspect the notebook. Without surprise, I discover that all remaining pages of my text are missing; last night's visit has left only his hieroglyphics behind. And mine? Now I am uncertain which of these symbols have been sketched by him, which by me. It doesn't matter. My belly groans with hunger. I ignore its sharp complaint; without moving, I wait for his arrival. His return. Only long after midnight do I decide that my vigil before the illuminated candle might deter his appearance. I must respect his modus operandi. After locking the door to invite him to unbolt it, after blowing out the candle to encourage him to light it, I place myself upon the pallet. Close eyes, feign sleep, await a touch that fails to make itself felt.

Your caresses were offered less and less frequently, were ever more glancingly bestowed, until they seemed only imagined before this actually became the case.

In grey morning light, the mirror reveals that his handprint has vanished from my shoulder along with its accompanying ache. This loss affects me more deeply than that of the last remnants of my text. I pound my fist against skin until it blooms with bruise; with satisfaction feel the return of a steady throb. Resulting relief allows me to settle at the desk and contemplate my notebook. Only dimly do I consider that my labour to complete the current manuscript has been intense during these past months in part because income from its sale is urgently required. There will soon be insufficient *pesetas* to pay for food and shelter. I dismiss this imminent crisis as unimportant. Instead, I draw hieroglyphics whose meaning remains concealed from me, whose value will certainly be unappreciated by the material world.

I should have been able to read your signs that spelled our inevitable end at the very start.

After several wakeful nights, I become convinced he will never return. My only possession of worth has been taken; nothing more remains for him to rob. One day my hand attempts to place legible language into the notebook--not from the belief that it might be possible to recreate lost text, but to offer him further material to steal, to sway him to arrive to effect the theft. Yet my pen refuses to form even remotely comprehensible words, insists on drawing obscure hieroglyphics still.

After hesitating over my hopeless effort, I rise to meet the mirror. It reflects that since his last intrusion my fists have decorated my body with several dozen bruises in a vain attempt to locate the secret spring of skin that would unlock the door to inner rooms as holy as those of the nearby church apparently entered by my visitor on the night of my pursuit. Has he yearned all along to step inside my similarly sacred space? He was unable to decode the instructions that allow such access? The language of my notebook's manual is as incomprehensible to him as his communication has been for me? Perhaps, maybe, possibly. Uncertainty is a luxury which current circumstance cannot afford. Suddenly, I become convinced that it lies within my power to beckon him to my rooms once more; on this final visit, he must be provided with directions, in his own language, which will clearly show him the way inside my body's temple. Yes, his hieroglyphics have always been details of a map waiting to be unscrambled. He was unable to arrange those clues himself; the job requires my assistance; it will be a wedded effort in the end. A decade's apprenticeship has taught me how to shape elements I do not understand into a form coherent to another's eyes: with one hand I hold a page of hieroglyphics; with the other, I carefully copy each symbol onto flesh yet unmarked by fists. Love whispers where they need to go. There is no margin for error; no chance for reconsideration. Taxing nights and days are required to transfer the notebook's total contents to their proper place upon my person. After completing this task, I light the candle for the last time, touch its flame with each now unneeded page, watch feathers of ash float to the floor. With satisfaction view swirls and shapes that cover my skin's entire surface. Without dismay see that, considered separately or as a whole, they withhold their meaning from me still: his eyes will understand. Already it is difficult to discern which marks have been imposed by fists and which by pen; already it is easy to understand the importance of not erasing with soap and water those that ink has drawn. After several days, my body begins to emit a scent similar to that smudged upon the air by his visits; it remains unclothed while I stir cautiously within the rooms, stays uncovered by blankets while I wait awake upon my pallet. It is vital not to conceal from his eyes the treasure map contained upon my skin. My body flutters beneath air's frozen hand; cold quivers a canvas of flesh. Although my stomach screams with hunger, I dare not step out even for a moment to purchase food. I must remain in my rooms in order to avoid missing his arrival. No eyes but his can be allowed to see the hieroglyphics that clothes would not completely cover; no mind but yours has the power to interpret them.

Him? You?

The distinction begins to blur, melt, dissolve.

You were always him; he was only ever you.

When rising from the pallet becomes impossible one day, this signals that you will find me soon. Occasionally, my starved body is wrenched by convulsions, beats weakly like a broken wing amid the perfumed pool of wastes. Otherwise, I wait patiently, at peace with this beauteous process. A bucket seems to bang at a great distance. From above, as though reaching across a decade, drift the faintest sounds of love. They become swallowed by prayers passing through the wall beside me. A choir sings inside my ears; the holy song swells. The world shifts farther away. My shrinking body seeks its final form. Reduces into essence, finds its necessary function. I am only hieroglyphics, in the end.

Hieroglyphics II: Only the Wing Knows Flight

DURING MY FIRST VIOLATION, I BELIEVE HE IS SLEEPING.

Only a faint indication of even breath, an intuition of occupied air, betray his presence upon the pallet. No light steals through tightly sealed shutters. The room is pitch black. With a touch whose sureness has been achieved through several decades of navigating darkness, I feel for the box of matches that rests beside the candle on the desk. These implements have been waiting; they urge me to interrupt the night. I scratch spark from sulphur, make flame cling to the candle. A circle of widening light reveals his face just below, just beside me; shadow carves features that appear as tightly clenched by anxiety as the blanket is by his left hand. Although he has apparently not been roused by my process of intrusion—key turning in lock, bolt withdrawing; door's click open, then shut—I fear my presence may disturb him now. Perhaps a chemical emission from my skin will call him from unconsciousness; the scent become detected by his sleeping senses. A blur of warmth bothers a chill dream. Yet he continues to lie motionless, breathing softly. I turn to the notebook spread open beneath the candle's glow.

His words will occupy as many as a hundred pages, I know. Three months of covert study have revealed that he writes steadily at the desk each day, often not rising until late evening from labour initiated shortly after dawn. With an invariable frown, he moves pen rapidly across paper. His head lifts occasionally, as though in response to sound from the world beyond his rooms. When his glance seeks the windows, shuttered even during day, I wonder if my presence in the courtyard has been detected. Does he feel the attention of an eye pressed to wood whose narrow slits scarcely permit him to be deciphered from inner dimness? Ostensibly unalarmed, he rotates his head back toward the notebook, wavers the flame of the candle that always burns at his elbow while he works.

Tonight I discover that his handwriting is surprisingly variable, shifting often in mid-paragraph from large, loosely formed letters to characters cramped, tight. The script slants now in one direction, now toward the other; yet it appears consistently neat and adheres strictly to the lines. If not for contradictory evidence acquired by observation, I might suspect that he alternates between writing with his left hand and his right to give each an opportunity to rest during extended composition. Or even suppose that several distinct beings have involved themselves with his notebook. In every one of its guises, the script appears illegible as a foreign language to my eyes.

Although I was prepared to encounter an inscrutable text, and remind myself that its withheld mystery does not subvert my purpose, this first vision of his words is dismaying. I am tempted to switch on lights to determine whether increased illumination will permit access to the meaning of his manuscript. No. He must not be wakened; he can't know I am here. It is essential that my turning to a blank notebook page and picking up his pen go unwitnessed. Surely nothing more than imagination suggests that the cheap plastic tube of ink retains his grip's warmth. Certainly only illusion encourages a sense that its mass-produced shape and weight and texture are unique, never known to any hands except his and now mine. It must be merely a variety of hallucination which makes me dream that I hold this pen precisely as he has clasped it, and that such knowledge allows me to feel his fingers entwined in mine.

My head shakes fantasy away. I sketch rapidly, destroy the purity of a page without hesitation. For thousands of nights, I have lain awake and mentally traced what ink must trace when the opportunity arrives. Intruding upon his notebook marks the first step in a process that will lead to an ultimate act of composition. This is more than some dress rehearsal, more than a rough draft. It requires my complete concentration, makes me forget that he is almost near enough to touch. A forbidden, unwitting hum forms in my throat. I stifle the sound just in time, preserve the late-night silence. No noise carries from the narrow street, deserted at this hour, and the nuns next door are surely sleeping.

The candle burns, ink flows, a blank page fills.

When my task has been completed, I turn to look at him again. Have his limbs rearranged themselves beneath the blanket since my earlier regard? Does the hand that clutched the woollen cover rest loosely upon it now? I rise from the desk. My body feels cold and stiff. The hand I have been writing with yearns to touch his face. I bend down and graze an exposed hint of smooth shoulder. He doesn't stir. Alarmed by my act of weakness, I steal from his room. Leave the door unlocked, the candle burning on the desk. Leave the notebook open to my hieroglyphic promise.

I have searched for him through the length and width of many lands, across a span of twenty years. At first I believed it would not take long to find him. I might have given up if I had known how difficult my quest would be. I might have feared success lay beyond my strength. In the beginning, it often seemed he stayed a single tantalizing step ahead of me: his departure from Paris occurs on the day before my arrival; his flight rises above Schiphol on the same afternoon mine touches Dutch ground. Again and again, I reach rooms he has just abandoned to encounter the disarray of his three- or six-month sojourn there. What is unnecessary, what would be a burden, has been left behind. I hunt for clues beneath the bed, at the bottom of drawers, behind bureaus. Despite the haste of his vanishings, no evidence illuminates their wake; my inability to obtain a sample of his handwriting proves especially disheartening. I try on his abandoned clothes, press my face into the pillow upon which his head has rested. Assume his space, learn his scent, feel texture that has touched him. Absorbing the scanty information, I wonder once more if he has been tipped off regarding my arrival. Does he possess means of knowing that I draw near which are as finely honed as my secret methods of pursuit?

Still young and strong, I am able to persuade myself that good reasons exist for my repeated disappointment. Quite likely, I am as unprepared to discover him as he is not ready to be found. Most probably, a premature encounter would be mutually disastrous, potentially fatal. This is not a series of unfortunate near misses, I assure myself. Instead, it has to be—it must be—the correct and necessary unfolding of a predetermined plan.

Then there came a time when his trail seemed to grow cold. Each of my instruments of pursuit—some blunt as sonar and radar, some subtle as implements of dream; others mysterious as the tools of desire—failed me at once. Shivering in the north, I believed he might be laughing anywhere where it was warm; sweltering in the south, I wondered if temperate breeze touched his face. Now I was tested, and now began years of aimless wandering. Only the remote possibility of stumbling upon him accidentally sustained my hope. Say I turn a corner in Cuernavaca to discover his form smudging the charcoal air. Glance across an Ios bar, spy him through miraculous smoke. I tried to convince myself that the moment my search was actively abandoned would be the same moment it found reward. Making bargains with belief, striking deals with chance: all the gambits that we desperately resort to; all those old tricks to con the heart to take another beat.

I couldn't give up.

I have always needed only him; he alone is able to receive my gift.

There has never been a choice.

Eventually, despite this knowledge, I am deluded that more than a single possibility for fulfillment might exist. I pretend that approximations of him will be enough; perhaps easily encountered, imperfect imitations can serve my purpose. In deceiving darkness, I attempt to transfigure the body within my arms through the force of fervor, to translate its clumsy movements into divine love's unspoken language. Some flimsy resemblance to his still unglimpsed shape, the inexact taste of his yet untouched lips, a slight similarity of scent: in the end, such imprecise echoes increase the weight of desire's undelivered burden. Render it leaden, back-breaking, unbearable.

And then:

Drifting through a southern Spanish city at another summer's end, loitering in what seems the most unlikely location, I am stopped in my tracks.

To my left, in the narrow cobbled passage, three nuns emerge from a door whose heavy wood is painted dark brown and studded with brass. As the trio files toward a church rising at the shadowed alley's reach, I notice that, adjacent to the one just opened and still ajar, an identical door stands closed. Gloom swallows three grey habits. My eyes ponder the fastened door.

Power coiled by several yearning decades releases a swift, sharp arrow; precisely aimed, it pierces my mind with inexorable understanding.

He breathes behind this barrier.

Cobblestones sway beneath my feet; the air wavers, bends, twists.

Danger leaks from dimness; shadows flood me with fear.

I immediately walk away. Emotion must be controlled; excitement contained. This single chance is too fragile to be fumbled, too vital to be lost.

As soon as I escape his narrow street, the situation feels less unsafe.

Now that he has been found, there is no threat of him fleeing.

As long as I proceed correctly.

For three months, I prepare for my first visit in the night. Satisfy myself with no more than several glimpses through his sealed shutters; steal those brief visions on days carefully spaced apart. It does not escape my notice that he has chosen to reside in a building whose other apartments are more or less uninhabited. The *pisos* on his ground floor, as well as those on two higher storeys, surround a central patio in sustained silence. Only infrequently does a young couple visit the place directly above his to make loud love for several hours in the afternoon. Only once a week does a cleaning woman arrive to slap a mop over the structure's common stairs and courtyard. Although it might seem that this address was selected because of its obscurity, I suspect that it was really to provide me with an opportunity to violate it without a witness. A single night-time reconnoitre, prior to the first intrusion, reveals how his body is tightly clenched even while unconscious on the pallet. I recognize this particular rigidity from personal experience, know it betrays the tension between a need to stay concealed and an equally urgent longing to be found.

I refuse to give in to my desire to follow him on his occasional forays from his rooms. Now I can be as patient as the Sphinx, careful as a surgeon of the heart. On several disconcerting instances, however, he strays into my vicinity before I know it has been infiltrated. At a kiosk in the Plaza de la Encarnación, beneath the almond trees, I skim headlines of distant battles. My back senses a gaze; my head turns one cautious inch. Across the square, he sits amid old benched men who drowse over newspapers or tilt faces toward a sun that each week weakens further with approaching winter. At the same moment my eyes find him, his close as if to dilute danger by erasing sight of it; when they open, a moment later, I am halfway up Calle Hortaleza, indeed absent from sight. This incident pricks my plan's perfect skin. A sliver of uncertainty needles me to acknowledge a suspicion that I have been followed since the start of my search. Before my apprehension can be dismissed, it receives reinforcement. Motionless in the flow of early-evening promenaders in San Eloy that passes at the end of his street, I face a *papelería* window filled with pens and notebooks and wells of ink. Sink into a spell of anticipation for the night when such objects will be exploited, when my possession of him at last begins. He passes behind me; his sleeve brushes my back. The left sleeve, I immediately know. Wheeling around at his touch, shivering with an ascent of sensation through my spine, I see his right hand rub his other arm, where the flesh burns beneath the cloth from our glancing contact. A distant church bell signals evening mass. Starlings rise with outraged screams from orange trees. He becomes swiftly swallowed by the throng.

Who is following who?

Careful, I tell myself.

Watch out, danger warns.

For several days after this near encounter, I stayed away from his hiding place. Allowed time to erase any inkling he might have of me; reformulated the correct equation between hunter and prey. From belief that my mental waves had the power to carry across the city and blemish the innocence of his air, I eschewed even fantasies of him. Denied myself the pleasure of conjuring his image into this shabby room, deep inside the Macarena's twisting maze, which suffices as my base of operation here. Refrained from musing upon the fact that when revealed to me—finally, after forever, at long last—his face failed to inspire the intense emotion that might have been expected. How I have not dwelled on shape of lips, colour of eyes; how neither architecture of bone nor features' arrangement dictate my waking dreams. His whole canvas is my concern, I realize with the force of renewed revelation, gazing into the pearled flame of a candle at rest on my dark room's desk. Yes, the entire expanse of his skin waits to receive my gift. Yes, the potential of this flesh exposed itself five days after happening on him, when I spied his naked surface still sheened by the shower, a flash and gleam through his dim domain. In the courtyard where I watched, this sight caused my left hand to clench and unclench; my fingers curled with desire to wield the instrument that would exact my art. With satisfaction, I noted that his skin has not been tainted by tattoos; only several scars from injury and faint lines of age decorate this breathing paper in a way that does not decrease its usefulness but renders it precious and unique.

On the day after my first visit in the night, certain of its success, I reward myself with contemplation of his alarmed waking. How he finds that a candle blown out before bed burns unaccountably at dawn. A door believed to have been bolted stands unlocked. He searches for explanation of these ciphers, wonders whether they result from falling upon the pallet in an unsettled state of mind the night before. Had writing in the notebook been especially disturbing? Some aspect of those words provoked preoccupation to the point that the candle was left illuminated, the door carelessly unlocked? Then he discovers that his notebook was violated in the darkness. Neither burning candle nor unfastened door is a result of his oversight, he understands now. No. While he was sleeping, an intruder withdrew the bolt, lit the wick, placed hieroglyphics upon a page. Who? He bends over my precisely presented symbols, seeks to decipher them. His lips move in an attempt to solve mystery by shaping it. Abruptly, he rises from the desk and crosses the room with three strides. Flings open the shutters, peers into the patio, bangs slatted wood shut again.

A knock interrupts my contemplation. Without waiting for an invitation, the *pension*'s owner opens the door. Señora X, I baptized the woman upon arriving here. My lack of luggage roused suspicion since heightened by an extended stay. When I find myself compelled to speak my plan out loud, to air what otherwise curls silently inside me, Señora X listens from the passage beyond. She investigates the room during my brief absences. Returning, I check that her inquisitive hands have not unearthed from hiding the tools that will be vital to my love's articulation.

"You had a visitor last night," says Señora X today.

Is there a knowing look in her eyes?

A sly expression as she adds that no message was left for me?

I am unable to summon back my former sense of his reaction to my visit. Can only muse vaguely whether he manages to dismiss evidence of an intruder as some quirk of the night. Has he found a way to resume his labour as if nothing alarming has occurred? Does he bend over the notebook, move pen rapidly across page after page? Continue to write in a script I cannot read? Create meaning I cannot understand?

I blame Señora X for destroying my seemingly clairvoyant vision of my lover. For keeping me from further insight into his current condition, from what would aid my effort to accomplish the second stage of possession with maximum efficiency. For distracting me with what must be a mistaken message. No one knows I inhabit this city. Except for fleeting strangers in the night, my whereabouts have been secret since my search for him began.

Later, I will doubt this conviction.

I will wonder: Did he not awaken alarmed after my first visit because he wasn't sleeping during it?

A sufficient amount of inviolate time must be allowed to pass after my inaugural intrusion. He has to be lulled into believing that the incident was nothing more than a freakish phenomenon; it is essential he regain a sense of safety in order for my next manoeuvre to be made without detection. Perhaps he wonders, during these dozen days, whether isolation has started to play pranks upon his mind. I have heard him mumble monologues in his vacant room. I have seen him stride the confined space in circles that grow increasingly tight until they leave him turning in place like an unsteady top. So well known to myself, these responses to solitude make me smile. I almost wish circumstances allowed me to share further strategies to survive seclusion, to defeat invasion. Certainly his measures of security are painfully ineffectual. Before bed, he checks and rechecks the door to ensure it has been locked; in the middle of night, his eyes open to divine whether a candle burns. Perhaps he measures the wand of wax at morning to satisfy himself its length has not been reduced by flame that flickered while he slept unaware. Peers at the pen to judge if ink has drained from it during darkness.

I run subjunctive scenarios through my mind, edit them in various order; splice them in a special way, study the flow of images in sensual slow motion.

Hold breath while Señora X haunts the hallway, play dead as she listens for informing noise to cement her apprehension.

My fingers itch. My skin burns.

During my second trespass on his sphere, he seems to sleep more deeply.

Lighting the candle and settling at the desk, I wonder if he has resorted to drugging himself before bed to encourage unconsciousness during a time of special strain. Is his breathing unusually heavy, suspiciously laboured? What I find in the notebook cancels out the question.

My page of hieroglyphics has been removed.

I glance into surrounding shadow, seek sight of a crumpled paper ball. Regard him with irritation; from frustration, sigh. The first night's work must be recreated; a primary step repeated. I am no nearer to approaching my real objective. With perfect memory, upon a fresh page, I trace hieroglyphics; surprisingly, they are more difficult to replicate than to originate. Too weary to proceed with my undertaking when this restoration has been completed, I am only able to examine his text.

Is his handwriting more legible because more familiar?

Am I almost able to understand one word here, half a phrase there?

Bird, I murmur to myself.

Wing knows flight.

Startling me, the candle spits.

I have risen from the desk to stand above the open notebook. Viewed from greater distance, his words seem to assume a collective shape, swim into some significant whole. My eyes blink, tear. I rip his last page of text from the notebook, stuff it in a pocket. The sound causes him to sigh and then stir; it pulls the prayers of insomniac nuns through stone wall, through my defence against desire. I bend over him. Touch his left shoulder, feel his bare skin. Allow my caress to linger long enough for its warmth to penetrate his dreams.

Steal past the burning candle, feather its flame in passing. Slip out into the hollow courtyard and look at the spread of sky two storeys above. A quarter moon carves a crescent upon squared darkness, influences me to leave his door ajar behind my back.

"He came looking for you again last night."

I close the door against the gleaming eyes of Señora X. Did she place ironic emphasis on the first word of her message? My mind fumbles with the question, fails to arrive at an answer; it feels clouded and dull this morning, as though impaired by excessive narcotics during the night. As I consider then reject asking Señora X to describe my visitor, I become aware that my left shoulder burns. The sensation is sufficiently strong to urge examination in the speckled mirror. Adequately intense that a reflection of unmarked flesh evokes surprise.

I inspect the page of text abducted from his notebook, speculate whether he simultaneously studies the leaf my hand adorned last night. Hope dwindles then dies that familiarity with his script might abet understanding of it: with protracted appraisal, his words cling more stubbornly to concealed meaning; nor does significance leap from their whole when the page is viewed from greater distance. A disquieting notion nudges my mind: could what I assumed to be words be a variety of hieroglyphics instead? Does he possess his own symbolic language? It has been placed into the notebook as an initial step of some operation involving me?

I hold the sheet of paper to the mirror, hope its contents decode when reflected in reverse. Drop the disappointing page upon the bed, watch it flutter downward like a broken wing, feel my body imitate the fall.

When I wake, the room is dark. I try to determine time by aural evidence. Sounds in the street beyond suggest late evening. I have slept too long on this crucial night; hours invaluable to the execution of my plan are lost. A panicked spring from bed rustles the page upon which my head has been dreaming, whispers words into the dark.

Only the bird knows the wing.

Switch on electricity, shake the non sequitur from my mind.

Does a scent of wax infiltrate the air?

Is the candle on my desk shorter than when I blew out its flame?

Less ink engorges the adjacent pen?

My left shoulder shoots with sharpened pain, as though pounded by fists during sleep?

From their hiding place, I collect the trio of tools that will be necessary tonight. My reflection in the mirror freezes me. Moist sleep has transferred a paper pillow's ink onto my face, patterned it with blue. Smudged tribal markings; enigmatic tattoos. An unknown owner's brand. I lean over the corner sink, scrub with soap and water. Re-inspect my image, assure myself its muted marks would be discernible only to a knowing glance. For example, that of Señora X. Her eyes narrow then widen as I rush by, as I fall into the demanding night.

Several things are different.

The candle burns upon his desk in anticipation of my return.

It illuminates that he has retired to the pallet fully clothed.

I smile at his vain attempt to equip himself to spring from bed upon feeling my touch, to pursue me without the delay of dressing. The vial in my pocket whispers a promise to vanquish his measure with its vapour. I touch the other pocket's softer shape, confirm that it scabbards a third tool. With satisfaction, note that my replicated hieroglyphics remain intact within the notebook.

Now these perfect signs and symbols may be copied upon his skin.

At last he will be branded permanently as mine.

My left hand twitches with excitement, removes the scalpel from its sheath, tests the sharpness of the blade.

Wait.

Something is wrong.

Does he lie too silently upon the pallet? Does he breathe at all?

In response to my uncertainty, prayer from next door once more penetrates the wall. This time it swims sickeningly around me. Sacred words chloroform the air before I can unscrew the vial and drench the handkerchief and press upon him the state of oblivion that will permit my artistry to be inflicted.

He has feigned sleep during each of my intrusions?

Dervish shadows whirl, the candle quivers crazily.

A sly smile curves his lips?

Song swells, air blurs, desk tilts. The notebook slides into my hands. I gather that a page of hieroglyphics has been added after mine. Flipping between the two sheets, I quickly become confused and panic from inability to distinguish his symbols from my own. Hymn rises rapturously around me, pollutes my perfect memory, renders both sets of shapes equally unfathomable.

I swiftly sketch new symbols, consume as many as twenty notebook pages, pray for significance to lift from them. Approaching dawn pressures me to work with haste, which puts in jeopardy several decades of judicious preparation. It is clear that inadequate hours remain to realize my dream tonight. It is obvious that no future opportunity for fulfillment will be afforded.

This is your last chance, chants the cresting choir.

Dropping the pen, I am aghast to confront only senseless scribble still.

I turn to his text with hope that meaning will emerge from it in fair compensation for vanishing from mine. I have always trusted in the purity of balanced equations. I have always worshipped the god of immaculate logic: his skin is blank so my hieroglyphics may adorn it; my blade is sharp so his surface can receive it. At this critical moment, when I need him most, my theoretic deity proves fickle, offers unacceptable equations.

My search for him has been precisely proportionate to his for me.

His flight from me has possessed the same value as mine from him.

I must abort my mission. I must adjust the plan. I must reverse an equation.

From the notebook, I rip pages that exactly number those left behind. Cunningly, he resists reacting to the tear of paper; a smirk still freezes his lips. When I reach down to shake his shoulder, he coldly continues to play dead. My prodding releases scent that rises around me, insinuating.

It is time to end a stalemated charade. Time to allow him reciprocal opportunity to realize our love. Time to flee a chant-filled room with twenty pages of his text in one hand, the scalpel in the other. To leave the door open wide behind my back. To invite him to pursue, find, possess.

Shining cobblestones evidence the effort of street cleaners who, late each night, when the pavement has been deserted by a sleeping population, unleash hoses and brooms to purify the city for another soiling day. My darting steps leave dry impressions upon a rough, damp surface; he has a distinct trail to follow. At the brief block's end, the *barrio* church looms in darkness. Laughing lightly, still believing in the beauty of algebra, I slip toward the building. My talent to escape easily equals his to capture. Hasn't his hunger for my skin been successfully outwitted for just as long as I have been driven by similar desire?

I spread twenty unnumbered pages across my bed, position them several ways, arrange them again. Love enlightens me when the correct order has been found, when the right moment has arrived. His hieroglyphics do not themselves receive my scrutiny. Their meaning has never been relevant to our purpose, sharply informs the scalpel's unsheathed blade.

It gleams upon the desk, insists on being exploited.

Here, now, at once.

A bucket clangs significantly beyond the door. When I returned here at dawn, Señora X asked when I would be leaving. Today? She posed the word less as a question than as a command.

Despite the pressure of time and the scalpel's impatience, I don't begin my work at once. I wish to savour this occasion; the right to relish each sacred second has surely been earned by now. Allow me to appreciate that this ceremony has been fated from the start. Let me feel his spirit with me, however far away his form may stray. Give me grace to guide him as he wanders lost within the distant *barrio* where I left him before morning; inspire me to sustain his stumble through tangled streets, which teem with forlorn gypsies and edgy addicts and scores of bodies for sale. Pity that he walked more and more slowly while darkness died; less and less certainly as hope of finding me waned. Bereft of bearings, he still hesitates on every corner, blindly searches thin boys awaiting buyers in each *bodega* doorway, attempts to incarnate one forlorn figure into me.

We don't need him to begin, whispered a scalpel in one hand.

All you require is us, twenty pages murmured in the other.

Walk away, advised my pocket's vial.

He can't find you unless he loses you, reminded my aphoristic god.

I left him then; I leave him now.

Move nakedly toward the beckoning blade, grasp its power in my hand, poise above the instructive bed.

Carve his cryptic shapes into the canvas of my skin. Slowly, carefully, precisely. No margin for error exists; no possibility to reconsider. This surface is limited to a single use; it is as precious as unique. My throbbing shoulder distracts me from fully feeling the scalpel; fresh pain encourages alertness, preserves attention. I discover how to slice skin for greatest effect: deeply enough to create an indelible impression, shallowly enough to discourage blood from muddying a beautiful design. I am ecstatic at my successful manipulation of this equation. Enthralled by the power of art. Elated that an incisive inscription of my torso has splattered a minimum of crimson drops on the blueprints scattered across the bed.

For a single pulse, his hieroglyphics release meaning: what my eyes could not interpret sings clearly from my skin.

Only the bird knows the wing.

The knob of my locked door rattles.

Only the wing knows flight.

"When are you going?" Señora X inquires impatiently from the hall.

"Soon," I shout.

She coughs in annoyance, moves heavily away.

Her interruption has cancelled comprehension. Never mind. The significance of his symbols lies beyond the sphere of my concern. Their presentation upon my skin is only for his understanding eyes.

For them to see his desire for me spelled out as it has never been before.

From the beginning this has been the hallowed plan; it receives lustration now.

In an *urbanización* at the far side of the city, where he has ended up, his head suddenly lifts. His nostrils quiver, detect the perfume of my plasma, draw him to its source.

The room descends into dimness, plummets into cold. I am reluctant to switch on electric light, to subject my exquisite art to harsh glare. A shaking hand lights the candle on the desk, seeks sustenance from the flame. Now his symbols must be peered at from an inch away so I may copy them onto my skin. The mirror is required to engrave my face. There, ink marks faintly visible from last night aid a delicate phase of operation, instruct the scalpel where to carve. My effort proves less than satisfactory. By now my left arm aches; its muscles twitch, complain. This key area of flesh should have received attention first. The scalpel grows heavy, my hand trembles, there is a bad gash in my right cheek. I reach for the handkerchief beside the vial on the desk. Dab blood that insists on flowing, that won't cease. My pulse pounds more rapidly; my manipulation of the scalpel turns panicked. A dozen separate sites spurt.

His pace increases as he leaves Nervión behind, reaches a run when Los Remedios approaches, hastens further through the fandango of Triana streets.

Señora X confers beyond the door. With someone whose voice sounds as familiar as hers in tone and timbre? As I strain to hear whether this muffled duet warns of immediate intrusion, it becomes swallowed by nearer sound. Psalms rise around me; sweet praise enfolds my body, entwines my head with tenderness. I waver on my feet as flame wavers above the desk.

Recover balance, transfer scalpel to the other hand. My right hand, my wrong hand. It is required to etch skin that could not otherwise be reached. My effort becomes increasingly awkward, wildly imprecise. Ribbons of blood unwind and sacred song unfurls and my interior chambers chill in exact symmetry to the warm, liquid glow upon their surface.

I am almost finished. I have done the best I can.

The choir crescendos as it aspires to divine conclusion.

He speeds across the swaying bridge, above the dividing river.

Rushes up San Eloy, along Amor de Dios, through La Alameda's sweep.

Time gushes with blood; both flow fast toward their end.

He enters La Macarena, turns onto my *pension's* block.

I reach toward the vial on the desk.

Carry handkerchief and bottle to bed, chorals the climaxing choir.

Wait, screams the scalpel as weak fingers fumble to unscrew a cap.

You forgot something.

One quick, deep slice replicates the last stroke that realizes his last hieroglyphic.

Cuts the throat of the choir in mid-note, silences its song, allows Señora X's shout to carry from the hall.

"Your visitor."

His blue symbols rustle the truth about love beneath my back, pool red proof upon my front.

Commotion occurs beyond the magic door.

Keys jangle like bells.

He's here.

The Truth about Love

THERE IS A TIME BOMB CONCEALED SOMEWHERE IN THE MINEFIELD OF our lives—in your heart, to be precise. I press my ear against your strong, broad chest and listen helplessly to its click. To diffuse this danger would be to dismantle your love, I know: the same mechanism caresses and kills. Steadily the ticking grows louder; sounds swells as that decisive, explosive moment nears when we will be blown into bits, scattered like fireworks through the sky. Sometimes I try to calculate how many weeks or months we have left together, you and me, before you are taken away. (Or are there only days?) Yes, it is you who they will handcuff and lock up; but, clearly, we will both pay for your crimes.

How we met, how we fell in love: seas of memory wash inside me, bubble in my blood. They are the same memories cherished by every lover, banal if spoken aloud, gold turned into dross when exposed to objective elements. We do not mention certain moments (our first kiss, for example); anniversaries pass without celebration. No photographs exist to remind me of the time we travelled deep into the desert and slept beneath the stars. That day we climbed a glacier, then built a fire against the cold. Evidence must not be allowed to gather, you have taught me; in the end, it will always be used against us, however innocent it appears. So the presents I gave you at the beginning, before I learned this lesson, you buried in the yard, where they could rot safe from sight, disintegrate into dust. And so we do not hold hands while walking together in the street; we offer no proof of ourselves as lovers to the world. Remember: once our very act of love was forbidden, illegal, punishable by imprisonment or worse.

From you I learned the value of silence, the purity of secrets. When you turn to me in darkness, without words, the gesture bears the weight of a thousand similarly unspoken movements, is heavy enough to prevent me from floating into the air. Once more our mute bodies move together. I receive private pleasure when you sigh or moan against your will. If I can make you cry out when you come, I count this as a triumph.

Later, I waken in your arms. You are talking in your sleep, mumbling what you dream. I listen carefully, hope you will drop a clue. One word that contains a whole story. A name, some Rosebud. Of course I have studied the information concealed inside your wallet. I know the thin data that defines your name and age and place of birth—but little else. Family, former friends and lovers--who were they, what did they mean to you, where are they now? Upon the blank slate of your silence I am free to draw versions of the past that make you who you are today: my man has a thousand distinct histories, a whole horde of buried identities. As I must have for you. I study one alternative then another, according to my mood, my need. No, I do not pretend to know or understand you completely; but my loving imagination can create a dozen approximations of who you really are, and each is dear to me. For this reason, and despite our isolation, we are not lonely. Our multiple selves crowd these tidy rooms: all the boys we once were, all those gap-toothed, grinning ghosts.

These days and nights pass beneath the most ordinary cloak. We waken and go to separate jobs. In the evenings, we share a meal, then stretch before the television, me in your arms or you in mine. We go to the gym and to the movies. Weekends are to clean the house and work in the yard. Domesticity. The telephone does not ring often; our doorbell insists upon silence. Outsiders pose danger, I have come to understand. They would bear witness in court, they would reveal what must stay hidden. As it is, our unknown neighbours will certainly speak to the television cameras upon discovery of your crimes; excited by brief, second-hand celebrity, they will offer mistaken impressions, skewed insights. ("They seemed such nice, quiet young men," those ignorant people will puzzle.) Anyway, I have no wish to share you; we need no one besides each other, I try to tell myself. I can condone your bloody acts for the way each one drives you deeper into only me; we are entangled inextricably within your web of guilt. Where do you leave off; where do I begin? Sometimes, half-asleep, I touch your arm in bed and think it's mine. It is that difficult to discern the line of separation: what you do, what I do.

By now I know the pattern. Twelve or fifteen or twenty days after your last crime, you grow restless, distracted, uninterested in making love. You complain of headache, and wear an inward expression as though inside your ears there were a buzzing you must silence any way you can. At our window you stand and search the dark, empty street. Out there is something you need that I can't give you: this is still difficult for me to accept. I wonder what it is I lack, how I could more completely fulfill your needs. (This is when I believe I am as guilty as you, a complete accomplice: I feel the shape and weight of your knife in my hand, see it slice and watch the red ribbons unfurl, share that satisfaction.) As it is, I can only sense you build toward dangerous excitement; I become excited by suspense myself. Always I am prepared for the night when you say you wish to go for a drive. "Want company?" I ask—must ask—hoping you will answer yes, hoping we will only drive along the river and observe lights shudder in the water. I must offer you this chance to detour from your violent path, even as I know that altering your route would, in fact, mean leaving me behind.

But you do not want my company, you long to go into the dark night alone. Are you protecting me, preserving my innocence? Or do you selfishly refuse to share your pleasure? You put on your coat and kiss me coldly at the door; already you heart has turned toward the next unknown, unsuspecting victim that waits. I listen to the car's engine turn over at your touch, hear you drive away. Sometimes you are gone for several hours; sometimes it is nearly dawn before you return. Then I will not notice the stain of blood on the hem of your jeans, the scratch on your arm hinting that this time there was a struggle. Afterward you are tired and full of need. There is always heightened passion then; whatever lay between us, separating us, has been eliminated. We move urgently toward our brief false death, then lie together slick with sweat. The scent of crushed blossoms hangs heavy in the air.

Do you suspect I know? There are times, moving above me, when your open eyes confess. You seek my understanding. And when I hold you tighter, grasping the muscles that wielded the knife, this is absolution. My hands stroke forgiveness. Be careful, I nearly say the next time you go out alone. Do it right. Then, while you sleep, I check your clothes and shoes for splashes of blood, eradicate a clue you may have overlooked. I retrieve the knife from the car's front seat to ensure that it is clean. Press its sharp blade against my throat as though I were both you and your victim at once.

Near the beginning, you deliberately dropped a clue, I suspect. You wanted me to know. Through narrowed eyes you watched warily to see how I would react to certain news stories on television. How I would respond to understanding their connection to you. You knew me well enough to be sure I would not telephone the police: such acuteness of intuition has, in part, saved you from discovery until now. Watching those images—the body draped with a white sheet, the sobbing family, the perplexed police— I matched your silence and calmness. Instead of fleeing from you in fear, I stayed to love you with greater fervour. That was the moment we became linked by unbreakable chains. Complete acceptance: this is what we all seek. This is my definition of love.

Details don't interest me. I am not curious to know if it is men or women or children you kill, or why you need them silenced. What you do with the bodies, before and afterward. If you like to hear them cry, beg, scream. How it feels. What it's like. I respect your secrets. After all, I have secrets of my own.

At first, it's true, I did feel jealous of your victims, of your special relationship with them. How their last earthly vision is of you. That interlocking of your eyes with theirs as they leave the world. How you carve out the shape of their unique destiny with your knife. Such shocking intimacy. But now I know you will always leave them to return to me. They hold your attention only briefly; our exchange lasts far longer than any death scream, any fading pulse.

Why I love you. After you are discovered (and the day draws nearer as surely as the next season), I will be the subject of curiosity--one more psychiatric specimen. They will hound me with questions, they will feed me drugs. Already I prepare for the silence I must maintain to preserve the holiness of our union. "Monster," they will label you in an attempt to pollute our mutual devotion. Perhaps they will present me with a detailed description of your acts. How you gouge out a victim's eye with your teeth, roll that firm ball in your mouth, bite through its resisting outer layer to the satisfying squish of softness, chew up all the visions this eye has seen. Inhuman, they will say, anxious to place your deeds on a plane separate from their own existence, unwilling to admit that in all of us there is the capacity to perform every kind of act, and that these acts, however horrible they appear, may be an expression of the most human emotions such as desire, and hate, and love.

"He is my lover," I will simply state. If they can't comprehend what this means, how the word wraps itself around everything you are, they will not be worthy of further information. If they had been just once inside your magic arms, they would not wonder at all. I will scorn them for accepting feeble, legal passion; I will mock their envy of our outsiders' ardour. It is simple to see how they will sensationalize and warp our story, but beneath their outrage will stir some glimpse of the true force of our love; really, this sight will disturb them more deeply than any of your actual crimes. It will drive them—the police, the courts, the media, the public—to hysteria. Without doubt they will work to prove that our love makes me an accessory to your crimes. They will not be able to leave me free.

The twisting of fate enthralls me. I see now that the inevitable end began long ago; the finale was written right there at the start. As a child my eyes hungrily swallowed dark-eyed boys who searched for trouble. Bad boys who did things I wished to do but could not do myself. There were never stains of dirt on my neatly pressed trousers; I did not dare cross the line that lies between what is and is not permitted. The misguided angels escaped from school, stole what they needed, drove with drunken recklessness through the night. At first their crimes seemed just an excess of boyish energy, a swagger of high spirits, such charming bravado; swiftly their needs turned darker, less innocent, and they flirted with Alcatraz, wooed severe sentences without parole. Danger burned inside them; I reached out for that heat, became branded a hundred times. There were handsome lovers and strong lovers, and lovers who carried me to all kinds of lawless lands and revealed to me any number of outlaw visions. Each of these dark desperados led directly to you. I followed their AWOL steps across the sand and found you there beside the sea, perched high upon the rocks, wind in your hair and salt sticking to your lips. Upon that shore we sealed an unbreakable pact, mixing our saliva and blood and semen.

We must take what we need. Every life you steal is a sacrifice offered only to me; our love is baptized upon an altar of blood. Certainly I do not pity your victims. I would stab them myself to keep you with me. Their lives are taken to preserve mine, I realize; if that seems a harsh equation, let me only say that all mathematics are cruelly precise. In fact, it is clear that your knife could easily press against my throat with the slightest shift of wind inside your heart. Anyone who doesn't know that even the strongest love must be this precarious is truly unenlightened.

Tonight the maple tree outside our window stirs and trembles. You look for car keys, you move toward the door. Suddenly my blood churns: their net may be drawn around you right now; this may be the night you don't return. The night you enter the magic door. When I do not visit you in prison, listen, you will understand: your spirit will escape its skin the moment you are captured; that body they guard with such care will be but an empty husk. Often I have caught your questioning glance: you wonder if I will be brave enough to slip from my skin also, and join you in the only place allowed for us to exist together. You'll never take us alive! we brag every outlaw's boast into the wind.

I don't know. I can feel impatient with abstractions that do not take into account the actual touch of your lips, the real pressure of your hands. Already I mourn your physical absence; knowledge of the brief time allotted for us here and now has made each glimpse of your tall form sweeter. Still, for a moment I am angry that you risk our earthly life together, court bodily separation enforced by iron bars. Is this what you finally want and need—to be apart from me in your lonely cell, your solitary confinement?

Fleetingly, I wonder what would happen if our roles were reversed: if I committed your crimes, would you be so understanding and accepting? While you pause in the doorway I doubt everything: you, me, us. I suspect your love is just another con job, one more grifter's sleight of hand. Have I been set up as the fall guy who will take the rap, while you dance away at liberty to seduce a score of men unsuspecting as me?

Don't go.

The words die on my lips, are swallowed by your goodbye kiss. No, finally I don't doubt, don't regret: I wouldn't change any of this even if I could. When you are gone into the demanding night, I hear steel doors clang, strong bolts slam, heavy keys rattle a dirge. Someone cries for mercy. A knife stabs my heart, my opened veins afford release, we drown together in the red sea of love.

Touching Darkness

FIRST THINGS FIRST:

You were not the prisoner; I was not the warden with the keys.

There was never a cage, never a cell. No bars of iron, no heavy chains.

Let's get that straight from the start.

Since appearances can be deceptive.

Once again, as originally, the room at the back of the house looks clean and neat and quite bare. The sparse furniture—a single bed, a night table, a wardrobe—is as unexceptional as its setting. A window, set fairly high in one wall, overlooks our backyard; even when they're closed, the venetian blinds let in light. The uncarpeted floor is laid with tiles, now faded or never bold, of an uninteresting design. White walls are decorated with several generic prints of ships at sea. A large closet contains a few unmarked cardboard boxes.

Undisturbed dust dreams in silence.

Unbreathed air waits to be consumed by throats, caressed by lungs.

Certainly not a sinister or disturbing place.

The room at the back of the house neither evokes nor deserves such a description.

Perhaps only I am able to detect the slight stain on the tiles to the rear.

The subtle scent that lingers like a memory or dream of love.

For years we use it as a spare room, a guest room, a room to hold odds and ends that don't belong in other rooms. You or I might look here without particular hope for something that's gone missing. The room possesses an air of neglect born of indifference; neither of us feels sufficient interest to invest it with his attention, his energy, his taste. We don't really need the space; it's almost beside the point. We can bear no heirs. Often I would forget that our house contains this room, as if it weren't there.

The infrequently entered door is kept closed. It has no lock or key.

As your last wish, you will wordlessly beg for those interdependent mechanisms that

deny entry.

Or that prevent escape.

Yet finally this unremarkable space will be spoken of in the most lurid language.

Chamber of Horrors.

Dungeon of Death.

(Never mind that the room is situated on the ground floor and not in the basement. Upon the prosaic surface of the earth, not in its murky depths. Outrage often eschews accuracy.)

Prison of Pain, they will inevitably howl.

You would smile, I know.

If you could.

When you begin to sleep in this room at the back of the house, I'm unconcerned. There have been occasions during our long union when one or the other of us has felt the need to sleep alone for a time. A night, a week; at most, a month. Such nocturnal separations are never the result of disharmony. Since there's no question of rejection or of withdrawal, the matter requires no explanation and can pass without comment: we are assured it will have a positive result. From a state of intimacy that to outside eyes might appear suffocating, we move apart in order to come back even more closely together. We learn to miss and to want and to need each other again. To tremble anew at a touch that was perhaps becoming overly familiar. To find fresh pleasure in the sensation of your body against mine, in the weight of my head upon your chest.

In simultaneous orgasms, syncopated sighs, osmotic dreams.

Our reconnection can possess the excitement of the first encounter, only heightened and enriched by a wealth of erotic knowledge gained from thousands of subsequent encounters.

But this time you do not return to our communal bed after a night, a week, a month.

I have no way of knowing that you will never share it with me again.

No understanding of what has ended, of what has begun.

During this time, I happen to be working while you are not. There's nothing unusual in that. We often alternate holding jobs. Our life of love has always been more important than the level of our income. One of us frees the other to assume the main burden of cooking and cleaning, and to tackle repairs and other projects around the house. More of our time together becomes available for the act of love. (In more than just a sense, though, each of our shared activities—putting up the storm windows in autumn, reseeding the lawn in spring—is an erotic exchange.)

The system has worked well for us.

Until now.

Because I sleep poorly without you beside me, I come home from work tired after the first night you spend in the back room. I don't have the energy to wonder why you haven't prepared supper. (This is precisely when you are apt to fix my favourite meal as reassurance, however unnecessary, of your unfaltering love.) Why you remain in the spare room instead of sharing the meal I end up making. Why you don't feel like going to the cinema, the café, the gym. You have already eaten, I think. You wish to spend a quiet evening at home, alone. When we don't join together physically, we often remain apart in other ways as well. I find myself listening for hints of your nearby presence, and shrug at the uninterrupted silence that leaks beneath the door you're behind. You are reading or resting or writing a letter. The spare room is closed each time I pass down the hallway. When I step into the backyard to turn the sprinkler off at ten o'clock, I notice your window is dark.

Mentally, I shrug again.

We've always respected each other's privacy.

As we grow closer, it becomes more important and necessary to avoid intruding upon our individual secrets.

The unknown is erotic. Darkness is an aphrodisiac.

The gap between what I don't know about your interior and all I know of your exterior can make me swoon.

Several days later, I suspect you rarely leave the spare room while I'm at work. The rest of the house lacks evidence of your presence. No crumbs litter the kitchen counter. No CD rests in the audio system. No damp towel drapes in the bathroom.

You continue to decline to share the meals I make, as you still don't wish to cook or clean or shop for groceries. While I'm at home, you remain behind the spare room door. You barely respond when I open it to say a few words at morning, after work, before bed.

Yes, you smile, when I ask if you're okay.

We have always told each other the truth.

Checking the odometer, I learn that your Jeep's mileage doesn't change from one day to the next.

Of course you aren't leaving the house if you aren't leaving the spare room.

The other room, as I begin to think of it.

As that room assumes greater importance, grows equal in significance to our room.

Or what was our room.

On the fifth or sixth day after we begin to sleep apart, I return from work to find the house filled with what seems like a new kind of silence and emptiness. It feels as though all traces of human presence have drained away through the walls. Immediately my heart relaxes; just as suddenly, I realize how tightly it has been clenched. Even without the reassurance of your Jeep in the driveway, I wouldn't be worried that you might have left me. I'm far from ready to conceive of the impossible. You are only strolling beside the river, or climbing the sweep of hill to where perfumed pines stir and moan in breeze. You have looked increasingly pale—I know it's as difficult for you as for me to sleep alone—and this June is especially fair. (The last June, I will later think, as though June has never come again, as though all months, including current ones, exist only as memories.) When I knock on the door of the other room, you don't answer. I open the door. You're sitting on the floor beside the bed, which looks as neat as if it hasn't been slept in for several nights. Your face is turned toward me. I suspect your eyes have been watching for the appearance of mine since I left for work ten hours ago. All day you have done nothing but wait for me.

For my touch.

Our sexual life has always been important. It's the principal reason we have remained together for the past twelve years. (Only those few—in my experience, they aren't many—who are willing to search through all five senses in the company of another human being, and who possess the particular talent for such exploration, are in any position to understand what a complete reason for sustained unity that journey can be.) Two strong, flexible bodies; swollen muscles and sleek skin; a pair of large penises: this forms the raw material for our unending expedition into each other. To preserve the instruments by which we make our exchange in perfect condition, and to keep our appetite for their use sharply honed, we take scrupulous care regarding diet, spend several hours in the gym each day, forsake smoke and drink and other drugs. What I wish to tell you about who I am, how I feel, what you mean to me: all this is said through the detailed language of touch. Your penis and then mine speaks now slowly and now quickly; the anus answers eagerly; mouths elaborate the point, and fingers stroke further meaning from it. Extended sentences of semen spill. Moans modulate into a dozen subtly different phrases. The few people to enter our life and observe us together invariably comment on the degree of silence between us. I doubt words could say more precisely or clearly what your hand conveys resting on the back of my neck as we drive into the mountains in search of the first or last snow of the ski season; what my multilingual lips say as they explore various countries of your skin. In private sign language, your caressing fingers spell endearments upon my back. Intricate concepts, complex emotions: this idiom of the senses is not simple.

Before finding each other, we both experienced lovers who did not wholly understand the speech of sex, the tongue of touch.

That early lack has allowed us to enjoy each other with special appreciation.

Now my first touch in five or six days tells you: I want you, I need you, I'll never leave you.

More, you say soundlessly, unsmilingly.

(But that was long ago. Sometimes now, when the rooms around me are most silent, and the clock ticks loudest, I can believe I inhabit this house alone. There's no sign of a second presence, except for the scarcely distinguishable yet permeating scent of rot that travels from the room in the back. I almost forget that in your ultimate, invisible form you remain with me here. Where you want to be. Need to be. Must be. Why? Love will forever remain the final puzzle of the world, the unsolved riddle of the Sphinx, our galaxy's last secret. I've had years now to muse upon the question of what became of us. Like reaching out to grab darkness and ending up with empty hands, the answer still eludes me.)

The tone of your touch has changed since five or six days ago. It speaks with new force about hunger and need. After our initial, urgent dialogue is complete, you turn from me and curl into a ball on the hard floor where we've come together. You want me to leave; before, our tactile conversation would continue long after the first explosion of white words.

Unlike me, the single bed remains undisturbed.

Leaving the room, I fail to realize the full significance of the bed's unrumpled state.

Or of your silence before, during, and after our act of love.

I come home the next day to find you've fastened heavy black cloth over the window of the other room in such a way that not even a crack of light enters. The following day marks my discovery that you have removed the bulb from the light socket in the ceiling. Two days after that, the room has been rid of its furniture, the walls of their prints, the closet of its cardboard boxes. You begin to use a bucket for your wastes. You no longer dress. When I enter the room, your naked body shrinks into the farthest corner from the light that falls in from the hall. Your eyes close until the door has shut and complete darkness returned. Only your body and the bucket prevent the space from being a void; there is nothing else that dilutes the vacant darkness. No clothes interfere with my touch. No objects separate us. No light distracts our eyes with unnecessary images. Now we see only each other. See through touch, through taste, through smell. To a lesser degree (quickened breath, contrapuntal groans), through sound.

But you have ceased speaking in words.

My voiced speech makes you cringe, as if it were fists.

The darkness is pure, your fingers spell upon my back.

The darkness is holy, they insist.

Would I have acted differently if I had known that I would never hear your voice again?

That you would never leave the dark room to appear before me in light again?

The heartbreak of hindsight.

Your touch soon informs me that it isn't necessary to bring the balanced meals I carefully prepare for you twice a day. You'll eat only a crust of bread, drink only a half cup of water. Nor is it important that I empty the bucket of waste regularly. All you want from me is my touch. As if this touch contains all light, all nourishment, all comfort you desire.

What do I desire?

The same thing as always: your happiness.

I give you what you want, what I can, what I have.

More, your touch demands.
Harder, it urges.
Don't stop.

Driving home, I fear what new development will await me. I park next to your Jeep and contemplate our shared home. From the outside, it appears more or less the same as the others on this quiet street. Innocent, innocuous. The old woman next door, whose sidewalk we shovel in winter and lawn we mow in summer, waves until I lift my arm in response. (We've taken pains to ingratiate ourselves with our neighbours in order to forestall unease they might otherwise feel from our presence, as in a foreign country one is careful to soothe potentially hostile natives.) A small boy pedals his tricycle up and down the sidewalk, rings its tinny bell repeatedly. A sprinkler pirouettes with perfect grace on green grass. Blue smoke from barbecues slants through the golden air of six o'clock. The scent of burning charcoal and cooking meat mixes with that of freshly cut lawns to produce the bouquet of suburbia.

The small boy's name is Billy. Often when you have worked in the yard, he has tagged at your heels, tugged at your sleeve, asked question after question. Changing the oil in your Jeep, you patiently explained each step, allowed him to hand you tools. He would stand beside you, scarcely reaching half-way up your long legs. His face tilts to find your eyes above. Your hand rests lightly upon his tawny head.

From what I understand, Billy has no father. My source of information, the old woman next door, shakes her head when speaking of the boy: plainly, she could say more.

I have seen the way you look at the son you'll never have.

It makes the strings of my heart knot, tangle, twist.

From the driveway's perspective and distance, it would be easy to summon terms such as "breakdown" and "psychosis" and "illness" to describe what is occurring inside our house. It seems obvious that intervention and assistance are required for you, of me. In the end, I will be asked why I didn't save you. That failure will be called a crime, given another name, turned into an act that demands punishment.

I won't try to explain that to drag you from the other room and call an ambulance would have meant failure to our eyes.

We have never lived for the world's eyes.

We have always lived for love alone.

Perhaps all lovers must believe they embark upon a unique adventure, undertake a brave new experiment, engage in unprecedented experience. You are daring me to follow you deep into the darkness. To search for the source of love, as elusive as that of the Nile, which lies far beyond practical procreation and sanctified desire and convenient passion; only there at its origin, before becoming contaminated by time and space, is love pure. Long ago, I suspect, you began preparing for this journey we're taking now. You waited patiently until you were able to bring it about; you always kept the larger picture in mind. An unremarkable house on a quiet street in a drowsy suburb far from the sleek centre of a city: this particular setting is important to the success of your meticulously conceived design—as the room at the back of the house, the old woman next door and the small boy half-way down the block form further crucial pieces of the puzzle you hold whole in your head. And you selected me specifically to participate in your experiment because you believed I would not fail its challenges, however difficult they might be. Several dozen images of you closely considering me form a montage. You are wondering if I am strong enough, brave enough, man enough to love.

The tricycle bell fades in the distance. I continue to feel you waiting within the house for me. For several days, I realize, I have come home hoping to find you gone. For one moment, I am tempted to turn the ignition key and restart the still-warm engine; to drive away and not return.

This is my last chance to leave you.

From here there is no going back.

Slowly I approach then enter our house.

Honey, I hysterically think of calling, *I'm home.*

Gradually I stop thinking of the space you occupy as "the other room."

It is simply "the room."

The original room, the only room.

As if no other room has ever existed.

Sometimes your silence taunts me.

Sometimes it shrilly screams.

Seduces, begs, insinuates, cajoles.

Increasingly, interpretation is all that remains for me.

Or rather: understanding that, in love, interpretation is all we ever have.

The adoring expression in his eyes, the tender tone of his voice: our own emotion, fatally subjective, elects the adjectives it requires to survive.

The air enclosed within the room becomes thick and heavy with the odour of your unbathed body, with the stench from the bucket of waste. It grows difficult to respond to your silent summons. I must remind myself that this aroma is produced by and is part of the being I love; therefore, I must love it also.

In love there can be no selective throwing out of chaff to keep the grain.

Take me as I am.

All or nothing.

In sickness and in health.

Till death do us part.

Threadbare clichés echo tinnily inside my head.

The darkness around you assumes the properties of solid matter. I stroke its skin; I squeeze its entrails. Rub darkness between my fingers, feel its texture. Touch it, learn it, know it.

Love it.

It requires increasing effort to touch you with the force you desire. I grow nostalgic for the days when the lightest pressure of my fingertips could make you quiver, cry out, come. In the Braille darkness, I read a historical romance that features your clean hair's scent, the gaze of two green eyes, the precise pitch of a laugh. More and more, I feel I'm making love with the past.

Or committing adultery with your ghost.

I wonder if our emphasis on touch as profound communication was misguided all along. As your silence lasts, I'm perversely compelled to speak to you in words, must fight to stifle that urge. When your birthday arrives, and then our anniversary, I feel helpless to convey the significance of these days. Especially since, exactly when subtlety is most needed, my touch becomes reduced to blunt blows.

Still harder, you mutely beg.

It's painful to realize that your powerful body is losing mass, your muscles their firm tone. In the second the door lies open, as I enter or leave the room, a glimpse reveals how pale you've become. Gaudy sores and cuts and bruises decorate your skin like the haphazard work of some tattoo artist suffering from a deficiency in concentration. Like the nails of your toes and fingers, your matted hair grows long. But in the darkness, your eyes shine more brightly than ever. Your touch tells me over and over that this is how you wish to live. Your previous experience was compromise.

Now you are completely satisfied.

Perfectly happy.

Summer passes slowly. I go to work each weekday. I visit you each evening. I mow the lawn and wave to neighbours and watch Billy pedal his blue tricycle back and forth in front of our house. He is hoping the sound of his bell will draw you to him. That you will play catch with him. Tell him about when you were a boy his age. Promise him that one day he'll grow to be as tall and strong as you. As loved as you.

When I return the emptied waste bucket to the room, you tend to shift it one or two feet from where I have placed it. After a moment, the metal's glint shows you have moved it half-way back to where it was. In my mind gleams a host of occasions from the time before the room, when you seemed to meditate on the position of some unimportant object, consult a blueprint in your head, then adjust the arrangement of the landscape to match. The blueprint is of the past; what seems unprecedented to me is in fact repetition: this has happened before. I slowly understand how crucial it is that your room is at the back, not the front of the house. That the woman next door is old rather than young. That, for purposes of replication, Billy's hair is tawny instead of dark.

In my dreams, I sponge your body until it sings with cleanliness. I cut your hair and clip your nails and dress your sores. I feed you, cradle you, croon to you.

In our dreams, we do what we're denied when awake.

Our telephone and doorbell have never rung often. We've always been enough—everything—for each other. Now when an acquaintance calls for you, I say you're at the gym, at the store, in the shower. When the old woman next door wonders why she hasn't seen you lately, I explain you're away on business for the summer. By autumn, I'll say that you've left me for good, that I don't know where you've gone. I leave the keys in your unlocked Jeep until it's stolen. I scrawl *Moved* on your mail and send it back. Telephone calls for you cease; with one exception, questions about you stop.

You have gone.

You are not here.

Like any dream erased by dawn.

In what was our room, on what was our bed, I study photographs of you. Once I would have said, with complete conviction, that it would never be necessary for me to do this, no matter how far you went away, no matter how long you stayed away. Light seeps from your snapshot skin, spills out of emerald eyes, escapes your Kodak smile. Women and other men turned in the street to catch that light; they didn't realize it was only a faint approximation of the dazzle to flood me when we're alone together. During our twelfth year, we have wanted each other more than during the first. In the supermarket, your broad shoulder would brush mine and nearly knock me off balance with the force of electric charge. Spotting you in the gym, my fingertips would graze your wrists and surge blood to the lush surface of your skin. Always the taste of your saliva bloomed in my mouth. Always from us wafted the spice of our mingled semen.

I do not possess a vial containing the precious essence of your original scent.

No recording of the voice that throbbed my blood.

Before or after the last leaf falls from the maple behind our house?

I don't realize precisely when I begin to think of you in the past as well as present tense. When the being in the room, though still "you," assumes an identity separate from the one I originally loved. You have divided into two parts—pre-darkness and post-light—like some organism capable, with only the assistance of time, of self-reproduction.

Which half of you received the indivisible heart?

Only Billy doesn't believe you've gone away. He persists in knocking on the front door and asking for you. As I explain your absence once again, he peers behind me, unconvinced. Dragging his heels, glancing over his shoulder, he leaves reluctantly. His face is pinched more sharply than ever with hunger.

At my least sound, you shake with such force I fear you will convulse. Now we do not even moan or grunt when we come together. There is only the dull thud of my fist against your face, the slap of my hand on your skin. My kick, my push, my shove: these gestures of love each produce their particular sound, speak their specific language. It's unfamiliar to me; I can't understand it. Only you are fluent in this idiom.

I wonder where and when you learned it.
With whom.

We've always been able to wear each other's clothes because, until recently, we've been the same size. Seeing you in my shirt would reinforce my feeling that we're interchangeable, identical, one. I would experience the same pleasurable confusion as of waking to wonder if the arm flung over my chest belongs to you or to me. Now I wear your clothes exclusively. At morning, I look in our closet and imagine what you would wish to wear today. The faded yellow sweatshirt with a small hole in the left shoulder— an old favourite? I like to believe my dressing in your clothes allows you to share my experience within them.

To live in light as well as in darkness.

In what was our room, I make loud, guilty love with your photographed self. I sense you stiffen with jealousy in the darkness across the wall. On my next visit, you retreat to the back of the closet and won't come out. Although I've ceased receiving pleasure from our physical contact (except in the sense that your pleasure is always mine), on this evening I leave the dark room overwhelmed by unsatisfied desire.

The autumn proves unusually mild, but I never feel warm in bed. I wonder if your body, naked upon bare tiles, suffers equally from cold. Beneath heavy blankets, I curl around my shivering self. The first time I waken to the sound of crying, I believe it comes through the wall. Then I understand this noise is produced by me. Soon I'm accustomed to being roused by weeping; it is no more extraordinary a nocturnal phenomenon than, say, darkness.

As you continue to deteriorate within the room, I grasp more tightly to life outside it. I never miss a day of work. I attend the gym religiously, read the newspaper thoroughly, clean the house carefully. Leaves fallen from the backyard maple are promptly raked; air freshener to combat the odour that leaks from beneath your door is purchased. I have my car tuned and my eyes examined and my teeth checked. Attentive to the calendar, I stock up on candy for Halloween. (This year Billy is a cowboy; last year he was an Indian.) I cook a Thanksgiving turkey with all the trimmings and eat enough for both of us. When the first snow falls, I'm aware that you must have no idea the world has become white. As perhaps you're uncertain whether it is Tuesday as opposed to Sunday, whether night has replaced day. (Or if in your dark zone have you developed strategies, based on sound reaching you from outside, to keep track of time as in the cemetery corpses are able to count off the weeks until their resurrection? Perhaps a blunting of senses allows me to bear the dark room but also prevents me from hearing, when inside it, the song of birds and calls of children beyond.) At Christmas, I'm at a loss as to the gift I can give you. On that silent, holy night, out of frustration with my failure to find a way to share a celebration of the season in a meaningful way with you, my hands draw your blood for the first time. At once I comprehend how much this excites and pleases you. You greedily lick the liquid spilling from your nose. I listen to the slurp, suck, slurp. I recall the time I entered the room and, in a second of revelation, saw you tilt the bucket of waste to your opened mouth. Then swallow, then lick lips, then burp.

Sometimes I wonder if my memory is confused. Was it me who unscrewed the bulb from the socket in the ceiling, removed the furniture, placed heavy black cloth over the window, and took away your clothes? My body almost seems to possess physical memory of having performed those actions. I shake my head. No. It has always been a challenge to distinguish where one of us begins and the other leaves off. What's done by you, what's done by me. That overlapping has caused me confusion now.

Rather than visit you in the darkness, could I remain with you there? Share it with you, as we've shared everything important?

I know this isn't possible.

I must remain in light so you can enjoy darkness.

I am the light, you are the darkness.

Complete love is the union of these opposite elements.

I repeat such formulae by rote, puzzle where I learned them, speculate that while I sleep someone stands beside the bed and whispers concepts and directives that sink through the darkness and into my subconscious to emerge as apparently my own thoughts upon waking.

There are moments, during daytime, when I can almost recall the sound of that instructive voice.

Its familiar tone, its known timbre.

Anyway, if we did love lastingly in the dark, our electricity would soon illuminate and destroy that element. Even now—still—sparks seem to shoot from our touch, swirl in haloes around our heads.

Repeatedly it strikes me how comfortable you are in your bare, pitch-black room.

As if you've lived this way before.

You are realizing in three dimensions the flat blueprint of the past that hovered for years inside your head.

(Sometimes, entering the room, I feel I am stepping into the dark chamber of your mind.)

Or, to take the longer view, your species has adapted, over centuries of evolution, to conditions that have finally become a natural environment for you to enjoy as well as endure.

Yet I can't permit myself to contemplate how you pass the hours while waiting for my next touch. What you remember of the past, what you experience in the present, what you hope for the future. I can't allow myself to calculate the number of dark hours you have survived so far. The thought causes a twinge of pain to shoot through my head.

Spring comes, spring goes. Suddenly it is a year since you entered the room. I mark the date by remembering:

The last words you spoke to me.

The last cup of coffee you made for me.

The last squint of your sun-drenched eyes.

If nostalgia is a second-rate emotion, surely sentimentality occupies a still lower plane.

In the backyard I catch Billy looking up at the window covered with heavy black cloth. He quickly runs away. The boy has always avoided me as much as he has inversely been drawn to you. He is aware that I know the truth about him. That I recognize the hunger in him. That I understand what he is prepared to do to save himself from starvation.

Need corrupts.

When you weren't looking, his innocent grey eyes leered at me.

His tongue has licked his pink petalled lips enticingly.

Billy lives with a relative of some kind. My neighbour says the old woman is an alcoholic recluse, a mean and twisted spirit. That's no excuse for the boy.

It could be much worse.

As I should know.

And as you, I'll learn, know better.

I abandon my habit of wearing your clothes. I don't want even to imagine that you are sharing the experiences and emotions I now have within them.

Certain stresses I must suffer and tensions I must bear because of the stupidity of the world.

Let's just say it has not been easy to sustain myself outside the room.

Arguably, you enjoy an easier existence within it.

Yet I do not resent the alignment of our roles.

Selfishly, unsuccessfully, I try to subvert your unspoken wishes and interfere with your undeniable happiness. At high volume I play certain music you have especially loved with the idea that it might draw you from the room. With similar hope, I prepare the one dish whose tantalizing aroma you have never been able to resist. For one week I refrain from bringing you bread and water. Going away for a weekend, I deprive you of several visits.

None of these stratagems works.

I can almost sense you smirk at the naïvete of my ploys.

Clearly you're the one in control here. The one to dictate the course of events.

I am merely your pawn.

Your prisoner.

Factor X in your investigation into the truth about love.

One evening, during the second year, you fail to shrink away when I enter the room. For once, the moment of light from the hallway does not seem to disturb you. Curious, I leave the door open and move silently toward your favourite spot at the rear of the room. When I wave my hands before your eyes, they don't blink. A clap near your ear fails to make you recoil.

You are blind, you are deaf.

Correspondingly, your touch becomes more urgent, more forceful, more demanding.

More, more, more. Each time leaving you, I am exhausted from trying to fulfill your need, surprised by the sustained vigor of your response. I doubt I possess the stamina to love you the way you need to be loved much longer.

Who is growing stronger?

Who weaker?

Yet I continue to close the door behind me upon entering or leaving the room. I can't bear to witness with my eyes what is difficult enough to be told by touch. Pus oozing from open sores, bones jutting sharply beneath skin coated with a second skin of dirt and blood, feces and urine. After each visit, I scrub myself mercilessly with powerful soap, but wonder if a trace of your decay clings to me still.

Unvanquished microbes.

Undislodged bacteria.

You have seeped into my skin, sunk deep inside my marrow, dripped into my DNA.

You're not deteriorating, I tell myself.

You are evolving.

I have still failed to rediscover how to sleep soundly alone. Perhaps this is a skill that, once unlearned, can never be acquired again? The place you occupied in our bed yawns like a bottomless pit beside which I huddle fearfully until dawn. (On the other side of the wall, are you awake too?) The voice that speaks to me in my sleep is waiting to pounce if I finally do drift off. Now it barks, growls, snarls obscene instructions. The morning mirror reveals a drawn, anxious face. My head throbs steadily. I fumble through the days as if half-blind, half-deaf. At work I continually make simple mistakes. My colleagues express concern. Those who have known about your presence in my life believe they witness evidence of suffering caused by your desertion.

It's not just a question of sleeping alone. I don't know if I am able to live alone. Millions do, I remind myself. Yes, but they have not known you. Often in the evening, battered by the pain in my head and the voice of my sleep, I sit on the hall floor, rest my back against your closed door, and from your presence beyond seek to draw sufficient strength to carry on for one more day.

Billy's blue tricycle becomes a green bicycle. One Saturday I see him bent over its prone frame. One of the pedals is broken. No, he replies when I ask if I can help. He looks at me with a mixture of suspicion and dislike and fear. He believes I have taken you from him. Made you disappear.

Perhaps I'm disappointed.

Perhaps I thought that, deprived of you, the boy would turn to me.

As if it was recently left there, or had been patiently awaiting discovery all along, a file concerning you, dated twenty-one years ago, appears at the bottom of the bag where you kept your hockey equipment. (I've been sorting through your things. *It's time*, snaps the voice of my sleep.) I glance quickly at the papers in the file. Medical reports, psychiatric records, police dossiers. Without assimilating the information, I stuff the papers back into the bag. If you had wanted me to know the contents of this file, you would have shared them with me. For reasons I can't articulate, it seems essential that I refrain from digging into your secrets now. The prospect makes the dull pain in my head sharpen.

We did not bring our pasts to our union. We were born anew with our first kiss. I've gathered that no parents or siblings or close friends peopled your existence before me; an uncrowded history was one more attribute we shared. No one will look for you now. Make inquiries. File a missing person's report. Even under these circumstances, it's astonishing that a human being could vanish without a murmur from the face of the earth. As if he had never been here at all.

A life melts away like snow that leaves no trace of itself behind.

Displaying what was there underneath all along.

After a certain point in the third year, there is no way to describe what passes between us in the room as sexual activity, however broad the scope encompassed by that term. Suddenly, swiftly, your touch grows weaker; you can no longer hold me, clutch me, grasp me. Eventually you do not have the strength to expel your wastes into the bucket, to swallow bread, to sip water. Your teeth have abandoned your gums. Your hair has deserted your head. Huge in your gaunt face, open wide, your blind eyes are covered with a film of white. Your limbs, apparently broken some time ago in the course of our meetings and never properly healed, dangle at odd angles from your torso of bereft bone. You become an inert mass on a tiled floor. Now I am required simply to enter the room and kick the shape of darkness. I must kick as hard as I can for you to feel the touch. That kick is all that keeps you alive.

It would be an act of violation, an explicit rape, to cradle you in my arms, rock you gently, whisper into your unhearing ears all the words of love that for three years have been building up inside me, festering like the pus that drips from your open sores.

Something snaps. With your last strength, you sever the unbreakable thread that has joined our physical selves for so long.

You perform this superhuman act for the sake of my survival—more exactly, since you are me, for our mutual survival. I no longer need to crouch outside the room in the evenings: what remains inside is dross; what is essential, our love, lives on within my walls of flesh. Although free from the contents of the room, from force of habit I can't help continuing to visit it, to consider it, to think of it as you.

Very carefully, I sweep the house of your belongings, wipe your finger-prints from each surface, destroy every piece of evidence that you were here. As a backyard fire consumes photographs of your face and pieces of identification from your wallet, as smoke from the liberating flames tears my eyes, I remind myself that I require no sentimental souvenirs, no nostalgic knick-knacks. Long ago, I repeat, you were imprinted upon my cells, written into their code. Every expression of love between us was an act of genetic engineering.

I frown with irritation. The file of documents I left in your hockey bag lies open on my bed. I distinctly recall taking the canvas bag, in a load of your other possessions, to the dump at the edge of town. I press my thumbs into the corners of my eyes; neither aspirin nor more potent medication relieves the pain of the headaches that have become a constant factor in my life. The dreaminess I have suffered since your entry into the room has steadily grown stronger; my job performance has been affected to the point that last week I was called in for an unpleasant interview with my supervisor. (Once the golden glow that surrounded me—the radiance created by the light of our love—caused this man to blush when I looked at him and to stammer when he spoke to me.) As a side effect of my headaches or my dreaminess, or under their combined influence, I've started to find myself places without the least idea of how I got there.

It's a disorienting experience.

Almost disturbing.

The other night I woke up (perhaps, more correctly, came to consciousness) outside the house half-way up the block where Billy lives. I could not recall the series of steps that led to my crouching there upon the dirt, beside the chinaberry bush, beneath his window. My most recent memory was of opening and then quickly closing the door of the room. For the first time failing to transform my disgust at the stench and filth of your remains into love for the substance that was its source. For the first time failing to enter the darkness and to satisfy what is left of its occupant. Beneath Billy's window, the spring dirt smelled amazingly rich. I'd describe the scent as a clean darkness. Through the pores of its skin, the earth beneath me breathed in, breathed out. Pulsing at the edge of the yard, crickets kept time like a clock in the May night and reminded ascendant stars they had hours to glitter the dew. The touch of a breeze against my face made me reel; the gleam of grass dilated my eyes; the hallucinogenic heavens swam, swirled, spun.

From the way the world overwhelmed my senses, I might have just emerged from three years within a dark, bare, fetid room.

From the nearest street lamp, a path of light carried my vision inside Billy's window, exposed his perfect, unmarked face upon the pillow. Although slightly flushed with sleep, his face appeared pale under this illumination. I could see his chest rise and fall, a pajama top patterned with what looked like superheroes; below, the covers tangled around his waist, left his concealed lower limbs to interpretation. The same breeze that touched my cheek lifted and released the curtain of Billy's open window, with a delicate gesture offering then taking away my view; tantalizing, teasing.

Suddenly I felt angry.

How careless to leave the window open like that.

How irresponsible.

Inviting anyone to enter.

Even a sleepy suburb like this isn't safe.

(Especially a sleepy suburb like this, I sometimes think.)

All at once, the pain in my head became much more severe. I blacked out; that must be what happened. I next found myself standing in the shower, scrubbing and scouring my skin of its stink with powerful soap.

Of your stink.

Apparently, at some point after leaving Billy, I overcame my revulsion and visited you. Perhaps my vision of Billy compelled the visit?

My vision, my experience.

I intuit that an image is missing from my memory: the absence nags. In the same way that the sound of Billy's bicycle bell reminds me of something I can't quite recall.

Something in the darkness I can't quite touch.

Something significant, I suspect.

Something known to the possessor of the voice that addresses me during sleep.

Trying to piece together what has happened during the blank spaces caused by the headaches causes the headaches to grow worse.

I feel caught within a closed circuit. The synapses in the circuit are produced by a struggle to escape it?

With reluctance, I pick up the file on the bed. Quietly, as if you can hear me from the other side of the wall, I examine its contents:

A physician's report concerning the physical condition of a boy who, it is estimated (see concurring police and psychiatric reports), spent seven years enclosed within a dark, bare room. Malnutrition: *severe*. Muscular coordination: *poor*. Sensory responses: *limited*. Inability to withstand light: *temporary*. Muteness: *see psychiatric report*. Recovery: *excellent* (underlined). Prognosis: *no permanent physical damage*.

The psychiatric diagnosis. Trauma: *severe*. Loss of speech: *temporary*. Loss of memory: *extensive; limited recovery anticipated.* Loss of affect: *severe, limited recovery probable.* Perception of reality: *poor.* Sexual fixations: *several.* Prognosis: *permanent psychological damage, eventual functioning at minimal levels.* (For detailed case analysis, see *International Journal of Psychiatry, Vol. XXIV, No. 3, pp 217–249.*)

Social services report. Placement of subject: *foster care.* Follow up visits: *social (home and school) difficulties noted.* Sexual disturbances: *acted out (see psychiatric records).* Discipline difficulties: *noted.* Concern of foster parents: *noted.* Status: *ongoing monitoring required.*

Police file. Efforts to establish identity of Case No. _____: *unsuccessful.* Investigation into circumstances of criminal confinement: *unsuccessful.* Possible suspects in confinement: *none.* Motives for confinement: *unknown.* Final status of case: *unsolved; closed.*

Court document: John Doe No. _____ will henceforth bear the legal name _____.

At the bottom of these documents lie petitions, dated eleven years later, for their release to subject.

I close the file.

In one sense, it has been closed for twenty-one years; in another, it's still open.

Do those twenty-one years form a blank space for you?

A synapse in your closed system?

A period of limbo between one bare, dark room and the next?

Between one dream and another?

On the other side of the wall, once more in darkness, you struggle to close the file.

Forever, for good.

If I did not know you better, this information might seriously disturb rather than briefly disappoint me. Initially, I must confess, I'm somewhat surprised by your failure to destroy, long ago, documents which are essentially without meaning, which obviously bear no real relation to our love. I wonder at your decision to allow them to survive for my discovery. To risk our special, intimate experience being polluted by the judgment of the uncomprehending world. Were my love for you less strong, it might now be soiled by the rough, clumsy touch of those systems which must always seek to control and to explain an existence as unique as ours.

Quickly correcting my mistaken sense of disappointment, I reject the documents as wholly as I reject the systems that produced them.

They mean nothing. They explain nothing. They illuminate only the incomprehension of the unevolved world around us.

The stupidity.

Clearly, you left this information for me to destroy.

Call it a final invitation to partake in your experience. A lover's last gift.

Once again, I am happy to comply with your wishes.

Another match scratches. More fire is fed.

Passing our house these days, Billy quickens his step, stares straight ahead. No longer looks lingeringly, hungrily toward where you once lived.

The smell of rot within the room is so intense I must hold my breath for the few moments I manage to withstand it. Although I continue to replace the bread and water that go untouched from one evening to the next, my visits are perfunctory at best. More would be unnecessary. The entity upon the tiled floor bears as little relation to our love as did the documents I have destroyed. Frankly, I grow impatient with this mass of blood and skin and bone that you have left behind. I am almost resentful at your delegating me to deal with it. There is a danger that if your remains linger too long they'll cloud the meaning of our love as much as the contents of the file briefly threatened to do. The most important act of love I could perform at the moment might very well be to free us entirely of this mute, motionless mess.

This matter, this muck.

The periods of darkness that befall me occur more frequently and last longer, as far as I can tell. Obviously, I am disinclined to seek relief from the medical profession for the blank spaces or for the worsening, accompanying headaches. The quacks and charlatans have done enough damage. Instead, I take the self-prescribed medication which, due to the stupidity of our legal system, I can obtain only with difficulty. Unfortunately, the substance renders me unable to pursue certain activities that have long played a central, stabilizing role in my life; for example, I'm no longer able to go to the gym. Also prevented from working, I take advantage of the considerable vacation time that has accumulated over the past three years.

The telephone rings unanswered.

Unopened mail accumulates.

Between the blank spaces, I visit the cash machine, the supermarket, the supplier of my medication. At a building supply store, I purchase a sack of lime, as the voice from my sleep has instructed. These excursions are necessarily brief: I must take care that the blank spaces occur as much as possible within the house; to fall into one of them outside exposes me to several kinds of risk. Yet there's continuing evidence that I still wander during dark episodes. Although I fail to remember coming to consciousness in places I have no memory of travelling to, that's hardly a relief. It only means I'm left in ignorance of where I go or what I do during times of blackness.

Guess, chuckles the voice from my sleep.

The unknown is dangerous, beats the pain in my head.

Of late, I have often "woken up" to find myself naked in the room. I'm not equipped to describe the appalling loneliness of that experience. How the darkness tells me only that I would do anything, even leave life, to escape it. (I have never liked the dark.) More than once, I have discovered my hands to be stained red, as if with bright blood; a bitter taste would haunt my mouth. For several days after my first encounter with these phenomena, I was puzzled by the elusive nature of their source.

Abruptly, unexpectedly, the explanation slid from the dark back of my mind to the front.

The house half way down the block.

The chinaberry bush.

Billy.

The obscure substance upon the tiles seems to produce a very weak, scarcely audible sound.

Mama.

Help.

Or so I think I hear.

The sound resembles the voice of a small boy who's frightened of the dark.

It is produced by my imagination, of course.

(The medication has more than several inconvenient side effects.)

The (imagined) voice does not speak again—at least, not while I'm in the dark room.

I must have accidentally cut myself during a recent fall from consciousness. There is a deep gash in the flesh of my inner arm. The sharp sting appears to cause the pain inside my head to recede, if only temporarily. Perhaps one hurt erases the other. I work my tongue into the wound as my penis stiffens.

In the backyard, I touch a match to a piece of cloth. It torn and soiled with what looks like the red juice of chinaberries. The pattern on the cloth shows men of comically exaggerated strength. They are patently capable of rescuing any situation no matter how desperate, of saving any being no matter how imperilled. Flames drop onto the ground by the back fence where ash indicates other flames have recently blazed. A nearby sound lifts my head. The old woman next door is watching from her back steps. Realizing that I notice her, she fades back into her house.

I wonder why I haven't seen Billy lately. Since school is out for the summer, he should be playing on the block during these sunny days. Perhaps he has gone away to a camp situated among green, scented pines, beside a blue lake of crystalline water. With other boys like him, he swims and hikes and canoes; after dark, they gather around a fire to sing sweetly. Their voices lift high into the clear night, reach to touch glittering stars.

I notice that I see better in the dark, as if my eyes have adapted to a prolonged lack of light. In the room, I believe I detect the matter at the back of the room stirs slightly. Bending closer, I realize this movement is that of worms wriggling in and out of liquefying flesh. Matter is changing form. I smile. This transmutation reminds me that our love has never been static; our love has always evolved. Progress keeps it vibrantly alive.

I waken to hear Billy's voice cry through the darkness. *Help, mama, help.* Something's happened to him at the summer camp beside a blue lake, amid green pines. An accident. He has drowned in crystalline water or has plummeted from a cliff. Long after its actual end, his voice continues to echo through the night. Although it travels from far away, the voice is as distinct and clear as a voice within this house.

The proliferation of wounds I find on my skin suggests that I must be clumsy when most heavily under the influence of medication. I must allow myself to become too close to sharp instruments. In the kitchen, silver knives wink knowingly. The axe leers from the back porch; seductively, a razor shimmers in bathroom light. Where opened to the air, my stinging flesh sings sweetly. My tongue tingles in anticipation.

Once such summer weather would have drawn me outdoors at every free moment, but each week I leave the house less frequently than the one before. It's not that I fear falling into dangerous darkness beyond these safe walls any more; there is no indication that I persist in undertaking journeys and performing actions without conscious knowledge: it seems that phase has ended. What needed to be done in darkness has been successfully accomplished, I assume.

(I can only speculate, at this point, upon developments occurring within and around me. Each new day I peek cautiously at whatever unexpected event unfolds. For you still control the execution of your secret master plan, and only the owner of the voice that speaks to me during sleep seems to share that privileged information in advance. *Kept in the dark*: this worn figure of speech acquires fresh potency as its figurative and its literal meanings rub against each other, set off a vibration I feel in my teeth. Clearly, both the darkness of the room and the darkness of my ignorance are preserved by you.)

Still my head pounds, still a voice snarls during my sleep, still the curtains stay closed. Medicated, I stumble through shadowed, scented rooms. The one or two times I venture outside, I don't bother to greet my neighbours with a friendly wave or to interpret and match their false expressions. The minor role played in my life by these unknowing people has been concluded; they don't matter any more. (However, someone should warn the old crone next door about the direction in which she watches from her window, from her steps. Too late, she might come to regret the unwise habit.) The street seems empty not only of Billy but of all children. It is the kind of absence that insists upon itself, like the silence that screams.

I'm not surprised when you begin to speak inside me. It's no secret that your essence entered mine some time ago: I have not mourned you because you did not leave. It does startle me, however, to recognize this interior voice as the same one that has been delivering instructions to my sleeping mind. Quickly I understand that a seeming harshness of tone was always due to the vocal force that is necessary to penetrate unconsciousness. For reasons not yet clear, your voice must communicate during daylight as well as in darkness now.

Of course, it is overwhelming to hear, after all that has happened over such a long time, the push of my lover's vowels, the catch of his consonants. At first I'm so enchanted by your voice that I disregard the words it forms. In some way, beyond the requirements of current circumstances, you sound different. I wonder if your voice has altered, if my memory of its timbre is incorrect, or if my interpretation of its qualities has changed. Beneath the erotic throb that lifts the hair on my arms cuts a cold, hard edge. Perhaps that edge was there all along. Carefully disguised, not perceived.

Hurry, it says.

The sack of lime, it insists.

Before it's too late, it commands.

The voice requires obedience. If its instructions are not carried out, I sense, the speaker will swiftly become enraged.

Summer heat has hastened the decomposition occurring within the room at the back of the house. The odour produced by this process is perceptible from the end of the driveway, from the farthest reaches of the backyard; slightly sweet, almost cloying, it mixes with a perfume of flowers grown by the old woman next door. Entering the room for the first time in several weeks, at your order, I notice at once that my approach raises numerous flies or gnats from the remains. The insects tremble above their source like visible ions of darkness. I see that the bones are nearly bare of flesh and surprisingly small. I bend nearer.

This is the skeleton of a child, not of a man.

Someone has secretly substituted a boy's bones for yours?

What are you waiting for? hisses your voice.

I sprinkle lime over the bones.

White sifts through the darkness like a child's midnight dream of snow. In the morning, we will toboggan down the big hill behind St Cecilia's. You ride in front; behind, I wrap my arms around your waist, hold on tight, and close my eyes as we speed faster and faster like the nuns' beads in the night. If we spill onto the snow, our arms will make angels until Sister Mary calls us in to feast on bread and water. That's all the nourishment needed by orphans who are always full with the sweetness of Jesus.

Pay attention, snaps your voice. *What are you doing?*

I shiver as an angel's wing brushes my shoulder in the dark.

Start as a heavy lid slams in my mind, seals St Cecilia's tight inside the coffin of the past.

Blink at my powdered fingers. Lick lime, taste chalk.

Rather than interfering with nature, I am helping to quicken its process.

I remember how we would never ingest steroids to stimulate our muscular growth by artificial means. For some reason, this memory strikes me as touching, tender.

It becomes necessary to turn more and more to my medication in order to silence the voice that otherwise speaks incessantly, steadily, scarcely pausing for breath. Yet you were never voluble; quite the opposite, in fact. Perhaps this stream of language is composed of all the words your voice did not speak during the dozen years before you entered the room.

Late at night, exhausted, I am prevented from sleeping by the constant chatter.

It is malicious, cynical, inimical.

It delights in enlightening me about the countless infidelities you committed from the very beginning of our union. It gleefully paints in pornographic detail every illicit fuck and suck you experienced, and how your excitement in each encounter was heightened by my ignorance of its occurrence. It droolingly describes what really gave you pleasure, how your true desires were never satisfied in our bed, the way you only went through the motions with me, why you considered yourself a skilled actor for stifling yawns of boredom both beneath and above me.

This voice can't be yours.

The possessor of this voice has only imitated you in order to deceive me.

You would never do the things this voice describes.

Sickening acts. Disgusting deeds.

The motive here is laughably obvious. It was clear from the start that the extraordinary combination we make would provoke inordinate jealousy and inspire every kind of attempt to sever us. In each other's arms, we used to joke about the pathetic efforts made by those who panted to come between us—the begging to join us in bed, the offers of large amounts of money to watch us. Instead of driving us apart, such machinations inspired us to dive more deeply inside each other.

The envious owner of this voice doesn't seem aware that now, more than ever, efforts to divide us are doomed to failure.

I'm able to reason my way through his ploy only with difficulty, as the venomous voice continues to scream inside me. It shrieks, over and over, that there was one obscene scenario you enjoyed above all others.

You don't believe me? shrills the impostor.

Ask the kid yourself. And why not give him a whirl, while you're at it. Afraid you might like it?

I am not offended by such an implication. I know what I have and have not done. Only that matters. It is interesting that, despite its purported omniscience, this voice isn't quite all-knowing: Billy's accident, that unfortunate fatality, seems to have eluded its notice. The real identity of the speaker is of negligible significance. Clearly, the voice is composed of all the frustrated longing, all the thwarted need, all the unsatisfied desire of all the cowards who throng the world around us. For the time being, for my own purposes, I'm content to allow the voice to believe it maintains the upper hand.

Naturally my feelings were hurt by not being invited to Billy's funeral. It appears I will not be informed even belatedly of his death; the sad event will be kept secret from me, like the weddings and anniversaries and baptisms that constantly take place beyond the edge of my vision. Despite this slight, I consider bringing a tasteful wreath to the woman halfway down the block who was charged with Billy's care. My impulse is quickly killed by anger that such a being would be given a child to raise. I have seen this sorry excuse for a human from a distance; I can guess, quite accurately, almost as if they happened to me, what sort of experiences Billy suffered at her hands. The kind of experiences that refuse to be buried, despite the passing of twenty-one or more long years. Maybe the boy is lucky to be out of it. I glare accusingly at the street from behind my window. The nondescript block lined with modest houses appears hushed, holding its breath, in suspense or in fear or in horror.

When I next enter the room (I'm not certain how much time has gone by; the medication interferes with my ability to calculate the passing of days), the remains on the tiles resemble perhaps finely crushed bone meal, perhaps the end product of the crematorium's furnace.

(Now my vision has grown poor, as if my eyes have strained too long to see in darkness.)

I sniff an unfamiliar odour—something acrid, acidic, chemical—the smothering smell of lime. A further substance has been added, by an anonymous assistant or by me, to encourage the disintegration of bone?

I allow the puzzle to pass unsolved. There are more important matters to worry about.

I dig the mixture into the flower beds that edge our back lawn.

The lawn is brown from lack of watering, I notice dully.

The flower beds are choked with weeds.

The simple task is almost beyond my strength. My movements are clumsy, my coordination poor.

Weakling, sneers the voice.

Patsy, it snipes.

I have no idea if this concoction of bone and lime and other ingredients will act as fertilizer or as poison.

Finish what you started, orders the voice.

I dispose of the waste bucket at the dump.

Remove the heavy black cloth from the window. Re-install the single bed, the night table, the boxes.

Hang the prints of ships upon the walls. Screw a bulb into the ceiling socket. Scrub the floor with disinfectant. Open the window to allow fresh air to enter.

Once again the room might appear very neat rather than quite bare.

Only a slight stain, perhaps invisible to unknowing eyes, remains on the tiles to the rear.

Despite the opened window, a subtle scent lingers like the memory of love.

For the first time in three years, I'm permitted to rest. Relieved of the painful pressure inside my head, apparently by the simple act of returning the room to its original state, I wander this shadowy house as if to reacquaint myself with it after an extended absence. I have been far away from here. During my long journey, the mirror informs, I have grown old. My face is pale and drawn and deeply lined. My hair is mostly grey; my eyes dull. My body is as cadaverous as a concentration camp victim. Beyond these physical effects, no souvenirs exist to speak of where my journey through love has taken me and what has happened to me there. There is no sign of what may have transpired within this house while I was away. What the world will call a crime. For which it will insist on finding a convenient scapegoat and on exacting harsh punishment.

I notice the outside of the house needs painting. Inside, the clock ticks more loudly than I remember.

I move down the hall, past the door that, though without lock or key, remains closed.

Behind it undisturbed dust dreams in silence.

Unbreathed air waits to be consumed by throats, caressed by lungs.

The voice that has spoken recently within these walls is silent. It has received what it wanted. Surely satisfied, it can now return to sleep behind the closed door. At least until the next time it is woken by desire.

Forgot something, teases the voice, with an approximation of a giggle, just when I become convinced it will stay dormant behind the door.

I look around again. I'm certain the house contains no evidence of the experience of love that has occurred during my seeming absence.

The latest experience; the most recent experiment.

I know now, as I have always known, that there have been experiences like this one in the past and that there will be more in the future.

There are always more.

If you can't figure out what you've overlooked, I'm not going to tell you, chortles the voice.

A clue has been left behind by the owner of the voice. A piece of evidence has been deliberately dropped to tie me to its actions.

I am its victim, after all. I will pay the price for the fulfillment of its desire.

The pain in my head returns with vicious vengeance. I reach for the medication, the instruments of injection. Pale blood swirls in the syringe.

The sting of the stab silences the voice.

I wait for the heavy fists to pound on the front door, the curious mob to gape from the sidewalk, the television cameras to capture the easy images, the surface truth.

Darkness, pure and holy, creeps up behind me. Softly, quietly. Shadows gently stroke, obscurity caresses. I wait for the absolving hands of darkness, its tender touch of love.

Mama.

Help.

Understand.

Forgive.

Pulsera

ESPERANZA WAS TWELVE, LIKE ME, BUT DIDN'T GO TO SCHOOL. SHE NEVER had. For as long as I could remember she'd spent each day on her chair at the end of the block, next to the coal man's stall, in front of six steps descending to a room where she and her older sister Selena lived. The cellar didn't have electricity. "Those poor girls," my mother would say, shaking her head. "It's dark as a tomb down there." Though blind, Esperanza didn't like the gloom. She preferred sitting out on the sidewalk with her work tray balanced across her knees. The twelve spools of coloured string there were always arranged the same way by Selena, but Esperanza could have found the one she wanted no matter where it was. After braiding friendship bracelets for six years, from fashioning all those thousands of *pulseras* with her fingers, she could identify the colours she worked with by touch. "Yellow feels different than green," Esperanza explained. It was easy to guess which colour was her favourite. The skirt and blouse she wore every day were blue, like her sweater when it turned chilly, and at least some blue had to be in all her *pulseras*. A vendor with a stall in the Plaza del Duque paid Selena two *pesetas* for each one. Throughout the city— across the river in Triana, up and down the Alameda, at the far side of Los Remedios—you could spy Esperanza's bracelets on wrists of Sevilla boys who bought them for each other or for themselves to wear like totems of some azure-adoring tribe. A quota of one hundred bracelets a day wasn't hard for Esperanza to meet. Her fingers were strong and deft; they twisted and pulled precisely. Her hand swooped down to pluck a string from the tray like a bird attracted by some shiny object on the ground. "I've done forty-six more since noon," Esperanza called, hearing me approach after school with a piece of meat wrapped in paper by my mother for those poor girls. "I'm almost there." Esperanza believed that upon braiding a million *pulseras* she'd be set free. She didn't say where she intended to go or what she planned to do after her liberation from the cellar and the sidewalk chair. I imagined Esperanza ascending into cerulean sky, in her similarly blue skirt and blouse, fingers fluttering like feathers. She soars toward the sun that she insisted was blue no matter what I tried to tell her. "It's blue as the stars," she said as we sneezed from the dust that drifted from next door whenever the coal man dug into his supply to sell half a kilo to a housewife. "I can feel it." At night the soot-filled stall diffused an acrid element into air already blurred by begonias growing in window pots up and down the narrow street. The complicated scent would pull me onto the latticed shelf of balcony off my bedroom to find the sky above the city strung with paths of stars leading to America. My right hand rubbed my other wrist, where naked skin itched to be adorned. In the cellar at the end of the block, Esperanza woke covered by a black film each morning, as though while asleep she burned with dreams whose ashes sifted over her like souvenirs of what blind eyes can see while closed.

No matter how many *pulseras* Esperanza completed, it was never enough to make her sister happy on returning home from work. The train station Selena scrubbed seven days a week was permanently filthy; no mop and broom could get it clean; a hundred years of drudgery wouldn't set Selena free. She moved heavily around the cellar in the evening, as though still dragging her pail of sour water. By candlelight she inspected another batch of bracelets. Each one had to be perfect to be worth two *pesetas*. No margin for mistakes existed; not a snippet of string could be wasted. There were no stray bits of blue to make into a free *pulsera* for me, and Esperanza would dismiss my offer of paying her to braid me one by swivelling her bare arms with disdain at such an idea. Yet I believe now that even then she realized how my left wrist ached more each month to be encircled, until it seemed I might be drawn by desire to the Plaza del Duque to buy a bracelet whose blues had been braided for sale to some stranger.

When I turned thirteen, I joined the club that rowed on the river running through the city. We met at a small dock below Calle Bétis three times a week after school. The other boys and I slid across the surface of the Guadalquiver in singles and pairs, fours and eights. Girls would drop flowers from bridges as we passed below; our oars made errant orange and purple petals swirl. There was still time to crouch on the sidewalk beside Esperanza before or after rowing. We never reached an end to our discussions of America or finished debating whether stars are really blue. Esperanza worked more quickly than ever. She seemed increasingly impatient to finish the million bracelets that would mean her release. Maybe she felt twinges of fear that the day would never come. Or Esperanza's fingers flew in an effort to tell me, while there was time, secrets that lay beyond spoken words, past any language I could understand. For instance, the art of rowing a boat into the sapphire stars.

Gradually then suddenly there was less time to spend with Esperanza. In the spring, the rowing club met more frequently and we often trained past nightfall for weekend regattas in Malaga or Marbella. I won ribbons that splashed my bedroom's white walls with blue and red. Hours on the river began to widen my shoulders and broaden my back. My bare wrists thickened. Esperanza often looked fretful now; her face was taking on a peevish cast. She didn't seem to enjoy discussing America as much. She no longer encouraged me to describe how neon from riverbank cafés could cast impossibly gaudy swathes across the black water below. When I mentioned spotting one of her blue *pulseras* on a boy in San Eloy, Esperanza's thin face would ripple like those reflections that insisted on glistening out of reach no matter how quickly I rowed toward them.

"Wait," said Esperanza one afternoon when I was about to leave for the river. She removed a *pulsera* from her pocket. "I mixed red with blue," she explained, "since second place will also win you any America you want." The bracelet had been made from Esperanza's most expensive string; its colours would remain rich despite time and weather and wear. I didn't ask Esperanza how she could afford this gift. The cost would be enormous, I suspected. She might have to braid another million *pulseras* to earn her freedom. "Let me," she said, fastening the band around my left wrist. Esperanza's touch was cool. Her fingers lingered on the vein below the knot, as though learning my pulse, counting the blood's beat. Waves washed across her face. Then Esperanza sat up straighter and squared her chin against the slanting light. Her hands reached toward her tray to begin another bracelet. As I walked away, she called in a voice clear as any carrying over water: "Even in California, promise you'll never take it off."

By the time I returned from the river that night, the cellar at the end of the block was empty. It must have been around dusk, as starlings begin their shrieking in the plane trees across the way, that a man followed Esperanza down into the dark room. No one saw him go in or come out. No one heard a thing, whispered *barrio* women gathered like perturbed pigeons on the corner. When Selena came home and found her, Esperanza wouldn't say who had done it, but she couldn't stop braiding air now smudged by shame as well as by soot. They needed to flee the cellar at once. In the asylum where Selena would leave her silenced sister, Esperanza's hands refused to cease speaking their secret language. The nuns took to tying down her wrists. One day she would no longer fight the knots, they prayed. "The poor things," my mother murmured, sautéing the ten o'clock *cena*. "It would have been better for both girls if the blind one hadn't lived."

For a long time, the world was a darkened place; colours seemed concealed by a sifting of black. Even on the river, air had an acrid taste. My right hand reached for my left wrist. The bracelet there felt smooth and rough at once. Esperanza had woven the blue and red strings so tightly they'd never loosen, never fray. I could hear a scarlet promise pulse beneath the band. Through veins as blue as any stars beat my secret vow.

The Laboratory of Love

"O NLY THE BIRD KNOWS THE WING," I REMIND MYSELF AT THE COMPLETION of another investigation into the truth about love.

After the latest specimen to participate in my decades-long study leaves the laboratory.

This moment is always delicate, dangerous.

My physical involvement in the experiment has caused my pulse to quicken, heart rate to elevate, temperature to rise.

The specimen's scent clings to my skin, his secretions stick and smear, the taste of him fills my mouth.

Electrical-biochemical reactions to our exertion continue in its aftermath. They're only powerful simulations of longing and loss, I reassure myself.

"It's all love," breathes the belly dancer, long before I find science, long before I leave the world, while we both stumble across deserts of desire, the same Saharas she searches still.

Immediately I embark on the series of steps which—followed in exact sequence, with full deliberation—permit me to move from being a necessary participant in an experiment to being the equally essential scientist who records what has been observed by his attentive eyes.

I endow order and grace to what is otherwise a wrenching, confusing transition. I follow standard procedures:

Change the sheets of the alcove mattress on which the investigation occurred.

Silence music and blow out candles and snuff out incense.

Switch on a bright light.

Swish potent mouthwash, spit in sink.

Beneath the shower, allow a river to wash over me.

(A whole Nile, before it was poisoned, when all of us dancers jangled silver and gold across the dark desert, fluttering flutes and veils, more swayed seduction upon the sand.)

As if, instead of scrupulous scientist, I were just another tired whore possessed by an ancient profession's mania to get clean. One more killer with an urgent need to wash off the blood that ties him to crime.

With antibacterial soap, exfoliate evidence. Scrub it off and let it descend through drain and pipe to the surface of the earth nine floors below; then further down, underneath, away, adding to sewer or sea, evaporating into air tonight, falling in rain upon my face tomorrow.

Steam rises around me as proof that processes of transmutation occur continually, occur now.

Liquid flays like hot lashes, for longer than a civilian shower lasts.

Afterward, veils of vapour float around the bathroom. Mist prowling the earth on its very first day, from which any original, unknown form of life might emerge.

Or me.

My physical self, having been enlisted into the service of science again, returns.

Hello, you've survived, you've come back.

Did you miss me? Do you still need me?

I dress in a clean, off-duty uniform of simply cut loose-fitting clothes.

I unlock a metal filing cabinet in the corner and remove the notebook in which current experiments are being recorded.

At the round white table, I prepare to enter data and observations.

Trace graphs, draw charts, solve equations.

My heart rate has slowed, my temperature has lowered.

I become calmer, cooler.

Like the scientist who has been here all along.

This post-experiment procedure has been developed according to sophisticated mathematical principles. Like any sequence of precisely ordered, perfectly repeated actions, it contains the power of ritual.

Moves me beyond science.

Allows me to live with the illusion that my body isn't smudged with fresh fingerprints; enables me to airbrush a million stubborn traces of strangers' oil and sweat from my skin.

To ignore the accumulated souvenirs from twenty years of hands-on investigative effort.

Glandular and chemical secretions, fractions of molecules and atomic particles, fragments of genetic material and broken chains of DNA.

I can almost believe that another tattoo—imperceptible to the unaided eye, as if drawn with invisible ink—has not been added to the numerous others that cover my flesh like a second skin I'll never slip from.

A species of shroud.

Ritual almost neutralizes the scent that clings to me despite my ablutions.

Procedure nearly cancels out a combination of concentrated odours.

The stench of twenty scientific years.

Tonight I fail to escape beyond reach of the senses. The scent of all the flesh experimented with in the laboratory of love rises in fumes from my notebook. My eyes inflame, my throat itches, my lungs burn. Warning signals puff through my mind: danger is coming, danger is near. The fumes still sicken as they dissolve. My belly clenches, the laboratory spins.

"Settle down," instructs the scientist inside me.

My sight shifts back into focus. My fingers grip the table's edge.

I remind myself that every investigation is challenging.

Methodology requires that I participate in procedures while simultaneously studying them with objectivity.

Control what is chaotic by nature for precise ends.

Manipulate activity that seeks to disrupt itinerary.

Work what is wild to a determined purpose.

Near the start of my project, I experimented with methodology by employing two "outside" specimens to comprise the pair required for my research. Physically removed from the equation, I hoped I could enhance the scientist's observations with my own.

Quickly I found this tactic unsatisfactory.

Incorporating a second subject into an experiment means having less control over an already unruly act.

Increased rewards of observation don't compensate for loss of critical data obtainable solely through experience.

I realized I had to overcome the challenges presented by my necessary involvement in my research.

I needed to trust that emotional makeup, physical constitution, and early experience had uniquely prepared me for success where most would fail.

I must continually reassure myself that I was chosen for this work.

Selected for sound, supportable reasons.

Not by accident, from whimsy, for fancy.

I tell myself varying stories about how the scientist found me.

Sometimes I suppose that twenty years ago I simply awoke one unwitting morning in the most recent of the cities in which I would pause during my flight from the boys I had once been. They persistently outwitted my escape; they continually clutched at my sleeve with hungry fingers. By this point, twenty years ago, they had already driven me back and forth across the globe countless times, jealously chased away every lover trying to claim me. My resources were drained, and my youth was exhausted. Now the weary light became clearer and truer on each of these afternoons in Tangier or Paris or Jakarta, always revealing more than the day before, as if I were moving from blindness to sight, from confusion to faith, from death to life. Yet for a while, I was unable to understand what my eyes newly saw. The purpose of an existence never before glimpsed remains obscure, even as its contours are created with clarity, without hesitation, in accordance with instructions murmured perhaps in sleep, directions offered by nightingales in the dark, apparently the echo of every lost lover's voice. An extensive number of complex factors worked together at this moment, twenty years ago, when they would at no other, to permit me to have received the muffled voice that grew increasingly audible during day as well as night, while the illumination it cast became more dazzling. My eyes weren't accustomed to such pure light; it took them time to adjust, to understand the purpose of the special landscape that my subconscious had been busily constructing. It was not until the first laboratory had been created—in exact obedience to his instructions—that the source of the voice materialized in brilliant light: I summoned the scientist by creating the correct air for him to breathe, I invoked him by establishing the appropriate setting to receive his words, his vocabulary, his language of love. Even as he carefully explained the goal of our experiments, the parameters within which we would conduct them, even as the scientist explained every shining law of my new life, I swooned inside his original seduction, the first syllables he slid into my ear:

Leave the world behind; come beyond with me. I will show you the dungeon, deep beneath your skin, whose hundred cells can hold a hundred boys in solitary confinement. I have the power to keep them down in that dark chamber below memory. As long as you remain loyal to the laboratory, they will never escape to haunt you again. Quid pro quo.

"This is only one more night," I try to convince the cold light that has surrounded me since I accepted the scientist's bargain.

My skin prickles, as when frozen flesh is invaded by blood during the painful process of thawing.

I listen for the image in the mirror to agree glassily: *Yes, this is just another night on the way to where we're going.*

From the outset, I understood that my investigations into love must be conducted through the medium of flesh: what I seek lies beneath the skin, below bone, under organs, deeper than blood, beyond scalpel's reach.

I accepted, too, that this path toward the truth would not travel through lush surfaces or shapely limbs.

(Pure science must always practice discrimination for which no apology is required; embracing one theory means coldly denying others.)

Human beings who are encased within less aesthetically fortunate shells have always provided the richest raw materials for research.

My thesis is built upon a single fundamental principle.

When desire denied too long is finally fulfilled, when withheld beauty is belatedly possessed, when longing for wing and flight are at last unshackled: such ecstatic experience can unleash extraordinary reactions that originate from the deeply buried, molten core of love.

My physical self, this form shaped and honed for satisfaction, provides the catalyst.

Bend your bones into a boomerang that will always return you to my arms.

Long before tonight, I learned to suppress distaste for the more physically unattractive subjects who participate in my project.

To stifle instinctual responses to rancid flesh and sagging skin and ominous rashes during intimate contact.

To disregard odours, to quell rising nausea, to bear dry heaves in the bathroom afterward.

("Aren't we the sensitive soul," sneers the scientist.)

To prize what appears repellent as especially valuable to my work.

To honour unpleasant surfaces that challenge me to dig deeper, to dig harder, to unearth from my own subterranean centre responses to what was once repugnant.

Slowly I grow to welcome the appearance at my laboratory door of a decomposing carcass.

I clasp carrion tightly within my arms.

Graze my lips in prayer over every inch of rotting flesh.

Bless each wrinkle, wart, imperfection.

On the evening, several years into my work, when I close my door against a subject brimming with youth and beauty and every other attraction, an embarrassment of physical riches, any doubt that I can successfully complete my experiment vanishes.

I leave longing behind, move beyond loss, enter a sacred zone.

Envision involvement with specimens of ever-decreasing beauty, according to an equation whose enactment can trace a straight line on a graph, until I embrace only beings with missing limbs, running sores, cancers.

I learn to kiss the abscessed eye, caress the encephalitic skull, enter the infected anus.

My study's final participants will be scarcely recognizable as human. They will resemble an appalling collection of genetic mistakes—a tongue for an ear, a seven-toed foot stemming from a shrunken head—of indefinable sex and age and race; more dead than alive; untouched by another hand, never blessed by a kiss.

This will provide the ultimate data for my investigation and illuminate the holy heart of love.

After seven childhood years in darkness, I couldn't see by light, I was able to negotiate the brush and fields only when the sky above was black save for stars that spelled a story about a dancing blonde, who with her striptease sidekick and her son orbits between showrooms and stages, who sometimes sings about a sailor: that was the real truth of before, not seven years inside a cage. Now the night revealed what followed the glitter; yes, this sea of sightless stumps came after the rouge.

There is no reason why this evening's encounter should threaten my controlled cocoon.

The specimen was unexceptional.

The experiment proceeded without incident to a satisfactory conclusion.

If anything, it was disappointingly mundane, unlikely to offer up startling insights or important revelations.

Unlike, for example, a session with a specimen who hates what he needs.

Who reacts violently upon receiving what he wants, upon satisfying what he despises.

Fists against my face, hands around my throat.

Boot in my back, blood in my mouth.

The scientist becomes excited by these instances. They permit him access to especially interesting expressions of love, provide opportunity to collect rare, precious data.

"Excellent," he enthuses as I spit a tooth.

Whether I find such intense experience personally pleasant or unpleasant has no relevance. Whether I am able to successfully defend myself from it with the knife concealed beneath the alcove mattress, is incidental.

I never asked who, I never asked why.

Still, every encounter, including the latest one, holds value. My investigative skills are, by this point, so highly evolved that I am able to uncover in the least promising material any number of minor points of interest which might, factored into earlier data, be of use.

My post-experiment disturbance tonight may, upon analysis, provide more important data than the activity in the alcove to precede it.

Even after twenty years of investigation, I remind myself, occasional unsettling responses to an encounter are only to be expected. These have always occurred. They have always proven to be isolated incidents, little more than freakish phenomena; nothing to worry seriously about, only a test of my strength.

"Love is our only religion," intones the belly dancer in Damascus dusk, interrupting her eternal prayer for his appearance. "We invoke his love with faith, we resurrect his ardour with our adoration, he saves our soul with his sex."

Instead of beginning to record, I warily study my laboratory. It resembles any of the studio apartments housed in any of the buildings that seek ascension above this city on the Pacific coast of North America. (The city's name is unimportant. This place is merely the latest in a long series to provide a setting for my research; except as a location for another laboratory, it holds no meaning.) Although I have been operating in this apartment for three years, it resembles one newly occupied, before the placement of furniture and hanging of prints and other evidence of a life.

One wall, facing south, is entirely windows; the others are bare white.

Between them, on clean hardwood floors, are visible the few articles necessary for research.

My apparatus:

A free-standing mirror, positioned at the end of the alcove, reflects visual data pertaining to what occurs on the mattress.

Besides the round white table of metal and single matching chair, besides the filing cabinet and portable CD player, the main room contains only a telephone through which potential subjects make contact with me.

There is little to snare the eye, claim attention, provide comfort.

No plants or rugs, no television or sofa.

Compact kitchen, spartan bathroom, closed closets.

Curtains and windows are also kept closed.

Antiseptic sharpens the air; formaldehyde hones its edge.

The telephone is usually silent; the CD player is not turned on unless an experiment is in session. It became necessary to cease listening to music for pleasure upon embarking on my project. The thinnest melody still evoked the most ridiculous responses in me, altered the chemistry of my emotions to counter effect, loosened and softened and encouraged to dream what must remain clear, hard, precise. Now music is merely a mathematical pattern of sound for my manipulation.

There is nothing to offer distraction from the essential procedures occurring between these walls.

Sometimes, upon entering my laboratory, a subject appears unsettled by the severity of the space. Realizing this disturbance could impact on our activity, I provide false assurance, say I live somewhere else, keep this apartment merely to meet men like him.

In a sense, this is true.

My laboratory is a setting only for controlled experiment, for pure science.

For love.

"Are you going to mope and moon all night?" interrupts the scientist.

Turn to a fresh page of my notebook.

Number and date tonight's experiment.

Identify time, temperature, weather.

Pinpoint phase of moon and tide, position of influential planets.

Target specimen's height, weight, age.

Ethnicity, race.

I record every word uttered by both specimen and myself, with deconstruction of syntax and vocabulary and grammar.

Every moan made, every sigh produced, with interpretation of timbre and tone.

From extensive experience, by means of highly evolved senses, I'm able to make finely calibrated estimations with conviction.

The exact temperature of his touch.

The precise key in which he groaned.

Alterations in barometric pressure at orgasm.

It was always foggy outside the blue room in Sidi Ifni where you found me. We couldn't see the ocean through its thickness; we could only hear the boom below, what went echoing against the hills behind, interrupting the meditation of camels in the desert beyond. Even the balcony was tiled blue. It floated in the fogged breath of all the boys who had drowned for love, it suspended us in silver that ascended from the depths, until I slipped away to Goulimine where you lost me to the dancer's dunes.

However powerfully developed, my senses remain subject to limitations. Once I considered the value of supplementing their capabilities with sophisticated technology, of exploiting audio, video, digital options. Exploring the possibilities of playback, frozen image, slowed motion, amplified sound, computer enhancement. But our investigation is observed best through unaided senses, documented best through the written word, the scientist insists. Commitment to process is key to every important endeavour, he stresses.

I refuse to consider that such insistence actually indicates something else. (Fixed philosophy, hardened ideology, limited vision.)

The eyes of the boy in the snow were frozen open, but he couldn't see.

Of course, I record the experiments in a constantly changing code. It is necessary to remain vigilant concerning security. While a fairly simple computer program could probably break my cryptography, precautionary measures must still be taken. Work in progress, particularly that of late—of increasing danger and of elevated intensity—needs to unfold and flower in secrecy.

When a cycle of completed experiments is ready to be offered to the world through publication, I painstakingly transcribe code into ordinary language.

Erase its complicated keys from my memory.

Destroy the original notebooks, dispose of their remains.

Bury them like atomic waste deep in earth above which ground burns, becomes barren.

We sleep in the thistles and weeds, dream of sailors navigating boats through the stars, steering toward a port of peace; it will resemble Eureka, California.

"What they don't know won't hurt them," the scientist explained amusedly when, early on, I wondered if the unwitting participation of subjects in our experiments raised an ethical question.

"They should feel honoured to be involved on any basis," he snapped the second time I expressed qualms.

They should understand that pure science operates in a sphere beyond muddy morality; in a space devoid of legal niceties, social conventions, polite parameters.

They should know that every act of love is an investigation, whether documented or not.

Upon my parchment skin you drew a treasure map to what you found beneath. It would become creased and soiled by ten thousand clumsy fingers, memorized by as many gold-fevered, glittering eyes.

Now a clear physical sensation runs down my right arm as I record. What transpired on the alcove mattress travels through my hand and onto the page.

Safely there, encased in code, it is removed from my memory, erased from my experience.

Dissociated from me.

I will be able to access this experiment only by reviewing the notebook that contains it.

From the start, I understood the impossibility of completing my long, difficult search for answers without the release that documentation provides.

Impossible for any being to bear the memory, prowling through his blood, of all the eyes that widened before his at the moment of truth.

He lay staring in the snow, a jagged grin gashed into his throat, a second mouth that couldn't tell who or why.

After recording an experiment, I typically study the notes from previous ones for purposes of contrast and correlation.

Tonight I fail to find release from the act of documenting; the encounter continues to perplex me. I close my notebook, unsoothed.

Each action has its reaction.

The air I've moved stirs the bills left on the table by the most recently departed specimen.

This donation will be slipped between the pages of one of the five volumes hidden at the back of the alcove closet, which contain the published records of early investigations, which function as my bank. For the moment, the money is disregarded, unimportant, beside the point.

It is never enough to sustain my work even on the most basic level: electricity and telephone always verge on disconnection; cupboards are too frequently bare; a single thin dime is all I have to make it through the night.

All money is magic, chanted the belly dancer from inside incense before swallowing another silver coin.

I rise from the white metal chair, move to the window.

As if responding to a muffled call from the world beyond the laboratory.

The call of my lost name, my real name, my secret name.

His summons thread through the imam's wail from the mosque in El Jadida and, as a Paseo de los Santos penitent, he prays eternally for my return and in far-flung airport terminals and train stations and bus depots, he crackles distorted directions back to his untrue eyes.

The curtains scratch open; the window opens with a resisting scrape. Behind me, the scientist clears his throat in disapproval. He doesn't have to tell me that I'm disobeying standard procedures. That science must almost always be conducted in secrecy.

A multitude of untitled research projects are currently underway at myriad unmarked locations upon the planet. Like mine, they deal with flammable material, tread hazardous ground. They are politically sensitive, morally risky, subject to sabotage. In the wrong hands, their findings could prove destructive on a catastrophic, global scale. They may be officially forbidden by governments that covertly fund them.

Denied by multinational corporations that instigate them.

Clandestine labs operating behind fronts in unmarked buildings at the edge of strip malls or inside industrial parks. Within gated compounds far off public roads, high up in mountains, deep in jungle or desert.

My current laboratory functions in similar anonymity.

In this undistinguished cement apartment building on this unexceptional street.

The intercom at the street door that is linked to the laboratory is labelled *Occupant.*

The laboratory door itself has triple locks.

The telephone number is unlisted.

In fact, there are two numbers, each with its distinct ring: One through which candidates for experiments make contact with the scientist, and a second, which allows access to the "front," behind which the scientist can safely operate.

To an assumed identity, an approximation of a civilian self, a construct.

A manipulation of tone of voice, facial expression, body language, behaviour.

A facade of fashion meticulously adopted from magazine layouts and advertisements.

It is essential, when outside the laboratory, that I blend in, escape attention.

Let's say I'm as much skilled thespian as scientist.

Say it suits my purpose that you judge me to be a prostitute or addict.

Damaged being, lost soul.

Zombie.

Whatever.

Sometimes he assumes another form in hope that it will be the one to dissolve my blinders, erode my shield, attract my eye. In a Tétouan derb, he impersonates a beggar; from rags reaches out a broken hand, whines for dirhams. On a plazita bench in Madrid, behind the church that's always locked, he clutches a cane as an ancient man. At the mall in Santa Monica, a skinny teen stunts a skateboard, rolls another blunt. He is the overly solicitous flight attendant during an Air India non-stop between Bombay and Algiers. He is the officer who conducts the

*strip search at Canadian customs. The cabbie who drives me into the ghetto of
my mind.*

Over the years, as I become more deeply immersed in investigative activities,
as the scope of my existence narrows to encompass only this sphere, less
communication unrelated to science occurs.

Each relocation of my base of operations, and corresponding changes of
telephone number and address, moves me further from reach of an earlier
life.

(When I was lost, until I was found, before I was set free.)

Because my research is funded with cash by its participants, I'm able to
avoid bank accounts, safety deposit boxes, credit cards. I pay no taxes; I have
no employment record. No health insurance. No driver's licence. I have a
criminal record only in several countries that are easily avoided; there are
no outstanding warrants. There are six passports, each issued to a different
name, each issued by a different government. All are false. The name I use at
any given period is likewise fictitious.

Except to telephone and electric companies, my address is unknown.

Except for bills from these two utilities, only advertisements are put
through the slot in my door.

Records concerning me do not inhabit filing cabinets or databases of private businesses or public agencies.

As much as possible—almost completely—I cease to exist in official as
well as private terms.

Slip through the cracks, off the face of the earth, from my original skin.

Did you miss me?
 Do you still need me?

The open window confronts me with a hundred apartment towers rising
through the night, confuses me with the lights of their ten-thousand rooms.
The same overwhelming number shines across the inlet, on the far side of
the bridge.

The light in which I stand is one of many, is just one more.

"Painted scenery," mocks the scientist at my elbow, "paper view."

Against the black velvet backdrop, purely silent and hallucinogenically near, an ascending aircraft illuminates a sloping line that replicates the graph of desire I have just traced in my notebook. The rising light hooks my eye, lifts it toward the spangle of stars above, the black ocean beyond.

We row across the moonlit lake toward Christmas Bay, each at an oar, bending backs in time while the train whistles midnight down the valley, pools its echo in the hollow of my bones until your tongue licks my eyes, our abandoned oars sway a waterdance, we drift and cluster, let cold dark current pull.

My skin ripples, as if in response to a subterranean disturbance. The scene before me shivers from stasis, emerges from muteness. Video screens flicker across darkness and distance; shapes shift in their strobe. The city breathes and traffic streams below; stars pulsate above.

"Moons and Junes and Ferris wheels," mutters the scientist.

Like an alarm, the telephone emits the three short rings which indicate another possible candidate for experiment is calling. I ignore the signal, though once I was always greedy to gather more research, keen to conduct a dozen experiments a day.

Lately, only one encounter an evening is usually possible; even the avid scientist does not advise attempting more.

"Stay away from the window," he suggests now, a sharper edge to his voice.

As the world outside surges into sound, roars like surf inside a shell, amplifies the echo of the distant ocean.

As the swelling air sharpens with salt, stings my skin.

A moment after falling silent, while its after-tone still intrudes upon the air's liquid hiss and foam, the telephone rings again. This time it emits only single rings, summoning not my scientific but my civilian self.

This is the first such summons since establishing this current laboratory,

I realize. The first in three years.

This realization vibrates like a plucked string inside my mind.

Quivers questions to life, triggers mental motion.

How many political systems have failed since I stepped out of time? Have wars been won and lost? Journeys made from here to stars?

(Who? I didn't wonder. And why? I didn't ask.)

As the ringing stops, I turn to the white table to record its occurrence.

Instead, my attention is drawn back to the rooms that illuminate the air outside.

Now I am able to detect that, like me, their occupants are poised before open windows.

They wave like flags, in greeting or in warning, call a thousand impersonations of his voice into the city's clamour.

You've survived, you've come back.

We lean into saline air, slant toward its suggestion of spring. In interior canyons, snow melts, uncovers, exposes. In the alley directly below my window stirs a shape darker than the darkness it fills. He magnetizes himself into a substance always attracted by my atoms.

My shoulders twitch; their muscles burn.

The scientist purses his lips.

Impossible that he has found me.

"Watch it," warns the scientist, his voice now pitched a single note away from the one that preludes punishment. The note that sounds as overture to finding myself slumped against the wall, its white surface stained from another night of cutting, the word *Help!* smeared with blood beside my head, the knife still in my hand and my sliced skin still singing, the scientist explaining once more that it hurts him more than it hurts me; if I followed standard procedures, this would be unnecessary.

Back away from the window, retreat from its clutch. Breathe the laboratory's familiar air; accept its acrid taste. The world's din fades then mutes. It must have been a mistaken call. One random voice thrown through the night. One incorrectly pressed digit among six others. No one knows where I am, who I am, that I am.

I will never keep you from flying, he whispered like a thousand oceans in my ear.

Varicoloured pills spill brilliantly upon the white table.

My fingers hover above possibilities, linger over choice, pluck blue.

Float its essence on my tongue, loll in its luxury, swallow with satisfaction.

"Another," seduces the scientist.

"Again," he purrs.

At the edge of my vision, where light meets darkness, where what is known melts into the unknown, his hand hovers in invitation. He wants me to join him on the balcony off the bedroom, beyond the French doors. Once more we will lean together against the iron rail above the narrow Macarena street during the hour when afternoon meets evening and the twang of a plucked guitar ascends from the music store below. Garlic from the corner café sautés geranium air; the slot machine in the bar halfway down our cobbled block pings tunes of chance. His arm across my shoulder holds me inside this winged moment at the same time as we soar above the azoteas and the spires, the river and its bridges, all the way to Matalascañas.

Daylight.

I am curled on the hardwood floor, in the corner of the laboratory far-thest from the alcove mattress, without blanket, pillow, clothes.

As usual.

Again.

(As a child, after what happens in the beginning, I form a dislike of beds. I'm afraid of sinking and smothering in asphyxiating softness and seek the safe surface of hard floor, preferring most of all the cube of partly contained darkness beneath a box spring. The people who say they are my parents worry. This is something else for them to whisper about in the next room; their clawed voices scratch through the wall. They consider returning me to the clinic, adding this latest unsettling behaviour to the records of others the doctors can't diagnose, can't cure. Instead, for my birthday, they buy me vibrant sheets patterned with bold superheroes against whose image any boy would like to sleep. They buy a firmer mattress for the bed. They tie me to its posts, fasten me in the harness, force more pills down my throat. Finally they give up, acknowledge one more defeat, accept something else they can't change. Something else from the cage I have to keep, something else too late to forsake.)

Gulls wheel through my line of sight, shriek that last night I neglected to close the windows, draw the curtains. My sleep has lasted longer than usual, the clock informs me; the setting of its alarm was shirked. I failed to return the notebook to the locked cabinet, to hide the donated dollars inside a book.

These minor lapses in discipline annoy my need for rigorous order.

The itinerary leading up to an experiment requires execution as exact as that which follows.

Stiffness in the muscles in my upper back, just below my shoulders, suggests that last night's encounter in the alcove was unusually demanding. Elements of wrestling were incorporated into the activity? Or of a more unusual sport of love?

What happened last night?

Something went wrong.

Something isn't right.

A wing of memory wheels across my mind as I shut the window. The trace of a dream swoops past the corner of my eye as I close the curtains. I rub the sockets of sleep, grind away its physical consequences, rid my vision of unscientific conceits.

Sleep is only a process required for physical and mental restoration.

Dreams are not permitted to invade my subconscious, to infiltrate my waking.

Traces of geranium are not allowed to linger in my sterilized air.

"Careful," murmurs the scientist, announcing that he too is awake.

Move cautiously through morning, as though I have wakened upon a landscape mined with the bones of all the ones who died for love.

As though their rigged, unmarked graves lurk to explode me into the sky.

I make allowances for the after-effects of last night's pre-sleep medication. The dosage, which I realize at the very beginning, functions as a tool in the pursuit of my investigation. Like the recording of experiments, a valuable device for release from them.

Obviously, I cannot afford to ingest substances that might negatively effect the mental clarity required to organize and cross-reference and analyze masses of detailed data, intricate formulae, sophisticated calculations.

No crude narcotics to damage the prime physique required for my research.

No tobacco, no alcohol.

No crank, crack, crystal.

Shoot up only the heroin of love.

I employ only substances refined with purity, designed with delicacy for precise effects, in laboratories as clinical as mine. After extensive trial and error, I discover those compatible with my most productive performance as scientist.

Certain nights require a pink pill.

(I record my intake precisely; monitor milligrams strictly.)

Other nights need silver powder.

(I remain on guard against the tendency toward an annihilating dosage, which the challenges of investigation can prompt.)

A blue pill is saved for extreme circumstances.

Upon discovery, after an experiment, of tear stains on the sheets, feces on my fist.

Last night I took two blue pills. Did the scientist double my dose in order to accomplish one of his special experiments?

The kind which, much to his displeasure, I still cannot bring myself either to participate in or witness?

Please, no.

Not again.

Maybe the blood I find in the morning isn't mine. There's still too much of it, a sickening surprise. My stomach heaves at the mess as the scientist shrieks, "Clean it up; it's the least you can do, excusing yourself from essential work with silly scruples, dreaming of valentines while I'm left to dispose of the remains."

I should feel relieved that the laboratory is not splattered with serum of brain or shreds of skull this morning.

Grateful to be spared the scientist's lengthy lecture concerning the long tradition allowing that lives must sometimes be sacrificed to the experiment in order to make important discoveries that outweigh such losses.

His rant that I am completely hopeless, quite unsatisfactory, he will find another associate if I don't shape up at once, there are a dozen boys bursting with promise on every block, he can pick and choose, who needs a weakling, a parasite, a nonentity like me.

His silence after a night that went wrong is suspicious.

Quite likely strategic.

After twenty years of intimate co-existence, we harbour few fantasies about each other, the scientist and me. I continue to be grateful that he saved me, that he set me free. But my blind devotion to his beliefs—when I worshipped at his feet and admired each of his ideas—has long passed. And it is many years since the scientist has been equally enamoured of me. At the beginning, he was ecstatic to have found the apparently perfect colleague for an unusual undertaking, after half a century of unsuccessful searching, after decades of disappointment. He was thrilled to have uncovered what was surely the ideal disciple. That was when I basked in his belief in me, delighted in showing him my fervour for his religion, burned with desire to embrace it as my own. I loved to exceed his wildest expectations. I adored making his jaw drop by drawing the richest data from specimens, by offering his eyes the most powerful articulations of love. Until, with astounding banality, as a surprising cliché, the honeymoon ended and the bubble of illusion burst. Gradually I learned that I can never satisfy the scientist. I discovered that he will ruthlessly use any weapon available to ensure the success of his experiment. He will employ a whole arsenal of unscrupulous effects to get what he wants. By turns he flatters or criticizes, encourages or exhorts, congratulates or condemns: always according to a concept that does not take into account my well-being except as it furthers his work. Yes, he is as temperamental and moody and selfish as any artist. Yes, I am intermittently resentful and restless as any prisoner. Ours is a complex union, subject to the stresses of extreme circumstances, intensified by uninterrupted intimacy. We bicker and nag. We humour each other, we ignore each other. I know that secretly the scientist despises me precisely because he needs me. I also know that, despite his protestations, he would abandon me in an instant, without a thought, if a more suitable assistant appeared. And while it has always been clear that my existence will end with the final experiment, as a necessary given, it seems the scientist will survive our endeavour undamaged. Once or twice he has let slip mention of a future experiment in which I will not be involved or needed. I do not deceive myself that he will miss me or mourn me in the usual sense. He has never pretended that the usual sense applies to us. We have left the usual sense behind. Beyond it, I have considered leaving him only once. If I did leave, he would unlock the dark dungeon inside me, release the boys who, after twenty years of solitary confinement, would kill for love.

I frown over last night's record, seek in its pages what has gone wrong. I am unable to decipher my own code; its key is missing from my mind.

"It doesn't matter," the scientist assures me.

Sometimes he censors an experiment that he decides isn't significant for our research or otherwise fails to meet his exacting standards.

"I know you'll make it up to me tonight."

An expression of forgiveness. A vote of confidence. A note of warning.

I ingest the first in a series of meals composed with dietary precision and accompanied by an exact assortment of supplements for maximum effect. Material to be chewed thoroughly and swallowed untasted at calculated intervals, Merely a combination of proteins and minerals, fibres and starches, carbohydrates and fats.

Solely the necessary means for maintaining the physical beauty that is my investigation's essential raw material.

"We have secrets," revealed the dancer. "Let me show you what we learn in the huzzelas *behind the bazaar, beyond the myrrh. How to magic into the magnet for his eye, how to incarnate into each image he needs to touch, how to create the illusion he loves to believe in. Let me show you tinctures and essences, powders and proteins. Roots and leaves, fire and ice, earth and sand and mud. We have secrets.*

Wait for the effects of nourishment to register.

Study the free-standing mirror, consider the body in it coldly. As always, it appears an alien entity, detached from myself; like its contents, donated to science.

Despite the inevitable processes of aging, despite damage presumably inflicted in my life before the laboratory as well as more recent injuries, still serviceable.

I trace the maze of scars, wonder where they lead.

"Don't start," advises the scientist.

I refocus on smooth taut skin flushed by veins visibly swollen with blood.

Ridges and mounds of muscle; curved and rippled flesh.

Large penis ready to engorge and lift.

My instrument, my equipment.

There is no physical evidence to suggest that I may not be able to continue my investigation indefinitely, whatever twists or turns it unexpectedly takes. I will see it through to the end.

I don't have to look at the face I cradle with my roughened hands at last; it has already been revealed to me by a thousand and one nights of sculpting your features from only air.

Telephone is silenced, laboratory is sealed. Minute adjustments made to apparatus to ensure its immaculate condition. I employ disinfectants and antibacterials, chemical solutions and compounds.

(Although insisting I perform them flawlessly, the scientist disdains such menial tasks, refuses to cook or clean at all. "We all have our own talents," he mutters, pondering hypotheses while I scrub the toilet. Privately, I wonder if he knows how to boil an egg, how he survived before meeting me.)

I put myself on autopilot and pretend that nothing is wrong.

Whatever has happened, I have lost only a single night of work. That's all, nothing more.

There is no significance to the fact that each week it takes me longer to summon the strength to begin work.

There is no indication that the correct execution of the proper series of steps will fail to prepare me for optimum participation in an experiment tonight.

"Your name is Billy," I baptized him too late.

Ominously, I don't feel stronger and clearer as morning reaches noon.

Perhaps this is one of those days when I find myself off balance without explanation, for reasons beyond cause and effect, inaccessible to logic. One of those difficult days when I wonder if my mood coincides with, say, the arrival of my forgotten date of birth, the erased anniversary of our first kiss, the unremembered time I last saw your eyes: information harboured within my cells, imprinted upon them like a genetic code whose key I have lost.

A closed curtain twitches.

A locked door strains to open.

I struggle to accept that I am always affected by invisible forces with the power to infiltrate the zone of sanctity around me.

They must be acknowledged, recognized, understood, factored in.

Nullify threat by naming it.

"Is Billy you?" they wondered in their white coats, waiting for my answer.

Such problematic days occurred most frequently during the second spring after I embraced science, when my first dedication to its holy commandments had abated, when I was still near enough to the world to hear the calls of boys as young as me outside the window, close enough to see their long-legged stride down the street. Those eager eyes, such frank faces, that absent arm an ache across my shoulder. In the midst of an experiment, I had to blink away an image of pink cheeks above the petalled O of promise, focus instead upon the specimen writhing below me like a snake desperate to shed its skin. In the hours between experiments, I had to erase the clean line of an adolescent neck from the April air, turn from the temptation of teenagers in trees. For a period of several months, it was uncertain whether I possessed the capacity of complete dedication demanded by my calling after all. The scientist made it clear that he had second thoughts about my suitability; I was on probation now, he let me understand. Certainly his supreme act of political cunning was to pretend ignorance of the two instances during that dangerous season when I sought selfish satisfaction, pursued private pleasure, sinned against science.

On both occasions I was conscious of the threat to which I was exposing the laboratory.

On both occasions such awareness conquered the power of the beauty in my arms, defeated my illicit enterprise.

When a third occasion presented itself, upon the appearance at the laboratory in Sydney of a corporeal composition of surf and sand and salt, I closed the door before he could surge inside and foam into my arms.

On that day I knew I was capable of saving every sigh of breath and ounce of semen for science.

Saving, not wasting.

The tattoo artist pricks patterns of Pisces upon my skin, colours constellations to orbit you into my arms.

As if a rainstorm were passing through me, I suddenly gush self-pity, stream torrents of tears upon the hardwood floor, wallow in the puddle.

I am getting old. Soon my hair will grey, my flesh sag, my skin cave. I will grow sick, weak, crippled; brittle bones will break. It will become increasingly challenging to maintain an illusion of the physical beauty required to catalyze experiments; eventually even the compassion of candlelight will not suffice. Specimens will leave ever smaller donations behind, then nothing at all. I will find it difficult and finally impossible to pay prosaic bills. The strongest dose of medication will fail to produce effect, the most forceful touch will not be felt, the final breath will pass unnoticed.

I am a victim of science, I am a dupe of delusion, I am a page of pathology.

An aging, addicted prostitute, an abortion of the world, a mistake of God.

Imminently, a body in a dumpster, a decapitation beside a dam.

A final tear forms in the corner of my eye. A harsh giggle emerges from my mouth. Who else but me can offer pity for myself?

Since I've fucked God to death.

The scientist finds this episode deplorable. He is aghast by such exhibitions;

he whistles tunelessly over his theorems until my self-indulgence has run its sorry course.

(They say the scars are the result of an accident. They say they were inflicted in an instant. They say they weren't produced systematically, slowly, deliberately during seven years behind locked bars.)

"You must leave life to know love," I mumble on this latest difficult morning, repeating by rote one of the old mantras that once cast clear, sharp light. As if making the sound realizes its meaning, actualizes it into the air, allows it to be seen and heard and held onto.

I cling to the knowledge of all the other beings working secretly across the world to uncover, illuminate, discover. I draw strength from their unwitnessed activity, their heroic sacrifices, however different than mine.

In Oslo, my attention is drawn to drapes closed across an apartment window in daylight, registers the palpable presence behind them, catches the subtlest tell of the curtain's twitch.

At the end of a dirt road in Macedonia, a dog barks on a chain before a cabin that is boarded up, though smoke rises from its chimney.

In a mall in Akron, Ohio, a blonde woman in a tennis dress ascends an escalator while, across the synthetic space, in perfect symmetry, I descend.

I am not alone.

There are many of us who have chosen to endure harsh circumstances to discover what the world has not yet dreamed of. Although we cannot meet, cannot even acknowledge each other, I take comfort in their existence. I know they read the published records of my research with understanding, absorb its information, augment it with their own insights.

You must lose love to find it, I chant to chase away my doubtful morning.

"Greeting card clichés," the scientist critiques.

"Dimestore platitudes," he pans.

"Hop to it," he instructs.

I visit the gym, several blocks away, in emptiest early afternoon. As usual, as though nothing were wrong.

Few forms move with mine among the weights and pulleys and chains.

Among machines which resemble crudely constructed instruments of torture whose pain must be endured for the sake of love.

The scientist is always mute in this setting. While he recognizes the vital importance of exercise, its repetitive nature bores him: he prefers to spend this time pursuing more intellectually stimulating activities. "They wouldn't interest you," he remarks loftily when I wonder. I shrug acceptingly, suspecting the scientist's silence in any location outside the laboratory stems secretly from fear. Removed from his controlled environment, he huddles within me like a frightened child inside a dark cage. I feel grateful for the respite from his demanding, critical attention.

For two and a half hours, I move between the mirrored walls.

Earlier inspection of my physical form, in the laboratory, has informed me which aspect of it must be developed today to create lines provocative of the greatest desire tomorrow.

Now I squint enough to see which muscles are manipulated with perfect form, for optimum result.

Not enough to notice my eyes.

Not enough to notice the forms that shift around me.

Upon my first appearance in a gym, several of these shapes will attempt to engage my attention.

My lack of response usually aborts such efforts.

Their immaculately developed surfaces, primed and pumped for love, render them useless for my purposes.

They do not sufficiently require my touch; they find satisfaction easily. When displays of interfering interest continue despite my dampening, I switch gyms.

Standard procedure.

He grins from the shower's steam. Tongues of vapour lick smooth skin I once licked. That tattooed butterfly above the hip, wing on bone, it made me soar. The body whose weight and length my arms measured precisely during a thousand and one nights has been extended by several inches, augmented by five or ten pounds. Eyes have been recoloured, hair dyed, foreskin cut. His false flesh drips deceit. He towels it dry, opens his mouth in invitation. Offers himself as the one who gives birth to love. Not the one who double-crosses desire.

I strain to lift unease. To handle it, control it, use it. Each dull clank of iron drives away the name called in the night.

Each drop of sweat defeats the power of geranium dreams.

Each heave of weight moves me surely toward ability to conduct the next experiment.

Heart rate increases, body temperature rises, pulse elevates, sweat forms.

This is a dress rehearsal for physiological phenomena that will occur during tonight's investigation.

I must push past the painful production of lactic acid, force released endorphins to shoot through my brain. Expel from my lungs exhausted oxygen to cloud the mirror, to conceal a pair of wakened, hungry eyes that look like mine, to blur the glass long after I have left the reflected space.

I cross the short distance between gym and laboratory unsteadily, as if exercise has weakened rather than strengthened me.

Train my eyes upon the sidewalk, see only enough to prevent me from stumbling into traffic, into some stranger's arms.

I protect myself from becoming daunted by the multitude of possible specimens for experiment, more than I will ever be able to use, too many to undertake. I blind myself from faces that turn in my direction, deafen my ears to following footsteps.

He has pursued me from our El Pozo balcony, back and forth across the globe, in and out of time. In a doorway across the street from the Lisbon apartment, he stamps his feet and shivers until I emerge at last into the iced evening. At the harbour of Naxos, he surveys the ageless Aegean in anticipation of my disembarking from the afternoon boat from the mainland. He suffers the heat of Havana until I appear as a darker shadow at the end of the shadowed arcade.

A murky shape at the end of the block emerges from bright daylight.

A vision of a pair of entwined lovers slaps my sight.

Once I would have been enraged to witness such ersatz ecstasy; once I harshly condemned all polite passion, civilized lust, legal longing. Filled with the fervour of any convert to a new religion, one more zealot, I took the pursuit of pale pleasure as a personal affront to my search for truth, saw it as a frivolous force against which my discoveries must strain for assertion. I had to learn to remind myself that against a background of unevolved exchanges, my message can only stand out more boldly, more brilliantly, more necessarily.

The two bodies press together, press against my eyes, insist upon recognition.

Are they familiar from before the laboratory or from inside it?

They separate into two slivers that waver away, vacate the wincing light.

At the bottom of my belly fists pound, feet kick.

Just moving mannequins, I try to convince myself. Cardboard city, tissue-paper trees.

From the little church on the opposite corner, across twenty or thirty feet of grass, a solo tenor ascends a hymn. The praise of God twists pitch, assumes every song of faith psalmed by the encaged, swivels my head. I perceive only darkness waiting beyond the ajar door.

Although its triple locks appear untampered with, my laboratory has been infiltrated during my absence at the gym. Even before studying the space for evidence of intrusion, I know it.

My scalp tingles in alarm, my stiffened hair registers danger.

Dusted surfaces would reveal fresh fingerprints not my own.

Infra-red equipment would register heat retained in the prints and betray that they were left only minutes ago.

Yet, at first glance, the laboratory appears undisturbed. The lock of the filing cabinet is, like the laboratory's door, intact. Last night's donation still rests on the round white table.

These signs that simple robbery did not motivate the invasion raise alarm. That the notebook for current investigations has been moved from the table elevates it further.

An inch of the notebook protrudes from beneath the alcove mattress— an incomplete attempt to bury, to hide. There is no way of knowing whether its code has been broken. If what I failed to understand has been understood by other eyes.

A miniature heart, drawn with red ink and in a steady hand, decorates the point where my record leaves off.

A single flower stains the exact centre of the alcove mattress scarlet. Geranium.

An imprint of unrouged lips smudges one corner of the mirror. Whose?

Only the kite knows the wind.
   Close the notebook, clean the mirror.
   Float a flower out of the window. Sigh it down into the empty alley.
   Only the sail knows the breeze.

I will have to leave this laboratory and relocate to a safe setting.

Usually I make geographic adjustments at my own will, in my own time.

Or upon the advice of the scientist, his insistence.

Sometimes I am motivated by intuition that Asia instead of Africa, for example, might contribute most usefully to my work.

Each shift requires a certain amount of adaptation: research conducted in a new language, maintained by another currency, enacted in altered air.

Close analysis reveals that the results of the experiments themselves are largely unaffected by modulations in language, culture, and political system.

The truth lies beyond primarily superficial differences.

The truth smelts such differences into substances as pure and essential as semen.

Once I am forced to move because of overly curious neighbours.

Once due to unwelcome attention from police.

On several instances because a subject persisted in pursuing me after participation in an experiment and refused to understand that only a single encounter was required of him.

Or I am driven over borders and across oceans for reasons less obvious, less tangible.

When the forbidden view outside a laboratory attaches itself to my sight like a lover's face that can never be studied long enough.

When the slope of a hill becomes his broad back I must lean into.

When the face of a child who plays in the park at the end of the block appears below me as I rock above a specimen.

When the child's voice emerges from the mature mouth at his moment of climax.

When such moments pierce the zone of purity necessary for my equilibrium, my dedicated existence. "Why don't you call the airport?" the scientist will suggest, trying to mask panic beneath a calming croon. "A change would do us both good."

I have relocated before, I remind myself.

There is no reason why I might not do so again.

And again.

And again.

Shaken like a leaf on its stem, stirred by the force of his breath, the kiss blown strong enough to break me from this branch.

Don't panic. Don't run.

Place last night's notebook in the filing cabinet.

Place last night's donation inside one of the five books at the back of the alcove closet.

Whatever happens, they will tell who and why.

Publishing early research has presented the only serious threat to my underground existence. It has created a subtle tension between exposure and concealment. I found it simple to present my manuscripts, transcribed from private code to public language, as the work of a fictitious author with a fictitious biography.

Simple to provide, for this author's photograph, a clipping from an obscure European magazine of a smiling young man advertising the beauty and joy of gin.

I am not interested in receiving reviews of these books.

However much I need it, I am not interested in the money offered in advance or generated by their sale. I insist, rather, that all earnings anonymously fund clinics—specifically, clinics which provide abortion on demand, without cost.

It won't stop crying however hard she shakes it, however loud she plays the music to drown it out, however long she shuts it in the storage shed outside. A mechanism that won't turn off, won't break. It's still crying on the floor when she returns from the bar the next morning. Ruth said, I told you so, and hung up after she asked if she could come back with it to Brale when it was two months old. The Jupiter Circuit had let her go in January; Diamond Lil had left for Vegas, the hotel was going to lock her out. Snow piles the tail end of dirty winter around the trailer that the bouncer lets her have if he can come by now and then. He didn't mention bringing his buddies. Didn't warn her of the spike on the table where she tries to change the baby. Something is wrong with it; it won't stop crying. Another headache pounds the solution that will make it end. You cross the highway, go through those fields that end in brush, follow the sound of the river. Walk away from the silence in the snow. You hear only the river; they won't find it until spring.

Because hesitation over unusual conditions imposed upon publication is overcome, because it is deemed worthwhile to make exceptions to standard business policies for its sake, I am encouraged, during moments of doubt in the real value of my research, to believe in it anew.

Until I realize that once again fact has been published as fiction.

Science presented as art.

Perhaps I don't find out for several springs. Except to pore over my encoded log books, I cease to read at the inception of my investigation: like music, words inspire fantasy and longing, which play no useful role in my essential occupation, but damage it instead.

I avoid bookstore and libraries, but accidents still happen.

Perhaps, after carefully avoiding the terminal's paperback kiosks, my sight stumbles upon a woman who sits facing me in the departure lounge at Schiphol for the next direct flight to LAX. She is reading the Dutch translation of the third volume of my research. The book is held in front of her to prevent the observation of her expression as she reads. She sits alone, posture erect, although the seats in this lounge are especially comfortable and invite ease. On the unoccupied seat beside her, carefully folded, lies her coat. Beside her feet rests a briefcase. I look up from it and meet, on the back of the book, the smile of the intoxicating young man who advertises gin.

The woman looks at me, looks away.

I will steal the book before our flight is over.

Add it to the first two volumes also abducted but rarely read.

I cannot afford the threat to my morale that even a quick glance at these published volumes evokes.

I am invariably disappointed by the crudeness of my early efforts.

The significance of the experiments seems diminished by translation from code to ordinary language.

Although only a scientist, I need the clarity of a seer and the power of an artist to communicate my results.

I am plagued by the doubt of publishing initial conclusions, which may be interpreted as final, though it is clear that my research is cumulative, always leading up to and preparing ground for the stunning revelations reached at the end.

I am conscious that I may not survive to express such conclusions.

I must balance these two conflicting concerns and realize the importance of disseminating preliminary research, however imperfectly, without delay.

Even misinterpreted, it still holds power, has use.

It serves the world better than untranscribed notebooks, which would appear to unevolved eyes as nothing more than gibberish, just desperate scratches into the surface of the cell, only hieroglyphics smeared with excrement upon the asylum wall.

They say that, technically, you were not locked inside a cage for seven years.

Since the key was always in your hand, the bars only in your brain.

The scars a product of your own knife.

Hesitantly, I open the first volume.

The text appears as untranscribed code.

Like last night's record, one whose key I have forgotten.

Worse, one whose key I have never known.

The other four published volumes are similarly indecipherable.

For my inability to create poetic effects, I have consoled myself with achieving the straightforward, the clear and exact.

If I fail to communicate the results of research on this basic level, my experiment is worthless.

"My?" interrupts the scientist with ironic emphasis.

"Not yours. Not even ours. Only mine."

The scientist seems as unperturbed by my loss of literacy as by the invasion of the laboratory. I sense with sudden force what I have often felt in flickers during our long association: I am involved in a scheme whose ultimate aim is kept secret from me; all along, the scientist has provided me with false or incomplete information in order to manipulate my involvement in an experiment that, in fact, has nothing to do with love, and everything to do with deception.

I am as ignorant as the unwitting specimens who visit the laboratory, only another specimen myself; we squirm together beneath the microscope, fry in its focal light.

Everything that is happening now has been arranged as perfectly as a poem to elicit my reactions to an experiment now inaccessible to my comprehension?

They want me to draw pictures, they want to talk about the pictures. Why the boy lies naked in the snow. Why he doesn't wear clothes, why he wears only one shoe. Why he doesn't move, why he doesn't breathe. Why a second mouth grins open on his throat. It looks like the lipstick with which Diamond Lil drew red hearts on the speckled mirrors, laughing.

Reaching farther back into the closet, I remove the valise that, despite the scientist's disapproval, I have carried with me since he found me. Some of its contents, I suspect, pertain to my forgotten life before the laboratory:

A plastic whistle, a Cracker Jack ring, a purple feather from a boa.

A shell that holds the echo of a sea, an envelope filled with grains of desert sand.

A postcard of Eureka, California, its message, *Miss you like crazy,* signed with a lipstick kiss.

Some of the valise's contents were, I believe, left behind by specimens when they left the laboratory. Dazed by their experience within my arms, scarcely able to remember their own names, they dropped pieces of themselves as they stumbled away.

Maybe I find a comb fallen beneath the table, sunglasses left beside the bathroom sink, or articles whose abandonment is puzzling, implausible:

A wedding band, a driver's licence, car keys, one shoe.

A wallet-sized snapshot of a family in front of a Christmas tree.

I turn all these objects over in my hands, feel which ones radiate the heat of meaning for me. It is difficult to judge which mementos pertain to my forgotten history and which hold value only for a stranger. I sift through uncertainty, wonder if in fact everything in the valise belongs to me, is a talisman of an experience that I have had but which the scientist has kept secret from me.

I have piloted an airplane, worked in an office, fished with friends.

I have danced at my own wedding, balanced my son on my shoulders.

Try on the wedding band, try on the single shoe. See if they fit, if they claim me. Imagine constructing a being who belongs to this assortment of disparate objects. Who would he be? What would he look like? How would he love?

The scientist peers over my shoulder, snorts in disgust.

"Do you really want to remember? Do you really want to know?"

I snap the valise shut, shove it back to the rear of the closet.

Knuckles knock the closed chambers of my heart.

Let me in, let me out.

I weave to the bathroom, claw at a vial.

No.

Medication at this hour would incapacitate me for tonight's experiment.

The correct response to this situation has been drilled into me:

A brief rest should place minor challenges into perspective, transform irritations into actual insignificance, restore what is still a perfect instrument for science.

Recuperation for which the hardwood floor appears inappropriate for once.

My alternative, the mattress in the alcove, is almost acceptably hard.

But it is disarming, deceptive, dangerous.

Even unoccupied, apparently innocuous within a skin of sterilized sheets, it throbs with the unmet longing of all the specimens who have squirmed upon its surface, it vibrates tensely with the undissolved energy of their unreleased desire, seethes with the toxins of their tears.

Even when I give them everything, it is never enough.

After, the dancer declaims, we are only the mirage of their oasis.

Even after they have sucked every drop of fluid from my spine, they slather thirstily.

Even after they have masticated each muscle of my heart, they drool hungrily.

It swamps the alcove mattress, my porous body would sponge it up.

Soak through bone, seep though cells, infiltrate blood, osmose into dreams.

Confuse me with belief that I am the specimens I study.

As though a single blossom resting briefly upon a surface has the power to permanently banish all fever beneath it, the power of a poppy opening its opium arms, offering perfumed invitation into the alcove, push into the drift and descent of dream.

Tap your cane blindly across the Algeciras square toward me and at Tarifa boom your voice beneath the surf beyond the green wall and drum your reach through beaten Morogoro night. Or its only a branch knocking against the cabin that turns the world in my arms, breathes you into my back. Only some pine outside, unsettled by a wind risen from the lake, swept down the valley. Only the Morse code of the indivisible dream.

The knocking isn't random.

It is a determined sequence of sounds.

A prearranged code to gain entrance.

Persistent, insistent.

The percussive pattern raps on my memory.

Let me in, let me out.

You knock on the stone wall that separates our cells for several dark years before I understand your coded language of love.

It takes too long to pour myself back into my sieved skin; the signal stops before my scattered bones gather themselves into a body, my cane hand gropes darkness too slowly.

I open the laboratory door upon an empty hallway as the elevator sighs shut, begins its hummed descent to the surface of the darkening world.

He was here again, he has gone again.

The echoed pattern of knocking unravels its code in my mind, informs me that I have been forced to alter my landscape with exponential frequency over the last ten years, each time toward an always narrower escape, away from always more dangerous circumstances. Informs me that, in fact, I have not inhabited this laboratory for three years. Informs me that, in fact, it has been only a matter of months since the last close call.

Since the last time I was found.

Or since the last body was found.

"If I conceal information from you," hisses the scientist, "it's for the greater good. If it weren't for your incompetence, relocation would never be necessary. So grease your lips and get ready for the salt mines, sissy."

Time lost to temptation, day lost to night.

Neglected procedures have left me hungry, dirty, disoriented. My shoulders' morning ache has turned into a throb, as if I have been heaving heavy burdens instead of resting.

Quick:

Flick switch, elicit light.

Shower, shave. Fix hair, fix face. Slope into uniform of seduction.

Make mirror hot with what they want to see, have to reach for, need to touch.

Ready for tonight's specimen, ready to receive his call.

It occurs within five minutes. I answer it correctly, on the second ring. As the correct identity. With words and voice which reel a participant in.

With modulated vowels and assumed accent, he attempts to pass himself off as a suitor for science initiating telephone contact. A catch in his tenor, a crack in its pitch, causes me to break the line in Toronto and Jakarta, in Ankara and Toulouse.

Shake my head, toss away its tricks.

Not his voice. Not my voice.

A suitable candidate for experiment. Yes. Perhaps even an especially interesting one. I provide him address, intercom code, floor, and door number. I'm not overly excited, not inappropriately pitched, not unfavourably flustered. I am as calm and blank as I need to be.

"You've done this ten thousand times before," soothes the scientist.

"Do it one last time until you need to do it again."

Dim lights, close windows, draw curtains, light candles, begin music.

The scientist coils on the metal chair, prepares to witness, watch, observe.

Should I remove from the alcove closet one of the props stored on its shelf? Did I intuit on the telephone that tonight's specimen might usefully respond to one of these implements?

Whips and chains, restraints and gags; variously sized and shaped objects of insertion.

Probes to delve deep into the truth as well as less obvious experimental aids:

Carefully chosen symbols with power and purity to evoke heightened responses, beyond rational proportion to their banal source.

Something as simple as the most ordinary article of clothing.

Any uniform of innocent youth, any carefree costume of athletic endeavour.

Pristine, perfect.

A skateboard aslant the hardwood floor. A dumbbell at rest before the window. A baseball glove to take him back, to release twenty-five years of longing, to expose the truth about love.

Like the one he wore playing catch with the boy across the street on summer evenings when the quality of air, its pressured composition, alters the pitch of their voices as they toss their secret back and forth, re-tunes what they call to one another into a newly discovered language, sharpening its note to one they have never before heard in their own voices across twenty or thirty feet of dampening grass. There is enough twilight now to blur faces, warm and cool at once, a medium for moths and the squeak of the Carpenter's screen door, for soft thuds against old leather.

I glance from the closet toward the scientist.

"No," he shakes his head, as knuckles tattoo the laboratory door. "Not tonight. Get ready," he repeats in the special tone, electric with excitement, that he adopts whenever he feels that my dedication to our cause might be wavering, whenever he wishes to falsely inspire me for one more unshared reason, whenever he wants to trick me into believing that the next experiment will be the final experiment, the one we have been working toward all these years, the one I was born to die for.

I'm not ready after all. Not ready to investigate his familiar eyes, not ready to admit what they ask. Not ready to watch him undress, expose his humble flesh, its erected need.

Its quarter-century of longing, its known lines.

The seam of scar across his throat.

The butterfly faded upon his left hip, frozen until I kiss breath into its wings, make them flutter with my tongue.

You don't have to watch, I'm the one who watches, it works best that way, you learned that long ago.

Once certain images would rustle the darkness after each experiment, interfere with required rest, despite recording—a drop of water falling from an oar, a curtain breathing before the balcony, his face against the snow—they would touch me where I didn't want to be touched, fondle what I didn't want felt, insist on squirming beneath the chemical blanket slid across my mind.

Until I trained my eyes to stay half-closed while rendering required kisses, while fulfilling fantasies of flesh.

Until I learned that what isn't seen won't be remembered.

Until I mastered standard procedure.

I have never stretched my bones around this shape, never curved its contours with my wrists, never sutured its wounds with my stapling lips, never heard my secret name breathed by this scarred throat across twenty or thirty feet of dampening grass as geranium explodes sharp as amyl nitrate through my wires, floods my circuits, overloads their sockets. This body pressed into my body shifts form again and again, transmutes into every form I have inflamed, evolves into every one not sparked. The knowing fingers find the mound of muscle on each of my shoulders, press both springed locks to allow what has lain beneath to unfold, expand, rustle.

Go away.

The words emerge from my mouth as a moan, inspire the shape beneath me to become further excited by this suggestion of passion, cause it to groan itself into my vision. Below me appears the face of a stranger, of any stranger, of every stranger. I squeeze it away with a squint.

Come back.

I stand above a body that lies naked upon the snow of sheets.

Why doesn't it move? Why doesn't it breathe?

Look closer.

Find him beside the creek, beyond the wooden bridge, where moss upholsters stones and roots, sponged green clings to winter water. Exposing spring has melted snow that covered him, melted flesh that draped him; his faith in me has faded with his breath, his bones have already bleached with broken trust; they don't believe in my approach across rusted needles fallen from the towering pines. The creek insists upon the exuberant season, throws itself upon your slate skull, splashes through your silence. Billy, it's me, remember? In the cage, my knuckles delivered an oath upon the wall between us: even if our escapes are individual, even if survival separates us, even if we alter into unrecognizable forms, I will always find you.

I nudge the body on the mattress with a fearful foot, apply cautious pressure with my heel.

Billy, it's me, remember?

The scientist's voice emerges harshly from my mouth. As at certain times of stress, when judging me unequal to the moment, he has decided to intervene, take over.

He spits: "Get up, get dressed, get out."

Snaps: "No use crying over spilt milk, splattered semen."

The body doesn't move.

The scientist's voice rises in pitch, assumes a shriek of fury, a scream beyond any language I understand, a howled code my mind can't break.

A sound like the one swelling from the snow, a sound I must stop.

I reach for the precautionary knife concealed beneath the mattress. Sieve my skin, unlock its pores, free its contents from their dark dungeon.

Dig harder, dig deeper.

Release the scent of plasma, sweet and rich and cloying.

Foetuses wriggle in the red pool like amoebae in a Petri dish.

They fight a losing battle for life as the scientist's scream wanes into a whine, weakens into a whimper.

Then a hum, then silence.

Goodbye, so long, miss you like crazy.

I am standing in a candlelit space which the illumination of leaving exposes to be a sparsely furnished apartment, small and shabby, with illegible graffiti scratched into its walls.

There is a man on the mattress before me; a butterfly pulses his hip. In the morning he will awaken to wonder who and where he is, what happened to him while he slept. With a mop he will eradicate the bloody evidence of an unknown, aborted past. He'll remove the valise from the closet, hold its contents in his hands, puzzle over which belong to him and which to a stranger. Turn the pages of five books, look for clues within them.

Until the light around him becomes stronger and clearer, until a voice emerges from that light to illuminate the meaning of his surroundings, their purpose.

How they will serve science, defeat memory, lead from life to love.

Before employing the power of my plumes, I wish to leave a message for this new associate of the scientist. Words for him to hold onto during what will be a long, difficult experience within the laboratory. A single sentence that will abbreviate and ease such an experience. I unlock the filing cabinet in the corner. On the round white table, beside the candle burning there, open the notebook to where my efforts to record the truth left off last night. Stare at the red heart beating on the page, then bend to write in the blank space beneath it.

Flame leaps from the candle, my new wings blaze.

Smoke enfolds me like mist at the very beginning of the world from which any original form of life might emerge.

"Love lifts," promised the belly dancer's final postcard from the pyramids, her last telegram from Tangier.

Throw open the window, invite air to stream inside the magic door. It feeds and fans my feathers of flame, enlarges and strengthens their span; encourages them to try the sky, to take a leap of faith, to trust in the end.

Ash falls into the alley, sparks ascend.

Sail me and my helium heart above the ocean of sky toward the upper port of peace.

Only the bird knows the wing, only the wing knows flight.

Compromise

THAT WE'VE ENDED UP IN THIS SALT-SPICED HOUSE SURROUNDED BY WILD gardens and crumbling stone walls presents a fresh surprise each day. Was it ever our wish to move over the earth's skin with such caution, always fearing further loss in an unlikely landscape? On May mornings I watch you descend the cliff to gather feathers fallen from Icarus's foolish wings. They float at the edge of the sea, they fill pillows upon which we no longer dare to dream. My arms can never hold you tightly enough and you will never look at me with Jesse's eyes. We have agreed not to ask each other for much; there is little left to give. Perhaps I offer you more coffee in the afternoon, or you wonder if I need anything in town. During restless nights, we refuse to hear wind stir the apple trees. At least it's peaceful, we think—while in darkness beyond our walls crickets shrilly complain against quiet. A newspaper delivered daily to the door describes distant battles; our nearest neighbours are far away. Jesse sails yachts around Adriatic islands or tosses lucky dice in Monte Carlo.

First he loved you, then he loved me; for a single season he loved us both. Of what was fleeting, photographs remain: Jesse always poses in the middle, careless arms around our shoulders, evasive eyes already shifting toward a summer absent of us—bleached Saturdays in Sicily, say. On that famous Barcelona balcony, our heartstrings vibrate beneath the same expert touch that strums his guitar, that commands an audience of other gypsies to gather in the street below. Jesse throws red and yellow roses down through flamenco darkness, one false flower for each of his betrayals in another Las Ramblas alley. Later, on the midnight ship to Formentera, his white teeth part to serenade the present with premature nostalgia, to wish on the starry wake for more and more. Even the two of us together are not enough for Jesse, as even Paris cannot satisfy his senses. He will leave no farewell note behind, he will leave us to each other: this was an act of compassion, I finally understand. Now I pass an open doorway to glimpse you sitting on the edge of our bed. Your arms emerge brown and veined from white sleeves, your large hands hold snapshots of Spain and Andorra. I continue toward the kitchen without intruding on the time and place to which you have boomeranged back. No, we never stride into each other's secrets; we share silent seasons separately. You don't mention how often I call out in sleep, and I don't ask if your lips on my throat hunger for taste of him. Waking beside empty space on hot August nights, I am spared the fear that you have obeyed a summons to search for Jesse in crowded California bars or on some beach in Mexico. I know you have only slipped past the rotting barn and entered our orchard to shift the sprinklers that keep grass lush and green even when there is no rain.

On Monday I do the laundry, and you steer the spitting iron through Tuesday, and every Wednesday we wash the windows that stare upon the sea. Already another year has passed. Waves do not stop breaking on the rocks below, the horizon has not neared. Sometimes town children come to play in these haunted gardens; their calls draw you out to wander through the long grass on the rise. We can bear no heirs. So it startles me to notice that suddenly—already—your Levis have faded like the sky before dusk. I try to smooth away lines etched around my mirrored eyes. Aren't we still young and strong? Haven't countless others survived defeat to continue fighting? I would tell Jesse that we do what we are able. We don't forget to wind the clocks or to split the wood for winter. Mail arrives at noon, and supper is at six. In June we tread the dusty lane, our sleeves brushing lightly, to where the stream still rages with spring.

Rorschach V: The Last Word

I LONG FOR THE LAST WORD SO BADLY I CAN TASTE IT.

Feel its weight and shape and texture in my mouth. Float the promise like a wafer on my tongue. Savour its sweet certainty. In advance, relish the reward.

Practice patience, advises Allah. Trust in time. After holding on for decades, you can cling a little longer to the surface of this planet. A multitude of additional words—as many as several hundred thousand—must be written before you reach the liberating one. Sustain yourself with the knowledge that each syllable placed on the page—including these few here—carries you nearer to release from the laboratory of love, closer to the end of the lonely dream.

It is hunger that prolongs our lives. Appetite for light compels us to waken at morning; yearning for beauty induces starving eyes to open. We continually crave the next breath, we thirst always for another day, we ache ceaselessly for solace. At the end of desire, I've discovered, one need remains. More urgent than all those preceding it, more essential than any already relinquished, my longing to leave our planet is so powerful it enthrals me in its sway. I shiver with anticipation of the moment of farewell, play it over and over in my mind, swoon before that seductive slow-motion vision.

I understand that my transmutation from dross into essence will not be permitted until the last word has been transcribed. I won't be free to dissolve beyond matter until I'm much lighter, when my spirit has been unburdened of all the stony words which currently anchor it here.

I will be released. My spirit will escape its sieve of skin, pass through a million imprisoning pores, ascend into the accepting sky.

I'll be paroled from paragraphs, freed from sentences, unchained from language.

Cold calculation suggests it should take three years, perhaps four, to complete the work required of me.

At that point, I'll have spoken sufficiently.

Enough, at least, to bargain my way out of the world.

With the movement of this pen, I'm writing a one-way ticket.

Goulimine, Tan-Tan, Laâyoune, I chant while some cold Canadian city mutters in sleep beyond the window.

My lips caress like beads the names of places which mark the route of the holy way home.

Smoura, Boukra, Galtat Zemmour.

Those various Stations of the Cross.

Here is the long goodbye.

When did the promise of the last word first appear? At what point did earthly existence become a state which needs to be eschewed rather than a precious gift that must be held onto and treasured for as long as possible? Aren't I still quite young—surely not old enough to begin considering the end? Isn't there some fatal flaw in my thinking? A gaping hole in my logic? Am I committing a crime, both moral and philosophical, against God, against myself? Does my choice insult all those who battle disease and stave off starvation and otherwise employ extraordinary efforts for the opportunity to draw one more breath? Finally, will my premeditated act be punished?

Allow me to explain that once I too fought with every available weapon for the chance to experience tomorrow. I've survived stroke and conquered cancer. Defeated poverty and triumphed over loneliness.

Please don't believe I'm giving up, throwing in the towel, cashing in my chips.

This is no headlong rush toward self-destruction. On the contrary, I take pains to preserve my physical and mental well-being in these circumstances. I don't smoke or drink. I attend a gym daily, practice yoga as frequently, eat only raw grains and fruits and vegetables. I need to be clean as sand in order to pursue my path.

It happens to lead into the desert; there the last word waits to be written.

(For me, it must be Africa, where my eyes were first opened; for you, it could be elsewhere, anywhere.)

Call this my scripture.

It seems my journey was embarked upon long before I realized a first step had been taken. I can see now that withdrawal from social structures, the severing of attachments to community, began well in advance of my comprehension of the purpose served by these actions. At the outset, before I had even an incomplete grasp of my destination, it was difficult to forsake family, painful to abandon friends, wrenching to relinquish each human relationship. Only gradually did I comprehend the importance, to a successful leaving, of there being no one to mourn my absence and, in return, no one for me to miss. It is essential that all grieving be completed in order to effect the transition from an ungainly bodily form to a more essential state; there is no space for anguished adieu, for a bathetic goodbye.

Yes, it was hard to break the habit of reaching out, of connecting, of sharing. It presented a formidable challenge to enter into and preserve myself within the lonely dream. You must grow accustomed to not hearing your name spoken, to never being glimpsed by eyes privy to your identity, to no longer feeling your skin touched by even careless hands. During the early phase of this withdrawal, full of appalling self-pity, I cried quantities of foolish tears for loss of the world outside the window; gave into unproductive nostalgia for the tinniest tunes and the cheapest of souvenirs to haunt my memory; spilled sloppy sentimentality for what was still visible, apparently within reach, yet at the same time, far removed, beyond my grasp. I learned it is possible to miss what is still present. At the beginning, against my will, I would sometimes feel drawn to a certain pair of slitted eyes, the timbre of a particular voice, a shoulder's specific line. I had to steel myself against the urge to move toward temptation. *Lighten up*, insinuated my rebellious shadow. What harm can come from one last kiss?

Each time my resolve threatened to waver, I would pack my bags and return to the desert to receive, through the medium of sky and sand and silence, an affirmation of my intentions: their validity, correctness, truth.

Each time my pen completes another text, I venture slightly farther into the expanse of sand, in anticipation of the ultimate expedition, when I will go too far to re-emerge.

Not yet, instruct the prophets whose voices bend like waves of heat beyond the last oasis, past the final palm.

There were times I became impatient.

If I already know the last word—it's so simple, common—why can't I write it immediately, and spare myself this protracted leave-taking? The answer, of course, is that I must understand the last word more fully before I am able to write it. I will gain such knowledge by creating the work which remains to be completed before I may depart. Say that through literary composition I learn to ascend. These words, however flimsy, represent my only choice, a single option, the sole route to the enticing end. I concede that my sincerity may be questioned; it will be assumed that I am playing with metaphor, engaging in literary conceits. After all, every previous attempt to tell my truth has been interpreted as fiction. Unpalatable as invention, my unvarnished vision will likely fail to find acceptance, will surely invite scorn. Mocking laughter echoing from the future has no power to bother me. *Only submit*, advises Allah.

It's been a quarter-century since I began to move purposefully from here to there upon the globe, always toward the end of placing greater distance between myself and every human to have known me. I'm careful to only open mail that appears completely safe; that is, impersonal, related strictly to business concerns. I have no telephone service or only an unlisted number, which is frequently changed. Just those individuals entrusted with the publication of my words are aware of my location at any given moment. Nothing except the production of those books implies that my existence continues.

With time, it has become easier to pass through the world without being pulled into its greedy arms. As if my corporeal dematerialization has already commenced, I seem to grow invisible already and exist beyond the power of human sight, transformed into an intangible entity. What is a ghost, after all, but a being who is never seen, never addressed, never touched?

"Are you still there?" I ask aloud, in a room on this side of the ocean or that, here or there, then or now.

(At the sound of my voice, I'm surprised it still works.)

Say finally I adhere to equations to achieve my ends.

The less contact I have with the world, the more powerful my yearning to leave it.

The more intent I become on reaching the last word, the less any activity except composition occupies my waking hours. My experiences away from my desk (currently an unsteady card table, always on the verge of collapse, discovered in the alley) have long been superfluous. I don't fear a lack of further human contact will negatively impact the task still to be completed; material has already been accumulated; it can be fulfilled in isolation, behind closed curtains, where my heart grows huge with clumsy attempts to convey through my remaining words what it was like to be alive.

The candle hisses at me: *Look.*

A stack of manuscript rests beside my right elbow; next to it are several book contracts, several sets of galley proofs. How much time has passed since I sat here with pad and pen? Has it been several days or several years? In a moment, I will step outside, check the date of a newspaper that it would serve no purpose to read: what occurs upon this planet is as alien to me as events unfolding up on Mars.

"You must leave life to find love," I mumble, resorting to that ancient mantra as the candle flame steadies.

What are you still doing here? interrupts an indistinct reflection hovering on the glass pane beyond which breathes the bay. *Sign,* demand the book contracts on this table. Sometimes I suspect that I've subverted the publication of words to postpone arriving at the final one. Not anymore. I've already stayed too long in this uncertain city beside the sea. If I linger further, the odds increase that my presence will be discovered; social systems might prevent me from proceeding with my purpose. They will intervene with dulling medication, enforced therapy, involuntary treatment: I'm aware that my *hégire* presents an affront to church and community and state. It offends reason and confronts the status quo. Disturbs, irritates, upsets.

So be it.

Bismillah.

The time has come at last for my final return into the desert, for one more voyage across beckoning waves of dune.

I glance around this nearly bare room. Except for manuscript, little needs to be brought with me. Travel light, travel right. Isn't the process I've undertaken one of letting go? Of becoming increasingly light, sufficiently unburdened to steal into sky?

Yes, I know the shape of the last word.

I've almost earned the right to spell it.

The still Sahara will allow my ears to hear the single syllable's insistent repetition in the pulsing of my blood, in the victorious voice of Allah.

Upon the blank page of a dune, I will trace this last word enough times to fill a final book entirely, to comprise its text completely.

Watch its divine design dissolve beneath hands of burning air, feel it raise me into the current and the rush.

Love.